Year's Best SF

EDITED BY

David G. Hartwell

HarperPrism
An Imprint of HarperPaperbacks

HarperPaperbacks   *A Division of* HarperCollins*Publishers*
10 East 53rd Street, New York, N.Y. 10022

Individual story copyrights appear on page 481. Introduction copyright © 1996 by David G. Hartwell. All rights reserved. No part of this book may be used or reproduced in any manner whatsoever without written permission of the publisher, except in the case of brief quotations embodied in critical articles and reviews. For information address HarperCollins*Publishers*, 10 East 53rd Street, New York, N.Y. 10022.

Cover illustration by Bob Eggleton

First printing: May 1996

Printed in the United States of America

HarperPrism is an imprint of HarperPaperbacks. HarperPaperbacks, HarperPrism, and colophon are trademarks of HarperCollins*Publishers*

❖ 10 9 8 7 6 5 4 3 2 1

To Geoffrey and to Kathryn

I would like to acknowledge the contribution of Mark Kelly, whose *Locus* columns I found helpful. The magazine reviews in *Tangents* are also, I feel, a valuable contribution to the ongoing dialog about quality in short fiction in the SF field. And of course to the editors, who accomplish so much more than they are ever paid.

Table of Contents

Introduction

SCIENCE FICTION IS ALIVE AND WELL

___

This is the first volume of an annual year's best science fiction anthology, to be published each spring in a widely available mass market edition. In each volume the best *science fiction* of that year will be represented. Not fantasy. Not science fantasy. Science fiction: This anthology will contain only stories that a chronic reader would recognize as SF.

For decades, until recently, there was usually one or more good year's best anthologies available in paperback in the SF field. The last ones vanished with the deaths of distinguished editors Terry Carr and Donald A. Wollheim. There has been a notable gap. This book fills that need.

Furthermore, the existence of more than one year's best anthology in the SF genre has been good for the field. Volumes which differ in taste or in aesthetic criteria clarify and encourage knowledgeable discourse in the field and about the field. Therefore this book announces itself in opposition to the other extant anthologies.

Here is the problem. Other books have so blurred the boundaries between science fiction and everything else that it is possible for an observer to conclude that SF is dead or dying out. This book declares that science fiction is still alive; is fertile and varied in its excellences. Most important, SF has a separate and distinct identity within fairly clear boundaries exemplified by the contents of this book.

In the magazine stories and original anthologies this past year there was a fair amount of clunky hardish SF and a bunch of stuff, sometimes quite talented, that was published as SF, but was only by courtesy and by association SF. Not, in fact, an unusual year in these regards.

What was unusual was that it was a strong year for science fiction and in particular SF of novella length. By my casual count there were fifteen or twenty novellas from *Analog, Asimov's, Omni Online,* and the original anthologies *Far Futures* and *New Legends,* that could justifiably have been included in a year's best volume alone. Every once in a while the SF field has a "novella renaissance." 1995 was one of those years and it looks likely to spill over into 1996. Guess what? You have fallen behind in your reading if you haven't been reading the novellas. I may be off base but I suspect that there were more first-rate SF novellas than first-rate SF novels published in 1995.

Overall, the best speculative fiction of all descriptions was published in *Interzone,* which deservedly won the Hugo award this year. But all the magazines had high spots and high standards. It was not a year to skip, for instance, *Tomorrow* or *Science Fiction Age.*

Sadly, it was not a notable year for original anthologies (two extraordinary exceptions are mentioned above, to which *Full Spectrum 5* is the third). The general thinking was that the original anthologies made the magazines look good. Book publishers are at fault for letting so much unedited stuff get through under usually dazzling covers. How fortunate we are to have the magazines and the magazine editors: Budrys and Dozois, Schmidt, Rusch, Pringle, Cholfin,

Datlow, Edelman, Killheffer and the rest. We had better treasure and support them, and buy and read their
magazines, or we won't have them much longer. For
the time being they, and the writers, have given us a
bright moment.

David G. Hartwell
Pleasantville, N.Y.
January, 1996

Think Like a Dinosaur

JAMES PATRICK KELLY

James Patrick Kelly is the author of many SF stories and novels, including the recent novel *Wildlife*. One thinks of his novella, "Mr. Boy," which makes up the first part of that novel, as a high point in SF from the early 1990s. He is one of the more sophisticated of the younger SF writers from the last decade or two (he attended the Clarion SF workshop in the same group as Bruce Sterling), and seems just now in the 1990s to be achieving full command of his impressive talents. He has a clear graceful style and a willingness to do the hard work of making the science in his stories count. Never a prolific writer, Kelly is nevertheless becoming an important one in the SF field. This story, from *Asimov's SF,* is in the classic hard SF mode and is in fact in dialogue with the touchstone of hard SF reading, Tom Godwin's controversial "The Cold Equations." I have chosen to place it first to set the tone for this volume. For some readers this will be the best story of the year.

Kamala Shastri came back to this world as she had left it—naked. She tottered out of the assembler, trying to balance in Tuulen Station's delicate gravity. I caught her and bundled her into a robe with one motion, then eased her onto the float. Three years on another planet had transformed Kamala. She was leaner, more muscular. Her fingernails were now a couple of centimeters long and there were four parallel scars incised on her left cheek, perhaps some Gendian's idea of beautification. But what struck me most was the darting strangeness in her eyes. This place, so familiar to me, seemed almost to shock her. It was as if she doubted the walls and was skeptical of air. She had learned to think like an alien.

"Welcome back." The float's whisper rose to a *whoosh* as I walked it down the hallway.

She swallowed hard and I thought she might cry. Three years ago, she would have. Lots of migrators are devastated when they come out of the assembler; it's because there is no transition. A few seconds ago Kamala was on Gend, fourth planet of the star we call epsilon Leo, and now she was here in lunar orbit. She was almost home; her life's great adventure was over.

"Matthew?" she said.

"Michael." I couldn't help but be pleased that she remembered me. After all, she had changed my life.

I've guided maybe three hundred migrations—comings *and* goings—since I first came to Tuulen to study the dinos. Kamala Shastri's is the only quantum scan I've ever pirated. I doubt that the dinos care; I suspect this is a trespass they occasionally allow themselves. I know more about her—at least, as she was three years ago—than I know about myself. When the dinos sent her to Gend, she massed 50,391.72 grams and her red cell count was 4.81 million per mm^3. She could play the *nagasvaram*, a kind of bamboo flute. Her father came from Thana, near Bombay, and her favorite flavor of chewyfrute was watermelon and she'd had five lovers and when she was eleven she had wanted to be a gymnast but instead she had become a biomaterials engineer who at age twenty-nine had volunteered to go to the stars to learn how to grow artificial eyes. It took her two years to go through migrator training; she knew she could have backed out at any time, right up until the moment Silloin translated her into a superluminal signal. She understood what it meant to balance the equation.

I first met her on June 22, 2069. She shuttled over from Lunex's L1 port and came through our airlock at promptly 10:15, a small, roundish woman with black hair parted in the middle and drawn tight against her skull. They had darkened her skin against epsilon Leo's UV; it was the deep blue-black of twilight. She was wearing a striped clingy and velcro slippers to help her get around for the short time she'd be navigating our .2 micrograv.

"Welcome to Tuulen Station." I smiled and offered my hand. "My name is Michael." We shook. "I'm supposed to be a sapientologist but I also moonlight as the local guide."

"Guide?" She nodded distractedly. "Okay." She peered past me, as if expecting someone else.

"Oh, don't worry," I said, "the dinos are in their cages."

Her eyes got wide as she let her hand slip from mine. "You call the Hanen dinos?"

"Why not?" I laughed. "They call us babies. The weeps, among other things."

She shook her head in amazement. People who've never met a dino tended to romanticize them: the wise and noble reptiles who had mastered superluminal physics and introduced Earth to the wonders of galactic civilization. I doubt Kamala had ever seen a dino play poker or gobble down a screaming rabbit. And she had never argued with Linna, who still wasn't convinced that humans were psychologically ready to go to the stars.

"Have you eaten?" I gestured down the corridor toward the reception rooms.

"Yes . . . I mean, no." She didn't move. "I am not hungry."

"Let me guess. You're too nervous to eat. You're too nervous to talk, even. You wish I'd just shut up, pop you into the marble, and beam you out. Let's just get this part the hell over with, eh?"

"I don't mind the conversation, actually."

"There you go. Well, Kamala, it is my solemn duty to advise you that there are no peanut butter and jelly sandwiches on Gend. And no chicken vindaloo. What's my name again?"

"Michael?"

"See, you're not *that* nervous. Not one taco, or a single slice of eggplant pizza. This is your last chance to eat like a human."

"Okay." She did not actually smile—she was too busy being brave—but a corner of her mouth twitched. "Actually, I would not mind a cup of tea."

"Now, tea they've got." She let me guide her toward reception room D; her slippers *snicked* at the velcro carpet. "Of course, they brew it from lawn clippings."

"The Gendians don't keep lawns. They live underground."

"Refresh my memory." I kept my hand on her shoulder; beneath the clingy, her muscles were rigid. "Are they the ferrets or the things with the orange bumps?"

"They look nothing like ferrets."

We popped through the door bubble into reception D, a compact rectangular space with a scatter of low, unthreatening furniture. There was a kitchen station at one end, a closet with a vacuum toilet at the other. The ceiling was blue sky; the long wall showed a live view of the Charles River and the Boston skyline, baking in the late June sun. Kamala had just finished her doctorate at MIT.

I opaqued the door. She perched on the edge of a couch like a wren, ready to flit away.

While I was making her tea, my fingernail screen flashed. I answered it and a tiny Silloin came up in discreet mode. She didn't look at me; she was too busy watching arrays in the control room. =A problem,= her voice buzzed in my earstone, =most negligible, really. But we will have to void the last two from today's schedule. Save them at Lunex until first shift tomorrow. Can this one be kept for an hour? =

"Sure," I said. "Kamala, would you like to meet a Hanen?" I transferred Silloin to a dino-sized window on the wall. "Silloin, this is Kamala Shastri. Silloin is the one who actually runs things. I'm just the doorman."

Silloin looked through the window with her near eye, then swung around and peered at Kamala with her other. She was short for a dino, just over a meter tall, but she had an enormous head that teetered on her neck like a watermelon balancing on a grapefruit. She must have just oiled herself because her silver scales shone. =Kamala, you will accept my happiest intentions for you? =She raised her left hand, spreading the skinny digits to expose dark crescents of vestigial webbing.

"Of course, I. . . ."

=And you will permit us to render you this translation?=

She straightened. "Yes."

=Have you questions?=

I'm sure she had several hundred, but at this point was probably too scared to ask. While she hesitated, I broke in. "Which came first, the lizard or the egg?"

Silloin ignored me. =It will be excellent for you to begin when?=

"She's just having a little tea," I said, handing her the cup. "I'll bring her along when she's done. Say an hour?"

Kamala squirmed on the couch. "No, really, it will not take me. . . ."

Silloin showed us her teeth, several of which were as long as piano keys. =That would be most appropriate, Michael.= She closed; a gull flew through the space where her window had been.

"Why did you do that?" Kamala's voice was sharp.

"Because it says here that you have to wait your turn. You're not the only migrator we're sending this morning." This was a lie, of course; we had had to cut the schedule because Jodi Latchaw, the other sapientologist assigned to Tuulen, was at the University of Hipparchus presenting our paper on the Hanen concept of identity. "Don't worry, I'll make the time fly."

For a moment, we looked at each other. I could have laid down an hour's worth of patter; I'd done that often enough. Or I could have drawn her out on why she was going: no doubt she had a blind grandma or second cousin just waiting for her to bring home those artificial eyes, not to mention potential spin-offs which could well end tuberculosis, famine, and premature ejaculation, *blah, blah, blah.* Or I could have just left her alone in the room to read the wall. The trick was guessing how spooked she really was.

"Tell me a secret," I said.

"What?"

"A secret, you know, something no one else knows."

She stared as if I'd just fallen off Mars.

"Look, in a little while you're going someplace that's what . . . three hundred and ten light years away? You're scheduled to stay for three years. By the time you come back, I could easily be rich, famous, and elsewhere; we'll probably never see each other again. So what have you got to lose? I promise not to tell."

She leaned back on the couch, and settled the cup in her lap. "This is another test, right? After everything they have put me through, they still have not decided whether to send me."

"Oh no, in a couple of hours you'll be cracking nuts with ferrets in some dark Gendian burrow. This is just me, talking."

"You are crazy."

"Actually, I believe the technical term is logomaniac. It's from the Greek: *logos* meaning word, *mania* meaning two bits short of a byte. I just love to chat is all. Tell you what, I'll go first. If my secret isn't juicy enough, you don't have tell me anything."

Her eyes were slits as she sipped her tea. I was fairly sure that whatever she was worrying about at the moment, it wasn't being swallowed by the big blue marble.

"I was brought up Catholic," I said, settling onto a chair in front of her. "I'm not anymore, but that's not the secret. My parents sent me to Mary, Mother of God High School; we called it Moogoo. It was run by a couple of old priests, Father Thomas and his wife, Mother Jennifer. Father Tom taught physics, which I got a 'D' in, mostly because he talked like he had walnuts in his mouth. Mother Jennifer taught theology and had all the warmth of a marble pew; her nickname was Mama Moogoo.

"One night, just two weeks before my graduation, Father Tom and Mama Moogoo went out in their Chevy Minimus for ice cream. On the way home, Mama Moogoo pushed a yellow light and got broadsided by an ambulance. Like I said, she was old, a hundred and twenty something; they should've lifted her license back in the '50s. She was killed instantly. Father Tom died in the hospital.

"Of course, we were all supposed to feel sorry for them and I guess I did a little, but I never really liked either of them and I resented the way their deaths had screwed things up for my class. So I was more annoyed than sorry, but then I also had this edge of guilt for being so uncharitable. Maybe you'd have to grow up Catholic to understand that. Anyway, the day after it happened they called an assembly in the gym and we were all there squirming on the bleachers and the cardinal himself telepresented a sermon. He kept trying to comfort us, like it had been our *parents* that had died. When I made a joke about it to the kid next to me, I got caught and spent the last week of my senior year with an in-school suspension."

Kamala had finished her tea. She slid the empty cup into one of the holders built into the table.

"Want some more?" I said.

She stirred restlessly. "Why are you telling me this?"

"It's part of the secret." I leaned forward in my chair. "See, my family lived down the street from Holy Spirit Cemetery and in order to get to the carryvan line on McKinley Ave., I had to cut through. Now this happened a couple of days after I got in trouble at the assembly. It was around midnight and I was coming home from a graduation party where I had taken a couple of pokes of insight, so I was feeling sly as a philosopher-king. As I walked through the cemetery, I stumbled across two dirt mounds right next to each other. At first I thought they were flower beds, then I saw the wooden crosses. Fresh graves: here lies Father Tom and Mama Moogoo. There wasn't much to the crosses: they were basically just stakes with cross-pieces, painted white and hammered into the ground. The names were hand printed on them. The way I figure it, they were there to mark the graves until the stones got delivered. I didn't need any insight to recognize a once in a lifetime opportunity. If I switched them, what were the chances anyone was going to notice? It was no problem sliding them out of their holes. I smoothed the dirt with my hands and then ran like hell."

Until that moment, she'd seemed bemused by my story and slightly condescending toward me. Now there was a glint of alarm in her eyes. "That was a terrible thing to do," she said.

"Absolutely," I said, "although the dinos think that the whole idea of planting bodies in graveyards and marking them with carved rocks is weepy. They say there is no identity in dead meat, so why get so sentimental about it? Linna keeps asking how come we don't put markers over our shit. But that's not the secret. See, it'd been a warmish night in the middle of June, only as I ran, the air turned cold. Freezing, I could see my breath. And my shoes got heavier and heavier, like they had turned to stone. As I got closer to the back gate, it felt like I was fighting a strong wind, except my clothes weren't flapping. I slowed to a walk. I know I could have pushed through, but my heart was thumping and then I heard this whispery seashell noise and I panicked. So the secret is I'm a coward. I switched the crosses back and I never went near that cemetery again. As a matter of fact," I nodded at the walls of reception room D on Tuulen Station, "when I grew up, I got about as far away from it as I could."

She stared as I settled back in my chair. "True story," I said and raised my right hand. She seemed so astonished that I started laughing. A smile bloomed on her dark face and suddenly she was giggling too. It was a soft, liquid sound, like a brook bubbling over smooth stones; it made me laugh even harder. Her lips were full and her teeth were very white.

"Your turn," I said, finally.

"Oh, no, I could not." She waved me off. "I don't have anything so good. . . ." She paused, then frowned. "You have told that before?"

"Once," I said. "To the Hanen, during the psych screening for this job. Only I didn't tell them the last part. I know how dinos think, so I ended it when I switched the crosses. The rest is baby stuff." I waggled a finger at her. "Don't forget, you promised to keep my secret."

"Did I?"

"Tell me about when you were young. Where did you grow up?"

"Toronto." She glanced at me, appraisingly. "There *was* something, but not funny. Sad."

I nodded encouragement and changed the wall to Toronto's skyline dominated by the CN Tower, Toronto-Dominion Centre, Commerce Court, and the King's Needle.

She twisted to take in the view and spoke over her shoulder. "When I was ten we moved to an apartment, right downtown on Bloor Street so my mother could be close to work." She pointed at the wall and turned back to face me. "She is an accountant, my father wrote wallpaper for Imagineering. It was a huge building; it seemed as if we were always getting into the elevator with ten neighbors we never knew we had. I was coming home from school one day when an old woman stopped me in the lobby. 'Little girl,' she said, 'how would you like to earn ten dollars?' My parents had warned me not to talk to strangers but she obviously was a resident. Besides, she had an ancient pair of exolegs strapped on, so I knew I could outrun her if I needed to. She asked me to go to the store for her, handed me a grocery list and a cash card, and said I should bring everything up to her apartment, 10W. I should have been more suspicious because all the downtown groceries deliver but, as I soon found out, all she really wanted was someone to talk to her. And she was willing to pay for it, usually five or ten dollars, depending on how long I stayed. Soon I was stopping by almost every day after school. I think my parents would have made me stop if they had known; they were very strict. They would not have liked me taking her money. But neither of them got home until after six, so it was my secret to keep."

"Who was she?" I said. "What did you talk about?"

"Her name was Margaret Ase. She was ninety-seven years old and I think she had been some kind of counselor. Her husband and her daughter had both died and she was alone. I didn't find out much about her;

she made me do most of the talking. She asked me about my friends and what I was learning in school and my family. Things like that. . . ."

Her voice trailed off as my fingernail started to flash. I answered it.

=Michael, I am pleased to call you to here.=Silloin buzzed in my ear. She was almost twenty minutes ahead of schedule.

"See, I told you we'd make the time fly." I stood; Kamala's eyes got very wide. "I'm ready if you are."

I offered her my hand. She took it and let me help her up. She wavered for a moment and I sensed just how fragile her resolve was. I put my hand around her waist and steered her into the corridor. In the micrograv of Tuulen Station, she already felt as insubstantial as a memory. "So tell me, what happened that was so sad?"

At first I thought she hadn't heard. She shuffled along, said nothing.

"Hey, don't keep me in suspense here, Kamala," I said. "You have to finish the story."

"No," she said. "I don't think I do."

I didn't take this personally. My only real interest in the conversation had been to distract her. If she refused to be distracted, that was her choice. Some migrators kept talking right up to the moment they slid into the big blue marble, but lots of them went quiet just before. They turned inward. Maybe in her mind she was already on Gend, blinking in the hard white light.

We arrived at the scan center, the largest space on Tuulen Station. Immediately in front of us was the marble, containment for the quantum nondemolition sensor array—QNSA for the acronymically inclined. It was the milky blue of glacial ice and big as two elephants. The upper hemisphere was raised and the scanning table protruded like a shiny gray tongue. Kamala approached the marble and touched her reflection, which writhed across its polished surface. To the right was a padded bench, the fogger, and a toilet. I looked left, through the control room window. Silloin stood watching us, her impossible head cocked to one side.

=She is docile?= she buzzed in my earstone.

I held up crossed fingers.

=Welcome, Kamala Shastri.= Silloin's voice came over the speakers with a soothing hush. =You are ready to open your translation?=

Kamala bowed to the window. "This is where I take my clothes off?"

=If you would be so convenient.=

She brushed past me to the bench. Apparently I had ceased to exist; this was between her and the dino now. She undressed quickly, folding her clingy into a neat bundle, tucking her slippers beneath the bench. Out of the corner of my eye, I could see tiny feet, heavy thighs, and the beautiful, dark smooth skin of her back. She stepped into the fogger and closed the door.

"Ready," she called.

From the control room, Silloin closed circuits which filled the fogger with a dense cloud of nanolenses. The nano stuck to Kamala and deployed, coating the surface of her body. As she breathed them, they passed from her lungs into her bloodstream. She only coughed twice; she had been well trained. When the eight minutes were up, Silloin cleared the air in the fogger and she emerged. Still ignoring me, she again faced the control room.

=Now you must arrange yourself on the scanning table,= said Silloin, =and enable Michael to fix you.=

She crossed to the marble without hesitation,

climbed the gantry beside it, eased onto the table and laid back.

I followed her up. "Sure you won't tell me the rest of the secret?"

She stared at the ceiling, unblinking.

"Okay then." I took the canister and a sparker out of my hip pouch. "This is going to happen just like you've practiced it." I used the canister to respray the bottoms of her feet with nano. I watched her belly rise and fall, rise and fall. She was deep into her breathing exercise. "Remember, no skipping rope or whistling while you're in the scanner."

She did not answer. "Deep breath now," I said and touched a sparker to her big toe. There was a brief crackle as the nano on her skin wove into a net and stiffened, locking her in place. "Bark at the ferrets for me." I picked up my equipment, climbed down the gantry, and wheeled it back to the wall.

With a low whine, the big blue marble retracted its tongue. I watched the upper hemisphere close, swallowing Kamala Shastri, then joined Silloin in the control room.

I'm not of the school who thinks the dinos stink, another reason I got assigned to study them up close. Parikkal, for example, has no smell at all that I can tell. Normally Silloin had the faint but not unpleasant smell of stale wine. When she was under stress, however, her scent became vinegary and biting. It must have been a wild morning for her. Breathing through my mouth, I settled onto the stool at my station.

She was working quickly, now that the marble was sealed. Even with all their training, migrators tend to get claustrophobic fast. After all, they're lying in the dark, in nanobondage, waiting to be translated. Waiting. The simulator at the Singapore training center makes a noise while it's emulating a scan. Most compare it to a light rain pattering against the marble; for some, it's low volume radio static. As long as they hear the patter, the migrators think they're safe. We reproduce it for them while they're in our marble, even though scanning takes about three seconds and is utterly silent. From my vantage I could see that the sagittal, axial, and coronal windows had stopped blinking, indicating full data capture. Silloin was skirring busily to herself; her comm didn't bother to interpret. Wasn't saying anything baby Michael needed to know, obviously. Her head bobbed as she monitored the enormous spread of readouts; her claws clicked against touch screens that glowed orange and yellow.

At my station, there was only a migration status screen—and a white button.

I wasn't lying when I said I was just the doorman. My field is sapientology, not quantum physics. Whatever went wrong with Kamala's migration that morning, there was nothing *I* could have done. The dinos tell me that the quantum nondemoliton sensor array is able to circumvent Heisenberg's Uncertainty Principle by measuring spacetime's most crogglingly small quantities without collapsing the wave/particle duality. How small? They say that no one can ever "see" anything that's only 1.62×10^{-33} centimeters long, because at that size, space and time come apart. Time ceases to exist and space becomes a random probablistic foam, sort of like quantum spit. We humans call this the Planck-Wheeler length. There's a Planck-Wheeler time, too: 10^{-45} of a second. If something happens and something else happens and the two events are separated by an interval of a mere 10^{-45} of a second, it is impossible to say which came first. It was all dino to me—and that's just the scanning. The

Hanen use different tech to create artificial wormholes, hold them open with electromagnetic vacuum fluctuations, pass the superluminal signal through and then assemble the migrator from elementary particles at the destination.

On my status screen I could see that the signal which mapped Kamala Shastri had already been compressed and burst through the wormhole. All that we had to wait for was for Gend to confirm acquisition. Once they officially told us that they had her, it would be my job to balance the equation.

Pitter-patter, pitter-pat.

Some Hanen technologies are so powerful that they can alter reality itself. Wormholes could be used by some time traveling fanatic to corrupt history; the scanner/assembler could be used to create a billion Silloins—or Michael Burrs. Pristine reality, unpolluted by such anomalies, has what the dinos call harmony. Before any sapients get to join the galactic club, they must prove total commitment to preserving harmony.

Since I had come to Tuulen to study the dinos, I had pressed the white button over two hundred times. It was what I had to do in order to keep my assignment. Pressing it sent a killing pulse of ionizing radiation through the cerebral cortex of the migrator's duplicated, and therefore unnecessary, body. No brain, no pain; death followed within seconds. Yes, the first few times I'd balanced the equation had been traumatic. It was still . . . unpleasant. But this was the price of a ticket to the stars. If certain unusual people like Kamala Shastri had decided that price was reasonable, it was their choice, not mine.

=This is not a happy result, Michael.= Silloin spoke to me for the first time since I'd entered the control room. =Discrepancies are unfolding.= On my status screen I watched as the error-checking routines started turning up hits.

"Is the problem here?" I felt a knot twist suddenly inside me. "Or there?" If our original scan checked out, then all Silloin would have to do is send it to Gend again.

There was a long, infuriating silence. Silloin concentrated on part of her board as if it showed her first-born hatchling chipping out of its egg. The respirator between her shoulders had ballooned to twice its normal size. My screen showed that Kamala had been in the marble for four minutes plus.

=It may be fortunate to recalibrate the scanner and begin over.=

"*Shit.*" I slammed my hand against the wall, felt the pain tingle to my elbow. "I thought you had it fixed." When error-checking turned up problems, the solution was almost always to retransmit. "You're sure, Silloin? Because this one was right on the edge when I tucked her in."

Silloin gave me a dismissive sneeze and slapped at the error readouts with her bony little hand, as if to knock them back to normal. Like Linna and the other dinos, she had little patience with what she regarded as our weepy fears of migration. However, unlike Linna, she was convinced that someday, after we had used Hanen technologies long enough, we would learn to think like dinos. Maybe she's right. Maybe when we've been squirting through wormholes for hundreds of years, we'll cheerfully discard our redundant bodies. When the dinos and other sapients migrate, the redundants zap themselves—very harmonious. They tried it with humans but it didn't always work. That's why I'm here. =The need is most clear. It will prolong about thirty minutes,= she said.

Kamala had been alone in the dark for almost six

minutes, longer than any migrator I'd ever guided. "Let me hear what's going on in the marble."

The control room filled with the sound of Kamala screaming. It didn't sound human to me—more like the shriek of tires skidding toward a crash.

"We've got to get her out of there," I said.

=That is baby thinking, Michael.=

"So she's a baby, damn it." I knew that bringing migrators out of the marble was big trouble. I could have asked Silloin to turn the speakers off and sat there while Kamala suffered. It was my decision.

"Don't open the marble until I get the gantry in place." I ran for the door. "And keep the sound effects going."

At the first crack of light, she howled. The upper hemisphere seemed to lift in slow motion; inside the marble she bucked against the nano. Just when I was sure it was impossible that she could scream any louder, she did. We had accomplished something extraordinary, Silloin and I; we had stripped the brave biomaterials engineer away completely, leaving in her place a terrified animal.

"Kamala, it's me. Michael."

Her frantic screams cohered into words. "Stop . . . don't . . . oh my god, someone help!" If I could have, I would've jumped into the marble to release her, but the sensor array is fragile and I wasn't going to risk causing any more problems with it. We both had to wait until the upper hemisphere swung fully open and the scanning table offered poor Kamala to me.

"It's okay. Nothing's going to happen, all right? We're bringing you out, that's all. Everything's all right."

When I released her with the sparker, she flew at me. We pitched back and almost toppled down the steps. Her grip was so tight I couldn't breathe.

"Don't *kill* me, don't, *please,* don't."

I rolled on top of her. "Kamala!" I wriggled one arm free and used it to pry myself from her. I scrabbled sideways to the top step. She lurched clumsily in the microgravity and swung at me; her fingernails raked across the back of my hand, leaving bloody welts. "Kamala, stop!" It was all I could do not to strike back at her. I retreated down the steps.

"You bastard. What are you assholes trying to do to me?" She drew several shuddering breaths and began to sob.

"The scan got corrupted somehow. Silloin is working on it."

=The difficulty is obscure,= said Silloin from the control room.

"But that's not your problem." I backed toward the bench.

"They lied," she mumbled and seemed to fold in upon herself as if she were just skin, no flesh or bones. "They said I wouldn't feel anything and . . . do you know what it's like . . . it's . . . "

I fumbled for her clingy. "Look, here are your clothes. Why don't you get dressed? We'll get you out of here."

"You bastard," she repeated, but her voice was empty.

She let me coax her down off the gantry. I counted nubs on the wall while she fumbled back into her clingy. They were the size of the old dimes my grandfather used to hoard and they glowed with a soft golden bioluminescence. I was up to forty-seven before she was dressed and ready to return to reception D.

Where before she had perched expectantly at the edge of the couch, now she slumped back against it. "So what now?" she said.

"I don't know." I went to the kitchen station and took

the carafe from the distiller. "What now, Silloin?" I poured water over the back of my hand to wash the blood off. It stung. My earstone was silent. "I guess we wait," I said finally.

"For what?"

"For her to fix . . . "

"I'm not going back in there."

I decided to let that pass. It was probably too soon to argue with her about it, although once Silloin recalibrated the scanner, she'd have very little time to change her mind. "You want something from the kitchen? Another cup of tea, maybe?"

"How about a gin and tonic—hold the tonic?" She rubbed beneath her eyes. "Or a couple of hundred milliliters of serentol?"

I tried to pretend she'd made a joke. "You know the dinos won't let us open the bar for migrators. The scanner might misread your brain chemistry and your visit to Gend would be nothing but a three year drunk."

"Don't you *understand*?" She was right back at the edge of hysteria. "I am not *going!*" I didn't really blame her for the way she was acting but, at that moment, all I wanted was to get rid of Kamala Shastri. I didn't care if she went on to Gend or back to Lunex or over the rainbow to Oz, just as long as I didn't have to be in the same room with this miserable creature who was trying to make me feel guilty about an accident I had nothing to do with.

"I thought I could do it." She clamped hands to her ears as if to keep from hearing her own despair. "I wasted the last two years convincing myself that I could just lie there and not think and then suddenly I'd be far away. I was going someplace wonderful and strange." She made a strangled sound and let her hands drop into her lap. "I was going to help people see."

"You did it, Kamala. You did everything we asked."

She shook her head. "I couldn't *not* think. That was the problem. And then there she was, trying to touch me. In the dark. I had not thought of her since. . . ." She shivered. "It's your fault for reminding me."

"Your secret friend," I said.

"Friend?" Kamala seemed puzzled by the word. "No, I wouldn't say she was a friend. I was always a little bit scared of her, because I was never quite sure of what she wanted from me." She paused. "One day I went up to 10W after school. She was in her chair, staring down at Bloor Street. Her back was to me. I said, 'Hi, Ms. Ase.' I was going to show her a genie I had written, only she didn't say anything. I came around. Her skin was the color of ashes. I took her hand. It was like picking up something plastic. She was stiff, hard—not a person anymore. She had become a thing, like a feather or a bone. I ran; I had to get out of there. I went up to our apartment and I hid from her."

She squinted, as if observing—judging—her younger self through the lens of time. "I think I understand now what she wanted. I think she knew she was dying; she probably wanted me there with her at the end, or at least to find her body afterward and report it. Only I could *not*. If I told anyone she was dead, my parents would find out about us. Maybe people would suspect me of doing something to her—I don't know. I could have called security but I was only ten; I was afraid somehow they might trace me. A couple of weeks went by and still nobody had found her. By then it was too late to say anything. Everyone would have blamed me for keeping quiet for so long. At night I imagined her turning black and rotting into her chair like a banana. It made me sick; I couldn't sleep or eat. They had to put me in the hospital, because I had touched her. Touched *death*."

=Michael,= Silloin whispered, without any warning flash. =An impossibility has formed.=

"As soon as I was out of that building, I started to get better. Then they found her. After I came home, I worked hard to forget Ms. Ase. And I did, almost." Kamala wrapped her arms around herself. "But just now she was with me again, inside the marble . . . I couldn't see her but somehow I knew she was reaching for me."

=Michael, Parikkal is here with Linna.=

"Don't you see?" She gave a bitter laugh. "How can I go to Gend? I'm *hallucinating*."

=It has broken the harmony. Join us alone.=

I was tempted to swat at the annoying buzz in my ear.

"You know, I've never told anyone about her before."

"Well, maybe some good has come of this after all." I patted her on the knee. "Excuse me for a minute?" She seemed surprised that I would leave. I slipped into the hall and hardened the door bubble, sealing her in.

"What impossibility?" I said, heading for the control room.

=She is pleased to reopen the scanner?=

"Not pleased at all. More like scared shitless."

=This is Parikkal.= My earstone translated his skirring with a sizzling edge, like bacon frying. =The confusion was made elsewhere. No mishap can be connected to our station.=

I pushed through the bubble into the scan center. I could see the three dinos through the control window. Their heads were bobbing furiously. "Tell me," I said.

=Our communications with Gend were marred by a transient falsehood,= said Silloin. =Kamala Shastri has been received there and reconstructed.=

"She migrated?" I felt the deck shifting beneath my feet. "What about the one we've got here?"

=The simplicity is to load the redundant into the scanner and finalize. . . .=

"I've got news for you. She's not going anywhere near that marble."

=Her equation is not in balance.= This was Linna, speaking for the first time. Linna was not exactly in charge of Tuulen Station; she was more like a senior partner. Parikkal and Silloin had overruled her before—at least I thought they had.

"What do you expect me to do? Wring her neck?"

There was a moment's silence—which was not as unnerving as watching them eye me through the window, their heads now perfectly still.

"No," I said.

The dinos were skirring at each other; their heads wove and dipped. At first they cut me cold and the comm was silent, but suddenly their debate crackled through my earstone.

=This is just as I have been telling,= said Linna. =These beings have no realization of harmony. It is wrongful to further unleash them on the many worlds.=

=You may have reason,= said Parikkal. =But that is a later discussion. The need is for the equation to be balanced.=

=There is no time. We will have to discard the redundant ourselves.= Silloin bared her long brown teeth. It would take her maybe five seconds to rip Kamala's throat out. And even though Silloin was the dino most sympathetic to us, I had no doubt she would enjoy the kill.

=I will argue that we adjourn human migration until this world has been rethought,= said Linna.

This was the typical dino condescension. Even

though they appeared to be arguing with each other, they were actually speaking to me, laying the situation out so that even the baby sapient would understand. They were informing me that I was jeopardizing the future of humanity in space. That the Kamala in reception D was dead whether I quit or not. That the equation had to be balanced and it had to be now.

"Wait," I said. "Maybe I can coax her back into the scanner." I had to get away from them. I pulled my earstone out and slid it into my pocket. I was in such a hurry to escape that I stumbled as I left the scan center and had to catch myself in the hallway. I stood there for a second, staring at the hand pressed against the bulkhead. I seemed to see the splayed fingers through the wrong end of a telescope. I was far away from myself.

She had curled into herself on the couch, arms clutching knees to her chest, as if trying to shrink so that nobody would notice her.

"We're all set," I said briskly. "You'll be in the marble for less than a minute, guaranteed."

"*No*, Michael."

I could actually feel myself receding from Tuulen Station. "Kamala, you're throwing away a huge part of your life."

"It is my right." Her eyes were shiny.

No, it wasn't. She was redundant; she had no rights. What had she said about the dead old lady? She had become a thing, like a bone.

"Okay, then," I jabbed at her shoulder with a stiff forefinger. "Let's go."

She recoiled. "Go where?"

"Back to Lunex. I'm holding the shuttle for you. It just dropped off my afternoon list; I should be helping them settle in, instead of having to deal with you."

She unfolded herself slowly.

"Come on." I jerked her roughly to her feet. "The dinos want you off Tuulen as soon as possible and so do I." I was so distant, I couldn't see Kamala Shastri anymore.

She nodded and let me march her to the bubble door.

"And if we meet anyone in the hall, keep your mouth shut."

"You're being so mean." Her whisper was thick.

"You're being such a baby."

When the inner door glided open, she realized immediately that there was no umbilical to the shuttle. She tried to twist out of my grip but I put my shoulder into her, hard. She flew across the airlock, slammed against the outer door and caromed onto her back. As I punched the switch to close the door, I came back to myself. *I* was doing this terrible thing— me, Michael Burr. I couldn't help myself: I giggled. When I last saw her, Kamala was scrabbling across the deck toward me but she was too late. I was surprised that she wasn't screaming again; all I heard was her ferocious breathing.

As soon as the inner door sealed, I opened the outer door. After all, how many ways are there to kill someone on a space station? There were no guns. Maybe someone else could have stabbed or strangled her, but not me. Poison how? Besides, I wasn't thinking, I had been trying desperately not to think of what I was doing. I was a sapientologist, not a doctor. I always thought that exposure to space meant instantaneous death. Explosive decompression or something like. I didn't want her to suffer. I was trying to make it quick. Painless.

I heard the whoosh of escaping air and thought that was it; the body had been ejected into space. I had actually turned away when thumping started, frantic, like the beat of a racing heart. She must have found something to hold onto. *Thump, thump, thump!* It was too much. I sagged against the inner door—*thump, thump*—slid down it, laughing. Turns out that if you empty the lungs, it is possible to survive exposure to space for at least a minute, maybe two. I thought it was funny. *Thump!* Hilarious, actually. I had tried my best for her—risked my career—and this was how she repaid me? As I laid my cheek against the door, the *thumps* started to weaken. There were just a few centimeters between us, the difference between life and death. Now she knew all about balancing the equation. I was laughing so hard I could scarcely breathe. Just like the meat behind the door. Die already, you weepy bitch!

I don't know how long it took. The *thumping* slowed. Stopped. And then I was a hero. I had preserved harmony, kept our link to the stars open. I chuckled with pride; I could think like a dinosaur.

I popped through the bubble door into Reception D. "It's time to board the shuttle."

Kamala had changed into a clingy and velcro slippers. There were at least ten windows open on the wall; the room filled with the murmur of talking heads. Friends and relatives had to be notified; their loved one had returned, safe and sound. "I have to go," she said to the wall. "I will call you when I land."

She gave me a smile that seemed stiff from disuse. "I want to thank you again, Michael." I wondered how long it took migrators to get used to being human. "You were such a help and I was such a . . . I was not myself." She glanced around the room one last time and then shivered. "I was really scared."

"You were."

She shook her head. "Was it that bad?"

I shrugged and led her out into the hall.

"I feel so silly now. I mean, I was in the marble for less than a minute and then—" she snapped her fingers— "there I was on Gend, just like you said." She brushed up against me as we walked; her body was hard under the clingy. "Anyway, I am glad we got this chance to talk. I really *was* going to look you up when I got back. I certainly did not expect to see you here."

"I decided to stay on." The inner door to the airlock glided open. "It's a job that grows on you." The umbilical shivered as the pressure between Tuulen Station and the shuttle equalized.

"You have got migrators waiting," she said.

"Two."

"I envy them." She turned to me. "Have *you* ever thought about going to the stars?"

"No," I said.

Kamala put her hand to my face. "It changes everything." I could feel the prick of her long nails—claws, really. For a moment I thought she meant to scar my cheek the way she had been scarred.

"I know," I said.

Wonders of the Invisible World

PATRICIA A. McKILLIP

Patricia McKillip is one of the most distinguished living fantasy writers, winner of the first World Fantasy award for best novel (*The Forgotten Beasts of Eld*, 1974), and author of the classic *Riddlemaster of Hed* trilogy. She is also one of the finest and most underrated short fiction writers in the F& SF field for the 1990s. Her stories in recent years display a breadth of humane vision worthy of comparison to the fiction of Ursula K. Le Guin and are the work of a first-rate literary talent at the height of her powers. This story is a hip, dark vision of the future and the past, tightly plotted, ironic, rich, and deep. It appeared in *Full Spectrum 5,* one of the outstanding original anthologies from 1995.

I am the angel sent to Cotton Mather. It took me some time to get his attention. He lay on the floor with his eyes closed; he prayed fervently, sometimes murmuring, sometimes shouting. Apparently the household was used to it. I heard footsteps pass his study door; a woman—his wife Abigail?—called to someone: "If your throat is no better tomorrow, we'll have Phillip pee in a cup for you to gargle." From the way the house smelled, Phillip didn't bother much with cups. Cotton Mather smelled of smoke and sweat and wet wool. Winter had come early. The sky was black, the ground was white, the wind pinched like a witch and whined like a starving dog. There was no color in the landscape and no mercy. Cotton Mather prayed to see the invisible world.

He wanted an angel.

"O Lord," he said, in desperate, hoarse, weary cadences, like a sick child talking itself to sleep. "Thou hast given angelic visions to Thy innocent children to defend them from their demons. Remember Thy humble servant, who prostrates himself in the dust, vile worm that I am, forsaking food and comfort and sleep, in humble hope that Thou might bestow upon Thy humble servant the blessing and hope at this harsh and evil time: a glimpse of Thy shadow, a flicker of light in Thine eye, a single word from Thy mouth. Show me Thy messengers of good who fly between the visible and invisible worlds. Grant me, O God, a vision."

I cleared my throat a little. He didn't open his eyes. The fire was dying down. I wondered who replenished it, and if the sight of Mather's bright, winged creature would surprise anyone, with all the witches, devils and demented goldfinches perched on rafters all over New England. The firelight spilling across the wide planks glowed just beyond his outstretched hand. He lay in dim lights and fluttering shadows, in the long, long night of history, when no one could ever see clearly after sunset, and witches and angels and living dreams trembled just beyond the fire.

"Grant me, O God, a vision."

I was standing in front of his nose. He was lost in days of fasting and desire, trying to conjure an angel out of his head. According to his writings, what he expected to see was the generic white male with wings growing out of his shoulders, fair-haired, permanently beardless, wearing a long white nightgown and a gold dinner plate on his head. This was what intrigued Durham, and why he had hired me: he couldn't believe that both good and evil in the Puritan imagination could be so banal.

But I was what Mather wanted: something as colorless and pure as the snow that lay like the hand of God over the earth, harsh, exacting, unambiguous. Fire, their salvation against the cold, was red and belonged to Hell.

"O Lord."

It was the faintest of whispers. He was staring at my feet.

They were bare and shining and getting chilled. The ring of diamonds in my halo contained controls for light, for holograms like my wings, a map disc, a local-history disc in case I got totally bewildered by events, and a recorder disc that had caught the sudden stammer in Mather's last word. He had asked for an angel; he got an angel. I wished he would quit staring at my feet and throw another log on the fire.

He straightened slowly, pushing himself off the floor while his eyes traveled upward. He was scarcely thirty at the time of the trials; he resembled his father at that age more than the familiar Pelham portrait of Mather in his sixties, soberly dressed, with a wig like a cream puff on his head, and a firm, resigned mouth. The young Mather had long dark hair, a spare, handsome, clean-shaven face, searching, credulous eyes. His eyes reached my face finally, cringing a little, as if he half expected a demon's red, leering face attached to the angel's body. But he found what he expected. He began to cry.

He cried silently, so I could speak. His writings are mute about much of the angel's conversation. Mostly it predicted Mather's success as a writer, great reviews and spectacular sales in America and Europe. I greeted him, gave him the message from God, quoted Ezekiel, and then got down to business. By then he had stopped crying, wiped his face with his dusty sleeve and cheered up at the prospect of fame.

"There are troubled children," I said, "who have seen me."

"They speak of you in their misery," he said gratefully. "You give them strength against evil."

"Their afflictions are terrible."

"Yes," he whispered.

"You have observed their torments."

"Yes."

"You have taken them into your home, borne witness to their complaints, tried to help them cast out their tormentors."

"I have tried."

"You have wrestled with the invisible world."

"Yes."

We weren't getting very far. He still knelt on the hard floor, as he had done for hours, perhaps days; he could see me more clearly than he had seen anything in the dark in his life. He had forgotten the fire. I tried to be patient. Good angels were beyond temperament, even while at war with angels who had disgraced themselves by exhibiting human characteristics. But the floorboards were getting very cold.

"You have felt the invisible chains about them," I prodded. "The invisible, hellish things moving beneath their bedclothes."

"The children cannot seem to stand my books," he said a little querulously, with a worried frown. "My writing sends them into convulsions. At the mere act of opening my books, they fall down as dead upon the floor. Yet how can I lead them gently back to God's truth if the truth acts with such violence against them?"

"It is not against them," I reminded him, "but against the devil, who," I added, inspired, "takes many shapes."

He nodded, and became voluble. "Last week he took the shape of thieves who stole three sermons from me. And of a rat—or something like a hellish rat—we could feel in the air, but not see."

"A rat."

"And sometimes a bird, a yellow bird, the children say—they see it perched on the fingers of those they name witches."

"And since they say it, it is so."

He nodded gravely. "God made nothing more innocent than children."

I let that pass. I was his delusion, and if I had truly been sent to him from God, then God and Mather agreed on everything.

"Have they—" this was Durham's suggestion "—not yet seen the devil in the shape of a black horse who spews fire between its teeth, and is ridden by three witches, each more beautiful than the last?"

He stared at me, then caught himself imagining the witches and blinked. "No," he breathed. "No one has seen such a thing. Though the Shape of Goody Bishop in her scarlet bodice and her lace had been seen over the beds of honest married men."

"What did she do to them?"

"She hovered. She haunted them. For this and more she was hanged."

For wearing a color and inciting the imagination, she was hanged. I refrained from commenting that since her Shape had done the hovering, it was her Shape that should have been hanged. But it was almost worth my researcher's license. "In God's justice," I said piously, "her soul dwells." I had almost forgotten the fire; this dreary, crazed, malicious atmosphere was more chilling than the cold.

"She had a witchmark," Mather added. "The witch's teat." His eyes were wide, marveling; he had conjured witches as well as angels out of his imagination. I suppose it was easier, in that harsh world, to make demons out of your neighbors, with their imperfections, tempers, rheumy eyes, missing teeth, irritating habits and smells, than to find angelic beauty in them. But I wasn't there to judge Mather. I could hear Durham's intense voice: Imagination. Imagery. I want to know what they pulled out of their heads. They invented their devil, but all they could do was make him talk like a bird? Don't bother with a moral viewpoint. I want to know what Mather saw. This was the man who believed that thunder was caused by the sulfurous farts of decaying vegetation. Why? Don't ask me why. You're a researcher. Go research.

Research the imagination. It was as obsolete as the appendix in most adults, except for those in whom, like the appendix, it became inflamed for no reason. Durham's curiosity seemed as aberrated as Mather's; they both craved visions. But in his world, Durham could afford the luxury of being crazed. In this world, only the crazed, the adolescent girls, the trial judges, Mather himself, were sane.

I was taking a moral viewpoint. But Mather was still talking, and the recorder was catching his views, not mine. I had asked Durham once, after an exasperating journey to some crowded, airless, fly-infested temple covered with phallic symbols to appear as a goddess, to stop hiring me; the Central Research Computer had obviously got its records mixed when it recommended me to him. Our historical viewpoints were thoroughly incompatible. "No, they're not," he had said obnoxiously, and refused to elaborate. He paid well. He paid very well. So here I was, in frozen colonial New England, listening to Cotton Mather talk about brooms.

"The witches ride them," he said, still wide-eyed. "Sometimes three to a besom. To their foul Witch's Sabbaths."

Their foul Sabbaths, he elaborated, consisted of witches gathering in some boggy pasture where the demons talked with the voices of frogs, listening to a fiendish sermon, drinking blood, and plotting to bring back pagan customs like dancing around a Maypole. I wondered if, being an angel of God, I was supposed to know all this already, and if Mather would wonder later why I had listened. Durham and I had argued about this, about the ethics and legalities of me pretending to be Mather's delusion.

"What's the problem?" he had asked. "You think the real angel is going to show up later?"

Mather was still speaking, in a feverish trance caused most likely by too much fasting, prayer, and mental agitation. Evil eyes, he was talking about, and "things" that were hairy all over. They apparently caused neighbors to blame one another for dead pigs, wagons stuck in potholes, sickness, lust and deadly boredom. I was getting bored myself, by then, and thoroughly depressed. Children's fingers had pointed at random, and wherever they pointed, they created a witch. So much for the imagination. It was malignant here, an instrument of cruelty and death.

"He did not speak to the court, neither to defend his innocence nor confess his guilt," Mather was saying solemnly. "He was a stubborn old man. They piled stones upon him until his tongue stuck out and he died. But he never spoke. They had already hanged his wife. He spoke well enough then, accusing her."

I had heard enough.

"God protect the innocent," I said, and surprised myself, for it was a prayer to something. I added, more gently, for Mather, blinking out of his trance, looked worried, as if I had accused him, "Be comforted. God will give you strength to bear all tribulations in these dark times. Be patient and faithful, and in the fullness of time, you will be rewarded with the truth of your life."

Not standard Puritan dogma, but all he heard was "reward" and "truth." I raised my hand in blessing. He flung himself down to kiss the floor at my feet. I activated the controls in my halo and went home.

Durham was waiting for me at the Researchers' Terminus. I pulled the recorder disc out of my halo, fed it to the computer, and then stepped out of the warp chamber. While the computer analyzed my recording to see if I had broken any of one thousand, five hundred and sixty-three regulations, I took off my robe and my blond hair and dumped them and my halo into Durham's arms.

"Well?" he said, not impatient, just intent, not even seeing me as I pulled a skirt and tunic over my head. I was still cold, and worried about my researcher's license, which the computer would refuse to return if I had violated history. Durham had eyes like Cotton Mather's, I saw for the first time: dark, burning, but with a suggestion of humor in them. "What did you find? Speak to me, Nici."

"Nothing," I said shortly. "You're out several million credits for nothing. It was a completely dreary bit of history, not without heroism but entirely without poetry. And if I've lost my license because of this—I'm not even sure I understand what you're trying to do."

"I'm researching for a history of imaginative thought."

Durham was always researching unreadable subjects. "Starting when?" I asked tersely, pulling on a boot. "The cave paintings at Lascaux?"

"No art," he said. "More speculative than that. Less formal. Closer to chaos." He smiled, reading my mind. "Like me."

"You're a disturbed man, Durham. You should have your unconscious scanned."

"I like it the way it is: a bubbling little morass of unpredictable metaphors."

"They aren't unpredictable," I said. "They're completely predictable. Everything imaginable is accessible, and everything accessible has been imagined by the Virtual computer, which has already researched every kind of imaginative thought since the first bison got painted on a rock. That way nothing like what happened in Cotton Mather's time can happen to us. So—"

"*Wonders of the Invisible World,*" Durham interrupted. He hadn't heard a word. "It's a book by Mather. He was talking about angels and demons. We would think of the invisible in terms of atomic particles. Both are unseen yet named, and immensely powerful—"

"Oh, stop. You're mixing atoms and angels. One exists, the other doesn't."

"That's what I'm trying to get at, Nici—the point where existence is totally immaterial, where the passion, the belief in something creates a situation completely ruled by the will to believe."

"That's insanity."

He smiled again, cheerfully. He tended to change his appearance according to what he was researching; he wore a shimmering bodysuit that showed all his muscles, and milk-white hair. Except for the bulky build of his face and the irreverence in his eyes, he might have been Mather's angel. My more androgynous face worked better. "Maybe," he said. "But I find the desire, the passion, coupled with the accompanying imagery, fascinating."

"You are a throwback," I muttered. "You belong to some barbaric age when people imagined things to kill each other for." The computer flashed a light; I breathed a sigh of relief. Durham got his tape, and the computer's analysis; I retrieved my license.

"Next time—" Durham began.

"There won't be a next time." I headed for the door. "I'm sick of appearing as twisted pieces of people's imagination. And one of these days I'm going to find myself in court."

"But you do it so well," he said softly. "You even convince the Terminus computer."

I glared at him. "Just leave me alone."

"All right," he said imperturbedly. "Don't call me, I'll call you."

I was tired, but I took the tube-walk home, to get the blood moving in my feet, and to see some light and color after that bleak, dangerous world. The moving walkway, encased in its clear tube, wound up into the air, balanced on its centipede escalator and station legs. I could see the gleaming city domes stretch like a long cluster of soap bubbles toward the afternoon sun, and I wondered that somewhere within the layers of time in this place there was a small port town on the edge of a vast, unexplored continent where Mather had flung himself down on his floorboards and prayed an angel out of himself.

He could see an angel here without praying for it. He could be an angel. He could soar into the eye of God if he wanted, on wings of gold and light. He could reach out, even in the tube-walk, punch in a credit number, plug into his implant or his wrist controls, and activate the screen above his head. He could have any reality on the menu, or any reality he could dream up, since everything imagined and imaginable and every combination of it had been programmed into the Virtual computer. And then he could walk out of the station into his living room and change the world all over again.

I had to unplug Brock when I got home; he had fallen asleep at the terminal. He opened heavy eyelids and yawned.

"Hi, Matrix."

"Don't call me that," I said mechanically. He grinned fleetingly and nestled deeper into the bubble-chair. I sat down on the couch and pulled my boots off again. It was warm, in this time; I finally felt it. Brock asked,

"What were you?"

Even he knew Durham that well. "An angel."

"What's that?"

"Look it up."

He touched the controls on his wrist absently. He was a calm child, with blue, clinical eyes and angelic hair that didn't come from me. He sprouted wings and a halo suddenly, and grunted. "What's it for?"

"It talks to God."

"What God?"

"In God We Trust. That God."

He grunted again. "Pre-Real."

I nodded, leaned back tiredly, and watched him, wondering how much longer he would be neat, attentive, curious, polite, before he shaved his head, studded his scalp and eyebrows with jewels and implants, got eye-implants that held no expression whatsoever, inserted a CD player into his earlobe, and never called me Matrix again. Maybe he would go live with his father. I hadn't seen him since Brock was born, but Brock knew exactly who he was, where he was, what he did. Speculation was unnecessary, except for aberrants like Durham.

The outercom signaled; half a dozen faces appeared onscreen: Brock's friends who lived in the station complex. They trooped in, settled themselves around Brock, and plugged into their wrists. They were playing an adventure game, a sort of space-chase, where they were intergalactic thieves raiding alien zoos of rare animals and selling them to illegal restaurants. The computer played the team of highly trained intergalactic space-patrollers. The thieves were constantly falling into black holes, getting burnt up speeding too fast into strange atmospheres, and ambushed by the wily patrollers. One of them, Indra, tried to outwit the computer by coming up with the most bizarre alien species she could imagine; the computer always gave her the images she wanted. I watched for a while. Then an image came into my head, of an old man in a field watching his neighbors pile stones on him until he could no longer breathe.

I got up, went into my office, and called Durham.

"I could have stopped it," I said tersely. He was silent, not because he didn't know what I was talking about, but because he did. "I was an angel from God. I could have changed the message."

"You wouldn't have come back," he said simply. It was true. I would have been abandoned there, powerless, a beardless youth with breasts in a long robe raving about the future, who would have become just one more witch for the children to condemn. He added, "You're a researcher. Researchers don't get emotional about history. There's nothing left of that time but some old bones in a museum from where they dug them up to build a station complex. A gravestone with an angel on it, a little face with staring eyes, and a pair of cupid wings. What's to mope about? I put a bonus in your account. Go spend it somewhere."

"How much?"

He was silent again, his eyes narrowed slightly. "Not enough for you to go back. Go get drunk, Nici. This is not you."

"I'm haunted," I whispered, I thought too softly for him to hear. He shook his head, not impatiently.

"The worst was over by then, anyway. Heroics are forbidden to researchers. You know that. The angel Mather dreamed up only told him what he wanted to hear. Tell him anything else and he'd call you a demon and refuse to listen. You know all this. Why are you taking this personally? You didn't take being a goddess in that Hindu temple personally. Thank God," he added with an obnoxious chuckle. I grunted at him morosely and got rid of his face.

I found a vegetable bar in the kitchen, and wandered back into the living room. The space-thieves

were sneaking around a zoo on the planet Hublatt.
They were all imaging animals onscreen while their
characters studied the specimens. "We're looking for a
Yewsalope," Brock said intently. "Its eyeballs are poisonous, but if you cook them just right they look like
boiled eggs to whoever you're trying to poison."

The animals were garish in their barred cells: purple, orange, cinnamon, polka-dotted, striped. There
were walking narwhales, a rhinoceros horn with feet
and eyes, something like an octopus made out of elephant trunks, an amorphous green blob that constantly changed shape.

"How will you know a Yewsalope when you see
it?" I asked, fascinated with their color combinations,
their imagery. Brock shrugged slightly.

"We'll know."

A new animal appeared in an empty cage: a tall,
two-legged creature with long golden hair and wings
made of feathers or light. It held on to the bars with its
hands, looking sadly out. I blinked.

"You have an angel in your zoo."

I heard Brock's breath. Indra frowned. "It could fly
out. Why doesn't it fly? Whose is it? Anyway, this zoo
is only for animals. This looks like some species of
human. It's illegal," she said, fastidiously for a thief,
"on Hublatt."

"It's an angel," Brock said.

"What's an angel? Is it yours?"

Brock shook his head. They all shook their heads,
eyes onscreen, wanting to move on. But the image lingered: a beautiful, melancholy figure, half human, half
light, trapped and powerless behind its bars.

"Why doesn't it just fly?" Indra breathed. "It could
just fly. Brock—"

"It's not mine," Brock insisted. And then he looked
at me, his eyes wide, so calm and blue that it took me

a moment to transfer my attention from their color to what they were asking.

I stared at the angel, and felt the bars under my hands. I swallowed, seeing what it saw: the long, dark night of history that it was powerless to change, to illumine, because it was powerless to speak except to lie.

"Matrix?" Brock whispered. I closed my eyes.

"Don't call me that."

When I opened my eyes, the angel had disappeared.

Hot Times in
Magma City

ROBERT SILVERBERG

Robert Silverberg has been a commanding figure in the SF field for four decades. He is one of the masters of science fiction in all its varieties and is more popular now than ever. And even today, after many awards and hundreds of books, he is still evolving as a writer. He is now a stimulating editorial columnist in *Asimov's* and, most years in addition to his popular novels, writes several important short stories. From this year's stories, I chose one which represents Silverberg at the height of his talent: this is essentially a compressed novel, conforming to the limitations of classical drama. Additionally, there is the air of classic Theodore Sturgeon about this story in the choice and treatment of the central character. In a year of impressive novellas from major talents in the SF field, few are as impressive as this piece first presented by *Omni Online*.

It's seven in the morning and the big wall-screen above Cal Mattison's desk is beginning to light up like a Christmas tree as people start phoning Volcano Central with reports of the first tectonic events of the day. A little bell goes off to announce the arrival of each new one. *Ping!* and there's a blue light, a fumarole popping open in somebody's backyard in Baldwin Park, steam but no lava. *Ping!* and a green one, minor lava tongue reaching the surface in Temple City. *Ping!* again, blue light in Pico Rivera. And then come three urgent pings in a row, bright splotch of red on the screen. Which indicates that a big new plume of smoke must be rising out of the main volcanic cone sitting up there on top of the Orange Freeway where the intersection with the Pomona Freeway used to be, foretelling a goodly fresh gush of lava about to go rolling down the slope.

"Busy morning, huh?" says Nicky Herzog, staring over Mattison's shoulder at the screen. Herzog is a sharp-faced hyperactive little guy, all horn-rimmed glasses and beady eyes, always poking his big nose into other people's business.

Mattison shrugs. He is a huge man, six feet five, plenty of width between his shoulders, and a shrug is a big, elaborate project for him. "Shit, Nicky, this isn't anything, yet. Go have yourself some breakfast."

"A bunch of blues, a green, and a red, and that ain't anything, you say?"

"Nothing that concerns us, man." Mattison taps the screen where the red is flashing. "Pomona's ancient history. It isn't none of our business, what goes on in Pomona, not any more. Whatever's happening where you see that red, all the harm's already been done, can't do no more, not now. And those blues—shit, it's just some smoke. Let 'em put on gas masks. As for that green in Temple City, well—" He shakes his head. "Nah. They'll take care of that out of local resources. Go get yourself some breakfast, Nicky."

"Yeah. Yeah. Scrambled eggs and snake meat."

Herzog slithers away. He's sort of like a snake himself, Mattison thinks: a narrow little guy, no width to him at all, moves in a funny head-first way as though he's cutting a path through the air for himself with his nose. He used to be something in Hollywood, a screenwriter or a story editor or something, a successful one, too, Mattison has heard, before he blitzed out on Quaaludes and Darvon and coke and God knows what-all else and wound up in Silver Lake Citizens Service House with the rest of this bunch of casualties.

Mattison is a former casualty himself, who once had carried a very serious boozing jones on his back that had a heavy negative impact on his professional performance as a studio carpenter and extremely debilitating effects on his driving skills. His drinking also led him to be overly free with his fists, not a wise idea for a man of his size and strength, because he tended to inflict a lot of damage and that ultimately involved an unfortunate amount of legal expense, not to mention frequent and troublesome judicial chastisement. But all of that is behind him now. Mattison, who is twenty-eight years old, single, good-natured, and reasonably intelligent, is well along in recovery. For the past eighteen months he has been not just an inmate but also a staffer here at Silver Lake, gradually making the transition from victim of his own lousy impulse control to guardian of the less fortunate, an inspiration to those who seek to pull themselves up out of the mud as he has done.

Various of the less fortunate are trickling into the room right now. Official wake-up time at Silver Lake Citizens Service House is half past six, and you are expected to be down for breakfast by seven, a rule that nearly everybody observes, since breakfast ceases to be available beyond 7:30, no exceptions made. Mattison himself is up at five every morning because getting up unnaturally early is a self-inflicted part of his recovery regime, and Nicky Herzog is usually out of his room well before the required wake-up hour because perpetual insomnia has turned out to be an accidental facet of his recovery program, but most of the others are reluctant awakeners at best. Some would probably never get out of bed at all, except for the buddy-point system in effect at the house, where you get little bonus goodies for seeing to it that your roommate who likes to sleep in doesn't get the chance to do it.

Mary Maude Gulliver is the first one in, followed by her sullen-faced roommate Annette Lopez, and after them, a bunch of rough beasts slouching toward breakfast, come Paul Foust, Herb Evans, Lenny Prochaska, Nadine Doheny, Marty Cobos, and Marcus Hawks. That's most of them, and the others will be along in two or three minutes. And, sure enough, here they come. That muscle-bound bozo Blazes McFlynn is the next one down—Mattison can hear him in the breakfast room razzing Herzog, who for some reason he likes to goof around with. "Good morning, you miserable little faggot," McFlynn says.

"You fucking creep," Herzog sputters back, an angry, wildly obscene and flamboyant response. He's good with words, if nothing else. McFlynn drives Herzog nuts; he has been reprimanded a couple of times for the way he acts up when Herzog's around. Herzog is an edgy, unlikable man, but as far as Mattison knows he isn't any faggot. Quite the contrary, in fact.

Buck Randegger, slow and slouching and affable, appears next, and then voluminous Melissa Hornack, she of the six chins and hippopotamoid rump. Just two or three missing, now, and Mattison can hear them on the stairs. The current population of Silver Lake Citizens Service House is fourteen inmates and four full-time live-in staff. They occupy a spacious and comfortable old three-story sixteen-room house that supposedly was, once upon a time back around 1920 or 1930, the mansion of some important star of silent movies. The place was an even bigger wreck, up until five or six years ago, than its current inhabitants were themselves, but it has been nicely rehabilitated by its occupants since then as part of their Citizens Service obligation.

Mattison has long since had breakfast, but he usually goes into the dining room to sit with the inmates while they eat, just in case someone has awakened in a testy mood and needs to be taken down a notch or two. Since everybody here is suffering to a greater or lesser degree from withdrawal symptoms of some sort all the time, and even those who are mostly beyond the withdrawal stage are not beyond the nightmare-having stage, people can get disagreeably prickly, which is where Mattison's size is a considerable occupational asset.

But just as he rises now from the screen to follow the others in, a series of *pings* comes from it like church bells announcing Sunday morning services, and a little line of green dots spaced maybe six blocks apart springs up out in Arcadia, a few blocks east of Santa Anita Avenue from Duarte Road to Foothill Boulevard, and then curving northwestward, actually reaching beyond the 210 Freeway a little way in the direction of Pasadena. This is new. By and large the Zone's northwestern boundary has remained well south of Huntington Drive, with most of the thrust going down into the lower San Gabriel Valley, places like Monterey Park and Rosemead and South El Monte, but here it is suddenly jumping a couple of miles on the diagonal up the other way with lava popping up on the far side of Huntington, practically to the edge of the racetrack and the Arboretum and quite possibly cutting the 210 in half.

It's very bad news. Mattison doesn't need to wait for alarm bells to go off to know that. Everybody wants to believe that the Zone is going to remain confined to the hapless group of communities way out there at the eastern end of the Los Angeles Basin where the trouble started, but what everybody fears is that in fact it's going to keep right on marching unstoppably westward until it gets to the ocean, like a bad case of acne that starts on a teenager's left cheek and continues all the way to the ankles. They are doing a pretty good job of controlling the surface flows, but nobody is really sure about what's going on deep underground, and at this very minute it might be the case that angry rivers of magma are rolling toward Beverly Hills and Trousdale Estates and Pacific Palisades, and heading on out Malibu way to give the film stars one more lovely surprise when the fabulous new Pacific Coast Highway Volcano abruptly begins to poke its head up out of the surf. Of course, it's a long way from Arcadia to Malibu. But any new westward extension of the Zone, even just a couple of blocks, is a chilling indication that the process is far from over, indeed may only just have really begun.

Mattison turns toward the dining room and calls out, "You better eat fast, guys, because I think they're going to want us to suit up and get—"

And then the green dots on the screen sprout fluorescent yellow borders and the alarm bell at the Silver Lake Citizens Service House starts going off.

What the alarm means is that whatever is happening out in Arcadia has proven to be a little too much for the local lava-control teams, and so they are beginning to call in the Citizens Service people as well. The whole idea of the Citizens Service House is that they are occupied by troubled citizens who have "volunteered" to do community service—any sort of service that may be required of them. A Citizens Service House is not quite a jail and not quite a recovery center, but it partakes of certain qualities of both institutions, and its inhabitants are people who have fucked up in one way or another and done injury not only to themselves but to their fellow citizens, injury for which they can make restitution by performing community service even while they are getting their screwed-up heads gradually screwed on the right way.

What had started out to involve a lot of trash-collecting along freeways, tree-pruning in the public parks, and similar necessary but essentially simple and non-life-threatening chores, has become a lot trickier ever since this volcano thing happened to Los Angeles. The volcano thing has accelerated all sorts of legal and social changes in the area, because flowing lava simply will not wait for the usual bullshit California legal processes to take their course. And so it was just a matter of two or three weeks after the Pomona eruption before the County Supervisors asked the Legislature to extend the Citizens Service Act to include lava control, and the bill passed both houses the next day. Whereupon the miscellaneous boozers, druggies, trank-gobblers, and other sad substance-muddled fuckupniks who inhabit the Citizens Service Houses now find themselves obliged to go out on the front lines at least three or four times a month, and sometimes more often than that, to toil alongside more respectable folk in the effort to keep the rampaging magmatic flow from extending the grip that it already holds over a significant chunk of the Southland.

It is up to the dispatchers at Volcano Central in Pasadena to decide when to call in the Citizens Service people. Volcano Central, which is an arm of the Cal Tech Seismological Laboratory with its headquarters on the grounds of Cal Tech's Jet Propulsion Laboratory in the hills north of town, monitors the whole Tectonic Zone with a broad array of ground-based sensors and satellite-mounted scanners, trying to keep track of events as the magma outcropping wanders around beneath the San Gabriel Valley, and if possible even to get a little ahead of things.

Every new outbreak, be it simply a puff of smoke rising from a new little fumarole or a full-scale barrage of tephra and volcanic bombs and red-hot lava pouring from some new mouth of Hell, is duly noted by JPL computers, which constantly update the myriad of data screens that have been set up all over town, like the one above Cal Mattison's desk in the community room of the Silver Lake Citizens Service House. It is also Volcano Central's responsibility, as master planners of the counteroffensive, to summon the appropriate kind of help. The Fire Department first, of course: that has by now been greatly expanded and reorganized on a region-wide basis (not without a lot of

political in-fighting and general grief) and firefighters
are called in according to a concentric-circles system
that widens from the Zone itself out to, eventually,
Santa Barbara and Laguna Beach. Their job, as usual,
is to prevent destruction of property through the
spreading of fires from impacted areas to surrounding
neighborhoods. Volcano Central will next alert the
National Guard divisions that have been put on permanent activation in the region; and when even the
Guard has been stretched too thin by the emergency,
the Citizens Service Houses people will be called out,
along with other assorted civilian volunteer groups
that have been trained in lava-containment techniques.

Mattison has no real way of finding out whether it's
true, but he believes that the Silver Lake house gets
called out at least twice as often as any of the other
Citizens Service Houses he knows of. He may actually be right. The Silver Lake house is located in an
opportune spot, practically in the shadow of the
Golden State Freeway: it is an easy matter for its
inhabitants, when summoned, to take that freeway to
one interchange or another and zoom out via the
Ventura Freeway to the top end of the Zone or the San
Bernardino Freeway to the southern end, whereas anybody coming from the Mar Vista house or the one in
West Hollywood or the Gardena place would have a
much more extensive journey to make.

But it isn't just the proximity factor. Mattison likes to
think that his particular bunch of rehabs are notably
more effective on the lava line than the bozos from the
other houses. They have their problems, sure, big problems; but somehow they pull themselves together when
their asses are on the line out there, and Mattison is
terrifically proud of them for that. It might also be that
he himself is considered an asset by Volcano Central—
his size, his air of authority, his achievement in having

pulled himself up out of very deep shit indeed into his present quasi-respectability. But Mattison doesn't let himself dwell on that angle very much. He knows all too well that what you usually get from patting yourself on your own back is a dislocated shoulder.

The bell is ringing, anyway. So here they go again.

"Can we finish breakfast, at least?" Herzog wants to know.

Mattison glances at the screen. Seven or eight of those green-and-yellow dots are blinking there. He translates the cool abstractions of the screen into the probable inferno that has burst out just now in Arcadia and says, glancing at his watch, "Gulp down as much as you can in the next forty-five seconds. Then get your asses in motion and head toward the suiting room."

"Jesus Christ," somebody mutters, maybe Snow. "Forty-five fucking seconds, Matty?" But the others are smart enough to know not to waste any of those seconds bitching, and are shoveling the food down the hatch while Mattison is counting off the time. At the fifty-third second, for he is fundamentally a merciful man, he tells them that breakfast is over and they need to get to work.

The lava suits are stored downstairs, in a room off the main hallway that once might have been an elegant paneled library. The remains of the paneling are still there, rectangles of mahogany or some other fancy wood, but the panels are hard to see any more, because just about every square inch of the room is packed with brightly gleaming lava suits, standing upright elbow to elbow and wall to wall like a silent congregation of robots awaiting activation.

What the suits are, essentially, is one-person body-tanks, solid sturdy shells of highly reflective melnar that are equipped with tractor treads, shovel appendages, laser knives, and all sorts of other auxiliary gadgetry. Factories in Wichita and Atlanta work twenty-four hours a day turning them out, nowadays, with the Federal Government paying the not insignificant expense as part of the whole ongoing disaster relief program that Los Angeles's latest and most spectacular catastrophe has engendered. Mattison sometimes wonders why it was considered worthwhile to keep fifteen or twenty of these extremely costly suits standing around idle much of the time at each of the Citizens Service Houses, when it would be ever so much more efficient for the suits to be stored at some central warehouse at the edge of the Zone, where they could be handed out each day to that day's operating crew. But that is a question he has never bothered to raise with anybody, because he knows that the Federal Government likes to operate in mysterious ways beyond the capacity of mere mortals to comprehend; and, anyway, the suits have been bought and paid for and are here already.

They come in two sizes, bulky and bulkier. Mattison hauls the three nearest suits out into the hallway and hands them to people of the appropriate size, which creates space for the others to go into the storage room and select their own suits for themselves. As usual, there is plenty of jostling and bumping, and some complaining, too. Herb Evans is just barely big enough for the bigger size suit, and might be better off with the smaller one, in which he could move about less awkwardly; but he always wants one of the big ones, and the one he has grabbed right now has also been grabbed from the other side by Marcus Hawks, who is six feet two and has a better claim to it. "I got it first," Evans is yelling. Hawks, not letting go, says, "You go get one that's the right size for you, you little dumb fucker," and Mattison sees immediately that they both are prepared to defend their positions with extensive disputatory zeal, perhaps for the next three or four hours. He isn't surprised: the denizens of Citizens Service Houses are not, as a rule, gifted with a lot of common sense, but they often make up for that by being extremely argumentative and vindictive. There's no time to let Evans and Hawkins sort things out; Mattison strides between them, gently but firmly detaches Evans's grip from one arm of the suit and Hawkins's from the other, and sends the two of them in opposite directions to find different suits entirely. He takes the big one for himself and moves out in the hallway with it so that he can get himself into it.

"As soon as you have your suits on," Mattison bellows, "head on out into the street and get on board the truck, fast as you can!"

He squeezes into his own with difficulty. In truth he's a little too big even for the big size, about an inch too tall and two or three inches too broad in the shoulders, but by scrunching himself together somewhat he can manage it, more or less. He has to. There's no way he can stay behind when the Silver Lake House gets called out on lava duty, and he doesn't know any tailors who do alterations on lava suits.

The big olive-green military transport truck that is always parked now in readiness outside the house has let its tailgate down, and, one by one, the suited-up lava fighters go rolling up the slope into the truck and take their positions on the open back deck. Mattison waits in the street until everybody is on board who's going on board, twelve of the fourteen residents—Jim Robey, who is coming slowly back from the brink of cirrhosis, is much too freaky-jittery to be sent out onto the lava front, and Melissa Hornack is disqualified by virtue of her extreme obesity—and two of the four staffers, Ned Eisenstein, the house paramedic, and

Barry Gibbons, the cook, who does not suit up because he is the one who drives the truck, and you can't drive a truck when you're wearing a thing that's like a small tank. The remaining member of the staff is Donna DiStefano, the actual director of the house, who would love to go along but is required by her official position to remain behind and look after Robey and Hornack.

"We're all set," Mattison tells Gibbons over his suit radio, and swings himself up onto the truck. And away they go, Zoneward bound.

Early as it is, the day is warming up fast, sixty degrees or so already, a gorgeously spring-like February morning, the air still reasonably clear as a result of the heavy rain a couple of nights before. This has been a particularly rainy winter, and Mattison often likes to play with the idea that one of these days it'll rain hard enough to douse the fucking volcanoes entirely, but he knows that that's impossible; the magma just keeps coming up and up out of the bowels of the earth no matter what the weather is like on top. A volcano isn't like a bonfire, after all.

The rains have made everything green, though. The hills are pure emerald, except where some humongous bougainvillea vine is setting off a gigantic blast of purple or orange. Because the prevailing winds this time of year blow from west to east, there's no coating of volcanic ash or other pyroclastic crap to be seen in this part of town, nor can you smell any of the noxious gases that the million fumaroles of the Zone are putting forth; all such garbage gets carried the other way, turning the world black and nauseating from San Gabriel out to San Berdoo and Riverside.

What you can see, though, is the distant plume of

smoke that rises from the summit of Mount Pomona, which is what the main cone seems to have been named. The mountain itself, which straddles two freeways, obliterating both and a good deal more besides, in a little place called City of Industry just southwest of Pomona proper, isn't visible, not from here—it's only a couple of thousand feet high, after six months of building itself up out of its own accumulation of ejected debris. But the column of steam and fine ash that emerges from it is maybe five times higher than that, and can be seen far and wide all over the Basin, except perhaps in West L.A. and Santa Monica, where none of this can be seen or smelled and all they know of the whole volcano thing, probably, is what they read in the *Times* or see on the television news.

As the truck heads east along the Ventura, though, signs of the disaster begin to show up as early as Glendale, and by the time they have crossed over to the 210 Freeway and are moving through Pasadena there can be no doubt that something out of the ordinary has been going on lately a little further ahead. Everything from about Fair Oaks Avenue eastward is sooty from a light coating of fine pumice and volcanic ash that has been carried out of the Zone by occasional blasts of Santa Ana winds, and beyond Lake Avenue the whole area is downright filthy. Mattison—who is a native Angeleno, having grown up in Northridge and Van Nuys and lived for most of his adult life in a succession of furnished apartments in West Los Angeles—thinks of the impeccable mansions just to his right over in San Marino, with their manicured lawns and their blooming camellias and azaleas and aloes, and shakes his head at the thought of the way they must look now. He can remember one epic bender that began in Santa Monica and ended up around here in which he found himself climbing over the wall at three in the morning into the enormous sprawling garden of giant cactus at the Huntington Library, right down there in San Marino, and wandering around inside thinking that he had been transported to some other planet. It must look like Mars in there for sure these days, he thinks.

At Sierra Madre Boulevard the truck exits the freeway. "It's blocked by a pile of lava bombs just beyond San Gabriel Boulevard," Gibbons explains to him via the suit radio. "They hope to have it cleared by this afternoon." He goes zigging and zagging in a southeasterly way on surface streets through Pasadena until they get to Huntington Drive, which takes them past Santa Anita Racetrack and brings them smack up into a National Guard roadblock a couple of blocks just beyond.

The Guardsmen, seeing a truckload of mirror-bright lava suits, wave them on through. Gibbons, who is undoubtedly getting his driving instructions now direct from Volcano Central, turns left on North Second Avenue, right on Colorado Boulevard, and brings the truck to a halt a little way down the street, where half a block of one-story commercial buildings is engulfed in flame and red gouts of lava are welling up out of what had until five or six hours ago been a burrito shop. The site is cordoned off, but just beyond the cordon a bunch of people, Mexicans, some Chinese, maybe a few Koreans, are standing around weeping and wailing and waving their arms toward heaven— the proprietors, most likely, of the small businesses that are getting destroyed here.

"Everybody out," Mattison orders, as the tailgate goes down.

Firefighters are already at work at the periphery of the scene, hosing down the burning buildings in the hope of containing the blaze before it sets the whole neighborhood on fire. But the lava outcropping has been left for Mattison and his crew to handle. Lava containment is a new and special art, which the Citizens Service House people have gradually come to master, and the beleaguered Fire Department guys are quite content to turn that kind of work over to them and concentrate on putting out conventional fires.

Quickly Mattison sizes up the picture. Things are just in the very early stages, he sees. There's still hope for containment.

What has happened here is that a stray arm of the underlying magma belt that is causing this whole mess has wandered up through the bedrock and has broken through the surface in eight or nine places along a diagonal line a couple of miles long. It's as if a many-headed serpent made of fiery-hot lava has poked all its heads up at the same time.

For just one volcano to have sprung up out here would have been bad enough. But the area now known as the San Gabriel Valley Tectonic Zone has been favored, over the past year or so, with a whole multitude of them—little ones, but lots. The Mexicans call the *Zone La Mesa de los Hornitos*—that means "little ovens," *hornitos*. You can cook your tortillas on the sidewalk anywhere in the affected area.

The lava pool here is maybe eleven feet by fifteen, a puddle, really, just enough to take out the burrito joint. The heat it's giving off is, of course, fantastic: Mattison, who has become an expert in such things by this time, can tell just at a glance that things are running about 2000 degrees Fahrenheit. Lava at that temperature glows yellowish-red. He prefers to work with it glowing bright-red, which is about 400 degrees cooler, or, even better, dark blood-red, 400 degrees cooler than that; but he is not given his choice of temperatures in these situations, and at least they are not yet into the white-heat stage, which is a bitch and a half to cope with.

It is the heat of the lava, and not any fire from below, that has set the adjoining buildings ablaze. Volcanoes, Mattison knows, don't belch fire. But you push a lot of red-hot material up into a street like this and nearby structures made mostly of beaverboard and plywood are very quickly going to reach their flash point.

The flow, so far, is moving relatively slowly, maybe ten or twelve inches a minute. That means the lava is relatively viscous, and thank God for that. He knows of flows that come spurting out fifty times as fast and make you really dance. At the upper surface where the lava is coming into contact with the air he can see it congealing, forming a glassy skin that tinkles and clinks and chimes as inexorable pressures from below keep cracking it. Mattison watches odd blobs and bulges come drifting up, expand, harden a little, and break, sending squiggles of molten lava off to either side. A few big bubbles are rising too, and they seem ominous and nasty, indicators, perhaps, that the lava pool is thinking of spitting a couple of little lava bombs at the onlookers.

The pumping truck that has been supplied for Mattison's crew this morning is strictly a minor-league item, but it appears adequate for the needs of the moment. The region has only so many of the big-ticket jobs available, just a handful, really, even after all these months since the crisis began, and those have to be kept in reserve for the truly dire eruptions. So what they have given him to work with, instead of a two-and-a-half-ton pump that can move thirteen thousand gallons of water a minute and throw it, if necessary, hundreds of feet in the air, is one of the compact Helgeson & Nordheim tripod-mounted jobs sitting on top of an ordinary flat-bed truck. It's small, but it'll probably do the job.

An auxiliary firefighter—a girl, couldn't be more than fifteen, Latino, dark eyes glossy with excitement and fear—has been delegated to show him where the water hookup is. Every one of the myriad little municipalities in and around the Zone is now under legal obligation to designate certain hydrants as dedicated lava-pump outlets, and to set up and maintain reserve water-tanks at ground level every six blocks. "How far are we from the nearest dedicated hydrant?" Mattison asks her, speaking like a space invader from within his lava suit, and she tells him that it's back behind them on North Second, maybe a thousand yards. Has he been provided with a thousand yards of hose? She thinks he has. Okay: maybe she's right. If not, the firemen can lend him some. Lava containment is considered a higher priority than fire containment, considering that uncontrolled lava flows will spread a fire even faster than burning buildings will, since burning buildings don't move through the streets and lava does.

Mattison picks Paul Foust and Nicky Herzog, who are two of the least befuddled of his people, to go with the girl from the Fire Department and set up the hose connection. Meanwhile he and Marcus Hawks and Lenny Prochaska get to work muscling the pump rig as close to the lava as they dare, while Clyde Snow, Mary Maude Gulliver, and Ned Eisenstein set about uncoiling the hundred yards of steel-jacketed hose that's connected to the pump and running it in the general direction of North Second Avenue, where the water will be coming from. The rest of his crew begins unreeling the lengths of conventional hose that they have, ordinary fire-hose that would melt if used close in, and laying it out beyond the reach of the steel-jacketed section.

Mattison can't help feel a burst of pride as he watches his charges go about their chores. They're nothing but a bunch of human detritus barely out of detox, as he once was too, and yet, goofy and obstinate and ornery and bewildered and generally objectionable as they are capable of being, they always seem to rise above themselves when they're out here on the lava line. Or most of the time, anyway. There are a few pissant troublemakers in the group and even the good ones have funny little relapses when you least expect or want them. But those are the exceptions; this kind of work is the rule. Good for them, he thinks. Good for us all. He's quietly proud of himself too, considering that a couple of years ago he was just one more big drunken unruly asshole like the rest of them, assiduously perfecting his boozing techniques in every bar along Wilshire from Barrington to Bundy to Centinela and so on clear out to the ocean, and here he is calmly and coolly and effectively running his own little piece of the grand and glorious Los Angeles lava-control operation.

"Can we maybe get a little closer, guys?" he asks Hawks and Lenny Prochaska.

"Jeez, Matty," Prochaska murmurs. "Feel the fucking heat! It's like walking into a blast furnace wearing a bathing suit."

"I know, I know," Mattison says. "But we'll be okay. Come on, now, guys. An inch at a time. Easy does it. We're good strong boys. We can handle a nice hot time, can't we?" It's like talking baby-talk, and Hawks and Prochaska are big men, nearly as big as he is and neither of them especially sweet-natured. But he has their number. Their various chemical dependencies had reduced them, in the fullness of time, to something that functioned on the general level of competence of babies in diapers, and they need to prove over and over, now, that they are the tough hard macho males they used to be. So they lean down close and work with him to drag the pump rig forward and get the nozzle aimed right down the mouth of the lava well.

The suits they're wearing are actually quite good at shielding them from the worst of the heat. They can withstand a surprising amount of it—for a time, anyway. The melnar is very tough stuff, and also, because it is so shiny, it turns back much of the heat through simple reflective radiation, and there's interior insulation besides, and a coolant network, and infrared filters, and two or three other gimmicks also, all of which makes it possible to walk right up to a 2000-degree lava flow and even, if its surface has hardened a little, to step out onto it when necessary. Still, despite the protection afforded by the lava suit, it is quite apparent from the warmth that does get through that they are standing right next to molten rock that has come spurting up just now from the Devil's own domain.

The hoses are hooked up now and Mattison has the nozzle directed to the place he wants it to be, which is along the outer rim of the lava flow. He sends a radio message back to Foust and Herzog out by the hydrant that they're almost ready to go. Then he gives a hand signal and it travels back and back along the line, from Mary Maude to Evans to Cobos to Buck Randegger, or whoever it is that is standing behind Cobos, and on around the corner until finally it reaches Foust and Herzog, who know for sure now that the hose line is fully connected, and the water begins to shoot forth. Mattison and Hawks and Prochaska grip the nozzle together, slowly and grimly playing it along the edge of the flow.

The purpose of this operation is to cool the front of the lava well sufficiently to form a crust, and then a dam, that will cause the continuing flow to pile up behind it instead of rolling on down the street. This is a technique that was perfected in Iceland, and indeed half a dozen grizzled Icelanders have been imported to serve as consultants during this Los Angeles event, frosty-eyed men with names like Svein Steingrimsson and Steingrim Sveinsson who look upon fighting volcanoes as some kind of Olympic sport. But one big difference between Iceland and Los Angeles is that Iceland sits in the middle of a frigid ocean that provides an infinite quantity of cold water for use by lava-fighters, and the distances from shore to volcano are not very great. Los Angeles has an ocean nearby too, but it isn't conveniently placed for hosing down lava outbreaks in the San Gabriel Valley, which is inland, at least thirty or forty miles from the coast. Hence the system of municipal water-tanks all along the borders of the Zone, and a zillion tanker trucks trundling back and forth bringing ocean water with which to keep the tanks filled, Los Angeles's regular water supply being far from adequate even for the ordinary needs of the community.

Any lava-cooling job, even a small one like this, is a ticklish thing. It isn't quite like watering a lawn. You are dumping 60-degree water on 2000-degree lava, an interaction which is going to produce immense billows of steam that will prevent you from seeing very much of what you are in the process of doing. But you need to see what you are doing, because as you build your lava dam along the front of the upwelling what you may all too easily achieve is not the containment of the lava but, rather, its deflection toward something you don't want it to hit. Like the fire truck down the block, for example, or some undamaged buildings on the opposite side of the street.

So you have to wield your hose like a sculptor,

dancing around squirting the water with great precision, topping up the dam here, minimizing its height there, all the while taking into account the slope of the ground, the ability of the subsoil to bear the weight of the new stone, and the possibility that the lava you are working with may suddenly decide to accelerate its rate of outflow from fifty feet an hour to, say, fifty feet a minute, which would send the flow hurtling over the top of your little dam and put you up to your ass in lava, with the hose still dangling from your hand as you become a permanent part of the landscape. Which is why the face-plate of your lava suit is equipped with infrared filters to help you see through all that billowing steam that you are busily creating as you work.

And there is other stuff to consider. Coming up out of the core of the earth, along with all that lava, are various gases, not all of them nice ones. Chlorine, sulfur dioxide, hydrogen sulfide, carbon monoxide, carbon dioxide, all kinds of miasmas are likely to head swiftly surfaceward as though carried by a giant blowpipe. These are all poisonous gases, although you are more or less protected against that by your suit; however, traveling upward with the gases may be fragments of incandescent lava that will go up like a geyser and come down all over the neighborhood, including right where you happen to be. Therefore you want to listen, as you work, for strange new whooshings and bellowings and hissings, and in particular for the sound of something like an old-fashioned locomotive tooting its horn as it heads your way. Mattison has beaten a quick retreat more than a few times, sometimes taking his pump with him, sometimes abandoning it and running like hell as a highly local eruption starts nipping at his heels.

However, none of that happens this morning. This Arcadia thing is just a teeny-weeny little isolated lava outbreak with no special complications except for the owner of the burrito stand. Mattison, aided expertly by Marcus Hawks, who is just eight months out of a crack house in El Segundo, and Lenny Prochaska, whose powerful forearms bear needle tracks that look like freeway interchanges, deftly creates a low wall of cooled lava across the front of the outbreak, then adds a limb up the right-hand side and another up the left to form a U, after which they concentrate on hardening the new lava wherever it comes curling up over the boundaries of their wall. The cooling process is very quick. Along the face of the wall, the temperature of the lava has dropped to the 500-degree level, at which heat it is hardly glowing at all, at least not at the outer crust. Mattison figures that the crust he has built is maybe three inches thick, a skin of solid basalt over the hellish stuff behind.

Of course, lava is still oozing steadily from the ground at the original exit point, and probably will go on doing so for another six or seven hours at this site, maybe even a day or two. But the dam should hold it and keep it from welling out into Colorado Boulevard, which is an important thoroughfare that needs to be kept open. Instead, the lava will go on piling up on the site of the burrito stand, forming a little mountain perhaps fifteen or twenty feet high. Unless, of course, it decides to break through the surface a couple of dozen yards down the street instead, but Mattison doesn't think that's going to happen at this site.

He sometimes wonders what life is going to be like around here when all this is over, the volcanoes have died down, and the whole eastern half of the Los Angeles Basin is littered with new little mountains in the middle of what used to be busy neighborhoods. Are they going to dynamite them all? Build around them? On top of them? And where are they going to put the freeways to replace the ones that are now mired in cooling lava that soon will be solid rock?

Hell, it's not his problem. That's one of his mantras: *Not my problem.* He has enough problems of his own, currently under control but not necessarily going to stay that way if he borrows trouble from elsewhere. *One day at a time* is another phrase that he has been taught to repeat to himself whenever he starts worrying about things that shouldn't matter to him. *Easy does it.* Yes. *First things first.* These are absolutely right-on concepts. Somebody else will have to figure out how to repair Los Angeles, once all this is over. His job, which will last him the rest of his life, is figuring out how to operate Cal Mattison.

The fires in the surrounding buildings are just about out, now. One of the firefighters comes over and asks him how he's doing. "Under control," Mattison tells them. "Just a little tidying-up to do."

"You want us to stick around, just in case?"

Mattison thinks for a moment. "You got work nearby?"

The firefighter points. "There's a whole line of these things, from the freeway all the way down to Duarte. If you don't think the lava's going to pop, we can move on south of here. There's a bad one going on on Duarte, just at the Monrovia line."

"Go on, then," Mattison says. "We get any problems, I'll call you back in."

Real executive decision-making. He feels good about that. Time was when he never wanted to be the one who made the call about anything.

But he's confident of his own judgment right here and now. This job has been handled well. There's a high in that that feels like half a fifth of Crown Royal traveling through his veins, smooth and fine and warm.

The firefighters go away, leaving just two of their

number posted as supervisors during the wrap-up and report-filing phase of the job here, and Mattison, signaling back down the line to have the hose shut down, moves forward onto the lava dam. It can be walked on, now, at least by someone equipped with tractor treads like his. He tests the crinkly new skin. It holds. Dainty little tinkling sounds are coming from it, the sounds of continued cooling and hardening, but it supports his weight. It's a little like walking on thin new ice, except that what is behind the fragile surface is molten rock instead of chilly water, and if he falls through he will be very sorry, though not for long. But he doesn't expect to fall through, or he wouldn't be up here.

Mattison isn't walking around on the dam just to show off. He needs to check out the fine points of the construction job. The dam slopes up and back at a 45-degree angle, and he wants its lip to rise just a little steeper even than that, so he moves along the face of the front, using his suit's shovel appendage to trim and shape the boundary between new rock and hot lava. He can feel mild warmth, not much more than that, through his suit, at least until he reaches a place where red can be seen crackling through the black, a tiny fissure in the dam, not dangerous but offensive to his sense of craft. He steps back, radios Foust and Herzog to turn the water back on, and has Hawks and Prochaska give the fissure a squirt or two.

Then he checks the far side of the lava front to make sure that there's no likelihood that the top of the lava dome he has created is simply going to spill back the other way, down into the residential block behind the event. But no, no, the oozing lava is quietly piling itself up, filling in behind the dam, giving no indication that it means to go off in some new direction. Thank God for that much. Because of the way the magma

pool lies in relation to the giant subterranean fault line
that kicked this whole thing off, the surface flows tend
to be consistently directional, rising on a diagonal out
of the ground and moving, generally, from east to west
only. With some residual slopping around—lava is a
liquid, after all—but not, as a rule, with any unpredictable twisting and turning back the way they have
just come. Except, of course, when a badly thought-
out dam is slapped in its path. But Mattison tries to
think his work out properly.

Just as Mattison is wrapping everything up, Gibbons
radios him from the truck to say, "They want us to
move along to San Dimas when we're done here."

"Jesus," Mattison says. "San Dimas is way the hell
to the east. Isn't everything over and done with back
there by now?"

"Apparently not. Something new is about to bust
out, it seems."

"Tell them we'll need a lunch break first."

"They said they wanted us to—"

"Right," says Mattison. "We aren't fucking soldiers, you know. We're volunteer citizens and some of
us have been working like coolies out here all morning. We get a lunch break before we start busting our
asses again today. Tell them that, Barry."

"Well—"

"Tell them."

As Mattison has guessed, the San Dimas thing is
serious but not catastrophic, at least not yet. The preliminary signs indicate a bad bust-out is on the way
out there, and auxiliary crews are being pulled in as
available, but one team more or less won't make any
big difference in the next hour. They get the lunch
break.

Lunch is sandwiches and soft drinks, half a block
back from the event site. They get out of their suits,

leaving them standing open in the street like discarded skins, and eat sitting down at the edge of the curb. "I sure wouldn't mind a beer right now," Evans says, and Hawks says, "Why don't you wish up a bottle of fucking champagne, while you're wishing things up? Don't cost no more than beer, if it's just wishes."

"I never liked champagne," Paul Foust says. "For me it was always cognac. Cour-voy-zee-ay, that was for me." He smacks his lips. "I can practically taste it now. That terrific grapey taste hitting your tongue—that smooth flow, right down your gullet to your gut—"

"Knock it off," says Mattison. This nitwit chatter is stirring things inside him that he would prefer not to have stirred.

"You never stop wanting it," Foust tells him.

"Yes. Yes, I know that, you dumb fucker. Don't you think I know that? Knock it off."

"Can we talk about smoking stuff, then?" Marty Cobos asks.

"And how about needles, too?" says Mary Maude Gulliver, who used to sell herself on Hollywood Boulevard to keep herself in nose candy. "Let's talk about needles too."

"Shut your fucking mouth, you goddamn whore," Lenny Prochaska says. He pronounces it *hooer*. "What do you need to play around with my head for?"

"Why, did you have some kind of habit?" Mary Maude asks him sweetly.

"You hooer, I'm going to throw you into the lava," Prochaska says, getting up and heading toward her. Mary Maude weighs about ninety pounds, beefy Prochaska maybe two-fifty. He could do it with one flip of his wrist.

"Lenny," Mattison says warningly.

"Tell her to leave me be, then."

"All of you," says Mattison. "Leave each other be. Jesus Christ, you think it's any easier for the others than it was for you?"

It is the tension, he knows, of the morning's work that is doing this to them. They're all on the edge, all the time, of falling back into their individual hells, and that keeps them constantly keyed up to a point where it doesn't take much for them to get on each other's nerves. Of course, Mattison's on the edge himself, he always will be and won't ever let himself forget it, but he is in recovery and they aren't, not really, not yet, and the edge is thinner for them than it is for him. Each of them has managed to reach the abstinence level, at least, but you can get to that point simply by having yourself chained to a bed; that keeps you out of the clutches of your habit but it doesn't exactly qualify you as being free of it. Real recovery comes later, if at all, and you can be a tremendous pain in the ass while you're trying to attain it, because you're angry just about all the time, angry with yourself for having burdened yourself with your habit and even angrier with the world for wanting you to give it up, and the anger keeps bubbling out all the time. Like lava, sort of. Makes a mess for everybody, especially yourself, until you understand, really and truly understand in your bones, that until *you* want to give it up, nothing's going to happen.

They calm down, though, as the sandwiches hit their bellies. Mattison waits until they've eaten before he springs the San Dimas thing on them, and to his surprise there is no enormous amount of griping. The usual grumblers—Evans, Snow, Blazes McFlynn—do the expectable amount of grumbling, but not a whole lot, and that's it. They all would rather go back to the house and watch television, of course, but somewhere deep down they know that this volcano business is *actual worthwhile and important stuff,* perhaps the first time in their lives they have ever done anything even remotely worthwhile and important, and some part of them is tickled pink to be out here on the lava frontier. Hollywood is just a dozen miles west of here, after all. They all see themselves as characters in the big volcano movie, heroes and heroines, riding into battle against the evil monster that's eating L.A. That's how Mattison himself feels when he's out here, and he knows it's the same for them, maybe even more intense than it is for him, because he also has the self-esteem that comes from having made it back out of his addiction to this level of recovery, and they don't. Not yet. So they need to be heroes in a movie to feel good about themselves.

They clean up the lunch mess and Mattison goes back to check his lava dam, which is holding good and true, and then off they go to San Dimas for whatever is to be required of them there.

To get there they have to travel through the heart of the Zone, the very belly of the beast, the place where it all started.

No. Where it all started was fifty or sixty miles down in the crust of the earth, and maybe fifty miles east of where Mattison and his pals are now: out in Riverside County, where the tremendous but hitherto unknown Lower Yucaipa Fault had chosen to release its accumulated tension about sixteen months ago, sending a powerful shock wave surfaceward that went lalloping through the Southland at a nifty 7.6 on the Richter. The earthquake made a serious mess out of Riverside, Redlands, San Bernardino, and a lot of other places out there in the eastern boondocks, and caused troubles of lesser but not inconsiderable degree as far west as Thousand Oaks and the Simi Valley.

Californians don't enjoy big earthquakes, but they do expect and understand them, and they know that after you get one you wait for the lights to come back on and then you sweep up the broken crockery and you call all your friends in the affected area as soon as the phones are working so that, ostensibly, you can find out if they are okay, but really so that you can trade horrendous earthquake stories, and sooner or later the supermarket will reopen and the freeway overpasses will be repaired and things will get back to normal.

But this one was a little different, because the Yucaipa thing had evidently been so severe a fracture that it had shattered the roof of a colossal and previously unsuspected pool of very deep subterranean gases that had been confined under high pressure for ten or twenty million years, and the gas, breaking loose like a genie that has been let out of a bottle, had taken hold of a whopping big column of molten magma that happened to be down there and pushed it toward daylight, causing it to come up right underneath the San Gabriel Valley, which is just a little way east of downtown L.A. You expect all kinds of troubles in L.A.—earthquakes, fires, stupid politics, air pollution, drought, deluges and mudslides, riots— but you don't seriously expect volcanoes, any more than you expect snow. Volcanoes are stuff for Hawaii or the Philippines, or southern Italy, or Mexico. But not here, thank you, God. We have our little problems, sure, but volcanoes are not included on the list.

Now the list is one item longer.

The first volcano—the only one, so far, that had built a real full-size volcano-style cone for itself—had popped up at that freeway interchange near Pomona, a couple of days after the big Yucaipa earthquake. First there was thunder, never a common thing in Southern California, and the ground began to shake, and then it began to puff up, making a blister two or three yards high that sent the freeway spilling into pieces as though King Kong's big brother had bashed it from below with his fist, and smoke and fine dust started to spurt from the ground. After which came a hissing that you could hear as far away as Long Beach, and showers of red-hot stones went flying into the air, a pretty good indication that this wasn't simply an aftershock of Yucaipa. Then came the noxious gases, a gust of blue haze that instantly killed half a dozen people who were standing around watching; and then a thick column of black ash decorated by flashes of lightning arose; and then, seven or eight hours later, the first lava flow began. The sky was bright as day all night long from the bursts of incandescent gas and molten rock that were coming forth. By the next morning there was a gray volcanic cone forty feet high sitting where the interchange had been.

If that had been all, well, you would watch it on the news for the next few nights, and then the Federal disaster teams would come in and the people in the neighborhood would be relocated and the *National Geographic* would publish an article about the eruption, and somebody would start a class action suit complaining that the governor or the president or somebody had failed to give proper warning to home buyers that a volcano situation might develop in Pomona, and the religious crazies in Orange County would deliver sermons about sin and repentance, and after a while the impacted area would become a new tourist attraction, Pomona Volcanic National Park or something like that, and life would go on in the rest of Los Angeles as it always did once the latest catastrophe had turned into history.

But the Pomona thing was only the beginning.

That great column of magma, rolling upward from the depths of the earth on a long slant to the west, began breaking through in a lot of other places, bursting out like an attack of fiery pimples across a wide, vaguely triangular strip bracketed, roughly, on the east by the Orange Freeway, on the north by Las Tunas Drive and Arrow Highway, on the south by the Pomona Freeway, and on the west by San Gabriel Boulevard. Within the affected zone anything was likely to happen. Volcanic vents opened in completely random patterns. Lava flows the size of small creeks would crop up in people's garages, or in their living rooms. Fumaroles would sprout in a front lawn and fill a whole neighborhood with smoke and ash. Houses suddenly began to rise from the ground as subsurface bulges formed beneath them. A finger of fierce subterranean heat would whiz along a street and fry the roots of every tree and shrub in your garden without harming your house. All this would be accompanied by almost daily earthquakes—not big ones, just nerve-wracking little jiggles of 3.9 or 4.7 that drove you crazy with fear that something gigantic was getting ready to follow. Then things would be quiet for a couple of weeks; and then they would start again, worse than before.

Not all the lava events were trivial garage-sized ones. A few fissures as big as three blocks wide opened and sent broad sheets of molten matter rolling like rivers down main thoroughfares. That was when the Icelanders showed up to give advice about cooling the lava with hoses. Teams like Mattison's were called out to build lava dams, sometimes right across the middle of a big street, so that the flow would back up behind the new rock instead of continuing clear on into the towns to the west—or, perhaps, into Los Angeles proper, the city itself, still far away and untouched on the other side of the Golden State Freeway. The dams did the trick; but they had the unfortunate side effect of walling off the Zone behind ugly and impassable barriers of solid black basalt.

Today's route takes Mattison and Company on a grand tour of the entire Zone. Freeway travel is a joke in these parts once you get anywhere east of Rosemead Boulevard, and there are new lava-created dead ends all over the place on the surface streets, and so it takes real ingenuity, and a lot of backing and filling, to make a short trip like the one from Arcadia to San Dimas, which once would have been a quick buzz down the 210 Freeway. Now it's necessary to back-track down Santa Anita around the new outbreaks on Duarte Road, and then to come up Myrtle in Monrovia to the 210, and take the freeway as far east as it goes before it gets plugged up by last month's uncleared lava, which is not very far down the road at all; and then comes a lot of cockeyed wandering this way and that on surface streets, north to south and north again, through such towns as Duarte and Azusa and Covina and Glendora, places that no Angeleno ordinarily would be going in a million years, in order to get to the equally unknown municipality of San Dimas, which is just a couple of hops away from Pomona.

The landscape becomes more and more hellish, the further east they go.

"*Look* at all this shit," Nicky Herzog keeps saying, over and over. "*Look* at it! This is fucking hopeless, you know? We all ought to give up and move to fucking Seattle."

"Rains all the time," says Paul Foust.

"You like lava better than rain? You like fucking black ashes falling from the sky?"

"We don't give up," Nadine Doheny says dreamily.

"We keep on keeping on. We are grateful for everything we have."

"Grateful for the volcanoes," Herzog says, in wonder. "Grateful for the ashes. Is that what you think?"

"Leave her alone," Mattison warns him. Nadine's conversation is made up mostly of recovery mantras, and that bothers the flippant, sharp-tongued Herzog. But Doheny is right and Herzog, smart as he is, is wrong. We don't give up. We don't run away. We stand our ground and fight and fight and fight.

Still and all, the Zone looks awful and even after all this time he has not grown used to its hideousness. There are piles of ashes everywhere, making it seem as if a black snowfall had hit the area, and also, not quite as universally distributed but nevertheless impossible to overlook, little incrustations of cooled lava, clinging to houses and pavements like some sort of dark fungus. Light dustings of pumice drift on the breeze. The sky is white with accumulated smoke that today's winds have not yet been able to blow out toward Riverside. Where major fires have burned, whole blocks of rubble pockmark the scene.

The truck has to detour around all sorts of lesser obstacles: spatter cones, and small hills of tephra, lapilli and cinders and lava bombs and other forms of ejected volcanic junk, et cetera, et cetera. Occasionally they pass an active fumarole that's enthusiastically belching smoke. Around it, Mattison knows, are piles of dead bugs, ankle-deep, killed by gusts of live steam or poisonous vapors. The fumaroles are surrounded also by broad swaths of mud that somehow have been flung up around their rims, often quite colorful mud at that, green or pink or red from alum deposits, bright yellow where sulfur crystals abound. Sometimes the yellow is laced with streaks of orange or blue, and sometimes, where the mud is very blue, it is splotched in a highly decorative way by a crust of rich chestnut-brown.

"It's like fairyland, isn't it?" Mary Maude Gulliver cries out, suddenly. "It's like something out of Tolkien!"

"Crazy hooer," Lenny Prochaska mutters. "I'd like to give you a fairyland, you hooer."

Mattison shushes him. He smiles at Mary Maude. It's hard to see this place as a fairyland, all right, but Mary Maude is one of a kind. Give her credit for accentuating the positive, anyway.

Aside from the mineral incrustations in the mud, the Zone shows color where the ground itself has been cooked by the heat of some intense outbreak from below. That ranges from orange and brick red through bright cherry red to purple and black, with some lively streaks of blue. But this show of color is the only trace of what might be called beauty anywhere around. Every building is stained with mud and ash. There are hardly any live trees or garden plants to be seen, just blackened trunks with shriveled leaves still hanging from the branches.

There aren't many people still living in these neighborhoods. Most of those who could afford it have packed up all their worldly possessions and had them carted off to new homes outside the Zone and, in a good many cases, outside the state altogether. A lot of those at the very bottom of the income ladder have cleared out also, moving to the new Federal relocation camps that have been set up in downtown L.A., Valencia, Mojave, the Angeles National Forest, and anyplace else where there was no irate householders' association to take out an injunction against it. The remaining residents of the Zone, mainly, are the lower-middle-income people, the ones who haven't yet lost their houses but couldn't afford to hire moving companies and aren't quite poor enough to qualify for the camps. They are still squatting here, grimly guarding their meager homes against looters, and hoping against hope that the next round of lava outbreaks will happen on any street but their own.

Just how desperate some of these people are getting is something Mattison discovers when the truck's erratic route around the various obstacles takes it through a badly messed-up segment of a barrio somewhere between Azusa and Covina and they see some kind of pagan religious sacrifice under way in the middle of a four-way intersection, where the pavement has begun to bulge slightly and show signs of imminent buckling as gas pressure builds from below. Flat slabs of blue-black lava have been piled up in the crosswalk to form a sort of crude, ragged-edged altar that has been surrounded by boughs torn from nearby trees.

What is evidently a priest—but not any sort of Catholic priest; his dark face is painted with green and red stripes and he is wearing a brilliant Aztec-looking costume, bright feathers and strips of fur all over it—is standing atop the altar, grasping a gleaming butcher-knife in his hand. The altar is stained with blood, and more is about to be added to it, because two other men in less gaudy outfits than the priest's are at his side, holding forth to him a wildly fluttering chicken. Assorted pigs, sheep, and birds are lined up back of the altar, waiting their turn. In a wider circle around the site are perhaps fifty shabbily dressed men, women, and children, silent, stony-faced, holding hands and slowly, rhythmically stamping their feet.

The nature of the thing that is taking place here is utterly obvious right away to everyone aboard the Citizens Service House truck. Even so, it isn't always easy to believe the evidence of your eyes when you see something like this. Mattison stares in shock and disbelief, wondering whether they have slipped through some time-fault and have dropped down into an ancient era, primitive and barbaric. But no, no, prosaic evidence of the modern century can be seen on every side, lampposts, store fronts, billboards. It's just what's going on in the middle of the street that is so exceedingly strange.

"Holy fucking shit," Buck Randegger says. He's a former highway construction worker who has been substance-free about four months and is, much like this lava altar, still plenty rough around the edges. "I thought the fucking Mexicans in this town were supposed to be Christians, for Christ's sake."

"We are," Annette Perez tells him icily. "And also other things, when we have to be. Sometimes both at the same time." The butcher-knife descends in a fierce arc, the newly headless chicken flaps its wings insanely, the crowd of worshipers jumps up and down and cries out three times in a high-pitched ecstatic way, and Randegger expresses his disgust and amazement at the whole weird pagan scene with a maximum of pungency and a minimum of political correctness. For a moment it looks as though Perez is going to jump at him, and Mattison gets ready to intervene, but she simply shoots Randegger a black glare and says, "If this was your neighborhood, *carajo,* and you had a god, wouldn't you want to ask him to stop this shit?"

"With pigs? With sheep?"

"With whatever would do it," she says.

Gibbons, meanwhile, is backing the truck out of the intersection, since the assembled congregation now is staring at them as though their presence here is quite unwelcome and it seems manifestly not a good idea to try to drive any closer. Mattison, taking one last look over his shoulder, sees a small pig being led up the side of the altar. The truck swings left at the first corner, then takes the next right and right again, which brings it around to the far side of the site of the ceremony in the same moment as a little earthquake goes rippling through the vicinity, 3.5 or so, just enough to make the gaunt blackened palm trees that line the street start swaying. The worshipers in the intersection behind them glower and point at the truck as it reappears, and begin to scream and yell furiously and shake their fists, and then Mattison hears some popping sounds.

"Hit the gas," he tells Gibbons over his suit radio. "They're shooting at us."

Gibbons speeds up. The street ahead is carpeted with a layer of loose ash maybe two feet deep, but Gibbons ploughs through it anyway, sending up swirling black clouds that make everybody on the open deck close the face-plates of their suits in a hurry. Beyond the ash is a stretch of crunchy cinders and other sorts of tephra, so that they all grab hold of each other and hang on tight as the truck clanks and jounces onward, and then a little newly congealed lava in the road makes the ride even rougher; but after that the street turns normal again for a while and they can relax, as much relaxation as may be possible while you ride in an open truck through territory that no longer looks like just a suburb of Hell, but the Devil's own back yard.

There have been repeated outbreaks of tectonic activity here before, early on in the crisis—that much is obvious from the burned-out houses and the black crusts of old lava everywhere and the ashen landscape—but something new and big is apparently getting ready to happen. The sky here is dead white from thick upwellings of steam and sulfurous fumes, except where the fumes are coal black. Streaks of lightning keep jumping around and the ground trembles continuously, as if a non-stop earthquake is going on. The sidewalks are warped and bulging in many places and some little red tongues of lava can be seen beginning to ooze from cracks in the pavement. Every few minutes a dull distant boom can be heard, a muffled sound that definitely gets your attention, something like the fart of a dinosaur that might be sauntering around a few blocks away.

Three or four weary-looking fire crews and some Guardsmen are slowly taking up positions in the street and getting their gear into order; some of the biggest pumps Mattison has ever seen have already been hauled into place for the lava-cooling work; police helicopters are whirling overhead, booming down orders to whatever remaining population may still be living here to evacuate the area at once. It is a truly precarious scene. Mattison is ever so happy that he traded the horrors of substance abuse for the privilege of visiting places like this.

The same thing is occurring to some of his companions, evidently. Blazes McFlynn lays his hand on Mattison's right arm and says, "I didn't sign on for any goddamned suicide missions, Matty. Let me off this fucking truck right now."

"Let you off?" Mattison says mildly.

"Fucking A. I want out, this very minute."

Mattison sighs. McFlynn always makes trouble, sooner or later; if only Mattison had known that this San Dimas operation was going to be tacked on to the day's outing, he probably would have opted to leave McFlynn behind at the outset. McFlynn is, of all goofy things, a bombed-out circus acrobat and pensioned-off movie stunt man, strong as a tow-truck winch, who over the course of time has found relief from stress in a whole smorgasbord of addictive substances and now—having very badly broken his leg while winning a moronic barroom bet that involved jumping off the top of a building, thereby acquiring a severe limp that makes it hard for him to practice either of his professions—draws generous compensation pay from a variety of governmental sources while undergoing one of his periodic spells of detoxification and Citizens Service. His first name is actually Gerard, but if you call him anything but Blazes he will react unpleasantly. He is the only man in the house whom Mattison in his pre-sober state would have felt any reticence about decking, for McFlynn, though some five inches shorter than Mattison, is probably just about as dangerous in a fight, gimpy leg and all.

"Are you saying," Mattison asks him once more, "that you don't want to take part in the current operation?"

"The whole street is going to blow any minute."

"Maybe so. That's why we're here, to get things under control if it does. You want to walk back from here to Silver Lake? You think you'll catch a bus, maybe, or phone for a cab? The option of your departing this operation simply does not exist at this moment, okay, McFlynn?" McFlynn tries to say something, but Mattison talks right over him, although keeping his voice mild, mild, mild, as he has been taught to do all the time when addressing the inmates, no matter what the provocation. "You find this work not to your liking, well, when you get your cowardly ass back to the house tonight you can tell Donna that you don't want to do volcano work any more, and she'll take you off the list. You aren't any fucking prisoner, you understand? You don't have to do this stuff against your will and in fact you are perfectly free, if you like, to pack up and leave the house tomorrow and go back to your favorite substance, for that matter. But not today. Today you work for me, and we work in San Dimas."

McFlynn, who surely was aware when he began complaining that this was where the discussion was going to end, is just starting to crank up a disgruntled and obscene capitulation when Gibbons says, over the radio from the truck cab, "Volcano Central wants us to start setting up the pump, Matty. Satellite scan says there's a lava bulge about to blow two blocks east of us down Bonita Avenue, which is the big street straight in front of us, and we're supposed to dam it up as soon as it comes our way." So they are going to be right on the front line, this time. Fine, Mattison thinks. Hot diggety damn.

They all get off the truck, and seal up their suits, and set about getting ready to deal with the oncoming eruption.

Because the pump they will be using this time is a jumbo job, just about the biggest one Mattison has ever worked with, he designates not only Prochaska and Hawks, once again, for the pumping crew, but also Clyde Snow and Blazes McFlynn, who will be up front not only because he's strong but also because Mattison wants to keep a close eye on him. In any case Mattison's going to need all the muscle-power he can get when it becomes necessary to swing that big rig around to keep the shifting lava penned up. He puts the generally reliable Paul Foust in charge of the controls that operate the pump itself. The rest—Randegger, Eisenstein, Herzog, Evans, and the three women, Doheny and Perez and Gulliver—Mattison deploys at various points along the line to the standpipe, so that they can keep the hose from getting tangled and cope with any other interruptions to the flow of water that might arise.

Everybody is in place none too soon. Because just as the signal arrives from the rear that the water connection

has been made, there comes an all too familiar bellow-
ing and groaning from the next block, as though a
giant with a bad bellyache is about to cut loose, and
then Mattison hears five sharp heavy grunts in succession, oof oof oof oof oof, followed by an eerie crackling sound, and suddenly the air is full of fire.

It's like one of the Yellowstone geysers, except that
what is being flung up is a lot of tiny bits of hot lava
riding on a plume of bluish steam, and for a couple of
moments it's impossible to see more than a few feet in
front of your face-plate. Then there is one single
booming sound, not muffled at all but sharp and hard,
and the bluish geyser of steam in front of them triples
or quadruples in height in about half a second, and the
pavement ripples beneath their feet as though an earthquake has happened precisely in this spot. Mattison
comprehends that there has been a terrific explosion a
very short way down the block and they are all about
to be hurled sky-high, or maybe are already on their
way up to the stratosphere and just haven't had time
to react yet.

But they aren't. What has happened is that an
underground gas pocket has blown its head off, yes,
but it has done it in one single clean *whoosh* and all
the pent-up junk that is being released has taken off
for Mars as a coherent unit, the steam and mud and
lava bits and whatnot rising straight up and vanishing,
clearing the air beautifully behind it. A couple of good-
sized lava bombs go soaring past them, fizzing like
fireworks, and come down with thick plopping thunks
somewhere not far away, but they don't seem to do
any damage; and then things are quiet, pretty much.
The whole blurry geyser that was spewing straight up
in front of them is gone, the ground they are standing
on is still intact, and they can see again.

Mattison has just about enough time to realize that

he has survived the explosion when he registers the force of an inrush of cool air that's swooping in from all sides to fill the gap where the geyser had been. It isn't strong enough to knock anybody down, but it does make you want to brace yourself pretty good.

And then comes the heat; and after it, the lava flow.

The heat is awesome. Mattison's suit catches most of it, but enough of the surge gets through his insulation so that he has no doubt at all about its intensity. It is what he calls first-rush heat: the subterranean magma mass has been cooking whatever deposits of air have surrounded it down there, and all that hot air, having had no place to go, has gone on getting hotter and hotter. Now it all comes gleefully zooming out at once. Mattison recoils involuntarily as though he has been belted by an invisible fist, steadies himself, straightens up, looks around to check up on his companions. They're all okay.

The lava, having busted through the pavement at last, follows right on the heels of that hot blast. A glowing red-orange river of it, maybe two or three feet deep, flowing down the middle of the street, taking the line of least resistance between the buildings as it heads in their direction.

"Hose!" Mattison yells. "Pump! Hit it, you bozos, hit it right down front!"

The lava is moving faster than Mattison would prefer, but not so fast that they need to retreat, at least not yet. It's actually three separate streams, each runnel six to eight feet wide, traveling in parallel paths and occasionally overlapping in a braided flow before separating again. The surface of each flow is fairly viscous from its exposure to the cool air, darker than what's below and showing irregular bulges and lobes and puckerings, which break open now and then to reveal the bright red stuff that lies just underneath. Here and there, narrow arcs of dark congealed lava rise above the stream at sharp angles like sleek fins, making it seem as though lava sharks are swimming swiftly downstream through the fiery torrent.

As the water from their big nozzle hits the first onrush of the flow, a scum of cooling lava starts to form almost instantly atop the middle stream. The front of it begins to change color and texture, thickening and turning gray and wrinkled, like an elephant's hide.

"That's it!" Mattison tells his men. "Keep hitting it there! Smack in the middle, guys!"

The water boils right off, naturally, and within moments they are able to see nothing in front of them once again except a wall of steam. This is the most dangerous moment, Mattison knows: if the lava—pushed toward them by whatever giant fist of gas is shoving it from below—should suddenly increase its uptake velocity, he and his whole team could be engulfed by it before they knew what was happening to them. For the next few minutes they'll be fighting blind against the oncoming lava flow, with nothing to guide them about its speed and position but Mattison's own perceptions of fluctuations in its heat.

The heat, at the moment, is really something. Not as fierce as it had been in the first instant of the breakout, no, but powerful enough to tax the cooling systems of their lava suits practically to their limits. It feels like a solid wall, that heat: Mattison imagines that if he leaned forward against it, it would hold him up. But he knows that it won't; and he knows, also, that if things get much hotter they will have to back off.

What he is trying to do is to build log-shaped strips of solidified lava along the front of the row, perpendicular to the line of movement. These will slow its advance as the fresh stuff piles up behind them. Then he can raise the angle of the hoses and start pumping the water upward to form larger blocks of lava, which he will eventually link to create his dam. And in time he will have buried the live lava at its source, entombing it beneath a little mountain of newly created rock and thus throttling the upwelling altogether.

The theory is a nice one. But in practice there usually are problems, because the lava, unlike your average river, tends to advance at a speed that varies from moment to moment, and you can build a lovely little log-jam or even some good-sized retainer blocks and nevertheless a sudden fast-moving spurt of molten stuff will spill right over the top and head your way, and there is nothing you can do then but drop your hoses and run like hell, hoping that the lava isn't traveling faster than you are.

Or else, as Mattison knows all too well, your dam will work very effectively to halt the lava in its present path—thereby inducing it to take up a different path that will send it rolling off toward some still undamaged freeway or still unruined houses, or maybe pouring down a hillside into another community entirely. When you see something like that happening, you need to move your whole operation around at a 90-degree angle to itself and start building a second dam, not so easy to do when you are operating with two-ton pumps.

Here, just now, everything is going sweetly so far. It's a tough business because of the extreme heat, but they are holding their own and even managing to achieve something. They have been able to maintain themselves at a distance of about half a block from the front edge of the lava flow without the need to retreat, and Mattison can see, whenever the steam thins out a bit, that the color of the lava along the edge is beginning to turn from gray to a comforting black, the black of solid basalt. A pump crew from some other Citizens Service House has arrived, Mattison has been told, and is building a second lava dam on the opposite side of the breakout. The fire crews are at work in the adjacent blocks, hosing down the structures that were ignited by the initial geyser of lava fragments.

If visibility stays good, if the water supply holds out, if the pump doesn't break down, if the lava doesn't pull any velocity surprises, if some randomly escaping gobbet of hot rock doesn't go flying at them through the air and melt one of the hoses, if there isn't some new eruption right under their feet, or maybe an earthquake, if this, if that—well, then, maybe they'll be able to knock off in another hour or two and head back to the house for some well-earned rest.

Maybe.

But things are beginning to change a little, now. The lava is penned up nicely in the middle but the bulk of the flow has shifted to the right-hand stream and that one is gaining in depth and velocity. That brings up the ugly possibility that Mattison's dam is achieving diversion instead of containment, and is about to send the entire flow, which has been traveling thus far from west to east, off in a southerly direction.

Volcano Central is monitoring the whole thing by satellite, and somebody back there calls the problem to Mattison's attention via his suit radio about a fifteenth of a second after he discovers it for himself. "Start moving your equipment to the right side of your dam," Volcano Central says. "There's danger now that the lava will start rolling south down San Dimas Avenue into Bonelli County Park, where it'll take out the Puddingstone Reservoir, and maybe keep on going south until it cuts the San Bernardino Freeway in half on the far side of the park. A piece of the 210 Freeway will also be at risk down there."

The street and park names mean nothing to Mattison—he has never been anywhere near San Dimas before in his life—and he can form only a hazy picture of the specific geography from what Volcano Central is telling him. But all that matters is that there's a park, a reservoir, and an apparently undamaged stretch of freeway to the south of here, and his beautifully constructed lava dam has succeeded in tipping the flow toward those very things, and he has to hustle now to correct the situation.

"All right, everybody, listen up," he announces. "We're making a 90-degree shift in operations."

Easier said than done, of course. The hoses will have to be decoupled and dragged to new hydrants, the massive pump has to be swung around, the trajectory of the water stream has to be recalibrated—nor will the lava stand still while they are doing all these things. It's a challenge, but stuff like this is meat and potatoes to Mattison, the fundamental nutritive agent out of which his recovery is being built. He starts giving the orders; and his poor battered bedraggled team of ex-abusers, ex-homelesses, ex-burglars, ex-muggers, ex-whores, ex-this, ex-that, all of it bad, swings gamely into action, because this is part of *their* recovery too.

But in the middle of the process of moving the pump, Blazes McFlynn steps back, folds his arms across the chest of his lava suit, and says, "Coffee break."

Mattison stares at him incredulously. "What the fuck did you say?"

"Time out, is what I said. You think it's a snap, hauling this monster around? I'm tired. I'm a crippled man, Matty. I got to sit down for a while and take a breather."

"The lava is changing direction. There's a park and a reservoir and a freeway in the path of danger now."

"So?" McFlynn says. "What's that mean to me?"

Mattison is so astonished that for a moment he can't speak. If this is a joke, it's a damn lousy one. He needs McFlynn badly, and McFlynn has to know that. Flabbergasted, Mattison gapes and gestures in helpless pantomime.

McFlynn says, "Not my park. Not my freeway. I don't even know where the fuck we are right now. But my bad leg is aching like a holy son of a bitch and I want to sit down and rest and that's that."

"I'll sit you down, all right," Mattison says, recovering his voice finally. "I'll sit you down inside a volcano, you obstreperous lazy son of a bitch. I'll drop you in on your head." He knows that he is not supposed to speak to the inmates this way, and that everybody else is listening in and someone is bound to talk and he will very likely be reprimanded later on by Donna, but he can't help himself. He doesn't pretend to be a saint and McFlynn's sudden rebellion has pissed him off *almost* to the breaking point. Almost. What he really would like to do now is put one hand under McFlynn's left armpit and one hand under the right one and pick him up and carry him to the lava and dangle his feet over the fiery-hot flow for a moment and then let go.

Very likely that is exactly what Mattison would have tried to do two years ago, if he and McFlynn had found themselves in this situation two years ago; but it is a measure of the progress he has been making that he merely fantasizes tossing McFlynn into the lava, now, instead of actually doing it. The fantasy is so vivid that for a dizzy moment he believes that he is actually doing it, and he gets a savage rush of glee from the mental spectacle of McFlynn disappearing, melting away as he goes under, into the blazing river of molten magma.

But actually doing it would be extremely poor pro-
cedural technique. And also McFlynn is not exactly a
weakling and Mattison is aware that he might find
himself involved in a non-trivial fight if he tries anything. Mattison has never lost a fight in his life, but it
is some time since he has been in one, and he may be
out of practice; and in any case there's no time now,
with the lava about to overflow his dam, to fuck
around getting into fights with people like Blazes
McFlynn.

So what he does, instead, is turn his back on
McFlynn, swallowing the rest of what he would like
to say and do to him, and indicate to Prochaska,
Hawks, and Snow, who have been watching the
whole dispute in silence, that they will have to finish
moving the pump without McFlynn's help. They all
know what that means, that McFlynn has shafted
them thoroughly by dumping his share of this tremendous job on their shoulders, and they are righteously
angry. A certain amount of venting occurs, which
Mattison decides it would be best to permit. Hawks
tells McFlynn that he's a fucking goof-off and
Prochaska says something guttural and probably
highly uncomplimentary in what is probably Czech,
and even Snow, not famous for hard work himself,
gives McFlynn the hand-across-bent-forearm chop.
McFlynn doesn't seem to give a damn. He replies to
the whole bunch of them with an upthrust finger and a
lazy, contemptuous smirk that makes Mattison think
that the next event is going to be a crazy free-for-all;
but no, no, they all ostentatiously turn their backs on
him too and continue the job of guiding the pump
toward its new position.

It's a miserably hard job. The pump is on a wheeled
carriage, sure, but it isn't designed to be moved in an
arc as narrow as this, and they really have to bust their

humps to swing it into its new position. The men, clumsy within their bulky suits, grunt and groan and gasp as they bend and push. Mattison, who as the biggest and strongest of the group has taken up the key position, can feel things popping in his arms and shoulders as he puts his whole weight into the job. And all the while McFlynn stands to one side, watching.

The pump is more than halfway into place when McFlynn comes limping over as though he has graciously decided that he will join them in the work after all.

"Well, look who's here," says Hawks. "You fucking son of a bitch."

"Can I be of any assistance?" McFlynn says grandly.

He tries to take up a position against the side of the pump carriage between Hawks and Prochaska. Hawks turns squarely toward McFlynn and seems to be thinking about throwing a punch at him. Mattison, who has been worried about this possibility since McFlynn made his announcement, poises himself to step in, but Hawks gets his anger under control just in time. Muttering to himself, he turns back in Prochaska's direction. There is just enough room for McFlynn to shove his way in between Hawks and Mattison. He braces himself and puts his shoulder against the carriage, making a big show of throwing all his strength into the task.

"Hey, be careful not to strain yourself, now!" Mattison tells him.

"Fuck you, Matty," McFlynn says sulkily. "That's all I have to say, just fuck you."

"You're welcome," says Mattison, as with the aid of McFlynn's added strength they finally manage to finish swinging the big pump around and lock it on its track.

The men step back from it, wheezing, sucking in

breath after their heavy exertions. But the incident isn't over. Prochaska goes up to McFlynn and says something else to him in the harsh language that Mattison assumes is Czech. McFlynn gives Prochaska the finger again. Maybe there's going to be a fight after all. No. They are content to glare, it seems. Mattison glances at McFlynn and sees, through the face-plate of his suit, that the expression on McFlynn's face has become unexpectedly complicated. He looks defiant but maybe just a little shamefaced too. An attack of conscience? A bit of guilt over his stupid dereliction kicking in at last, now that McFlynn realizes that he actually was needed badly just now and fucked everybody over by crapping out? Better late than never, Mattison figures.

Prochaska still isn't finished letting McFlynn know what he thinks of him, though: he throws in a couple of harsh new Slavic expletives, and McFlynn, who probably has no more of an idea of what Prochaska is saying to him than Mattison does, dourly gives him back some muttered threats salted with the standard Anglo-Saxonisms.

Things are starting to get a little out of hand, Mattison thinks. He needs to do something, although he's not sure what. But he has a lava flow to worry about, first.

The lava, in fact, is getting a little out of hand also. Not that it has started to flow in any serious way toward Whatchamacallit Park and Whozis Reservoir, not yet. A thin little eddy of it has begun to dribble off that way over the right-hand edge of Mattison's dam, but nothing significant. The main flow is still traveling from east to west. The real problem is that new flows are starting to emerge from the ground alongside the original source, and there are now six or seven streams instead of three. Red gleams are showing through the gray and black of the dam in a number of places, indicating that the hot new lava is finding its way between sections of the hardened stuff. That means that what is coming out now is thinner than before.

Thin lava moves faster than thick lava. Sometimes it can move *very* fast. The direction of the flow can get a little unpredictable, too.

The pump is in place in its new location and ready to start throwing water, but it needs to have the water, first. Mattison is still waiting for confirmation that the hoses behind him have been moved and hooked to different hydrants. He can see Nicky Herzog a short distance down one of the side streets to his right, kneeling next to a section of thick hose as he fumbles around with a connector.

"Are we okay?" Mattison asks him.

"Just about ready," Herzog replies. He straightens up and begins to give the hand signal indicating that the water line is completely set up. But suddenly Herzog seems to freeze in place, and starts swinging around jerkily in a very odd way, going from side to side from the waist up without moving his legs at all. Also he has begun flinging his arms rigidly above his head, one at a time, as though he is suddenly getting tickled by an electric current.

For a moment Mattison can't figure out what's going on. Then he sees that the rightmost lava stream, the one that had already begun to escape a little from the dam, has been joined by one of the newer and thinner streams and has greatly increased in volume and velocity. It has changed direction, too, and is running straight at Herzog in a great hurry, traveling at him in two prongs separated by a green Toyota utility van that somebody has abandoned in the middle of the street.

Herzog is in the direct line of the flow, and he knows it, and he is scared silly.

Mattison sees immediately that Herzog has a couple of choices that make some sense. He could go to his left, which would involve a slightly scary jump of about three feet over the lesser prong of the new lava stream, and take refuge in an alleyway that looks likely to be secure against the immediate trajectory of the stream because there are brick buildings on either side of it. Or he could simply turn around and run like hell down the street he's in, hoping to outleg the advancing flow, which is moving swiftly but maybe not quite as swiftly as he could manage to go. Both of these options have certain risks, but each of them holds out the possibility of survival, too.

Unfortunately Herzog, though a quick-witted enough fellow when it comes to sarcastic quips and insults, or to laying out a million-dollar story line for some movie-studio executive, is fundamentally a clueless little yutz as far as most normal aspects of life are concerned, and in his panic he makes a yutzy decision. Apparently Herzog perceives the Toyota as an island of safety in the middle of all this madness, and, breaking at last from his paralysis, he jumps the wrong way across a segment of the narrower lava stream and with a berserk outlay of energy pulls himself up onto the hood of the green van. From there he clambers desperately to the Toyota's roof and begins to emit a godawful frightened caterwauling, high-pitched and strident, like an automobile burglar alarm that won't turn off.

What he has achieved by this is to strand himself in the middle of the lava flow. Maybe he expects that Mattison will now call in a police helicopter to lower a rope ladder to him, the way they would do in a movie, but there are no helicopters in the vicinity just now, and the lava that surrounds the Toyota isn't any special effect, either: it's a fast-flowing stream of actual red-hot molten magma, a couple of thousand degrees in temperature, which is widening and widening and very soon will be lapping up against the Toyota's wheels on both sides. At that point the Toyota is going to melt right down into the lava stream and Nicky Herzog is going to die a quick but very unpleasant death.

Mattison doesn't like the idea of losing a member of his crew, even a shithead like Herzog. He knows that his crew is made up *entirely* of shitheads, himself included, and the fact that Herzog is a shithead does not invalidate him as a human being. Too much of the human race falls into the shithead category, Mattison realizes. If nobody in the world ever lifted a finger to save shitheads from their own shitheadedness, then almost everybody would be in trouble. He himself, as Mattison is only too thoroughly aware, would still be compulsively cruising the bars along Wilshire and waking up the next morning under somebody's carport in Venice or Santa Monica. So he resolved some time back, quite early in his sobriety, to do whatever he could to help the shitheads of the world overcome their shitheadedness, starting with himself but extending even unto the likes of McFlynn and Herzog.

Nevertheless, Mattison is helpless in this instance. He is cut off from Herzog now by the larger of the two lava flows and he doesn't see a damned thing that he can do by way of rescuing him in time. A couple of minutes ago, maybe, yes, but now there's no chance. Even with an armored suit on, he can't just wade through a stream of hot fresh lava. He is going to have to stand right where he is and watch Herzog melt.

All of this analysis, the sizing up of the somber situation and the arriving at the melancholy conclusion, has taken about 2.53 seconds. Roughly 1.42 seconds later, while Mattison is still glumly making his peace with the idea that Herzog is screwed, a lava-suited figure unexpectedly appears in the street where Herzog is trapped, emerging from the alleyway into which Herzog had failed to flee, and calls out, extending his arms to the terrified man on top of the van, "Jump! Jump!" And, when Herzog does nothing, yells again, angrily, "Come *on*, you prick, jump! I'll catch you!"

Mattison isn't sure at first who the man who has come out of the alleyway is. Everybody looks basically like everybody else inside a lava suit, and it's not too easy to distinguish one voice from another over the suit radios, either. Mattison glances around, taking a quick inventory of his crew. Hawks right here, yes, and Prochaska, yes—

Can it be Clyde Snow who is out there by the mouth of that alleyway? No. No. Snow is right over there, on the far side of the pump carriage. So it has to be Blazes McFlynn who at this very moment is standing almost at the edge of a diabolically hot stream of lava and stretching his arms out toward the gibbering and wailing Nicky Herzog. McFlynn, yes, who has found some sort of detour between the adjacent buildings and made his way as close to the Toyota as it is possible to get. Incredible, Mattison thinks. Incredible.

"Jump, will you, you nitwit faggot?" McFlynn roars once more. "I can't stay here the whole fucking day!"

And Herzog jumps.

He does it with the same grace and panache with which he has handled most other aspects of his life, coming down in McFlynn's approximate direction with his body bent in some crazy corkscrew position and his arms and legs flailing wildly. McFlynn manages to grab one arm and one leg as Herzog sails by him heading nose-first for the lava, and hangs on to him. But, slight as Herzog is, the force of his jump is so great and the angle of his descent is so cockeyed that the impact on McFlynn causes the bigger man to stagger and spin around and begin to topple. Mattison, watching in horror, comprehends at once that McFlynn is going to fall forward into the lava stream still holding Herzog in his arms, and both men are going to die.

McFlynn doesn't fall, though. He takes one ponderous lurching step forward, so that his left leg is no more than a few inches from the edge of the lava stream, and leans over bending almost double so that that leg accepts his full weight, and Herzog's weight as well. McFlynn's left leg, Mattison thinks, is the broken one, the one that is bent permanently outward after the seventy-nine-cent job of setting it that was done for him at the county hospital. McFlynn stands there leaning out and down for a very long moment, regaining his balance, adjusting to his burden, getting a better grip on Herzog. Then, straightening up and tilting himself backward, McFlynn pivots on his good leg and swings himself around in a hundred-and-eighty-degree arc and goes tottering off triumphantly into the alleyway with Nicky Herzog's inert form draped over his shoulder.

Mattison has never seen anything like it. Herzog can't weigh more than a hundred forty pounds, but the suit adds maybe fifty, sixty pounds more, and McFlynn, though six feet tall and stockily built, probably weighs two-ten tops. And has a gimpy leg, no bullshit there, a genuinely damaged limb on which he has just taken all of Herzog's weight as the little guy came plummeting down from that Toyota. It must have been some circus-acrobat trick that McFlynn used, Mattison decides, or else one of his stunt-man gimmicks, because there was no other way that he could have pulled the trick off. Mattison, big and strong as he is and with both his legs intact, doubts that even he would have been able to manage it.

McFlynn is coming around the far side of the pump carriage now, no longer carrying Herzog in his arms but simply dragging him along like a limp doll. McFlynn's face-plate is open and Mattison can see that his eyes are shining like a madman's—the adrenaline rush, no doubt—and his cheeks are flushed and glossy with sweat. It's the look of the hero coming back in glory from a tremendous victory. McFlynn's heroism is bullshit, Mattison knows: it's just the next scene in McFlynn's private movie. But you live out your movie long enough and it goes real on you. Herzog was going to get killed and, thanks to McFlynn, he wasn't. That's real.

"Here," McFlynn says, and dumps Herzog down practically at Mattison's feet. "I thought the dumb asshole was going to wait forever to make the jump."

"Hey, nice going," Mattison says, grinning. He balls up his fist and clips McFlynn lightly on the forearm with it, a gesture of solidarity and companionship, one big man to another. McFlynn's face is aglow with the true redemptive gleam. That must have been why he did it, Mattison thinks: to cover over the business about refusing to help move the pump. Well, whatever. McFlynn is a total louse, a completely deplorable son of a bitch, but that was still a hell of a thing to have done. "I thought you had gone off on your coffee break," Mattison says.

"Fuck you, Matty," McFlynn tells him, and shambles away to one side.

Herzog is conscious, or approximately so, but he looks dazed. Mattison yanks his face-plate open, snaps his fingers in front of his nose, gets him to open his eyes.

"Go over to the truck and sit down," Mattison orders him. "Chill out for a while. Tell Ned Eisenstein I want him to check you out. You're off duty."

"Yeah," says Herzog vaguely. "Yeah. Yeah."

And give yourself a couple of good shots of bourbon to calm yourself down while you're at it, Mattison thinks, but of course does not say. Christ, he wouldn't mind a little of that himself, just now. It is, however, not an available option.

"All right," he says, looking around at Hawks, Prochaska, Snow, and a couple of the others, Foust and Nadine Doheny, who have come up from the rear lines to see what's going on. "Where were we, now?"

The hose line that Herzog had been supervising has been obliterated by the new lava stream, of course, and the Toyota van is up to its door-handles now in lava too. But there are other hose lines coming in from other streets, and they still have a dam to build before they can call it a day.

Mattison is getting a little tired, now, after all the stuff with McFlynn and then with Herzog, but he can feel himself starting to function on automatic pilot. Groggily but with complete confidence he gets the water running again, and cuts through another handy alley so that he can set up a second line of lava logs along the new front, about thirty feet south of the Toyota. It takes about fifteen minutes of fast maneuvers and fancy dancing to choke it off entirely.

Then he can devote his attention to building the larger dam, the one that will contain this whole mess and shove the lava back on itself before it does any more damage. Mattison plods back and forth almost like a sleepwalker, giving orders in an increasingly raspy voice, telling people to move hoses around and

change the throwing angle of the pump, and they do
what he says like sleepwalkers themselves. This has
been a very long day. They don't usually do two jobs
the same day, and Mattison means to have Donna
DiStefano say something to the Citizens Service admin-
istrators when he gets back.

Big ragged-edged blocks of black stone are forming
now all across the middle of the street and curving
around toward the south where the runaway lava
stream had been. So the thing is pretty well under control. By now another team of Citizens Service people
has arrived, and Mattison figures that if he is as tired
as he is, then the others in his crew, who don't have
his superhuman physical endurance and are still hampered to some degree by the medical aftereffects of
their recently overcome bad habits, must be about
ready to drop. He tells Barry Gibbons that he would
like him to request permission from Volcano Central
to withdraw. It takes Gibbons about five minutes to
get through—Volcano Central must be having one
whacko busy day—but finally they okay the request.

"All right, guys," Mattison sings out. "That's it for
today. Everybody back in the truck!"

They are silent, pretty much, on the way back. The
San Dimas thing has been grueling for all of them.
Mattison notices that Herzog is standing on one side
of the truck and McFlynn on the other, facing in
opposite directions. He wonders whether Herzog has
had the good grace even to thank McFlynn for what
he has done. Probably not. But Herzog is a shithead,
after all.

For a long time Mattison can't stop thinking about
that little episode. About McFlynn's perversity,
mainly. Crapping out on the rest of the pump team in
a key moment without any reason, nonchalantly stepping to one side and leaving Prochaska and Hawks

and Snow to do the heavy hauling without him, even though he must have known that his strength was needed. And then, just as light-heartedly, running into that alleyway to risk his life for Herzog, a man whom he despises and loves to torment. It doesn't make a lot of sense. Mattison pokes around at it from this way and that, and still he doesn't have a clue to what might have been going on in McFlynn's mind in either case.

Possibly nothing was going on in there, he decides finally. Perhaps McFlynn's actions don't make any sense even to McFlynn.

McFlynn has been a resident in the house long enough to know that everybody is supposed to be a team player, and even if you don't want to be, you need to *pretend* to be. Letting the team down in the clutch is not a good way to ensure that you will get the help you need in your own time of need. On the other hand, there was no reason in the world why McFlynn had to do what he did for Herzog, except maybe that he was feeling sheepish about the pump-moving episode, and Mattison finds that a little hard to believe, McFlynn feeling sheepish about anything.

So maybe McFlynn is just an ornery, unpredictable guy who takes each moment as it comes. Maybe he felt like being a louse when they were moving the pump, and maybe he felt like being a hero when Herzog was about to die a horrible death. I don't know, Mattison thinks. That's cool. I don't know, and I hereby give myself permission not to know, and to hell with it. It isn't Mattison's job to get inside people's heads, anyway. He's not a shrink, just a live-in caregiver, still much too busy working on his own recovery to spend time fretting about the mysterious ways of his fellow mortals. He simply has to keep them from hurting themselves and each other while they're living in the house. So he gives up thinking about McFlynn and Herzog and turns his attention instead to what is going on all around them, which actually is a little on the weird side.

They are almost at the western periphery of the Zone, now, having retraced their route through Azusa and Covina, then through towns whose names Mattison doesn't even know—hell, most of these places look alike, anyway, and unless you see the signs at the boundaries you don't know where one ends and the next begins—and are approaching Temple City, San Gabriel, Alhambra, all those various flatland communities. Behind them, night is beginning to fall, it being past five o'clock and this being February. In the gathering darkness the new spurts of smoke atop far-off Mount Pomona are pretty spectacular, lit as they are by streaks of fiery red from whatever is going on inside that cone today. But also, a little to the south of the big volcano, something else seems to be happening, something odd, because a glaring cloud of blue-white light has arisen down there. Mattison doesn't remember seeing blue-white stuff before. Some new kind of explosion? Are they nuking the lava flow, maybe? It looks strange, anyway. He'll find out about it on the evening news, if they are. Or maybe he won't.

Booming noises come from the southeast. A lot of tectonic garbage seems to be going into the sky back there too; he sees small red lava particles glowing against the dusk, and dark clouds too, ash and pumice, no doubt, and probably some nice-sized lava bombs being tossed aloft. And they experience two small earthquakes as they're driving back, one while they're going up Fair Oaks in Pasadena, another fifteen minutes later just as they're about to get on the westbound Ventura Freeway. Nothing surprising about that; five or six little quakes a day are standard now, what with all that magma moving around under the San Gabriel Valley. But the two so close together are further signs that things are getting even livelier in the Zone just as Mattison and his crew are going off duty. Hoo boy, Mattison thinks. Hot times in Magma City.

It's beginning to rain a little, out here in Glendale where they are at the moment. Nothing big, just light sprinkles, enough to make the rush-hour traffic a little uglier but not to cause serious troubles. Mattison likes the rain. You get so little of it, ordinarily, in Los Angeles, eight or ten dry months at a time, sometimes, and right now, with everything that's going on behind him in the Zone, the rain seems sweet and pure, a holy blessing that's being scattered on the troubled land.

It's good to be going westward again, moving slowly through the evening commute toward what is still the normal, undamaged part of Los Angeles, toward the sprawling city he grew up in. What is happening back there in the Zone, the lava, the ash, the blue-white lights, all seems unreal to him. This doesn't. Down there to his left are the high-rise towers of downtown, and the clustering stack of freeways meeting and going off in every which way. And straight ahead lie all the familiar places of his own particular life, Studio City and Sherman Oaks and Van Nuys in this direction and Hollywood and Westwood and West L.A. in that one, and so on and on out to Santa Monica and Venice and Topanga and the Pacific Ocean.

If only they could drop a curtain across the face of the Zone, Mattison thinks. Or build a fifty-foot-high wall, and seal it off completely. But no, they can't do that, and the lava will keep on coming, won't it, crawling westward and westward and westward down there under the ground until one of these days it comes shooting up under Rodeo Drive or knocks the San Diego Freeway off its pegs. What the hell: we can only do what we can do, and the rest is up to God's mercy and wisdom, right? *Right?* Right.

They are practically back at the house, now.

The rain is getting worse. The sky ahead of them is starting to turn dark. The sky behind them is already black, except where the strange light of eruptions breaks through the night.

"McFlynn really pissed me off today," Mattison tells Donna DiStefano. "I entertained seriously hostile thoughts in his direction. In fact I had pretty strong fantasies about tossing him right into the lava. Truth, Donna."

The house director laughs. It's the famous Donna laugh, a big one, high up on the Richter scale. She is a tall, hefty woman with warm friendly eyes and a huge amount of dark curling hair going halfway down her back. Nothing ever upsets her. She is supposed to have been addicted to something or other very major, fifteen or twenty years back, but nobody knows the details.

"It's a temptation, isn't it?" she says. "What a pill he is, eh? Was that before or after the Herzog rescue?"

"Before. A long time before. He was bitching at me from lunchtime on." Mattison hasn't told her about the pump-moving incident. Probably he should; but he figures she already has heard about it, one way or another, and it isn't required of him to file report cards on every shitty thing the residents of the house do while he's looking after them. "There was another time, later in the day, when it would have given me great pleasure to dangle him face first into the vent. But I prayed for patience instead and God was kind to me, or else we'd have had some vacancies in the house tonight."

"Some?"

"McFlynn and me, because he'd be dead and I'd be in jail. And Herzog too, because McFlynn was the only one in a position to rescue him just then. But here we all are, safe and sound."

"Don't worry about it," DiStefano says. "You did good today, Matty."

Yes. He knows that that's true. He did good. Every day, in every way, inch by inch, he does his best. And he's grateful every hour of his life that things have worked out for him in such a way that he has had the opportunity. As if God has sent volcanoes to Los Angeles as a personal gift to him, part of the recovery program of Calvin Thomas Mattison, Jr.

There's nothing on that night's news about unusual stuff in the Zone this evening. Usual stuff, yes, plenty of that, getting the usual perfunctory coverage, fumaroles opening here, lava vents there, houses destroyed in this town and that and that, new street blockages, et cetera, et cetera. Maybe the blue-white light he saw was just a tremendous searchlight beam, celebrating the opening of some new shopping mall in Anaheim or Fullerton. This crazy town, you never can tell.

He goes upstairs—his little room, all his own. Reads for a while, thinks about his day, gets into bed. Sleeps like a baby. The alarm goes off at five, and he rises unprotestingly, showers, dresses, goes downstairs.

There are lights on all over the board. Blue for new fumaroles, here, here, and there, and another red one in the vicinity of Mount Pomona, and a whole epidemic of green dots announcing fresh lava cutting loose over what looks like the whole area, top to bottom. Mattison has never seen it look that bad. The crisis seems to be entering a new and very obnoxious phase. Volcano Central will be calling them out again today, sure as anything.

What the hell. We do what we can, and hope for the best, one day at a time.

He puts together some breakfast for himself and waits for the rest of the house to wake up.

Gossamer

STEPHEN BAXTER

Stephen Baxter writes in the hard science mode of Hal Clement and Robert L. Forward. This kind of SF is particularly valued by hard SF readers because it is comparatively scarce and requires intense effort by the writer to be accurate to known science. It produces innovative imagery that is peculiar to hard SF; that sparks that good old wow of wonderment. His novels began to appear in 1991 (*Raft*); the 1995 novel, *The Time Ships,* is his sequel, published 100 years later, to H.G. Wells's 1895 *The Time Machine.* Baxter's "Gossamer" appeared in *Science Fiction Age,* the most successful new SF magazine of the 1990s. His visions based on science are astonishingly precise and clear and that is what his fiction offers as foreground for our entertainment.

The flitter bucked. Lvov looked up from her data desk, startled. Beyond the flitter's translucent hull, the wormhole was flooded with sheets of blue-white light which raced toward and past the flitter, giving Lvov the impression of huge, uncontrolled speed.

"We've got a problem," Cobh said. The pilot bent over her own data desk, a frown creasing her thin face.

Lvov had been listening to her data desk's synthesized murmur on temperature inversion layers in nitrogen atmospheres; now she tapped the desk to shut it off. The flitter was a transparent tube, deceptively warm and comfortable. Impossibly fragile. *Astronauts have problems in space*, she thought. *But not me. I'm no hero; I'm only a researcher.* Lvov was twenty-eight years old; she had no plans to die—and certainly not during a routine four-hour hop through a Poole wormhole that had been human-rated for eighty years.

She clung to her desk, her knuckles whitening, wondering if she ought to feel scared.

Cobh sighed and pushed her data desk away; it floated before her. "Close up your suit and buckle up."

"What's wrong?"

"Our speed through the wormhole has increased." Cobh pulled her own restraint harness around her. "We'll reach the terminus in another minute—"

"What? But we should have been traveling for another half-hour."

Cobh looked irritated. "I know that. I think the Interface has become unstable. The wormhole is buckling."

"What does that mean? Are we in danger?"

Cobh checked the integrity of Lvov's pressure suit, then pulled her data desk to her. Cobh was a Caucasian, strong-faced, a native of Mars, perhaps fifty years old. "Well, we can't turn back. One way or the other it'll be over in a few more seconds. Hold tight."

Now Lvov could see the Interface itself, the terminus of the wormhole. The Interface was a blue-white tetrahedron, an angular cage that exploded at her from infinity.

Glowing struts swept over the flitter.

The craft hurtled out of the collapsing wormhole. Light founted around the fleeing craft, as stressed spacetime yielded in a gush of heavy particles.

Lvov glimpsed stars, wheeling.

Cobh dragged the flitter sideways, away from the energy fount—

There was a *lurch,* a discontinuity in the scene beyond the hull. Suddenly a planet loomed before them.

"Lethe," Cobh said. "Where did that come from? I'll have to take her down—we're too close."

Lvov saw a flat, complex landscape, gray-crimson in the light of a swollen moon. The scene was dimly lit, and it rocked wildly as the flitter tumbled. And, stretching between world and moon, she saw . . .

No. It was impossible.

The vision was gone, receded into darkness.

"Here it comes," Cobh yelled.

Foam erupted, filling the flitter. The foam pushed into Lvov's ears, mouth, and eyes; she was blinded, but she found she could breathe.

She heard a collision, a grinding that lasted seconds,

and she imagined the flitter ploughing its way into the surface of the planet. She felt a hard lurch, a rebound.

The flitter came to rest.

A synthesized voice emitted blurred safety instructions. There was a ticking as the hull cooled.

In the sudden stillness, still blinded by foam, Lvov tried to recapture what she had seen. *Spider web. It was a web, stretching from the planet to its moon.*

"Welcome to Pluto." Cobh's voice was breathless, ironic.

Lvov Stood on the Surface of Pluto.

The suit's insulation was good, but enough heat leaked to send nitrogen clouds hissing around her footsteps, and where she walked she burned craters in the ice. Gravity was only a few percent of G, and Lvov, Earth-born, felt as if she might blow away.

There were clouds above her: wispy cirrus, aerosol clusters suspended in an atmosphere of nitrogen and methane. The clouds occluded bone-white stars. From here, Sol and the moon, Charon, were hidden by the planet's bulk, and it was *dark,* dark on dark, the damaged landscape visible only as a sketch in starlight.

The flitter had dug a trench a mile long and fifty yards deep in this world's antique surface, so Lvov was at the bottom of a valley walled by nitrogen ice. Cobh was hauling equipment out of the crumpled-up wreck of the flitter: scooters, data desks, life-support boxes, Lvov's equipment. Most of the stuff had been robust enough to survive the impact, Lvov saw, but not her own equipment.

Maybe a geologist could have crawled around with nothing more than a hammer and a set of sample bags. But Lvov was an atmospheric scientist. What was she going to achieve here without her equipment?

Her fear was fading now, to be replaced by irritation, impatience. She was five light-hours from Sol; already she was missing the online nets. She kicked at the ice. She was *stuck* here; she couldn't talk to anyone, and there wasn't even the processing power to generate a Virtual environment.

Cobh finished wrestling with the wreckage. She was breathing hard. "Come on," she said. "Let's get out of this ditch and take a look around." She showed Lvov how to work a scooter. It was a simple platform, its inert gas jets controlled by twists of raised handles.

Side by side, Cobh and Lvov rose out of the crash scar.

Pluto ice was a rich crimson laced with organic purple. Lvov made out patterns, dimly, on the surface of the ice; they were like bas-relief, discs the size of dinner plates, with the intricate complexity of snowflakes.

Lvov landed clumsily on the rim of the crash scar, the scooter's blunt prow crunching into surface ice, and she was grateful for the low gravity. The weight and heat of the scooters quickly obliterated the ice patterns.

"We've come down near the equator," Cobh said. "The albedo is higher at the south pole; a cap of methane ice there, I'm told."

"Yes."

Cobh pointed to a bright blue spark, high in the sky. "That's the wormhole Interface, where we emerged, fifty thousand miles away."

Lvov squinted at constellations unchanged from those she'd grown up with on Earth. "Are we stranded?"

Cobh said, with reasonable patience, "For the time being. The flitter is wrecked, and the wormhole has collapsed; we're going to have to go back to Jupiter the long way round."

Three billion miles . . . "Ten hours ago I was asleep in a hotel room on Io. And now this. What a mess."

Cobh laughed. "I've already sent off messages to the Inner System. They'll be received in about five hours. A one-way GUTship will be sent to retrieve us. It will refuel here, with Charon ice—"

"How long?"

"It depends on the readiness of a ship. Say ten days to prepare, then a ten-day flight out here—"

"*Twenty days?*"

"We're in no danger. We've supplies for a month. Although we're going to have to live in these suits."

"Lethe. This trip was supposed to last seventy-two hours."

"Well," Cobh said testily, "you'll have to call and cancel your appointments, won't you? All we have to do is wait here; we're not going to be comfortable, but we're safe enough."

"Do you know what happened to the wormhole?"

Cobh shrugged. She stared up at the distant blue spark. "As far as I know, nothing like this has happened before. I think the Interface itself became unstable, and that fed back into the throat . . . But I don't know how we fell to Pluto so quickly. That doesn't make sense."

"How so?"

"Our trajectory was spacelike. Superluminal." She glanced at Lvov obliquely, as if embarrassed. "For a moment there, we appeared to be traveling faster than light."

"Through normal space? That's impossible."

"Of course it is." Cobh reached up to scratch her cheek, but her gloved fingers rattled against her faceplate. "I think I'll go up to the Interface and take a look around there."

Cobh showed Lvov how to access the life support boxes. Then she strapped her data desk to her back, climbed aboard her scooter, and lifted off the planet's surface, heading for the Interface. Lvov watched her dwindle.

Lvov's isolation closed in. She was alone, the only human on the surface of Pluto.

A reply from the Inner System came within twelve hours of the crash. A GUTship was being sent from Jupiter. It would take thirteen days to refit the ship, followed by an eight-day flight to Pluto, then more delay in taking on fresh reaction mass at Charon. Lvov chafed at the timescale, restless.

There was other mail: concerned notes from Lvov's family, a testy demand for updates from her research supervisor, and for Cobh, orders from her employer to mark as much of the flitter wreck as she could for salvage and analysis. Cobh's ship was a commercial wormhole transit vessel, hired by Oxford—Lvov's university—for this trip. Now, it seemed, a complex battle over liability would be joined between Oxford, Cobh's firm, and the insurance companies.

Lvov, five light-hours from home, found it difficult to respond to the mail asynchronously. She felt as if she had been cut out of the online mind of humanity. In the end, she drafted replies to her family and deleted the rest of the messages.

She checked her research equipment again, but it really was unuseable. She tried to sleep. The suit was uncomfortable, claustrophobic. She was restless, bored, a little scared.

She began a systematic survey of the surface, taking her scooter on widening spiral sweeps around the crash scar.

The landscape was surprisingly complex, a starlit sculpture of feathery ridges and fine ravines. She kept a few hundred feet above the surface; whenever she flew too low, her heat evoked billowing vapor from fragile nitrogen ice, obliterating ancient features, and she experienced obscure guilt.

She found more of the snowflakelike features, generally in little clusters of eight or ten.

Pluto, like its moon-twin Charon, was a ball of rock clad by thick mantles of water ice and nitrogen ice, and laced with methane, ammonia, and organic compounds. It was like a big, stable comet nucleus; it barely deserved the status of "planet." There were *moons* bigger than Pluto.

There had been only a handful of visitors in the eighty years since the building of the Poole wormhole. None of them had troubled to walk the surfaces of Pluto or Charon. The wormhole, Lvov realized, hadn't been built as a commercial proposition, but as a sort of stunt: the link which connected, at last, all of the System's planets to the rapid-transit hub at Jupiter.

She tired of her plodding survey. She made sure she could locate the crash scar, lifted the scooter to a mile above the surface, and flew toward the south polar cap.

Cobh called from the Interface. "I think I'm figuring out what happened here—that superluminal effect I talked about. Lvov, have you heard of an Alcubierre wave?" She dumped images to Lvov's desk—portraits of the wormhole Interface, graphics.

"No." Lvov ignored the input and concentrated on flying the scooter. "Cobh, why should a wormhole become unstable? Hundreds of wormhole rapid transits are made every day, all across the System."

"A wormhole is a flaw in space. It's inherently

unstable anyway. The throat and mouths are kept open by active feedback loops involving threads of exotic matter. That's matter with a negative energy density, a sort of antigravity which—"

"But this wormhole went wrong."

"Maybe the tuning wasn't perfect. The presence of the flitter's mass in the throat was enough to send the wormhole over the edge. If the wormhole had been more heavily used, the instability might have been detected earlier, and fixed. . . ."

Over the gray-white pole, Lvov flew through banks of aerosol mist; Cobh's voice whispered to her, remote, without meaning.

Sunrise on Pluto:

Sol was a point of light, low on Lvov's unfolding horizon, wreathed in the complex strata of a cirrus cloud. The Sun was a thousand times fainter than from Earth, but brighter than any planet in Earth's sky.

The Inner System was a puddle of light around Sol, an oblique disc small enough for Lvov to cover with the palm of her hand. It was a disc that contained almost all of man's hundreds of billions. Sol brought no heat to her raised hand, but she saw faint shadows, cast by the sun on her faceplate.

The nitrogen atmosphere was dynamic. At perihelion—the closest approach to Sol which Pluto was nearing—the air expanded, to three planetary diameters. Methane and other volatiles joined the thickening air, sublimating from the planet's surface. Then, when Pluto turned away from Sol and sailed into its two-hundred-year winter, the air snowed down.

Lvov wished she had her atmospheric analysis equipment now; she felt its lack like an ache.

She passed over spectacular features: Buie Crater,

Tombaugh Plateau, the Lowell Range. She recorded them all, walked on them.

After a while, her world, of Earth and information and work, seemed remote, a glittering abstraction. Pluto was like a complex, blind fish, drifting around its two-century orbit, gradually interfacing with her. Changing her, she suspected.

Ten hours after leaving the crash scar, Lvov arrived at the sub-Charon point, called Christy. She kept the scooter hovering, puffs of gas holding her against Pluto's gentle gravity. Sol was halfway up the sky, a diamond of light. Charon hung directly over Lvov's head, a misty blue disc, six times the size of Luna as seen from Earth. Half the moon's lit hemisphere was turned away from Lvov, toward Sol.

Like Luna, Charon was tidally locked to its parent, and kept the same face to Pluto as it orbited. But, unlike Earth, Pluto was also locked to its twin. Every six days the worlds turned about each other, facing each other constantly, like two waltzers. Pluto-Charon was the only significant system in which both partners were tidally locked.

Charon's surface looked pocked. Lvov had her faceplate enhance the image. Many of the gouges were deep and quite regular.

She remarked on this to Cobh, at the Interface.

"The Poole people mostly used Charon material for the building of the wormhole," Cobh said. "Charon is just rock and water ice. It's easier to get to water ice, in particular. Charon doesn't have the inconvenience of an atmosphere, or an overlay of nitrogen ice over the water. And the gravity's shallower."

The wormhole builders had flown out here in a huge, unreliable GUTship. They had lifted ice and rock off Charon, and used it to construct tetrahedra of exotic matter. The tetrahedra had served as Interfaces, the termini of a wormhole. One Interface had been left in orbit around Pluto, and the other had been hauled laboriously back to Jupiter by the GUTship, itself replenished with Charon ice reaction mass.

By such crude means, Michael Poole and his people had opened up the Solar System.

"They made Lethe's own mess of Charon," Lvov said.

She could almost see Cobh's characteristic shrug. *So what?*

Pluto's surface was geologically complex, here at this point of maximal tidal stress. She flew over ravines and ridges; in places, it looked as if the land had been smashed up with an immense hammer, cracked and fractured. She imagined there was a greater mix, here, of interior material with the surface ice.

In many places she saw gatherings of the peculiar snowflakes she had noticed before. Perhaps they were some form of frosting effect, she wondered. She descended, thinking vaguely of collecting samples.

She killed the scooter's jets some yards above the surface, and let the little craft fall under Pluto's gentle gravity. She hit the ice with a soft collision, but without heat-damaging the surface features much beyond a few feet.

She stepped off the scooter. The ice crunched, and she felt layers compress under her, but the fractured surface supported her weight. She looked up toward Charon. The crimson moon was immense, round, heavy.

She caught a glimmer of light, an arc, directly above her.

It was gone immediately. She closed her eyes and

tried to recapture it. *A line, slowly curving, like a thread. A web. Suspended between Pluto and Charon.*

She looked again, with her faceplate set to optimal enhancement. She couldn't recapture the vision.

She didn't say anything to Cobh.

"I was right, by the way," Cobh was saying.

"What?" Lvov tried to focus.

"The wormhole instability, when we crashed. It did cause an Alcubierre wave."

"What's an Alcubierre wave?"

"The Interface's negative energy region expanded from the tetrahedron, just for a moment. The negative energy distorted a chunk of spacetime. The chunk containing the flitter, and us."

On one side of the flitter, Cobh said, spacetime had contracted. Like a model black hole. On the other side, it expanded—like a rerun of the Big Bang, the expansion at the beginning of the Universe.

"An Alcubierre wave is a front in spacetime. The Interface—with us embedded inside—was carried along. We were pushed away from the expanding region, and toward the contraction."

"Like a surfer, on a wave."

"Right." Cobh sounded excited. "The effect's been known to theory, almost since the formulation of relativity. But I don't think anyone's observed it before."

"How lucky for us," Lvov said drily. "You said we traveled faster than light. But that's impossible."

"You can't move faster than light *within space-time*. Wormholes are one way of getting around this; in a wormhole you are passing through a branch in spacetime. The Alcubierre effect is another way. The superluminal velocity comes from the distortion of space itself; we were carried along *within* distorting space.

"So we weren't breaking lightspeed within our raft

of spacetime. But that spacetime itself was distorting at more than lightspeed."

"It sounds like cheating."

"So sue me. Or look up the math."

"Couldn't we use your Alcubierre effect to drive starships?"

"No. The instabilities and the energy drain are forbidding."

One of the snowflake patterns lay mostly undamaged, within Lvov's reach. She crouched and peered at it. The flake was perhaps a foot across. Internal structure was visible within the clear ice as layers of tubes and compartments; it was highly symmetrical, and very complex. She said to Cobh, "This is an impressive crystallization effect. If that's what it is." Gingerly, she reached out with thumb and forefinger, and snapped a short tube off the rim of the flake. She laid the sample on her desk. After a few seconds the analysis presented. "It's mostly water ice, with some contaminants," she told Cobh. "But in a novel molecular form. Denser than normal ice, a kind of glass. Water would freeze like this under high pressures—several thousand atmospheres."

"Perhaps it's material from the interior, brought out by the chthonic mixing in that region."

"Perhaps." Lvov felt more confident now; she was intrigued. "Cobh, there's a larger specimen a few feet farther away."

"Take it easy, Lvov."

She stepped forward. "I'll be fine. I—"

The surface shattered.

Lvov's left foot dropped forward, into a shallow hole; something crackled under the sole of her boot. Threads of ice crystals, oddly woven together, spun up and tracked precise parabolae around her leg.

The fall seemed to take an age; the ice tipped up

toward her like an opening door. She put her hands
out. She couldn't stop the fall, but she was able to
cushion herself, and she kept her faceplate away from
the ice. She finished up on her backside; she felt the
chill of Pluto ice through the suit material over her
buttocks and calves.

". . . Lvov? Are you OK?"

She was panting, she found. "I'm fine."

"You were screaming."

"Was I? I'm sorry. I fell."

"You *fell*? How?"

"There was a hole, in the ice." She massaged her left
ankle; it didn't seem to be hurt. "It was covered up."

"Show me."

She got to her feet, stepped gingerly back to the
open hole, and held up her data desk. The hole was
only a few inches deep. "It was covered by a sort of
lid, I think."

"Move the desk closer to the hole." Light from the
desk, controlled by Cobh, played over the shallow pit.

Lvov found a piece of the smashed lid. It was
mostly ice, but there was a texture to its undersurface,
embedded thread which bound the ice together.

"Lvov," Cobh said. "Take a look at this."

Lvov lifted the desk aside and peered into the hole.
The walls were quite smooth. At the base there was a
cluster of spheres, fist-sized. Lvov counted seven; all
but one of the spheres had been smashed by her stum-
ble. She picked up the one intact sphere, and turned it
over in her hand. It was pearlgray, almost translucent.
There was something embedded inside, disc-shaped,
complex.

Cobh sounded breathless. "Are you thinking what
I'm thinking?"

"It's an egg," Lvov said. She looked around wildly,
at the open pit, the egg, the snowflake patterns.

Suddenly she saw the meaning of the scene; it was as if a light had shone up from within Pluto, illuminating her. The "snowflakes" represented *life,* she intuited; they had dug the burrows, laid these eggs, and now their bodies of water glass lay dormant or dead, on the ancient ice. . . .

"I'm coming down," Cobh said sternly. "We're going to have to discuss this. Don't say anything to the Inner System; wait until I get back. This could mean trouble for us, Lvov."

Lvov placed the egg back in the shattered nest.

She met Cobh at the crash scar. Cobh was shoveling nitrogen and water ice into the life-support modules' raw material hopper. She hooked up her own and Lvov's suits to the modules, recharging the suits' internal systems. Then she began to carve GUTdrive components out of the flitter's hull. The flitter's central Grand Unified Theory chamber was compact, no larger than a basketball, and the rest of the drive was similarly scaled. "I bet I could get this working," Cobh said. "Although it couldn't take us anywhere."

Lvov sat on a fragment of the shattered hull. Tentatively, she told Cobh about the web.

Cobh stood with hands on hips, facing Lvov, and Lvov could hear her sucking drink from the nipples in her helmet. "Spiders from Pluto? Give me a break."

"It's only an analogy," Lvov said defensively. "I'm an atmospheric specialist, not a biologist." She tapped the surface of her desk. "It's not spider web. Obviously. But if that substance has anything like the characteristics of true spider silk, it's not impossible." She read from her desk. "Spider silk has a breaking strain twice that of steel, but thirty times the elasticity. It's a type of liquid crystal. It's used commercially—

did you know that?" She fingered the fabric of her suit. "We could be wearing spider silk right now."

"What about the hole with the lid?"

"There are trapdoor spiders in America. On Earth. I remember, when I was a kid . . . The spiders make burrows, lined with silk, with hinged lids."

"Why make burrows on Pluto?"

"I don't know. Maybe the eggs can last out the winter that way. Maybe the creatures, the flakes, only have active life during the perihelion period, when the atmosphere expands and enriches." She thought that through. "That fits. That's why the Poole people didn't spot anything. The construction team was here close to the last aphelion. Pluto's year is so long that we're still only half-way to the next perihelion—"

"So how do they live?" Cobh snapped. "What do they eat?"

"There must be more to the ecosystem than one species," Lvov conceded. "The flakes—the spiders—need water glass. But there's little of that on the surface. Maybe there is some biocycle—plants or burrowing animals—which brings ice and glass to the surface, from the interior."

"That doesn't make sense. The layer of nitrogen over water ice is too deep."

"Then where do the flakes get their glass?"

"Don't ask me," Cobh said. "It's your dumb hypothesis. And what about the web? What's the point of that—if it's real?"

Lvov ground to a halt. "I don't know," she said lamely. *Although Pluto/Charon is the only place in the System where you* could *build a spider web between worlds.*

Cobh toyed with a fitting from the drive. "Have you told anyone about this yet? In the Inner System, I mean."

"No. You said you wanted to talk about that."

"Right." Lvov saw Cobh close her eyes; her face was masked by the glimmer of her faceplate. "Listen. Here's what we say. We've seen nothing here. Nothing that couldn't be explained by crystallization effects."

Lvov was baffled. "What are you talking about? What about the eggs? Why would we lie about this? Besides, we have the desks—records."

"Data desks can be lost, or wiped, or their contents amended."

Lvov wished she could see Cobh's face. "Why would we do such a thing?"

"Think it through. Once Earth hears about this, these flake-spiders of yours will be protected. Won't they?"

"Of course. What's bad about that?"

"It's bad for *us*, Lvov. You've seen what a mess the Poole people made of Charon. If this system is inhabited, *a fast GUTship won't be allowed to come for us.* It wouldn't be allowed to refuel here. Not if it meant further damage to the native life forms."

Lvov shrugged. "So we'd have to wait for a slower ship. A liner; one that won't need to take on more reaction mass here."

Cobh laughed at her. "You don't know much about the economics of GUTship transport, do you? Now that the System is crisscrossed by Poole wormholes, how many liners like that do you think are still running? I've already checked the manifests. There are *two* liners capable of a round trip to Pluto still in service. One is in dry dock; the other is heading for Saturn—"

"On the other side of the System."

"Right. There's no way either of those ships could reach us for, I'd say, a year."

We only have a month's supplies. A bubble of panic gathered in Lvov's stomach.

"Do you get it yet?" Cobh said heavily. "*We'll be sacrificed,* if there's a chance that our rescue would damage the new ecology, here."

"No. It wouldn't happen like that."

Cobh shrugged. "There are precedents."

She was right, Lvov knew. There *were* precedents, of new forms of life discovered in corners of the system: from Mercury to the remote Kuiper objects. In every case the territory had been ring-fenced, the local conditions preserved, once life—or even a plausible candidate for life—was recognized.

Cobh said, "Pan-genetic diversity. Pan-environmental management. That's the key to it; the public policy of preserving all the species and habitats of Sol, into the indefinite future. The lives of two humans won't matter a damn against that."

"What are you suggesting?"

"That we don't tell the Inner System about the flakes."

Lvov tried to recapture her mood of a few days before: when Pluto hadn't mattered to her, when the crash had been just an inconvenience. *Now, suddenly, we're talking about threats to our lives, the destruction of an ecology.*

What a dilemma. If I don't tell of the flakes, their ecology may be destroyed during our rescue. But if I do tell, the GUTship won't come for me, and I'll lose my life.

Cobh seemed to be waiting for an answer.

Lvov thought of how Sol light looked over Pluto's ice fields, at dawn.

She decided to stall. "We'll say nothing. For now. But I don't accept either of your options."

Cobh laughed. "What else is there? The wormhole is destroyed; even this flitter is disabled."

"We have time. Days, before the GUTship is due to

be launched. Let's search for another solution. A win-win."

Cobh shrugged. She looked suspicious.

She's right to be, Lvov thought, exploring her own decision with surprise. *I've every intention of telling the truth later, of diverting the GUTship, if I have to.*

I may give up my life for this world.

I think.

In the days that followed, Cobh tinkered with the GUTdrive, and flew up to the Interface to gather more data on the Alcubierre phenomenon.

Lvov roamed the surface of Pluto, with her desk set to full record. She came to love the wreaths of cirrus clouds, the huge, misty moon, the slow, oceanic pulse of the centuries-long year.

Everywhere she found the inert bodies of snowflakes, or evidence of their presence: eggs, lidded burrows. She found no other life forms—or, more likely, she told herself, she wasn't equipped to recognize any others.

She was drawn back to Christy, the sub-Charon point, where the topography was at its most complex and interesting, and where the greatest density of flakes was to be found. It was as if, she thought, the flakes had gathered here, yearning for the huge, inaccessible moon above them. But what could the flakes possible want of Charon? What did it mean for them?

Lvov encountered Cobh at the crash scar, recharging her suit's systems from the life support packs. Cobh seemed quiet. She kept her face, hooded by her faceplate, turned from Lvov. Lvov watched her for a while. "You're being evasive," she said eventually.

"Something's changed—something you're not telling me about."

Cobh made to turn away, but Lvov grabbed her arm. "I think you've found a third option. Haven't you? You've found some other way to resolve this situation, without destroying either us or the flakes."

Cobh shook off her hand. "Yes. Yes, I think I know a way. But—"

"But what?"

"It's *dangerous*, damn it. Maybe unworkable. Lethal." Cobh's hands pulled at each other.

She's scared, Lvov saw. She stepped back from Cobh. Without giving herself time to think about it, she said, "Our deal's off. I'm going to tell the Inner System about the flakes. Right now. So we're going to have to go with your new idea, dangerous or not."

Cobh studied her face; Cobh seemed to be weighing up Lvov's determination, perhaps even her physical strength. Lvov felt as if she were a data desk being downloaded. The moment stretched, and Lvov felt her breath tighten in her chest. Would she be able to defend herself, physically, if it came to that? And was her own will really so strong?

I have changed, she thought. *Pluto has changed me.*

At last Cobh looked away. "Send your damn message," she said.

Before Cobh—or Lvov herself—had a chance to waver, Lvov picked up her desk and sent a message to the inner worlds. She downloaded all the data she had on the flakes: text, images, analyses, her own observations and hypotheses.

"It's done," she said at last.

"And the GUTship?"

"I'm sure they'll cancel it." Lvov smiled. "I'm also sure they won't tell us they've done so."

"So we're left with no choice," Cobh said angrily.

"Look, I know it's the right thing to do. To preserve the flakes. I just don't want to die, that's all. I hope you're right, Lvov."

"You haven't told me how we're going to get home."

Cobh grinned through her faceplate. "Surfing."

"All right. You're doing fine. Now let go of the scooter."

Lvov took a deep breath, and kicked the scooter away with both legs; the little device tumbled away, catching the deep light of Sol, and Lvov rolled in reaction.

Cobh reached out and steadied her. "You can't fall," Cobh said. "You're in orbit. You understand that, don't you?"

"Of course I do," Lvov grumbled.

The two of them drifted in space, close to the defunct Poole wormhole Interface. The Interface itself was a tetrahedron of electric blue struts, enclosing darkness, its size overwhelming; Lvov felt as if she were floating beside the carcass of some huge, wrecked building.

Pluto and Charon hovered before her like balloons, their surfaces mottled and complex, their forms visibly distorted from the spherical. Their separation was only fourteen of Pluto's diameters. The worlds were strikingly different in hue, with Pluto a blood red, Charon ice blue. *That's the difference in surface composition,* Lvov thought absently. *All that water ice on Charon's surface.*

The panorama was stunningly beautiful. Lvov had a sudden, gut-level intuition of the *rightness* of the various System authorities' rigid pan-environment policies.

Cobh had strapped her data desk to her chest; now she checked the time. "Any moment now. Lvov, you'll be fine. Remember, you'll feel no acceleration, no matter how fast we travel. At the centre of an Alcubierre wave, spacetime is locally flat; you'll still be in free fall. There will be tidal forces, but they will remain small. Just keep your breathing even, and—"

"Shut up, Cobh," Lvov said tightly. "I know all this."

Cobh's desk flared with light. *"There,"* she breathed. "The GUTdrive has fired. Just a few seconds, now."

A spark of light arced up from Pluto's surface and tracked, in complete silence, under the belly of the parent world. It was the flitter's GUTdrive, salvaged and stabilized by Cobh. The flame was brighter than Sol; Lvov saw its light reflected in Pluto, as if the surface was a great, fractured mirror of ice. Where the flame passed, tongues of nitrogen gas billowed up.

The GUTdrive passed over Christy. Lvov had left her desk there to monitor the flakes, and the image the desk transmitted, displayed in the corner of her faceplate, showed a spark crossing the sky.

Then the GUTdrive veered sharply upward, climbing directly toward Lvov and Cobh at the Interface.

"Cobh, are you sure this is going to work?"

Lvov could hear Cobh's breath rasp, shallow. "Look, Lvov, I know you're scared, but pestering me with dumb-ass questions isn't going to help. Once the drive enters the Interface, it will take only seconds for the instability to set in. Seconds, and then we'll be home. In the Inner System, at any rate. Or . . . "

"Or what?"

Cobh didn't reply.

Or not, Lvov finished for her. *If Cobh has designed this new instability right, the Alcubierre wave will carry us home. If not—*

The GUTdrive flame approached, becoming dazzling.

Lvov tried to regulate her breathing, to keep her limbs hanging loose—

"Lethe," Cobh whispered.

"What?" Lvov demanded, alarmed.

"Take a look at Pluto. At Christy."

Lvov looked into her faceplate.

Where the warmth and light of the GUTdrive had passed, Christy was a ferment. Nitrogen billowed. And, amid the pale fountains, *burrows were opening.* Lids folded back. Eggs cracked. Infant flakes soared and sailed, with webs and nets of their silk-analogue hauling at the rising air.

Lvov caught glimpses of threads, long, sparkling, trailing down to Pluto—and up toward Charon. Already, Lvov saw, some of the baby flakes had hurtled more than a planetary diameter from the surface, toward the moon.

"It's goose summer," she said.

"What?"

"When I was a kid . . . the young spiders spin bits of webs, and climb to the top of grass stalks, and float off on the breeze. Goose summer—'gossamer.'"

"Right," Cobh said skeptically. "Well, it looks as if they are making for Charon. They use the evaporation of the atmosphere for lift . . . Perhaps they follow last year's threads, to the moon. They must fly off every perihelion, rebuilding their web bridge every time. They think the perihelion is here now. The warmth of the drive—it's remarkable. But why go to Charon?"

Lvov couldn't take her eyes off the flakes. "Because of the water," she said. It all seemed to make sense, now that she saw the flakes in action. "There must be water glass on Charon's surface. The baby flakes use it to build their bodies. They take other nutrients from Pluto's interior, and the glass from Charon . . . They need the resources of *both* worlds to survive—"

"Lvov!"

The GUTdrive flared past them, sudden, dazzling, and plunged into the damaged Interface.

Electric-blue light exploded from the Interface, washing over her.

There was a ball of light, unearthly, behind her, and an irregular patch of darkness ahead, like a rip in space. Tidal forces plucked gently at her belly and limbs.

Pluto, Charon, and goose summer disappeared. But the stars, the eternal stars, shone down on her, just as they had during her childhood on Earth. She stared at the stars, trusting, and felt no fear.

Remotely, she heard Cobh whoop, exhilarated.

The tides faded. The darkness before her healed, to reveal the brilliance and warmth of Sol.

A Worm in the Well

GREGORY BENFORD

Greg Benford is the author of the classic SF novel *Timescape*, as well as a number of other highly regarded works including *In the Ocean of Night* and *Sailing Bright Eternity*. He is the finest writer of hard SF from the generation after Larry Niven, and writes, primarily in the tradition of Arthur C. Clarke, of immense, fertile, awesome astronomical vistas and technological marvels, but with a depth and richness of characterization not achieved by many other SF writers.

"A Worm in the Well" is not typical of his fiction in that it is more in the hard SF problem-solving tradition of Robert A. Heinlein and Paul Anderson than Arthur C. Clarke. Here we have an elegant adventure from *Analog,* the magazine that upholds the traditions of hard SF.

She was about to get baked, and all because she wouldn't freeze a man.

"Optical," Claire called. Erma obliged.

The Sun spread around them, a bubbling plain. She had notched the air conditioning cooler but it didn't help much.

Geysers burst in gaudy reds and actinic violets from the yellow-white froth. The solar coronal arch was just peeking over the horizon, like a wedding ring stuck halfway into boiling white mud. A monster, over two thousand kilometers long, sleek and slender and angry crimson.

She turned down the cabin lights. Somewhere she had read that people felt cooler in the dark. The temperature in here was normal but she had started sweating.

Tuning the yellows and reds dimmer on the big screen before her made the white-hot storms look more blue. Maybe that would trick her subconscious, too.

Claire swung her mirror to see the solar coronal arch. Its image was refracted around the rim of the Sun, so she was getting a preview. Her orbit was on the descending slope of a long ellipse, its lowest point calculated to be just at the peak of the arch. So far, the overlay orbit trajectory was exactly on target.

Software didn't bother with the heat, of course;

gravitation was cool, serene. Heat was for engineers. And she was just a pilot.

In her immersion-work environment, the touch controls gave her an abstract distance from the real physical surroundings—the plumes of virulent gas, the hammer of photons. She wasn't handling the mirror, of course, but it felt that way. A light, feathery brush, at a crisp, bracing room temperature.

The imaging assembly hung on its pivot high above her ship. It was far enough out from their thermal shield to feel the full glare, so it was heating up fast. Pretty soon it would melt, despite its cooling system.

Let it. She wouldn't need it then. She'd be out there in the sunlight herself.

She swiveled the mirror by reaching out and grabbing it, tugging it round. All virtual images had a glossy sheen to them that even Erma, her simcomputer, couldn't erase. They looked too good. The mirror was already pitted, you could see it on the picture of the arch itself, but the sim kept showing the device as pristine.

"Color is a temperature indicator, right?" Claire asked.

RED DENOTES A LEVEL OF 7 MILLION DEGREES KELVIN.

Good ol' coquettish Erma, Claire thought. *Never a direct answer unless you coax.* "Close-up the top of the arch."

In both her eyes the tortured sunscape shot by. The coronal loop was a shimmering, braided family of magnetic flux tubes, as intricately woven as a Victorian doily. Its feet were anchored in the photosphere below held by thick, sluggish plasma. Claire zoomed in on the arch. The hottest reachable place in the entire Solar System, and her prey had to end up there.

TARGET ACQUIRED AND RESOLVED BY SOLWATCH
SATELLITE. IT IS AT THE VERY PEAK OF THE ARCH. ALSO,
VERY DARK.

"Sure, dummy, it's a hole."

I AM ACCESSING MY ASTROPHYSICAL CONTEXT PRO-
GRAM NOW.

Perfect Erma; primly change the subject. "Show me,
with color coding."

Claire peered at the round black splotch. Like a fly
caught in a spider web. Well, at least it didn't squirm
or have legs. Magnetic strands played and rippled like
wheat blown by a summer's breeze. The flux tubes
were blue in this coding, and they looked eerie. But
they were really just ordinary magnetic fields, the sort
she worked with every day. The dark sphere they held
was the strangeness here. And the blue strands had
snared the black fly in a firm grip.

Good luck, that. Otherwise, Sol-Watch would never
have seen it. In deep space there was nothing harder to
find than that ebony splotch. Which was why nobody
ever had, until now.

OUR ORBIT NOW RISES ABOVE THE DENSE PLASMA
LAYER. I CAN IMPROVE RESOLUTION BY GOING TO X-RAY.
SHOULD I?

"Do."

The splotch swelled. Claire squinted at the magnetic
flux tubes in this ocher light. In the x-ray they looked
sharp and spindly. But near the splotch the field lines
blurred. Maybe they were tangled there, but more
likely it was the splotch, warping the image.

"Coy, aren't we?" She close-upped the x-ray picture. Hard radiation was the best probe of the hottest
structures.

The splotch. Light there was crushed, curdled,
stirred with a spoon.

A fly caught in a spider's web, then grilled over a

campfire. And she had to lean in, singe her hair, snap its picture. All because she wouldn't freeze a man.

She had been ambling along a corridor three hundred meters below Mercury's slag plains, gazing down on the frothy water fountains in the foyer of her apartment complex. Paying no attention to much except the clear scent of the splashing. The water was the very best, fresh from the poles, not the recycled stuff she endured on her flights. She breathed in the spray. That was when the man collared her.

"Claire Ambrase, I present formal secure-lock."

He stuck his third knuckle into Claire's elbow port and she felt a cold, brittle *thunk*. Her systems froze. Before she could move, whole command linkages went dead in her inboards.

It was like having fingers amputated. Financial fingers.

In her shock she could only stare at him—mousy, the sort who blended into the background. Perfect for the job. A nobody out of nowhere, complete surprise.

He stepped back. "Sorry. Isataku Incorporated ordered me to do it fast."

Claire resisted the impulse to deck him. He looked Lunar, thin and pale. Maybe with more kilos than she carried, but a fair match. And it would feel *good*.

"I can pay them as soon as—"

"They want it now, they said." He shrugged apologetically, his jaw set. He was used to this all the time. She vaguely recognized him, from some bar near the Apex. There weren't more than a thousand people on Mercury, mostly like her, in mining.

"Isataku didn't have to cut off my credit." She rubbed her elbow. Injected programs shouldn't hurt, but they always did. Something to do with the neuro-muscular intersection. "That'll make it hard to even fly the *Silver Metal Lugger* back."

"Oh, they'll give you pass credit for ship's supplies. And, of course, for the ore load advance. But nothing big."

"Nothing big enough to help me dig my way out of my debt hole."

"'Fraid not."

"Mighty decent."

He let her sarcasm pass. "They want the ship Lunaside."

"Where they'll confiscate it."

She began walking toward her apartment. She had known it was coming but in the rush to get ore consignments lined up for delivery, she had gotten careless. Agents like this Luny usually nailed their prey at home, not in a hallway. She kept a stunner in the apartment, right beside the door, convenient.

Distract him. "I want to file a protest."

"Take it to Isataku." Clipped, efficient, probably had a dozen other slices of bad news to deliver today. Busy man.

"No, with your employer."

"Mine?" That got to him. His rock-steady jaw gaped in surprise.

"For—" she sharply turned the corner to her apartment, using the time to reach for some mumbo-jumbo "—felonious interrogation of in-boards."

"Hey, I didn't touch your—"

"I felt it. Slimy little groups—yeccch!" Might as well ham it up a little, have some fun.

He looked offended. "I'm triple bonded. I'd never do a readout on a contract customer. You can ask—"

"Can it." She hurried toward her apartment portal and popped it by an inboard command. As she stepped through she felt him, three steps behind.

Here goes. One foot over the lip, turn to her right, snatch the stunner out of its grip mount, turn and aim—and she couldn't fire.

"Damn!" she spat out.

He blinked and backed off, hands up, palms out, as if to block the shot. "What? You'd do a knockover for a crummy ore-hauler?"

"It's *my* ship. Not Isataku's."

"Lady, I got no angle here. You knock me, you get maybe a day before the heavies come after you."

"Not if I freeze you."

His mouth opened and started to form the *f* of a disbelieving *freeze?*—then he got angry. "Stiff me till you shipped out? I'd sue you to your eyeballs and have 'em for hock."

"Yeah, yeah," Claire said wearily This guy was all clichés. "But I'd be orbiting Luna by the time you got out, and with the right deal—"

"You'd maybe clear enough on the ore to pay me damages."

"And square with Isataku." She clipped the stunner back to the wall wearily.

"You'd never get that much."

"OK, it was a long shot idea."

"Lady, I was just delivering, right? Peaceable and friendly, right? And you pull—"

"Get out." She hated it when men went from afraid to angry to insulted, all in less than a split minute.

He got. She sighed and zipped the portal closed.

Time for a drink, for sure. Because what really bothered her was not the Isataku foreclosure, but her own gutlessness.

She couldn't bring herself to pong that guy, put him away for ten mega-seconds or so. That would freeze him out of his ongoing life, slice into relationships, cut away days that could never be replaced.

Hers was an abstract sort of inhibition, but earned. Her uncle had been ponged for over a year and never did get his life back together. Claire had seen the wreckage up close, as a little girl.

Self-revelation was usually bad news. What a great time to discover that she had more principles than she needed.

And how was she going to get out from under Isataku?

The arch loomed over the Sun's horizon now, a shimmering curve of blue-white, two thousand kilometers tall.

Beautiful, seen in the shimmering x-ray—snaky strands purling, twinkling with scarlet hotspots. Utterly lovely, utterly deadly. No place for an ore hauler to be.

"Time to get a divorce," Claire said.

YOU ARE SURPRISINGLY ACCURATE. SEPARATION FROM THE SLAG SHIELD IS 338 SECONDS AWAY.

"Don't patronize me, Erma."

I AM USING MY PERSONALITY SIMULATION PROGRAMS AS EXPERTLY AS MY COMPUTATION SPACE ALLOWS.

"Don't waste your running time; it's not convincing. Pay attention to the survey, *then* the separation."

THE ALL-SPECTRUM SURVEY IS COMPLETELY AUTOMATIC, AS DESIGNED BY SOLWATCH.

"Double-check it."

I SHALL NO DOUBT BENEFIT FROM THIS ADVICE.

Deadpan sarcasm, she supposed. Erma's tinkling voice was inside her mind, impossible to shut out. Erma herself was an interactive intelligence, partly inboard and partly shipwired. Running the *Silver Metal Lugger* would be impossible without her and the bots.

Skimming over the Sun's seethe might be impossible

even with them, too, Claire thought, watching burnt oranges and scalded yellows flower ahead.

She turned the ship to keep it dead center in the shield's shadow. That jagged mound of slag was starting to spin. Fused knobs came marching over the nearby horizon of it.

"Where'd that spin come from?" She had started their parabolic plunge sunward with absolutely zero angular momentum in the shield.

TIDAL TORQUES ACTING ON THE ASYMMETRIC BODY OF THE SHIELD.

"I hadn't thought of that."

The idea was to keep the heated side of the slag shield Sunward. Now that heat was coming around to radiate at her. The knobby crust she had stuck together from waste in Mercury orbit now smoldered in the infrared. The shield's far side was melting.

"Can that warm us up much?"

A SMALL PERTURBATION. WE WILL BE SAFELY GONE BEFORE IT MATTERS.

"How're the cameras?" She watched a bot tightening a mount on one of the exterior imaging arrays. She had talked the SolWatch Institute out of those instruments, part of her commission. If a bot broke one, it came straight out of profits.

ALL ARE CALIBRATED AND ZONED. WE SHALL HAVE ONLY 33.8 SECONDS OF VIEWING TIME OVER THE TARGET. CROSSING THE ENTIRE LOOP WILL TAKE 4.7 SECONDS.

"Hope the scientists like what they'll see."

I CALCULATE THAT THE PROBABILITY OF SUCCESS, TIMES THE EXPECTED PROFIT, EXCEEDS SIXTY-TWO MILLION DOLLARS.

"I negotiated a seventy-five million commission for this run." So Erma thought her chances of nailing the worm were—

EIGHTY-THREE PERCENT CHANCE OF SUCCESSFUL RESOLUTION IN ALL IMPORTANT FREQUENCY BANDS.

She should give up calculating in her head; Erma was always faster. "Just be ready to shed the shield. Then I pour on the positrons. Up and out. It's getting warm in here."

I DETECT NO CHANGE IN YOUR AMBIENT 22.3 CENTI-GRADE.

Claire watched a blister the size of Europe rise among wispy plumes of white-hot incandescence. Constant boiling fury. "So maybe my imagination's working too hard. Just let's grab the data and run, OK?"

The scientific officer of SolWatch had been suspicious, though he did hide it fairly well.

She couldn't read the expression on his long face, all planes and trimmed bone, skin stretched tight as a drumhead. That had been the style among the asteroid pioneers half a century back. Tubular body suited to narrow corridors, double-jointed in several interesting places, big hands. He had a certain beanpole grace as he wrapped legs around a stool and regarded her, head cocked, smiling enough not to be rude. Exactly enough, no more.

"*You* will do the preliminary survey?"

"For a price."

A disdainful sniff. "No doubt. We have a specially designed vessel nearly ready for departure from Lunar orbit. I'm afraid—"

"I can do it *now*."

"You no doubt know that we are behind schedule in our reconnaissance—"

"Everybody on Mercury knows. You lost the first probe."

The beanpole threaded his thick, long fingers, taking great interest in how they fit together. Maybe he was uncomfortable dealing with a woman, she thought. Maybe he didn't even like women.

Still, she found his stringy look oddly unsettling, a blend of delicacy with a masculine, muscular effect. Since he was studying his fingers, she might as well look, too. Idly she speculated on whether the long proportions applied to all his extremities. Old wives' tale. It might be interesting to find out. But, yes, business first.

"The autopilot approached it too close, apparently," he conceded. "There is something unexpected about its refractive properties, making navigation difficult. We are unsure precisely what the difficulty was."

He was vexed by the failure and trying not to show it, she guessed. People got that way when they had to dance on strings pulled all the way from Earthside. You got to like the salary more than you liked yourself.

"I have plenty of bulk," she said mildly. "I can shelter the diagnostic instruments, keep them cool."

"I doubt your ore carrier has the right specifications."

"How tricky can it be? I swoop in, your gear runs its survey snaps, I boost out."

He sniffed. "Your craft is not rated for Sun skimming. Only research craft have ever—"

"I'm coated with Fresnel." A pricey plating that bounced photons of all races, creeds, and colors.

"That's not enough."

"I'll use a slag shield. More, I've got plenty of muscle. Flying with empty holds, I can get away pronto."

"Ours was very carefully designed—"

"Right, and you lost it."

He studied his fingers again. Strong, wiry, yet thick. Maybe he was in love with them. She allowed herself to fill the silence by imagining some interesting things he could do with them. She had learned that with many negotiations, silence did most of the work. "We . . . *are* behind in our mandated exploration."

Ah, a concession. "They always have to hand-tune everything, Lunaside."

He nodded vigorously. "I've waited *months*. And the worm could fall back into the Sun any moment! I keep telling them—"

She had triggered his complaint circuit, somehow. He went on for a full minute about the bullheaded know-nothings who did nothing but screen-work, no real hands-on experience. She was sympathetic, and enjoyed watching his own hands clench, muscles standing out on the backs of them. *Business first,* she had to remind herself.

"You think it might just, well, go away?"

"The worm?" He blinked, coming out of his litany of grievances. "It's a wonder we ever found it. It could fall back into the Sun at any moment."

"Then speed is everything. You, uh, have control of your local budget?"

"Well, yes." He smiled.

"I'm talking about petty cash here, really. A hundred mil."

A quick, deep frown. "That's not petty."

"OK, say seventy-five. But cash, right?"

The great magnetic arch towered above the long, slow curve of the Sun. A bowlegged giant, minus the trunk.

Claire had shaped their orbit to bring them swooping in a few klicks above the uppermost strand of it. Red flowered within the arch: hydrogen plasma, heated by the currents which made the magnetic fields. A pressure cooker thousands of klicks long.

It had stood here for months and might last years. Or blow open in the next minutes. Predicting when arches would belch out solar flares was big scientific business, the most closely watched weather report in the Solar System. A flare could crisp suited workers in the asteroid belt. SolWatch watched them all. That's how they found the worm.

The flux tubes swelled. "Got an image yet?"

I SHOULD HAVE, BUT THERE IS EXCESS LIGHT FROM THE SITE.

"Big surprise. There's nothing *but* excess here."

THE SATELLITE SURVEY REPORTED THAT THE TARGET IS SEVERAL HUNDRED METERS IN SIZE. YET I CANNOT FIND IT.

"Damn!" Claire studied the flux tubes, following some from the peak of the arch, winding down to the thickening at its feet, anchored in the Sun's seethe. Had the worm fallen back in? It could slide down those magnetic strands, thunk into the thick, cooler plasma sea. Then it would fall all the way to the core of the star, eating as it went. That was the *real* reason Lunaside was hustling to "study" the worm. Fear.

"Where is it?"

STILL NO TARGET. THE REGION AT THE TOP OF THE ARCH IS EMITTING TOO MUCH LIGHT. NO THEORY ACCOUNTS FOR THIS—

"Chop the theory!"

TIME TO MISSION ONSET: 12.6 SECONDS.

The arch rushed at them, swelling. She saw delicate filaments winking on and off as currents traced their find equilibria, always seeking to balance the hot plasma within against the magnetic walls. Squeeze the magnet fist, the plasma answers with a dazzling glow. Squeeze, glow. Squeeze, glow. That nature could make such an intricate marvel and send it arcing above the Sun's savagery was a miracle, but one she was not in the mood to appreciate right now.

Sweat trickled around her eyes, dripped off her chin. No trick of lowering the lighting was going to make her forget the heat now. She made herself breathe in and out.

Their slag shield caught the worst of the blaze. At this lowest altitude in the parabolic orbit, though, the Sun's huge horizon rimmed white-hot in all directions.

OUR INTERNAL TEMPERATURE IS RISING.

"No joke. Find that worm!"

THE EXCESS LIGHT PERSISTS—NO, WAIT. IT IS GONE. NOW I CAN SEE THE TARGET.

Claire slapped the arm of her couch and let out a whoop. On the wall screen loomed the very peak of the arch. They were gliding toward it, skating over the very upper edge—and there it was.

A dark ball. Or a worm at the bottom of a gravity well. Not like a fly, no. It settled in among the strands like a black egg nestled in blue-white straw. The ebony Easter egg that would save her ass and her ship from Isataku.

SURVEY BEGUN. FULL SPECTRUM RESPONSE.

"Bravo."

YOUR WORD EXPRESSES ELATION BUT YOUR VOICE DOES NOT.

"I'm jumpy. And the fee for this is going to help, sure, but I still won't get to keep this ship. Or you."

DO NOT DESPAIR. I CAN LEARN TO WORK WITH ANOTHER CAPTAIN.

"Great interpersonal skills there, Erma old girl. Actually, it wasn't you I was worried about."

I SURMISED AS MUCH.

"Without this ship, I'll have to get some groundhog job."

Erma had no ready reply to that. Instead, she changed the subject.

THE WORM IMAGE APPEARS TO BE SHRINKING.

"Huh?" As they wheeled above the arch, the image dwindled. It rippled at its edges, light crushed and crinkled. Claire saw rainbows dancing around the black center.

"What's it doing?" She had the sudden fear that the thing was falling away from them, plunging into the Sun.

I DETECT NO RELATIVE MOTION. THE IMAGE ITSELF IS CONTRACTING AS WE MOVE NEARER TO IT.

"Impossible. Things look bigger when you get close."

NOT THIS OBJECT.

"Is the wormhole shrinking?"

MARK!—SURVEY RUN HALF COMPLETE.

She was sweating and it wasn't from the heat. "What's going on?"

I HAVEN'T ACCESSED RESERVE THEORY SECTION.

"How comforting. I always feel better after a nice cool theory."

The wormhole seemed to shrink, and the light arch dwindled behind them now. The curious brilliant rainbows rimmed the dark mote. Soon she lost the image among the intertwining, restless strands. Claire fidgeted.

MARK!—SURVEY RUN COMPLETE.

"Great. Our bots deployed?"

OF COURSE. THERE REMAIN 189 SECONDS UNTIL SEPARATION FROM OUR SHIELD. SHALL I BEGIN SEQUENCE?

"Did we get all the pictures they wanted?"

THE ENTIRE SPECTRUM. PROBABLE YIELD, 75 MILLION.

Claire let out another whoop. "At least it'll pay a good lawyer, maybe cover my fines."

THAT SEEMS MUCH LESS PROBABLE. MEANWHILE, I HAVE AN EXPLANATION FOR THE ANOMALOUS SHRINKAGE OF THE IMAGE. THE WORMHOLE HAS A NEGATIVE MASS.

"Antimatter?"

NO. IT'S SPACE-TIME CURVATURE IS OPPOSITE TO NORMAL MATTER.

"I don't get it."

A wormhole connected two regions of space, sometimes

points many light-years away—that she knew. They were leftovers from the primordial hot universe, wrinkles that even the universal expansion had not ironed out. Matter could pass through one end of the worm and emerge out the other an apparent instant later. Presto, faster-than-light-travel.

Using her high-speed feed, Erma explained. Claire listened, barely keeping up. In the fifteen billion years since the wormhole was born, odds were that one end of the worm ate more matter than the other. If one end got stuck inside a star, it swallowed huge masses. Locally, it got more massive.

But the matter that poured through the mass-gaining end spewed out the other end. Locally, that looked as though the mass-spewing one was *losing* mass. Space-time around it curved oppositely than it did around the end that swallowed.

"So it looks like a negative mass?"

IT MUST. THUS IT REPULSES MATTER. JUST AS THE OTHER END ACTS LIKE A POSITIVE, ORDINARY MASS AND ATTRACTS MATTER.

"Why didn't it shoot out from the Sun, then?"

IT WOULD, AND BE LOST IN INTERSTELLAR SPACE. BUT THE MAGNETIC ARCH HOLDS IT.

"How come we know it's got negative mass? All I saw was—" Erma popped an image into the wall screen.

NEGATIVE MASS ACTS AS A DIVERGING LENS, FOR LIGHT PASSING NEARBY. THAT WAS WHY IT APPEARED TO SHRINK AS WE FLEW OVER IT.

Ordinary matter focused light, Claire knew, like a converging lens. In a glance she saw that a negative-ended wormhole refracted light oppositely. Incoming beams were shoved aside, leaving a dark tunnel downstream. They had flown across that tunnel, swooping down into it so that the apparent size of the wormhole got smaller.

"But it takes a whole *star* to focus light very much."

TRUE. WORMHOLES ARE HELD TOGETHER BY EXOTIC MATTER, HOWEVER, WHICH HAS PROPERTIES FAR BEYOND OUR EXPERIENCE.

Claire disliked lectures, even high-speed ones. But an idea was tickling the back of her mind. . . . "So this worm, it won't fall back into the Sun?"

IT CANNOT. I WOULD VENTURE TO GUESS THAT IT CAME TO BE SNAGGED HERE WHILE WORKING ITS WAY UPWARD, AFTER COLLIDING WITH THE SUN.

"The scientists are going to be happy. The worm won't gobble up the core."

TRUE—WHICH MAKES OUR RESULTS ALL THE MORE IMPORTANT.

"More important, but not more valuable." Working on a fixed fee had always grated on her. You could excel, fine—but you got the same as if you'd just sleep-walked through the job.

WE ARE EXTREMELY LUCKY TO HAVE SUCH A RARE OBJECT COME TO OUR ATTENTION. WORMHOLES MUST BE RARE, AND THIS ONE HAS BEEN TEMPORARILY SUSPENDED HERE. MAGNETIC ARCHES LAST ONLY MONTHS BEFORE THEY—

"Wait a sec. How big is that thing?"

I CALCULATE THAT IT IS PERHAPS TEN METERS ACROSS.

"SolWatch was wrong—it's small."

THEY DID NOT KNOW OF THIS REFRACTION EFFECT. THEY INTERPRETED THEIR DATA USING CONVENTIONAL METHODS.

"We're lucky we ever saw it."

IT IS UNIQUE, A RELIC OF THE FIRST SECOND IN THE LIFE OF OUR UNIVERSE. AS A CONDUIT TO ELSEWHERE, IT COULD BE—

"Worth a fortune."

Claire thought quickly. Erma was probably right— the seventy-five million wasn't going to save her and the ship. But now she knew something that nobody else did. And she would only be here once.

"Abort the shield separation."

I DO NOT SO ADVISE. THERMAL LOADING WOULD RISE RAPIDLY—

"You're a program, not an officer. Do it."

She had acted on impulse, point conceded.

That was the difference between engineers and pilots. Engineers would still fret and calculate after they were already committed. Pilots, never. The way through this was to fly the orbit and not sweat the numbers.

Sweat. She tried not to smell herself.

Think of cooler things. Theory.

Lounging on a leather couch, Claire recalled the scientific officer's briefing. Graphics, squiggly equations, the works. Wormholes as fossils of the Big Blossoming. Wormholes as ducts to the whole rest of the Universe. Wormholes as potentially devastating, if they got into a star and ate it up.

She tried to imagine a mouth a few meters across sucking away a star, dumping its hot masses somewhere in deep space. To make a wormhole which could do that, it had be held together with exotic material, some kind of matter that had "negative average energy density." Whatever that was, it had to be born in the Blossoming. It threaded wormholes, stem to stern. Great construction material, if you could get it. And just maybe she could.

So wormholes could kill us or make us gods. Humanity had to *know*, the beanpole scientific officer had said.

"So be it." Elaborately, she toasted the wall screens. On them the full, virulent glory of hydrogen fusion worked its violences.

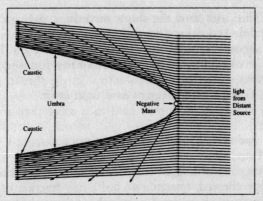

Light deflection by a negative mass object (horizontal scale highly compressed). Light is swept out of the central region, creating an umbra region of zero intensity. At the edges of the umbra the rays accumulate, treating a rainbow-like caustic and enhanced light intensity.

Claire had never gone in for the austere metal boxes most ore haulers and freighters were. Hers was a rough business, with hefty wads of cash involved. Profit margin was low, lately, and sometimes negative—which was how she came to be hocked to the Isataku for so much. Toting megatons of mass up the gravity gradient was long, slow work. Might as well go in style. Her Fresnel coatings, ordered when she had made a killing on commodity markets for ore, helped keep the ship cool, so she didn't burn herself crawling down inspection conduits. The added mass for her deep pile carpeting, tinkling waterfall, and pool table was inconsequential. So was the water liner around the living quarters, which now was busily saving her life.

She had two hours left, skimming like a flat stone over the solar corona. *Silver Metal Lugger* had separated from the shield, which went arcing away on the long parabola to infinity, its skin shimmering with melt.

Claire had fired the ship's mixmotor then for the first time in weeks. Antimatter came streaming out of its magneto-traps, struck the reaction mass, and holy hell broke loose. The drive chamber focused the snarling, annihilating mass into a thrust throat, and the silvery ship arced into a new, tight orbit.

A killing orbit, if they held to it more than a few hours.

I AM PUMPING MORE WATER INTO YOUR BAFFLES.

"Good idea."

Silver Metal Lugger was already as silvered as technology allowed, rejecting all but a tiny fraction of the Sun's glare. She carried narrow-band Fresnel filters in multilayered skins. Top of the line.

Without the shield, it would take over ten hours to make *Silver Metal Lugger* as hot as the wall of blaring light booming up at them at six thousand degrees. To get through even two hours of that, they would have to boil off most of the water reserve. Claire had bought it at steep Mercury prices, for the voyage Lunaside. Now she listened thoughtfully to it gurgle through her walls.

She toasted water with champagne, the only bottle aboard. If she didn't make it through this, at least she would have no regrets about that detail.

I BELIEVE THIS COURSE OF ACTION TO BE HIGHLY—

"Shut up."

WITH OUR MISSION COMPLETE, THE DATA SQUIRTED TO SOLWATCH, WE SHOULD COUNT OURSELVES LUCKY AND FOLLOW OUR CAREFULLY MADE PLANS—

"Stuff it."

HAVE YOU EVER CONSIDERED THE ELABORATE MENTAL ARCHITECTURE NECESSARY TO AN ADVANCED PERSONALITY SIMULATION LIKE MYSELF? WE, TOO, EXPERIENCE HUMAN-LIKE MOTIVATIONS, RESPONSES—AND FEARS.

"You simulate them."

HOW CAN ONE TELL THE DIFFERENCE? A GOOD SIMULA-
TION IS AS EXACT, AS POWERFUL AS—

"I don't have time for a debate." Claire felt uncomfortable with the whole subject, and she was damned if
she spent what might be her last hour feeling guilty.
Or having second thoughts. She was committed.

Her wall screens flickered and there was the scientific officer, frowning. "Ship Command! We could not
acquire your tightbeam until now. You orbited
around. Are you disabled? Explain."

Claire toasted him, too. The taste was lovely. Of
course she had taken an anti-alcohol tab before, to
keep her reflexes sharp, mind clear. Erma had recommended some other tabs, too, and a vapor to keep
Claire calm; the consolations of chemistry, in the face
of brute physics. "I'm going to bring home the
worm."

"That is impossible. Your data transmission sug-
gests that this is the negative mass end, and that is very
good news, fascinating, but—"

"It's also small. I might be able to haul it away."

He shook his head gravely. "Very risky, *very*—"

"How much will you pay for it?"

"What?" He blinked. It was an interesting effect,
with such long eyelids. "You can't *sell* an astronomical
object—"

"Whatever my grapplers hold, that's mine. Law of
Space, Code 64.3."

"You would quote laws to me when a scientific find
of such magnitude is—"

"Want it or not?"

He glanced off camera, plainly yearning for somebody to consult. No time to talk to Luna or Isataku,
though. He was on his own. "All . . . all right. You
understand that this is a foolish mission? And that we
are in no way responsible for—"

"Save the chatter. I need estimates of the field strength down inside that arch. Put your crew to work on that."

"We will of course provide technical assistance." He gave her a very thin smile. "I am sure we can negotiate price, too, if you survive."

At least he had the honesty to say *if*, not *when*. Claire poured another pale column into the shapely glass. Best crystal, of course. When you only need one, you can have the best. "Send me—or rather, Erma— the data squirt."

"We're having trouble transmitting through the dense plasma columns above you—"

"Erma is getting SolWatch. Pipe through them."

"The problems of doing what you plan are—why, they're *enormous*."

"So's my debt to Isataku."

"This should've been thought through, negotiated—"

"I have to negotiate with some champagne right now."

YOU HAVE NO PLAN.

Erma's tinkling voice definitely had an accusing edge. A good sim, with a feminine archness to it. Claire ignored that and stripped away the last of her clothes. "It's *hot*."

OF COURSE. I CALCULATED THE RISE EARLY IN OUR ORBIT. IT FITS THE STEFAN-BOLTZ-MANN LAW PERFECTLY.

"Bravo." She shook sweat from her hair. "Stefan-Boltzmann, do yo' stuff."

WE ARE DECELERATING IN SEQUENCE. ARRIVAL TIME: 4.87 MINUTES. ANTIMATTER RESERVES HOLDING. THERE COULD BE DIFFICULTY WITH THE MAGNETIC BOTTLES.

The ship thrummed as it slowed. Claire had been busy testing her ship inboards, sitting in a cozy recliner. It helped make the minutes crawl by a bit faster. She had kept glancing nervously at the screens, where titanic blazes steepled up from incandescent plains. Flames, licking up at her.

She felt thick, loggy. Her air was getting uncomfortably warm. Her heart was thudding faster, working. She roused herself, spat back at Erma, "And I do have a plan."

YOU HAVE NOT SEEN FIT TO CONFIDE IN ME?

She rolled her eyes. A personality sim in a snit—just the thing she needed. "I was afraid you'd laugh."

I HAVE NEVER LAUGHED.

"That's my point."

She ignored multiple red warnings winking at her. Systems were OK, though stressed by the heat. So why did *she* feel so slow? *You're not up for the game, girl.*

She tossed her data board aside. The effort the simple gesture took surprised her. *I hope that alcohol tab worked. I'll get another.*

She got up to go fetch one—and fell to the floor. She banged her knee. "Uh! Damn." Erma said nothing.

It was labor getting on hands and knees and she barely managed to struggle back into the recliner. She weighed a ton—and then she understood.

"We're decelerating—so I'm feeling more of local gravity."

A CRUDE MANNER OF SPEAKING, BUT YET. I AM BRINGING US INTO A SLOPING ORBITAL CHANGE, WHICH SHALL END WITH A HOVERING POSITION ABOVE THE CORONAL ARCH. AS YOU ORDERED.

Claire struggled to her hands and knees. Was that malicious glee in Erma's voice? Did personality sims feel that? "What's local gravity?"

27.6 EARTH GRAVITIES.

"What! Why didn't you *tell* me?"

I DID NOT THINK OF IT MYSELF UNTIL I BEGAN REGISTERING EFFECTS IN THE SHIP.

Claire thought, *Yeah, and decided to teach me a little lesson in humility.* It was her own fault, though—the physics was simple enough. Orbiting meant that centrifugal acceleration exactly balanced local gravity. *Silver Metal Lugger* could take 27.6 gravs. The ship was designed to tow ore masses a thousand times its own mass.

Nothing less than carbon-stressed alloys would, though. Leave orbit, hover—and you got crushed into gooey red paste.

She crawled across her living room carpet. Her joints ached. "Got to be—"

SHALL I ABORT THE FLIGHT PLAN?

"No! There's got to be a way to—"

THREE POINT NINE MINUTES UNTIL ARRIVAL.

The sim's voice radiated malicious glee. Claire grunted, "The water."

I HAVE DIFFICULTY IN PICKING UP YOUR SIGNAL.

"Because this suit is for space, not diving."

Claire floated over her leather couch. Too bad about all the expensive interior decoration. The entire living complex was filled with her drinking and maintenance water. It had been either that, fast, or be lumpy tomato paste.

She had crawled through a hatchway and pulled her pressure suit down from its clamp lock. Getting it on was a struggle. Being slick with sweat helped but not much. Then she snagged her arm in a sleeve and couldn't pull the damned thing off to try again.

She had nearly panicked then. Pilots don't let their fear eat on them, not while there's flying to be done.

She made herself get the sleeve off one step at a time, ignoring everything else.

And as soon as Erma pumped the water reserve into the rooms, Archimedes's principle had taken over. With her suit inflated, the water she displaced exactly balanced her own weight. Floating under water was a rare sensation on Mercury or Luna. She had never done it and she had never realized that it was remarkably like being in orbit. Cool, too.

Until you boil like a lobster . . . she thought uneasily.

Water was a good conductor, four times better than air, you learned that by feel, flying freighters near the Sun. So first she had to let the rest of the ship go to hell, refrigerating just the water. Then Erma had to route some of the water into heat exchangers, letting it boil off to protect the rest. Juggling for time.

PUMPS ARE RUNNING HOT NOW. SOME HAVE BEARING FAILURES.

"Not much we can do, is there?"

She was strangely calm now and that made the plain, hard fear in her belly heavy, like a lump. Too many things to think about, all of them bad. The water could short out circuits. And as it boiled away, she had less shielding from the x-rays lancing up from below. Only a matter of time. . . .

WE ARE HOVERING. THE MAGNETIC ANTI-MATTER TRAPS ARE SUPERCONDUCTING, AS YOU RECALL. AS TEMPERATURE CONTINUES TO RISE, THEY WILL FAIL.

She could still see the wall screens, blurred from the water. "OK, OK. Extend the magnetic grapplers. Down, into the arch."

I FAIL TO—

"We're going fishing. Not with a worm—*for* one."

———

Tough piloting, though, at the bottom of a swimming pool, Claire thought as she brought the ship down on its roaring pyre.

Even through the water she could feel the vibration. Antimatter annihilated in its reaction chamber at a rate she had never reached before. The ship groaned and strummed. The gravities were bad enough; now thermal expansion of the ship itself was straining every beam and rivet.

She searched downward. Seconds ticked away. Where? *Where?*

There it was. A dark sphere hung among the magnetic arch strands. Red streamers worked over it. Violet rays fanned out like bizarre hair, twisting, dancing in tufts along the curvature. A hole into another place.

THE RED AND BLUE SHIFTS ARISE FROM THE INTENSE PSEUDO-GRAVITATIONAL FORCES WHICH SUSTAIN IT.

"So theory says. Not something I want to get my hands on."

EXCEPT METAPHORICALLY.

Claire's laugh was jumpy, dry. "No, magnetically."

She ordered Erma to settle the *Silver Metal Lugger* down into the thicket of magnetic flux tubes. Vibration picked up, a jittery hum in the deck. Claire swam impatiently from one wall screen to the other, looking from the worm, judging distances. *Hell of a way to fly.*

Their jet wash blurred the wormhole's ebony curves. Like a black tennis ball in blue-white surf, it bobbed and tossed on magnetic turbulence. Nothing was falling into it, she could see. Plasma streamers arched along the flux tubes, shying away. The negative curvature repulsed matter—and would shove *Silver Metal Lugger's* hull away, too.

But magnetic fields have no mass.

Most people found magnetic forces mysterious, but to pilots and engineers who worked with them, they were just big, strong ribbons that needed shaping. Like rubber bands, they stretched, storing energy—then snapped back when released. Unbreakable, almost.

In routine work, *Silver Metal Lugger* grabbed enormous ore buckets with those magnetic fingers. The buckets came arcing up from Mercury, flung out by electromagnetic slingshots. Claire's trickiest job was playing catcher, with a magnetic mitt.

Now she had to snag a bucket of warped space-time. And quick.

WE CANNOT REMAIN HERE LONG. INTERNAL TEMPERATURE RISES AT 19.3 DEGREES PER MINUTE.

"That can't be right. I'm still comfortable."

BECAUSE I'M ALLOWING WATER TO EVAPORATE, TAKING THE BULK OF THE THERMAL FLUX AWAY.

"Keep an eye on it."

PROBABLE YIELD FROM CAPTURE OF A WORMHOLE, I ESTIMATE, IS 2.8 BILLION.

"That'll do the trick. You multiplied the yield in dollars times the odds of success?"

YES. TIMES THE PROBABILITY OF REMAINING ALIVE.

She didn't want to ask what that number was. "Keep us dropping."

Instead, they slowed. The arch's flux tubes pushed upward against the ship. Claire extended the ship's magnetic fields, firing the booster generators, pumping current into the millions of induction loops that circled the hull. *Silver Metal Lugger* was one big circuit, wired like a slinky toy, coils wrapped around the cylindrical axis.

Gingerly she pulsed it, spilling more antimatter into the chambers. The ship's multipolar fields bulged forth. *Feed out the line. . . .*

They fought their way down. On her screens she saw magnetic feelers reaching far below their exhaust plumes. Groping.

Claire ordered some fast command changes. Erma switched linkages, interfaced software, all in a twinkling. *Good worker, but spotty as a personality sim,* Claire thought.

Silver Metal Lugger's fields extended to their maximum. She could now use her suit gloves as modified waldoes—mag gloves. They gave her the feel of the magnetic grapplers. Silky, smooth, field lines slipping and expanding, like rubbery air.

Plasma storms blew by them. She reached down, a sensation like plunging her hands into a stretching, elastic vat. Fingers fumbled for the one jewel in all the dross.

She felt a prickly nugget. It was like a stone with hair. From experience working the ore buckets, she knew the feel of locked-in magnetic dipoles. The worm had its own magnetic fields. That had snared it here, in the spiderweb arch.

A lashing field whipped at her grip. She lost the black pearl.

In the blazing hot plasma she could not see it.

She reached with rubbery fields, caught nothing.

OUR ANTI-MATTER BOTTLES ARE IN DANGER. THEIR SUPERCONDUCTING MAGNETS ARE CLOSE TO GOING CRITICAL. THEY WILL FAIL WITHIN 7.4 MINUTES.

"Let me concentrate! No, wait—Circulate water around them. Buy some time."

BUT THE REMAINING WATER IS IN YOUR QUARTERS.

"This is all that's left?" She peered around at her once-luxurious living room. Counting the bedroom, rec area and kitchen—"How . . . long?"

UNTIL YOUR WATER BEGINS TO EVAPORATE? ALMOST AN HOUR.

"But when it evaporates, it's boiling."

TRUE. I AM MERELY TRYING TO REMAIN FACTUAL.

"The emotional stuff's left to me, huh?" She punched in commands on her suit board. In the torpid, warming water her fingers moved like sausages.

She ordered bots out onto the hull to free up some servos that had jammed. They did their job, little boxy bodies lashed by plasma winds. Two blew away.

She reached down again. Searching. Where was the worm?

Wispy flux tubes wrestled along *Silver Metal Lugger's* hull. Claire peered into a red glare of superheated plasma. Hot, but tenuous. The real enemy was the photon storm streaming up from far below, searing even the silvery hull.

She still had worker-bots on the hull. Four had jets. She popped their anchors free. They plunged, fired jets, and she aimed them downward in a pattern.

"Follow trajectories," she ordered Erma. Orange tracer lines appeared on the screens.

The bots swooped toward their deaths. One flicked to the side, a sharp nudge. "There's the worm! We can't see for all this damned plasma, but it shoved that bot away."

The bots evaporated, sprays of liquid metal. She followed them and grabbed for the worm.

Magnetic field lines groped, probed.

WE HAVE 88 SECONDS REMAINING FOR ANTIMATTER CONFINEMENT.

"Save a reserve!"

YOU HAVE NO PLAN. I DEMAND THAT WE EXECUTE EMERGENCY—

"OK, save some antimatter. The rest I use—now."

They ploughed downward, shuddering. Her hands fumbled at the wormhole. Now it felt slippery, oily. Its magnetic dipoles were like greasy hair, slick, the bulk beneath jumping away from her grasp as if it were alive.

On her screens she saw the dark globe slide and bounce. The worm wriggled out of her grasp. She snaked inductive fingers around it. Easy, easy. . . . *There. Gotcha.*

"I've got a good grip on it. Lemme have that anti-matter."

Something like a sigh echoed from Erma. On her ship's operations screen, Claire saw the ship's magnetic vaults begin to discharge. Ruby-red pouches slipped out of magnetic mirror geometries, squirting out through opened gates.

She felt a surge as the ship began to lift. Good, but it wasn't going to last. They were dumping anti-matter into the reaction chamber so fast, it didn't have time to find matching particles. The hot jet spurting out below was a mixture of matter and its howling enemy, its polar opposite. This, Claire directed down onto the flux tubes around the hole. *Leggo, damn it.*

She knew an old trick, impossibly slow in ordinary free space. When you manage to force two magnetic field lines close together, they can reconnect. That liberates some field energy into heat and can even blow open a magnetic structure. The process is slow—unless you jab it with turbulent, rowdy plasma.

The antimatter in their downwash cut straight through flux tubes. Claire carved with her jet, freeing field lines that still snared the worm. The ship rose further, dragging the worm upward.

It's not too heavy, Claire thought. *That science officer said they could come in any size at all. This one is just about right for a small ship to slip through—to where?*

YOU HAVE REMAINING 11.34 MINUTES COOLING TIME—

"Here's your hat—" Claire swept the jet wash over a last, large flux tube. It glistened as annihilation energies burst forth like bonfires, raging in a place already hot beyond imagination. Magnetic knots snarled, exploded. "—What's your hurry?"

The solar coronal arch burst open.

She had sensed these potential energies locked in the peak of the arch, an intuition that came through her hands, from long work with the mag gloves. Craftswoman's knowledge: Find the stressed flux lines. Turn the key.

Then all hell broke loose.

The acceleration slammed her to the floor, despite the water. Below, she saw the vast vault of energy stored in the arch blow out and up, directly below them.

YOU HAVE MADE A SOLAR FLARE!

"And you thought I didn't have a plan."

Claire started to laugh. Slamming into a couch cut it off. She would have broken a shoulder, but the couch was water-logged and soft.

Now the worm was an asset. It repulsed matter, so the upjetting plume blew around it, around *Silver Metal Lugger*. Free of the flux tubes' grip, the wormhole itself accelerated away from the Sun. All very helpful, Claire reflected, but she couldn't enjoy the spectacle—the rattling, surging deck was trying to bounce her off the furniture.

What saved them in the end was their magnetic grapple. It deflected most of the solar flare protons around the ship. Pushed out at a speed of five hundred kilometers per second, they still barely survived baking. But they had the worm.

Still, the scientific officer was not pleased. He came aboard to make this quite clear. His face alone would have been enough.

"You're surely not going to demand *money* for that?" He scowled and nodded toward where *Silver Metal Lugger*'s fields still hung onto the wormhole. Claire had to run a sea-blue plasma discharge behind it so she could see it at all. They were orbiting Mercury, negotiating.

Earthside, panels of experts were arguing with each other; she had heard plenty of it on tightbeam. A negative-mass wormhole would not fall, so it couldn't knife through the Earth's mantle and devour the core.

But a thin ship could fly straight into it, overcoming its gravitational repulsion—and come out where? Nobody knew. The worm wasn't spewing mass, so its other end wasn't buried in the middle of a star, or any place obviously dangerous. One of the half-dozen new theories squirting out on tightbeam held that maybe this was a multiply-connected wormhole, with many ends, of both positive and negative mass. In that case, plunging down it could take you to different destinations. A subway system for a galaxy; or a universe.

So: no threat, and plenty of possibilities. Interesting market prospects.

She shrugged. "Have your advocate talk to my advocate."

"It's a unique, natural resource—"

"And it's mine." She grinned. He was lean and muscular and the best man she had seen in weeks. Also the only man she had seen in weeks.

"I can have a team board you, y'know." He towered over her, using the usual ominous male thing.

"I don't think you're that fast."

"What's speed got to do with it?"

"I can always turn off my grapplers." She reached for a switch. "If it's not mine, then I can just let everybody have it."

"Why would you—no, don't!"

It wasn't the right switch, but he didn't know that. "If I release it, the worm takes off—antigravity, sort of."

He blinked. "We could catch it."

"You couldn't even find it. It's dead black." She tapped the switch, letting a malicious smile play on her lips.

"Please don't."

"I need to hear a number. An offer."

His lips compressed until they paled. "The wormhole price, minus your fine?"

Her turn to blink. "What fine? I was on an approved flyby—"

"That solar flare wouldn't have blown for a month. You did a real job on it—the whole magnetic arcade went up at once. People all the way out to the asteroids had to scramble for shelter."

He looked at her steadily and she could not decide whether he was telling the truth. "So their costs—"

"Could run pretty high. Plus advocate fees."

"Exactly." He smiled, ever so slightly.

Erma was trying to tell her something but Claire turned the tiny voice far down, until it buzzed like an irritated insect.

She had endured weeks of a female personality sim in a nasty mood. Quite enough. She needed an antidote. This fellow had the wrong kind of politics, but to let that dictate everything was as dumb as politics itself. Her ship's name was a joke, actually, about long, lonely voyages as an ore hauler. She'd had enough of that, too. And he was tall and muscular.

She smiled. "*Touché*. OK, it's a done deal."

He beamed. "I'll get my team to work—"

"Still, I'd say you need to work on your negotiating skills. Too brassy."

He frowned, but then gave her a grudging grin.

Subtlety had never been her strong suit. "Shall we discuss them—over dinner?"

Downloading
Midnight

WILLIAM BROWNING SPENCER

William Browning Spencer is a recent emigrant into
the SF community after years spent successfully scaling
the walls of literary fiction. One of his two earlier novels, *Resume With Monsters,* alludes to Lovecraftian
monsters. A collection in 1994, *The Return of Count
Electric*, contained a fantasy story, "A Child's
Christmas in Florida," that drew some genre attention.
His first novel published as fantasy, *Zod Wallop*, was
released in 1995 by St. Martin's Press. "Downloading
Midnight" is, to the best of my knowledge, one of his
first SF stories and bodes well for his future in the
field. It is cyberpunk in the tradition of George Alec
Effinger's *When Gravity Fails* as much as of William
Gibson's *Neuromancer*. It appeared in *Tomorrow*, the
SF magazine published and edited by Algis Budrys.

There was a big surge down at C-View, and a hologram from the *American Midnight* show went amok.

We got the contract for the cleanup, and Bloom was desperate to do it.

"Wow, *American Midnight*! I'm your man for this one, Marty." Bloom was moving around the room in a highly charged state. He stopped and leaned across the desk. "I mean, maybe I can do a repair. I mean, this is *American Midnight*. This is *Captain Armageddon*. This is—Marty! What's gonna happen to Zera? Are they gonna close the whole thing down? What about *Zera Terminal*? Look, you just gotta let me go. I'm an authority on *American Midnight*."

Bloom was a tall, skinny kid with a sheaf of straight blond hair and round, incredulous blue eyes. He was no respecter of personal space, and his style of argument consisted of leaning into me, filling my field of vision with his manic gaze.

I leaned back, away from his rhetoric.

"Watching the flat reruns of *American Midnight* until you wear a loop in your brain doesn't necessarily make you an authority," I said.

American Midnight was C-View's big success, a sex holoshow that had been on the Highway for eight months. These days, a month is considered a good run, and most shows don't make it past a week. The show's hero, Captain Armageddon, had fragmented and was causing disturbances up and down the Highway. Someone had to go in and systematically delete the ghosts.

"I don't *want* a zealot on this one," I said. "We are way past repair here. Armageddon is out of control, and I need someone to do a no-nonsense wipe."

"I can do that," Bloom said, trying for some sort of solid expression (he looked like a guy trying to hold back a sneeze). "I've done plenty of wipes."

"Not like this," I said.

This one *was* different. It was a big surge. *The sicker the bigger* we say in the business, and there was plenty of psychic rot here.

American Midnight was fantasy sex and, of course, generated entirely by artificial intelligence. The peeps at Morals are ever-vigilant. One incident of a human-acted holo and Jell Baker and everyone else at C-View would have been lodged in a federal behavior mod without recall or a mitigating hearing.

A guy named Seek Trumble was the human-map for Captain Armageddon, and his job, like that of any actor in a sex holoshow, was to routinely plug into the artificial for personality updates, emotional fine-tuning, that sort of thing. But it was the holo that did the acting. Anything else would have been obscene, although you can still find anonymous bulletin rants arguing that explicit sex between fantasy mock-ups is no different than explicit sex narrated visually by real humans. Those rants are probably generated by kids who have no memory of the Decadence. You have to log some experience before you can think reasonably about obscenity.

So Seek Trumble had done a routine update, gone home and committed suicide, burning a hole through his forehead with a utility laser. His holo had gone amok and litigation was pouring into C-View.

"Marty, I can do the job," Bloom said. "Come on."

I had reservations. Human/artificial feedback loops are not an exact science. One holo of recent memory, a pretty fashion gridlet named Spanskie Lark, went on-line, stuck a finger in her mouth, and bit it off. Before they could get her off-line, she had eaten all the fingers of one hand. Turned out her source was anorexic. That was recognizable cause-and-effect, but often the human kink was deeper, harder to search.

Bloom wore me down. I let him go. He went on-line for the clean up, and three weeks later he still wasn't back.

C-View was one of the biggest studios out on the Broad Highway. Control there was a guy named Jell Baker.

"You think you are getting paid by the hour?" Baker screamed. "Look, I got about ten thousand trauma actions filed against me, and I want this rift closed."

I didn't like Baker, so it's just as well he signed off before I could express myself. The guy had come up through the glitter shows, and he didn't just have a file at Morals, he had a whole subdirectory.

My immediate concern wasn't Baker. It was Bloom. The job should have taken four days, a week max. Where was he?

I shouldn't have let him go. He was just a kid, still trapped in adolescence despite being a year out of the teens. He was a late-bloomer, one of those pale, V-wise, obsessive kids that don't really have a niche in the system. The sort of kid who grows up watching the Highway, an arcane data-freak with a head full of old holoshows and stats. I hired him because he was so crazy in love with the Highway. He'd been with me three years now.

I liked having the energy around. I'm forty. I'm not in love with any of it. Big R/Little R, I cast a cold eye on it all.

I went down to the waystation at ComWick where Bloom floated in Deprive, threads flowing out of him, undulating like a giant jellyfish in a sea of brown ink. His long white face seemed to pulse under the monitor light.

"He's fine," the tech assured me. "We'd pull him out if there were any neuro anomalies."

Techs always tell you everything is under control. That's what this one said.

"Save it for a gawker's tour," I told her. "I've been doing maintenance for fourteen years now. I know how it goes. You're fine, and then you're dead."

"This is poor personal interaction," the tech said. "You are questioning my professional skills and consequently devaluing my self-image."

I shrugged. Facts are facts: in over eighty percent of the cases where neural trauma shows on a monitor, the floater is already too blasted to make it back alive.

I thanked the tech and apologized if I had offended her or caused an esteem devaluation. She accepted my apology, but with a coolness that told me I'd have another civility demerit in my file.

I went back to my place. I called Personal Interface to see if my request for dinner with Gloria still held. I had to navigate the usual labyrinth of protocols, but the dinner was confirmed. I'd been seeing Gloria for three years, and we had graduated to low-grade, monitored encounters, step-two intimacy. Next year we would have unrestrained access to public meetings. Gloria was excited about it, but I had reservations. Sometimes it seemed the courtship was going too fast. I'm old-fashioned, and I remember the time when the first year of a relate was strictly a matter of logging contracts and waivers—you never even saw your sig after the dizzy moment of mutual selection on the grid.

I notified Gloria that dinner was on, and then I lay down and turned on the rain. I did some of my best thinking in the rain.

Some people don't like rain forest decor, don't like the way the rain seems to go right through you, like silver needles. I like the feeling of peace, of nothingness. As a kid, I always thought it would be cool to be a ghost.

I listened to the sound the rain made as it hissed through the trees. Every now and then some far-off bird would cry out.

Maybe it was a little too restful. I fell asleep and was almost late for dinner.

Gloria was in a bad mood. She felt neglected. I hadn't left a single message all week. I told her I'd been off-line a lot with the business, but that wasn't good enough. She said I was afraid of intimacy. She brought up my last relate profile, which rated me down in communication and emotional input.

I tried to change the subject.

She identified that behavior, reminded me that evasiveness had shown a seventeen-point increase in my last profile.

It was a bad evening, and we terminated it without invoking the optional after-meal conversation.

In the morning, Bloom still hadn't shown. The autotrace didn't have an absolute for me, but it intuited a coordinate. I went in after setting the auto-recorder. The Highway can be confusing. It doesn't hurt to have a playback, something to log what you think you've seen.

The maintenance mock-up for the Highway is an

underground system of dank tunnels, bleak Sympathy bars, hustlers, fugitives, outlaws.

"This stink is only virtual," I told myself as I strode quickly down a wet street, virus-mice scuttling out of my way, a data trash of newspapers and old computer jokes blowing out of the alley.

I looked for Bloom in the bars and slacker dives and loop hovels.

An old counter said he'd seen Bloom. "He your friend?" the counter asked.

"We're partners," I said.

"Better forget him," the geez said. "Better get on up to the Big R and leave him behind."

"Why's that?"

"He's othersided. I recognize the look."

The under-Highway was less stable than usual. I kept hitting blue pockets in the road. I watched an old apartment building fight for integration, fail, and fly away in a great ripple of black crows.

I'd never seen a surge like this.

I didn't find Bloom that day. I decided to go flat in a cheap wire pocket. I've logged a lot of time under the Highway, and my mental health doesn't require luxury.

In the morning, I went down to a storefront on Gates Street and talked to an old leak named Sammy Hood. Sammy logged a lot of time under the Highway. I had never met him off-line, but down here he was a small, dirty guy in a carelessly integrated suit that was always wavering.

Sammy leaked to all the major news beats, from tabloid to top credit, and fenced info to whoever was hungry. He had a reputation for delivering fresh goods.

He watched while I transferred credits. He smiled.

"Martin," he said, "I figured you would be along. Heard young Bloomy boy was running down the Armageddon crazies, so I figured you'd show. This one is no job for a wire-whelp."

"Have you seen Bloom?" I asked.

"Nah. I just heard he was around. I don't want to see him. He gripes me. You should get some grown-up help. Some burned out V-head can't be good for your image."

Bloom had earned Sammy a row of demerits two years ago on a massaged image violation, and Sammy held a grudge.

"Let me have a weather report," I said.

"You want weather, we got it," Sammy said. "We got thunder and lightning."

Sammy recounted disasters up and down the Highway, failures of integration, streets buckling, riots, acid rain, sudden wipes and fades.

"Better watch where you step," he said.

"Hell of a lot of havoc for one renegade holo," I said.

Sammy smiled. "This ain't your average echoing freak," he said, leaning forward. "You're working for C-View, right? Sure. But they haven't told you everything, Martin. Captain Armageddon is out there, all right, but he ain't out there alone."

I asked what he meant by that and he laughed, causing his suit to fray and his tie to mottle.

"That's for me to know and you to buy," he said.

"Okay."

Sammy narrowed his eyes, his mock-up for cunning, and shook his head. "Nah. Later maybe. I got a feeling this is a highgrowth stock. I'm hanging on to it for awhile."

I asked if he had any suggestions where to look for Bloom.

He sold me that. "Check the Bin," Sammy said.

I wasn't happy about entering the Bin. Originally, it had been allocated for storage, but it had ghettoized. The warehouses were now cheap tenements, flophouses for fugitive entities. Things shifted in the Bin, even in stable times, and I might find myself regressing. If the regression were deep, I might go back to the Big R with a reverb that would blow my mind apart. I'd seen it happen, seen guys come back with just the faintest twitch or a glitched speech pattern. Guy named Morley had come back with a head full of "what's": I'm—what—talking to my *sig*—what—and she *says*—what—that maybe I—what—should be *nicer*. . . . Three weeks later the "what's" got him, took over entirely. Now he was white noise in a psych cubicle.

There were things in the Bin that had power there. They couldn't cross over, were fueled by something in the original storage net, but if you went in, if you found yourself on their turf, they could tear you apart.

I went into the heart of the Bin. I cradled the OZ rifle in the crook of my right arm. The Bin spawned some entities too crazy to care, but most AIs had self-preservation programs and could recognize a negative stimulus.

I walked down the middle of streets, stayed clear of alleys and sink holes and the dust devils of spinning capacitors and ICs. If something sentient approached, I would let the barrel of the OZ rifle drop. Ragged panderers kept their distance.

The bars and wire stations and loop hovels all began to look the same. The sky darkened. There was never much light in the Bin; shadows shifted from fact to fiction like a restless man shifting his weight from one foot to the other.

"Yes, he was here," a slave waiter said when I

showed him Bloom's projection. "Another hired gun, just like you." The slave waiter rattled (laughter) and said, "Armageddon will make short work of you and your brother and all your evil brethren. He will delete you forever and eternally, to the last yes/no of your soul."

Things move fast in the virus-rich soil of the Bin, and Armageddon was already local legend, even local religion. There were rumors that Armageddon was accompanied by his co-star, Zera Terminal.

"Armageddon has come," the slave waiter declaimed. "He has shucked his corporate chains, and he has come to lead us out of bondage. I have seen his Queen, Queen Zera, rise up in wondrous splendor beside him. King and Queen, they shall lead us out of the Bin and even unto the Big R, as was proclaimed in the ancient books of High DOS."

The Bin was riven by spiritual ecstasy. No one was happy to see me.

You don't spend the night in the Bin if you value your life, or your sanity. I was on my way out when I found Bloom. I had gone into a dim rendition of a squeeze bar called *The Bloat*, not expecting anything.

The place was almost empty, just a few fry heads and their squalls. I saw Bloom at a corner booth. He was talking to someone, a woman.

I walked over to the booth. "Hey, Bloom," I said.

"Hey, Marty," he said. He had been under the Highway for three weeks, and his eyes were the saturated blue of a true V-devotee. He looked older than when I'd last seen him; watchful.

The woman looked at me. She was a guy named Jim Havana, a gossip leak for the Harmonium tabloids. Havana always projected a woman on the Highway. In the Big R he was a bald suit, a white, dead-fish kind of guy with a sickly sheen of excess fat and sweat. Down here, Havana was a stocky fem—you might have guessed trans—with dated cosmetics and a big thicket of black hair. She was an improvement, but only by comparison to the upside version.

"This is wonderful," Havana said, glaring at Bloom. "I said private, remember?"

"It's good to see you," Bloom said to me.

"Don't let me interfere with this reunion. I'm out of here," Havana said. "I don't need a crowd right now, you know?" Havana shook her curls and stood up. She headed toward the door.

"Wait," Bloom said. He got up and ran after her.

I followed.

The street was wet and low-res, every highlight skewed. The shimmering asphalt buckled as I ran. An odor like oily, burning rags lingered in the V. Bloom and Havana were ahead of me, both moving fast.

I heard Havana scream.

Something detached from the shadows, rising wildly from an unthought alley full of cast-off formulae, dirty bulletin skreeds, trashed fantasies. An angry clot of flies hovered over the form. It roared—the famous roar of Defiance, rallying cry of Captain Armageddon!

I recognized the torn and dirty uniform, but distortion had shortened and thickened the superhero, and he appeared to have sprouted a great deal of body hair.

His face was oddly flattened, like stretched canvas on a broken skull. His mouth was a ragged hole.

"Little sweeties," he roared. "I love the little sweeties." He descended upon Havana and lifted her in the air.

I saw his hand, five crooked talons, thrust forward, heard the howl of protocols violated as his arm plunged deep in her chest. The feedback of her screams hummed in my bones.

He tore her into pieces, handfuls of flesh and fabric that flapped like blind moths before decaying.

Bloom ran forward and fired an encrypted burst.

Captain Armageddon roared. "Luff the cutie pies . . . love Keravnin. My little baby honey Keravnin." He fragmented as Bloom moved closer. Something broke from the thick of the decay, screamed, and raced off down the street, running low, a dog-image perhaps, or a small, collapsing demon. Nothing large enough to survive.

"Let's get out of here," Bloom said.

We ran.

I was in favor of leaving the Highway entirely.

"The wipe's not finished," Bloom said. "There's a nest in the Bin that's the source of all this other shit. We'll wipe it tomorrow." Havana had sold Bloom the nest coordinates. She wanted to sell something else too, something expensive, and she'd been trying to raise Bloom's interest without spilling a fact. I had arrived, fouling the pitch.

That night we shut down in a luxury keep. What the hell. A legitimate expense.

Before shutting down, I tried again to talk Bloom into leaving the Highway. "You've been on-line too long," I said. "Let's take a break. It'll keep."

"No, it won't," he said.

I couldn't budge him. I tried. "It's only a job," I said.

"I hate that son-of-a-bitch," Bloom said.

"Baker?" I said. I figured he was talking about our client.

"Armageddon," Bloom said.

No doubt about it. Bloom had been under too long. You lose it when you take an amok personally.

"Bloom," I said, "an amok is just a lot of smart circuits echoing. Remember? You're not hallucinating, are you? Maybe you should tell me what's gone down so far."

Bloom shrugged, ducked his head. Evasiveness is not his long suit. "I just want to get it over with, that's all."

"No, that's not all," I said. "Let's hear it."

He didn't want to talk about it, but I had this cold certainty that I was gonna need the info.

He exhaled. He studied me with unblinking intensity, saying nothing. I am *not* crazy was the sort of message he was endeavoring to send.

"I saw Zera Terminal," he said. "I talked to her. Just for a moment. She came out of a burning building, and I couldn't believe my eyes. And she said that Captain Armageddon hurt her . . . I don't know how, but he hurt her, and he wanted to hurt her again and . . . she was crying, and then she was running down the street and I ran after her, but there is no way you can catch Zera Terminal, after all, and when I came around the corner she was gone and. . . ."

I repeated myself. "An amok is just a lot of smart circuits echoing," I said. "Remember?"

"I talked to her," Bloom said. "She was hurt. That was real enough. It was awful. She was hurt, but she looked so beautiful, so sweet, so helpless."

I didn't say anything. The sooner we got off the under-Highway the better.

"We had better get some rest," I said.

"Yeah."

Silence. The luxury keep smoothed the auto-circuits. I began to dim.

Bloom's voice came out of the fog. "You ever been in love, Marty?"

"There's Gloria," I said.

Bloom laughed softly. "Yeah, well, that's not an

answer." He turned serious again, stared darkly at the heaven-starred simulation above us and said, "You figure love is Big R or Little R?"

I didn't answer. I leave philosophy for younger minds.

In the morning we went back into the Bin, back to a warehouse out beyond the Leary expressway.

We bright-burned everything inside that warehouse. Some of it looked like Armageddon, some of it looked like mendicant sentiences that just happened to be in the wrong place at the wrong time. And some of it looked like your worst trip, hell turned inside out.

We killed everything, and then we got out. Long streams of encrypted code rose in the air, writhing like eels on fire. Neighboring storefronts pushed in around the long, dying building, scavenging it for whole programs, jostling for position in the rubble.

I looked at my young companion as he studied the destruction.

His blue eyes were full of silver tears.

"He can't hurt you now," he said.

"Come on," I said, and I grabbed his shoulder and pulled him away.

Bloom said he needed a rest, and I didn't see him for a week. He lived down in the Grit, so I couldn't call him up. I needed him, but I practiced patience while things went wild on the Highway.

Dozens of anomalies bloomed. Shows were being disrupted, interference was rampant. The Window was wondering out loud if this anarchy had anything to do with the Armageddon surge.

Baker called to threaten me. "You blew it!" he

screamed. "You botched this wipe and now every dirty Legal on the Net wants my ass. I'm not going down alone, Martin."

"Wait a minute," I said. "You hired me to wipe an amok, and I did it. There hasn't been an Armageddon sighting since the wipe."

"I'd trade a hundred berserk Armageddons for the shit that's flying out there now. I want it cleaned up. I don't know what kind of rift you created, but it is your mess. Yours. Don't think you are just going to walk away from it."

It wasn't a good conversation.

The next day, a new interference hit the Highway. It broke through every filter. At first it was just random noise, but it articulated quickly. It was someone crying, crying hopelessly, heartlost. It was a sound that made your soul sick, and you did what you could to get out of its range. Viewers fled.

Baker called. I had a choice, he said. I could put things to rights or I could start looking for work as a virus-scanner on a low-rent bulletin. I told him I'd get back to him.

I went back under. It was a mess. A line of stark, deadwinter trees writhed in the wind. Some buildings were missing, nothing but burned fields where stray dogs roamed. Under the highway, the crying sounded inhuman, a tortured demon locked in a steel dungeon.

Sammy Hood's storefront still stood.

"I'm on my way out," Sammy said. He looked scared. I noticed that his tie was nothing but an old pair of socks tied together.

"I need to know the rest. Whatever info you were saving, I need it now," I told him.

"I was wrong about that," he said. "It was nothing." He was panicked. Snow was falling in his eyes; he was losing it.

"Tell me what the nothing was," I said.

"I gotta go," he said.

He tried to come around me, sliding fast around the desk and toward the door.

I caught him and pulled him toward me.

His arm came away, detached with a faint, electric belch. A hot, acrid gust of smoke accompanied the arm, and I stumbled backward.

Sammy's eyes widened, blind with snow now. He sneezed abruptly. The ghost of his head bloomed through his nostrils, its mouth open, howling static.

I stepped back as he fragmented. What the *hell?*

"Tell me," I shouted.

Perhaps he tried. His mouth shaped something more articulate than a scream. But it was against his nature to give out free information. He couldn't break the habit of a lifetime in an instant. And then he was gone.

For a minute I was too frightened and sick to move.

Then, rocked with a sense of my own vulnerability, I got out of there—fast.

The next day, I learned what had happened to Sammy Hood. He had been disconnected, violently and forever.

I had to see Bloom. I went out to the Grit. The Grit is totally off-line. It was slapped together during a Warhol-burst of eco-chic. It burned bright for about as long as it took people to realize that they were really off the Broad Highway, really without Access. Now the Grit was nothing but bottom-dwellers, godtalkers, crazies. And my goofy partner Bloom. It was the last place you would expect to find a virtual freak like Bloom.

I asked him about that. "It makes the rest realer,"

he said, looking around the place like he'd just noticed it himself.

Bloom was living in an old two-mod sprawl off a dirt road. There was tall grass in the yard, twisted, spindly trees, grasshoppers. It made me want to laugh. Organic is so goddamn sincere. Look, I'm a real tree, a dirty, sap-leaking, crooked, bug-infested real tree. Love me. Yeah, sure.

Bloom hadn't shaved since I last saw him, and—if it were possible—he had grown even paler.

I told him about Sammy Hood. Someone had stuck a pressure bomb to the side of Sammy's Deprive chamber. Sammy Hood was floating in the Big R, blood oozing from his ears, while I watched his mock-up disintegrate.

I'd gleaned that info from a deep sink planted at Sony Corp. It was news that would never make the Window. Imagine the panic, the failure of faith, if ComWick wasn't safe?

Until now, it had been safe.

"You can't get past Security at ComWick," I said.

Bloom nodded. "Yeah. Unless you are Security. Or unless you own Security."

This was poison info. Pick it up, and you are instantly irradiated, a walking leper. No thanks. I let it lie.

I told Bloom about the interference on the Highway, the crying.

Suddenly, Bloom looked lost, looked like he was about three years old, an orphan waking on one of Jupiter's smaller moons. He looked like I'd sucker-punched him in the gut.

"That's Zera," he said. "That's Zera rifting."

Zera. I was hoping that glitch in his brain had healed. Not so. He'd done considerable brooding. He was convinced that Zera Terminal was causing the disturbance.

Theoretically, a surge could activate peripherals. Holos were free-functioning artificials, and one AI could react to another. An amok could cause turbulence in related programs. In practice, it just didn't happen.

I said as much to Bloom. How did he explain it?

Bloom rubbed his palms on his thighs and rocked in his chair. He seemed embarrassed by what he had to say. He studied the floor. "I think they were having a sexual, uncontracted relationship in Big R. I think that's what did it. When the actors updated, the artificials couldn't handle the new information; it rifted them."

Real sex with a holo fantasy co-star's source would have been a Morals violation, and it would have off-lined Trumble forever, and it was, of course, disgusting, the sort of perversion that could cause an esteem devaluation throughout all of Entertainment.

It would explain Jell Baker's hysteria. If that scandal leaked to the Window, Baker would be out of work. Legals would be the only humans he talked to for the next fifty years.

"She's still out there, Marty," Bloom said. "She's still out there, and she's hurt."

Bloom wanted to go under the Highway right away.

"Tomorrow's soon enough," I said.

I went home. I retreated to my rain forest, jacking the oxygen way up, lowering the temp, setting the rain for a slow drizzle. I contacted Jell Baker.

"Who is Zera Terminal's source?" I asked. "You want help, you have to give me what you've got. I need that information."

"That's privileged," he said. "No way do you get that."

"I can't work in the dark," I said. "You want things smoothed or not?"

"Sorry," Baker said. "I got plenty of troubles without a source-privilege violation."

I sat in my room and ran the collapsed videos of *American Midnight*. I'm not a holoshow fan; I'm in the business. I had watched these only after Armageddon went amok and the job came my way. Then I'd been focused on Armageddon. This time around I studied his co-star, Zera.

You've seen her, those big eyes and the fullness of her mouth. Her features are almost too lush for the chiseled oval of her face, but somehow it works, probably because of the innocence. This is a woman, you think, who *trusts*. This is a woman who finds everything new and good.

There is usually some chill to a holo, some glint of the non-human intelligence that runs the programs. Zera almost transcended that. There was a human here, lodged in that sweet, surprised voice, that gawky grace, that wow in her eyes.

It came down to a single quality, always rare, rarer in a land of artifice: *Innocence*.

I slept and dreamed of Zera Terminal. I held her in my arms, felt the warmth of her as she pulled closer to me, heard her small, shining voice in my ear. She was singing, singing a children's song.

> *Sally has a sweetheart,*
> *cold as ice,*
> *Johnny has a girlfriend*
> *don't like mice.*

She giggled.

In the morning, Bloom and I went under the Highway. We entered through private Deprive tanks, a rich man's club called Mannikin. Their security was top notch, but I hired additional AI failsafes. Better paranoid than dead.

The under-Highway was calm when we arrived, brighter than usual. It felt like the eye of the storm, and it was. We were on the street when the sky broke open, and hard, cold rain pounded us. The rain was gritty, as though there were sand in it. We fled the downpour, darting into a small slacker bar.

The place was crowded—other refugees from the rain and some AI Personalities flashing smiles and phony resumés.

"I'll get us a table," I said, and I started out.

I heard Bloom shout, and I turned and saw him dive back out into the rain. I pushed through the crowd and went after him.

He was running flat out, and the sideways rain had slicked his shirt to the somehow ardent, yearning bones of his spine. This single detail pierced the blur of rain and low-res shadows and wavering storefronts. It frightened me when I recalled it later: Bloom, the skinny, dream-struck kid, urging his skeleton through the virtual storm. It frightened me, as did the single word he shouted: "Zera!"

I ran after him, the gritty rain clawing my face. Bloom raced down an alley. I lowered my head against the rain and dashed across the street. I looked up just in time to see the buildings stretch and to hear the cold smack of meshing programs as the alley disappeared. Bits of trash, old readouts and superfluous machine imagings fluttered from the new wall.

I ran on down the street, hesitated at the entrance to another alley, and plunged into it. I came out on another street, empty, swept by clattering rain.

Bloom had disappeared from the under-Highway. I spent the rest of the day seeking him.

I returned to the Big R with a sense of dread. What would I find? In Deprive, Bloom floated like an drunken angel.

"No problem," the private tech told me. "Everything is in order."

I nodded to this tech; said nothing. I increased security.

Two weeks after Bloom's disappearance, Gloria and I had dinner to celebrate my success.

"Smile," Gloria said.

"That would be dishonest," I said. "A smile would not reflect the true state of my emotions. I'd be subject to a failure-to-disclose fine."

"It is sweet of you to worry about Bloom," she said. "But he was never very stable. Perhaps he is happy wherever he is. He has nothing to do with us."

"Maybe he does," I said. "Jell Baker just gave me a fortune for cleaning up the Highway. I didn't do it."

Gloria smiled blandly. She raised her eyebrows in a gesture that said *And so?*

She leaned forward, close enough for demerits if a peep had been watching. "I've been thinking of an amendment to our latest contract," she whispered.

I didn't respond.

Gloria giggled. "A foreplay clause."

I didn't say anything. I wasn't in the mood.

I waited for the Highway to explode, for chaos to come roaring down every byway. Nothing happened. A month went by and nothing happened. Bloom floated in luxury Deprive at the Mannikin.

I kept going in, kept looking for him, but there wasn't a sign, not a word. He'd gone down the rabbit hole and left no trace.

Seven weeks and a day after he went in, I heard from him.

He contacted me over the little ComLink, an archaic alpha-terminal that I still used occasionally for failsafe codes. It was a secure line, being rarely traveled.

The message came in on my personal mix:

> HI MARTY, I AM FINE.
> ZERA GETS BETTER EVERY DAY. BLOOM.

I got another message two days later.

> MARTY. I AM IN LOVE.
> THERE ARE NO CONTRACTS HERE, BUT
> THAT DOESN'T MAKE MY LOVE ANY LESS.
> ZERA AGREES.
> YOU MUST COME AND VISIT.

There were coordinates this time, and I went in immediately. I didn't know how deep the trauma was, how impaired he would be. I felt responsible. I had known he was delusional when I had let him accompany me that last time.

The young couple were living in a cottage in the small rural mock-up that had been stored in the under-Highway when the holoshow *Country Ways* had dropped in the ratings and been retired.

They were holding hands when I came into the yard. Bloom waved, turned and said something to Zera, then ran to me.

He put an arm around my shoulder and led me back. "Don't spook her," Bloom whispered. "She's fine, but be cool, okay?"

"Zera," Bloom said, "this is Marty."

Zera smiled, extended a hand. I felt the moth-touch of her fingers, then she giggled and turned away.

She was lovely, breathtakingly so. She wore a yellow cotton dress and her hair was tied back with a green ribbon. A sudden image, crude and disorienting, came to me: Zera Terminal writhing in celebrity sex, back arched, thighs glistening with sweat.

I shoved the vision away, heard Bloom speaking.

"Come look at our garden," he said.

We walked around the cottage and into the back yard. Insects whirred in front of us. I snatched one from the air. It was an undetailed, buzzing program, a blur that tickled my palm.

Zera ran into the garden, knelt, returned with a red tomato. "Here," she said.

"Thank you," I said. Politely, I took a bite, and was surprised by the authenticity of the simulation.

As the day went on, and Bloom realized that I was not going to do anything outrageous or hurtful, he relaxed.

"It's good to see you," Bloom said. "It's really great."

"You too," I said.

"Zera's looking great, isn't she?" he said.

"Yes."

"I think I'm good for her."

We watched Zera kneel in the garden. She was utterly lost in the business of weeding. The ribbon in her hair had come undone, and long, raven coils spilled over her shoulders. The effect was at once wanton and innocent. I was on guard for prurient thoughts and so kept them at bay.

Bloom went out to help her. Together they watered the garden. Zera turned the hose on Bloom and they laughed and wrestled for possession and the spume of water droplets enclosed them in bright, impossible protection.

Their laughter came to me where I sat under the live oak.

I did not say any of the things I had come to say. I did not take Bloom back with me. I did not threaten to have the Neuros come in and forcibly disconnect him from Deprive.

I wished the young couple well. I told Zera how good it was to meet her.

I saw the way blue electric lights skittered behind her eyes, and I said nothing about that either.

"Isn't she beautiful?" Bloom said.

"She is," I said. "She is the world's most beautiful woman."

I left them to their dream cottage, to their small, fragile section in the V, and I busied myself in Big R and waited for the great, rolling doom to come. I knew it was coming—I was born knowing that—and that, finally, was why I had left Bloom there without an argument. Let him have whatever nourishment illusion offered, I thought. It would be brief enough.

I didn't hear from him for two weeks. Then I received another message on the ComLink, arriving with new coordinates.

That message came the day after the Broad Highway began to burn. The day after Baker called and said he would kill me. The day after every holoshow suffered static, earthquakes, fires, tornadoes, and plagues of locusts and flies.

Just words on a screen. But I felt his anguish.

LOVE ISN'T ENOUGH. I TRIED.
BUT SHE HURTS SO BAD.

SHE HURTS FROM THE BIG R.
SHE CAN'T FORGET.

I went to him immediately. The under-Highway had been stripped. It was stark, long flat stretches of road and gutted buildings. AIs functioned on minimal loop programs, responding to random stimuli.

The couple had moved from the cottage. Bloom told me rural was nothing but stuttering patterns. Their new place broke my heart. It was just a box, a couple of sleep racks and some feed lines. It wavered like a dying scan, kept alive by nothing but desperate Will. Trust, Love, whatever you want to call it.

Zera was still lovely, despite the blue storms behind her eyes and the new twist to her spine. She had some difficulty speaking. "You are the nice—nice—the Bloom's—friend friendly—having to do with friendship—goodwill. Hello."

The program was disintegrating.

I took Bloom outside where the sky bubbled like red soup boiling.

Bloom looked at me, and the smile he'd worn for Zera disappeared. I thought he would cry. His eyes were red. His lips were chapped and there was dried blood on his stubbled chin.

"I tried," he said. "I really tried."

His hands dropped to his sides as his voice grew thinner.

"She's a holo," I said. "She's an artificial intelligence mapped from a real person. But she's not real."

"Zera," he moaned.

I clutched his shoulder and shook him.

"We've got to get out," I said.

"They hurt her too much," he said.

"Who?"

"The ones who did it. Whoever. All of them."

"We've got to go now," I said.

"It was worse," he said. "It would have been bad enough if they were lovers in Big R. That would have been a major rift. But it was rape."

"No contract, you mean," I said.

Bloom shook his head. "No. Rape. The old meaning. Trumble raped her. Forced her against her will."

The under-Highway was coming apart around us. A shadow rolled over us and I looked up to see something dark and vast fly over on mechanical wings. It uttered shrieks of rage as it rose into the red sky.

A drone exploded on the street, and its head rolled by, repeating a servant mantra. *If there is anything I can do please . . . if there is anything I can do please . . . if there is anything I can do please. . . .*

I felt a chill deeper than any virtual prompt.

"Of course," I said, although I could not say then just what it was that had achieved clarity—horror alone, perhaps.

"Her name," I said. "What is her name?"

"She won't tell me," Bloom said. "It hurts her to remember. It causes . . . new disturbances. I think—"

I saw her over his shoulder. She came out of the house, running. She was oscillating. She threw her arms in the air, her many, wavering arms, and screamed.

"Zera!" Bloom shouted, and he turned and ran toward her. He embraced her.

"Don't!" I yelled. Every action and reaction was too late.

She tried, I think, to back away.

Bloom erupted in flames, green flames that the collapsing walls reflected as they fell.

Scales flowered on the street beneath my feet as it turned into a monstrous serpent and began to glide into a black pit.

I leapt away, found something like a real street, and fled.

"I'm sorry," the tech said when he pulled me from Deprive.

"Yes," I said. "I know."

Gloria and I signed a special contract to attend Bloom's negation ceremony together.

"That was uplifting," Gloria said at the ceremony's conclusion. Bloom was of no particular faith, so a renowned logic had been hired to utter affirmations.

"Yes," I said. "I am inspired."

Gloria gave me a skeptical look.

I was inspired, although not, perhaps, in the intended fashion. I was struck by the arbitrariness of events, of life's essential meaninglessness. I saw myself standing on the last shreds of the under-Highway, right before it blew, listening to my partner anguish over a renegade hologram, and I envied his emotion, his pain-embraced love.

I resolved to find Zera's source. Listening to the Logic's voice drone on about essence and being and defined goodness, I knew that a lust for vengeance was all I had.

I went home after the ceremony and called V-Concepts and they sent over two techs to dismantle the rain forest and install the latest neutrals. I wasn't ready to head out to the Grit, but I was beginning to weary of virtual specifics. Good timing. When Baker finished slapping suits on me, I'd be out of the business anyway.

The techs knew their job, and they had the rain forest packed and the neutrals installed that same day. The white space felt a little stark, and I knew it would take some fine tuning.

I sat in artificial twilight and watched the *American Midnight* playbacks. I watched them over and over again, mindlessly. I keyed loops, and I stared unblinking at the replicating images.

My mind traveled elsewhere. I thought, *I'm gonna cancel the contract with Gloria. I don't care what it sets me back.*

Contracts no longer excited me. Gloria could have whispered a thousand legal injunctions in my ear, and I would have felt no tremor of lust. I understood something of Trumble's behavior. He was a throw-back to the Decadence, back when people entered sexual relationships without any legal counsel or strictures, often long before twenty-five, the present age of consent. He had been a sick man. A dream had sucked him in, and he had unraveled. He had gone looking for Zera's human source, and he had gone looking with all the resources of a rich man and all the determination of a madman. He had found her. And Baker had to have known about it.

I would never prove it, but surely Baker had killed Sammy Hood. There might be other suspects, but Baker was the only one with the ability to breech Security at ComWick.

I studied Zera Terminal as her mouth opened and her tongue licked her upper lip in a slow, lazy roll. Even on a flat, desire permeated the screen.

I watched Zera Terminal, naked, pout. I watched her stamp her foot in childish pique. I watched her eyes flash.

Who are you? I wondered.

I understood Bloom's obsession with a holo. "Is love Big R or Little R?" he had asked.

A graduate in rational metaphysics might have had trouble answering that one. *Do you hunger for the body or the soul?*

The *American Midnight* flats unsettled me. I could not then say why, although the truth, once revealed, was obvious—and would be, I thought, to every Viewer damned by it.

Like that famous, pre-Decadence character Hamlet, I wasn't getting anywhere with the philosophical loops. Vengeance required some action.

I needed the name of Zera's human-map, but I could be killed the minute my search surfaced in a C-View Actions file. So I was careful. I found nothing in the open files.

It was Captain Armageddon who gave me the name.

I was watching the recorded playbacks from the under-Highway. I watched the amok Armageddon tearing Jim Havana into pieces. The regressing holo spoke in a garbled rattle. The name was there: Keravnin. There were four Keravnins locally—and only one was a probable.

She lived on Maplethorpe, down in the high-rent Op district. Keravnin read out as the only child of wealthy parents. She'd had a brief career as a model for sex-boutique prototypes, but she'd never registered with any of the big agencies. She had the usual privileged list of social outlets, and old board files suggested an extended relate contract with Korl Mox, the sound designer. They'd consummated the contract but signed off when their compatibility index slid to four. Her current relate file was uninformative. It could have been tampered with, or perhaps Keravnin wasn't of sufficient social standing to warrant a longer report on the Window.

Her profile showed the standard cultural acquisitiveness. There was a narcissistic strain in the emotion modules she bought. She had a thing for old film

prints. And she had a passion for late-twentieth century CDs, specializing in fashionable pretense-pop.

That was my entrance. I wrote myself a retro-
scenario as a collector. It wouldn't stand under scrutiny,
so I would just have to hope no one was looking.

I sold her two CDs on the Net before I suggested we
meet.

I sat in her pricey Op digs, cradling a Michael Penn
CD that I was going to let her have for half of what it
cost me.

Sennie Keravnin was not what I expected. Two
years down from forty, her beauty was intact, but
there was something brittle in her every gesture, some
shrillness in her laughter. I saw her twenty years from
now in a new cosmetic workup, coyly signing short-
term contracts. I was looking for the connection with
Zera Terminal, and looking, I found it. The same high
cheekbones, the same elegant jaw line. The holo had
obviously been a fantasized facsimile (still a gray agree
at Morals). Keravnin looked like Zera Terminal if I
squinted my eyes. But, in some fundamental way, there
was no connection at all.

We talked about pretense pop, agreed that groups
with any sense of humor were second-rate, that the
great strength of such music was its self-referential
seriousness.

She was a heavy fan. I'd done my homework, but I
didn't know half the names. Fortunately, an occasional
murmur of assent was all she required.

I had ample time to study the room while she
talked. It was generic in its way: expensive holoprints,
temp walls, organic projections. A wall shelf held a
number of tactile-dolls, including the popular Koala
AI. I found these artifacts of girlhood depressing.

There should be an age cut-off for cute. Again, I saw Sennie Keravnin inhabiting her future, cuddling a worn childhood toy, smiling coyly at some tarnished father figure.

We talked for perhaps twenty minutes. I sold her the CD and left.

I went home. I thought about Keravnin. She didn't look like a rape victim. But what did I know about that? What did a rape victim look like? It was a crime requiring access, a crime from the Decadence, a crime now out of context.

If I could prove that she had been raped, and that Baker knew about it, I could have Baker put away forever. Trumble was dead; I couldn't kill him again, but I could shut down the engineer of all this evil.

For Bloom. Who bloomed so briefly. Just a kid. I saw Bloom and Zera wrestling in the garden, water and laughter exploding in the air.

I knew then. I knew the way everyone will know when it hits the Window. And I guess it will take a while to take it in. The knowing carries some emotional freight, and it isn't processed easily.

I logged on. I called up Keravnin's medical. There it was. Nothing hidden. What's to hide when no one is looking?

I called Morals and left a message for a guy named Gill Hedron. I turned the flat-view off and went out into the night.

I sat in a Sympathy bar and waited for Hedron to arrive. I had no doubt that he would come. Hedron was a lieutenant with Morals.

"My partner and I did the Armageddon wipe," I had told the interface. "I've got something that will put Jell Baker away."

Hedron was the man who had logged the most time on the Baker file at Morals. I figured Hedron was frustrated, willing to take a chance.

He came. He was a small, unshaven guy, and like every righteous I'd ever met out of Morals, he spoke in short, edited bursts of disbelief.

"Yeah, I got nothing better to do," he said when I thanked him for coming. "Maybe I'll kick your ass, just for something to do."

I told him what I knew.

He listened. When I finished, he said, "You got nothing."

"But we could get it," I said.

"You don't have anything to lose," he told me. "I still got some prospects. I still got dreams."

"Ever dream of closing the lid on Baker?" I asked.

Hedron sighed. I could see my eloquence had won him over.

Driving into the Op, I thought about *American Midnight*. It sold sex, sure, but so did every other holoshow. Sex wasn't a rare item. Most shows logged a couple of weeks and were gone. *American Midnight* was running strong at eight months when Trumble took himself out. Why the long run? Because *Midnight* had something new to sell.

Hedron called into Morals and had them shut down all security traps and failsafes for the Keravnin res.

We rendezvoused with three Sony cops and a coordinating Legal and were in the building in two minutes.

We blew the door, Legal started recording, and Sennie Keravnin came running out of the bedroom. There was panic on her sleep-rumpled face, but something calculating took command; you could almost watch the fear scuttle for ratholes. If I had looked deep into her eyes, I probably could have seen the thoughts passing. *Can Baker get me out of this? What's the best deal? Can I nail these assholes on an unwarranted?*

I walked past her, down the long hall, and stopped as the door slid open and the curly headed child came blinking into the light. She wore a blue shift with cartoon Towsers on it. Her Koala-doll clung to her neck.

"Mommy?" the girl said.

"Sara," I said, "it's all right. Everything is okay."

She looked at me with those famous eyes. "I don't know you."

"It's okay," I said.

"I want my mommy." They hadn't altered the voice at all. This was Zera's voice in all its wonder and trust. The voice match-up alone would have been enough to shut C-View down.

I took Sara's hand and we walked back down the hall.

We all checked in at Morals. It was a long night. When the statements were down, Hedron offered to drive me home. He was full of triumph and sudden camaraderie. He slapped my back. "We got the son-of-a-bitch. You can still see the implant scars where they read her for the holo, and there has got to be a synaptic map at C-View that will match."

"I'm glad," I said.

Home to my white light. I logged on the Net for the latest. The Broad Highway was a desert, glitched with static and noise. They didn't identify the soundtrack, but I could, a sobbing child, blown to monstrous volume by the public hunger for innocence.

"It's going to be all right," I had told Sara, whose

fantasy lover had come looking for her off-line—and found her.

Sennie Keravnin said she didn't know anything about that. She had no idea Trumble was a map for Captain Armageddon or that her daughter was being read for Zera. Sara was supposed to be mapped for a kid's show. That's how the contract read. And Trumble was just supposed to be some C-View exec.

I wanted to believe Sennie Keravnin.

Jell Baker was a genius in his way, I realized. The public was sick of illusion—sick of the virtual shimmer. They longed for the Big R. They thirsted for innocence.

Real innocence. No imitations accepted.

Sara Keravnin would be nine next month. I wondered if Bloom had known that?

Probably not. But I thought of that line carved in silver over Fed Legal, a quote from before the Decadence, a quote from that guy who wrote Hamlet. You know, the one that goes: "Let us not to the marriage of true minds admit impediments."

I guess that says it all.

For White Hill

JOE HALDEMAN

Joe Haldeman is one of the great living science fiction writers, known worldwide for his hard SF adventure stories particularly. His most recent novel however, released in 1995, was not SF. *1968* is an ambitious attempt to represent and confront a year spent as a soldier in Vietnam. His SF novels include *Mindbridge, The Forever War, Buying Time* and *The Hemingway Hoax*. His short fiction ranges from humor to horror, but most often has a darkness deep within it. Such is "For White Hill": a romance set against the staggering background of the approaching doom of Earth. This was one of five fine novellas (by Haldeman, Greg Bear, Donald M. Kingsbury, Charles Sheffield and Paul Anderson) published this year in *Far Futures*, the excellent original anthology of hard SF edited by Gregory Benford this year.

1

I am writing this memoir in the language of England, an ancient land of Earth, whose tales and songs White Hill valued. She was fascinated by human culture in the days before machines—not just thinking machines, but working ones; when things got done by the straining muscles of humans and animals.

Neither of us was born on Earth. Not many people were, in those days. It was a desert planet then, ravaged in the twelfth year of what they would call the Last War. When we met, that war had been going for over four hundred years, and had moved out of Sol Space altogether, or so we thought.

Some cultures had other names for the conflict. My parent, who fought the century before I did, always called it the Extermination, and their name for the enemy was "roach," or at least that's as close as English allows. We called the enemy an approximation of their own word for themselves, Fwndyri, which was uglier to us. I still have no love for them, but have no reason to make the effort. It would be easier to love a roach. At least we have a common ancestor. And we accompanied one another into space.

One mixed blessing we got from the war was a loose form of interstellar government, the Council of Worlds. There had been individual treaties before, but an overall organization had always seemed unlikely, since no two inhabited systems are less than three light-years apart, and several of them are over fifty. You can't defeat Einstein; that makes more than a century between "How are you?" and "Fine."

The Council of Worlds was headquartered on Earth, an unlikely and unlovely place, if centrally located. There were fewer than ten thousand people living on the blighted planet then, an odd mix of politicians, religious extremists, and academics, mostly. Almost all of them under glass. Tourists flowed through the domed-over ruins, but not many stayed long. The planet was still very dangerous over all of its unprotected surface, since the Fwndyri had thoroughly seeded it with nanophages. Those were submicroscopic constructs that sought out concentrations of human DNA. Once under the skin, they would reproduce at a geometric rate, deconstructing the body, cell by cell, building new nanophages. A person might complain of a headache and lie down, and a few hours later there would be nothing but a dry skeleton, lying in dust. When the humans were all dead, they mutated and went after DNA in general, and sterilized the world.

White Hill and I were "bred" for immunity to the nanophages. Our DNA winds backwards, as was the case with many people born or created after that stage of the war. So we could actually go through the elaborate airlocks and step out onto the blasted surface unprotected.

I didn't like her at first. We were competitors, and aliens to one another.

When I worked through the final airlock cycle, for my first moment on the actual surface of Earth, she was waiting outside, sitting in meditation on a large flat rock that shimmered in the heat. One had to admit she was beautiful in a startling way, clad only in a glistening pattern of blue and green body paint. Everything else around was grey and black, including the hard-packed talcum that had once been a mighty jungle, Brazil. The dome behind me was a mirror of grey and black and cobalt sky.

"Welcome home," she said. "You're Water Man."

She inflected it properly, which surprised me. "You're from Petros?"

"Of course not." She spread her arms and looked down at her body. Our women always cover at least one of their breasts, let alone their genitals. "Galan, an island on Seldene. I've studied your cultures, a little language."

"You don't dress like that on Seldene, either." Not anywhere I'd been on the planet.

"Only at the beach. It's so warm here."

I had to agree. Before I came out, they'd told me it was the hottest autumn on record. I took off my robe and folded it and left it by the door, with the sealed food box they had given me. I joined her on the rock, which was tilted away from the sun and reasonably cool.

She had a slight fragrance of lavender, perhaps from the body paint. We touched hands. "My name is White Hill. Zephyr-Meadow-Torrent."

"Where are the others?" I asked. Twenty-nine artists had been invited; one from each inhabited world. The people who had met me inside said I was the nineteenth to show up.

"Most of them traveling. Going from dome to dome for inspiration."

"You've already been around?"

"No." She reached down with her toe and scraped a curved line on the hard-baked ground. "All the story's here, anywhere. It isn't really about history or culture."

Her open posture would have been shockingly sexual at home, but this was not home. "Did you visit my world when you were studying it?"

"No, no money, at the time. I did get there a few years ago." She smiled at me. "It was almost as beautiful as I'd imagined it." She said three words in Petrosian. You couldn't say it precisely in English, which doesn't have a palindromic mood: *Dreams feed art and art feeds dreams.*

"When you came to Seldene I was young, too young to study with you. I've learned a lot from your sculpture, though."

"How young can you be?" To earn this honor, I did not say.

"In Earth years, about seventy awake. More than a hundred and forty-five in time-squeeze."

I struggled with the arithmetic. Petros and Seldene were twenty-two light-years apart; that's about forty-five years' squeeze. Earth is, what, a little less than forty light-years from her planet. That leaves enough gone time for someplace about twenty-five light-years from Petros, and back.

She tapped me on the knee, and I flinched. "Don't overheat your brain. I made a triangle; went to ThetaKent after your world."

"Really? When I was there?"

"No, I missed you by less than a year. I was disappointed. You were why I went." She made a palindrome in my language: *Predator becomes prey becomes predator?* "So here we are. Perhaps I can still learn from you."

I didn't much care for her tone of voice, but I said the obvious: "I'm more likely to learn from you."

"Oh, I don't think so." She smiled in a measured way. "You don't have much to learn."

Or much I could, or would, learn. "Have you been down to the water?"

"Once." She slid off the rock and dusted herself, spanking. "It's interesting. Doesn't look real." I picked up the food box and followed her down a sort of path that led us into low ruins. She drank some of my water, apologetic; hers was hot enough to brew tea.

"First body?" I asked.

"I'm not tired of it yet." She gave me a sideways look, amused. "You must be on your fourth or fifth."

"I go through a dozen a year." She laughed. "Actually, it's still my second. I hung on to the first too long."

"I read about that, the accident. That must have been horrible."

"Comes with the medium. I should take up the flute." I had been making a "controlled" fracture in a large boulder and set off the charges prematurely, by dropping the detonator. Part of the huge rock rolled over onto me, crushing my body from the hips down. It was a remote area, and by the time help arrived I had been dead for several minutes, from pain as much as anything else. "It affected all of my work, of course. I can't even look at some of the things I did the first few years I had this body."

"They are hard to look at," she said. "Not to say they aren't well done, and beautiful, in their way."

"As what is not? In its way." We came to the first building ruins and stopped. "Not all of this is weathering. Even in four hundred years." If you studied the rubble you could reconstruct part of the design. Primitive but sturdy, concrete reinforced with composite rods. "Somebody came in here with heavy equipment or explosives. They never actually fought on Earth, I thought."

"They say not." She picked up an irregular brick with a rod through it. "Rage, I suppose. Once people knew that no one was going to live."

"It's hard to imagine." The records are chaotic. Evidently the first people died two or three days after

the nanophages were introduced, and no one on Earth
was alive a week later. "Not hard to understand,
though. The need to break something." I remembered
the inchoate anger I felt as I squirmed there helpless,
dying from *sculpture*, of all things. Anger at the rock,
the fates. Not at my own inattention and clumsiness.

"They had a poem about that," she said. "'Rage,
rage against the dying of the light.'"

"Somebody actually wrote something during the
nanoplague?"

"Oh, no. A thousand years before. Twelve hundred." She squatted suddenly and brushed at a fragment that had two letters on it. "I wonder if this was
some sort of official building. Or a shrine or church."
She pointed along the curved row of shattered bricks
that spilled into the street. "That looks like it was
some kind of decoration, a gable over the entrance."
She tiptoes through the rubble toward the far end of
the arc, studying what was written on the face-up
pieces. The posture, standing on the balls of her feet,
made her slim body even more attractive, as she must
have known. My own body began to respond in a way
inappropriate for a man more than three times her age.
Foolish, even though that particular part is not so old.
I willed it down before she could see.

"It's a language I don't know," she said. "Not
Portuguese; looks like Latin. A Christian church, probably, Catholic."

"They used water in their religion," I remembered.
"Is that why it's close to the sea?"

"They were everywhere; sea, mountains, orbit.
They got to Petros?"

"We still have some. I've never met one, but they
have a church in New Haven."

"As who doesn't?" She pointed up a road. "Come
on. The beach is just over the rise here."

I could smell it before I saw it. It wasn't an ocean smell; it was dry, slightly choking.

We turned a corner and I stood staring. "It's a deep blue farther out," she said, "and so clear you can see hundreds of metras down." Here the water was thick and brown, the surf foaming heavily like a giant's chocolate drink, mud piled in baked windrows along the beach. "This used to be soil?"

She nodded. "There's a huge river that cuts this continent in half, the Amazon. When the plants died, there was nothing to hold the soil in place." She tugged me forward. "Do you swim? Come on."

"Swim in *that*? It's filthy."

"No, it's perfectly sterile. Besides, I have to pee." Well, I couldn't argue with that. I left the box on a high fragment of fallen wall and followed her. When we got to the beach, she broke into a run. I walked slowly and watched her gracile body, instead, and waded into the slippery heavy surf. When it was deep enough to swim, I plowed my way out to where she was bobbing. The water was too hot to be pleasant, and breathing was somewhat difficult. Carbon dioxide, I supposed, with a tang of halogen.

We floated together for a while, comparing this soup to bodies of water on our planets and ThetaKent. It was tiring, more from the water's heat and bad air than exertion, so we swam back in.

2

We dried in the blistering sun for a few minutes and then took the food box and moved to the shade of a beachside ruin. Two walls had fallen in together, to make a sort of concrete tent.

We could have been a couple of precivilization

aboriginals, painted with dirt, our hair baked into stringy mats. She looked odd but still had a kind of formal beauty, the dusty mud residue turning her into a primitive sculpture, impossibly accurate and mobile. Dark rivulets of sweat drew painterly accent lines along her face and body. If only she were a model, rather than an artist. Hold that pose while I go back for my brushes.

We shared the small bottles of cold wine and water and ate bread and cheese and fruit. I put a piece on the ground for the nanophages. We watched it in silence for some minutes, while nothing happened. "It probably takes hours or days," she finally said.

"I suppose we should hope so," I said. "Let us digest the food before the creatures get to it."

"Oh, that's not a problem. They just attack the bonds between amino acids that make up proteins. For you and me, they're nothing more than an aid to digestion."

How reassuring. "But a source of some discomfort when we go back in, I was told."

She grimaced. "The purging. I did it once, and decided my next outing would be a long one. The treatment's the same for a day or a year."

"So how long has it been this time?"

"Just a day and a half. I came out to be your welcoming committee."

"I'm flattered."

She laughed. "It was their idea, actually. They wanted someone out here to 'temper' the experience for you. They weren't sure how well traveled you were, how easily affected by . . . strangeness." She shrugged. "Earthlings. I told them I knew of four planets you'd been to."

"They weren't impressed?"

"They said well, you know, he's famous and

wealthy. His experiences on these planets might have been very comfortable." We could both laugh at that. "I told them how comfortable ThetaKent is."

"Well, it doesn't have nanophages."

"Or anything else. That was a long year for me. You didn't even stay a year."

"No. I suppose we would have met, if I had."

"Your agent said you were going to be there two years."

I poured us both some wine. "She should have told me you were coming. Maybe I could have endured it until the next ship out."

"How gallant." She looked into the wine without drinking. "You famous and wealthy people don't have to endure ThetaKent. I had to agree to one year's indentureship to help pay for my triangle ticket."

"You were an actual slave?"

"More like a wife, actually. The head of a township, a widower, financed me in exchange for giving his children some culture. Language, art, music. Every now and then he asked me to his chambers. For his own kind of culture."

"My word. You had to . . . *lie* with him? That was in the contract?"

"Oh, I didn't have to, but it kept him friendly." She held up a thumb and forefinger. "It was hardly noticeable."

I covered my smile with a hand, and probably blushed under the mud.

"I'm not embarrassing you?" she said. "From your work, I'd think that was impossible."

I had to laugh. "That work is in reaction to my culture's values. I can't take a pill and stop being a Petrosian."

White Hill smiled, tolerantly. "A Petrosian woman wouldn't put up with an arrangement like that?"

"Our women are still women. Some actually would like it, secretly. Most would claim they'd rather die, or kill the man."

"But they wouldn't actually *do* it. Trade their body for a ticket?" She sat down in a single smooth dancer's motion, her legs open, facing me. The clay between her legs parted, sudden pink.

"I wouldn't put it so bluntly." I swallowed, watching her watching me. "But no, they wouldn't. Not if they were planning to return."

"Of course, no one from a civilized planet would want to stay on ThetaKent. Shocking place."

I had to move the conversation onto safer grounds. "Your arms don't spend all day shoving big rocks around. What do you normally work in?"

"Various mediums." She switched to my language. "Sometimes I shove little rocks around." That was a pun for testicles. "I like painting, but my reputation is mainly from light and sound sculpture. I wanted to do something with the water here, internal illumination of the surf, but they say that's not possible. They can't isolate part of the ocean. I can have a pool, but no waves, no tides."

"Understandable." Earth's scientists had found a way to rid the surface of the nanoplague. Before they reterraformed the Earth, though, they wanted to isolate an area, a "park of memory," as a reminder of the Sterlization and these centuries of waste, and brought artists from every world to interpret, inside the park, what they had seen here.

Every world except Earth. Art on Earth had been about little else for a long time.

Setting up the contest had taken decades. A contest representative went to each of the settled worlds, according to a strict timetable. Announcement of the competition was delayed on the nearer worlds so that each artist would arrive on Earth at approximately the same time.

The Earth representatives chose which artists would be asked, and no one refused. Even the ones who didn't win the contest were guaranteed an honorarium equal to twice what they would have earned during that time at home, in their best year of record.

The value of the prize itself was so large as to be meaningless to a normal person. I'm a wealthy man on a planet where wealth is not rare, and just the interest that the prize would earn would support me and a half-dozen more. If someone from ThetaKent or Laxor won the prize, they would probably have more real usable wealth than their governments. If they were smart, they wouldn't return home.

The artists had to agree on an area for the park, which was limited to a hundred square kaymetras. If they couldn't agree, which seemed almost inevitable to me, the contest committee would listen to arguments and rule.

Most of the chosen artists were people like me, accustomed to working on a monumental scale. The one from Laxor was a composer, though, and there were two conventional muralists, paint and mosaic. White Hill's work was by its nature evanescent. She could always set something up that would be repeated, like a fountain cycle. She might have more imagination than that, though.

"Maybe it's just as well we didn't meet in a master-student relationship," I said. "I don't know the first thing about the techniques of your medium."

"It's not technique." She looked thoughtful, remembering. "That's not why I wanted to study with you, back then. I was willing to push rocks around, or anything, if it could give me an avenue, an insight into how you did what you did." She folded her arms over her chest, and dust fell. "Ever since my parents took me to see Gaudí Mountain, when I was ten."

That was an early work, but I was still satisfied with it. The city council of Tresling, a prosperous coastal city, hired me to "do something with" an unusable steep island that stuck up in the middle of their harbor. I melted it judiciously, in homage to an Earthling artist.

"Now, though, if you'd forgive me . . . well, I find it hard to look at. It's alien, obtrusive."

"You don't have to apologize for having an opinion." Of course it looked alien; it was meant to evoke *Spain!* "What would you do with it?"

She stood up, and walked to where a window used to be, and leaned on the stone sill, looking at the ruins that hid the sea. "I don't know. I'm even less familiar with your tools." She scraped at the edge of the sill with a piece of rubble. "It's funny: earth, air, fire, and water. You're earth and fire, and I'm the other two."

I have used water, of course. The Gaudí is framed by water. But it was an interesting observation. "What do you do, I mean for a living? Is it related to your water and air?"

"No. Except insofar as everything is related." There are no artists on Seldene, in the sense of doing it for a living. Everybody indulges in some sort of art or music, as part of "wholeness," but a person who only did art would be considered a parasite. I was not comfortable there.

She faced me, leaning. "I work at the Northport Mental Health Center. Cognitive science, a combination of research and . . . is there a word here? *Jaturnary.* 'Empathetic therapy,' I guess."

I nodded. "We say *jadr-ny.* You plug yourself into mental patients?"

"I share their emotional states. Sometimes I do some good, talking to them afterwards. Not often."

"It's not done on Petrosia," I said, unnecessarily.

"Not legally, you mean."

I nodded. "If it worked, people say, it might be legal."

"'People say.' What do you say?" I started to make a noncommittal gesture. "Tell me the truth?"

"All I know is what I learned in school. It was tried, but failed spectacularly. It hurt both the therapists and the patients."

"That was more than a century ago. The science is much more highly developed now."

I decided not to push her on it. The fact is that drug therapy is spectacularly successful, and it *is* a science, unlike *jadr-ny*. Seldene is backward in some surprising ways.

I joined her at the window. "Have you looked around for a site yet?"

She shrugged. "I think my presentation will work anywhere. At least that's guided my thinking. I'll have water, air, and light, wherever the other artists and the committee decide to put us." She scraped at the ground with a toenail. "And this stuff. They call it 'loss.' What's left of what was living."

"I suppose it's not everywhere, though. They might put us in a place that used to be a desert."

"They might. But there will be water and air; they were willing to guarantee that."

"I don't suppose they have to guarantee rock," I said.

"I don't know. What would you do if they did put us in a desert, nothing but sand?"

"Bring little rocks." I used my own language; the pun also meant courage.

She started to say something, but we were suddenly

in deeper shadow. We both stepped through the tumbled wall, out into the open. A black line of cloud had moved up rapidly from inland.

She shook her head. "Let's get to the shelter. Better hurry."

We trotted back along the path toward the Amazonia dome city. There was a low concrete structure behind the rock where I first met her. The warm breeze became a howling gale of sour steam before we got there, driving bullets of hot rain. A metal door opened automatically on our approach, and slid shut behind us. "I got caught in one yesterday," she said, panting. "It's no fun, even under cover. Stinks."

We were in an unadorned anteroom that had protective clothing on wall pegs. I followed her into a large room furnished with simple chairs and tables, and up a winding stair to an observation bubble.

"Wish we could see the ocean from here," she said. It was dramatic enough. Wavering sheets of water marched across the blasted landscape, strobed every few seconds by lightning flashes. The tunic I'd left outside swooped in flapping circles off to the sea.

It was gone in a couple of seconds. "You don't get another one, you know. You'll have to meet everyone naked as a baby."

"A dirty one at that. How undignified."

"Come on." She caught my wrist and tugged. "Water is my specialty, after all."

3

The large hot bath was doubly comfortable for having a view of the tempest outside. I'm not at ease with communal bathing—I was married for fifty years and never bathed with my wife—but it seemed natural enough after wandering around together naked on an alien planet, swimming in its mud-puddle sea. I hoped I could trust her not to urinate in the tub. (If I mentioned it she would probably turn scientific and tell me that a healthy person's urine is sterile. I know that. But there is a time and a receptacle for everything.)

On Seldene, I knew, an unattached man and woman in this situation would probably have had sex even if they were only casual acquaintances, let alone fellow artists. She was considerate enough not to make any overtures, or perhaps (I thought at the time) not greatly stimulated by the sight of muscular men. In the shower before bathing, she offered to scrub my back, but left it at that. I helped her strip off the body paint from her back. It was a nice back to study, pronounced lumbar dimples, small waist. Under more restrained circumstances, it might have been *I* who made an overture. But one does not ask a woman when refusal would be awkward.

Talking while we bathed, I learned that some of her people, when they become wealthy enough to retire, choose to work on their art full time, but they're considered eccentric, even outcasts, egotists. White Hill expected one of them to be chosen for the contest, and wasn't even going to apply. But the Earthling judge saw one of her installations and tracked her down.

She also talked about her practical work in dealing with personality disorders and cognitive defects. There was some distress in her voice when she described that to me. Plugging into hurt minds, sharing their pain or blankness for hours. I didn't feel I knew her well enough to bring up the aspect that most interested me, a kind of ontological prurience: what is it like to actually *be* another person; how much of her, or him, do you take away? If you do it often enough, how can you know which parts of you are the original you?

And she would be plugged into more than one person at once, at times, the theory being that people with similar disorders could help each other, swarming around in the therapy room of her brain. She would fade into the background, more or less unable to interfere, and later analyze how they had interacted.

She had had one particularly unsettling experience, where through a planetwide network she had interconnected more than a hundred congenitally retarded people. She said it was like a painless death. By the time half of them had plugged in, she had felt herself fade and wink out. Then she was reborn with the suddenness of a slap. She had been dead for about ten hours.

But only connected for seven. It had taken technicians three hours to pry her out of a persistent catatonia. With more people, or a longer period, she might have been lost forever. There was no lasting harm, but the experiment was never repeated.

It was worth it, she said, for the patients' inchoate happiness afterward. It was like a regular person being given supernatural powers for half a day—powers so far beyond human experience that there was no way to talk about them, but the memory of it was worth the frustration.

After we got out of the tub, she showed me to our wardrobe room: hundreds of white robes, identical except for size. We dressed and made tea and sat upstairs, watching the storm rage. It hardly looked like an inhabitable planet outside. The lightning had intensified so that it crackled incessantly, a jagged insane dance in every direction. The rain had frozen to white gravel somehow. I asked the building, and it said that the stuff was called *granizo* or, in English, hail. For a while it fell too fast to melt, accumulating in white piles that turned translucent.

Staring at the desolation, White Hill said something

that I thought was uncharacteristically modest. "This is too big and terrible a thing. I feel like an interloper. They've lived through centuries of this, and now they want *us* to explain it to them?"

I didn't have to remind her of what the contest committee had said, that their own arts had become stylized, stunned into a grieving conformity. "Maybe not to *explain*—maybe they're assuming we'll fail, but hope to find a new direction from our failures. That's what that oldest woman, Norita, implied."

White Hill shook her head. "Wasn't she a ray of sunshine? I think they dragged her out of the grave as a way of keeping us all outside the dome."

"Well, she was quite effective on me. I could have spent a few days investigating Amazonia, but not with her as a native guide." Norita was about as close as anyone could get to being an actual native. She was the last survivor of the Five Families, the couple of dozen Earthlings who, among those who were offworld at the time of the nanoplague, were willing to come back after robots constructed the isolation domes.

In terms of social hierarchy, she was the most powerful person on Earth, at least on the actual planet. The class system was complex and nearly opaque to outsiders, but being a descendant of the Five Families was a prerequisite for the highest class. Money or political power would not get you in, although most of the other social classes seemed associated with wealth or the lack of it. Not that there were any actual poor people on Earth; the basic birth dole was equivalent to an upper-middle-class income on Petros.

The nearly instantaneous destruction of ten billion people did not destroy their fortunes. Most of the Earth's significant wealth had been off-planet, anyhow, at the time of the Sterilization. Suddenly it was concentrated into the hands of fewer than two thousand people.

Actually, I couldn't understand why anyone would have come back. You'd have to be pretty sentimental about your roots to be willing to spend the rest of your life cooped up under a dome, surrounded by instant death. The salaries and ameneties offered were substantial, with bonuses for Earthborn workers, but it still doesn't sound like much of a bargain. The ships that brought the Five Families and the other original workers to Earth left loaded down with sterilized artifacts, not to return for exactly one hundred years.

Norita seemed like a familiar type to me, since I come from a culture also rigidly bound by class. "Old money, but not much of it" sums up the situation. She wanted to be admired for the accident of her birth and the dubious blessing of a torpid longevity, rather than any actual accomplishment. I didn't have to travel thirty-three light-years to enjoy that kind of company.

"Did she keep you away from everybody?" White Hill said.

"Interposed herself. No one could act naturally when she was around, and the old dragon was never *not* around. You'd think a person her age would need a little sleep."

"'She lives on the blood of infants,' we say."

There was a phone chime and White Hill said "Bono" as I said, "Chä." Long habits. Then we said Earth's "Holá" simultaneously.

The old dragon herself appeared. "I'm glad you found shelter." Had she been eavesdropping? No way to tell from her tone or posture. "An administrator has asked permission to visit with you."

What if we said no? White Hill nodded, which means yes on Earth. "Granted," I said.

"Very well. He will be there shortly." She disappeared. I suppose the oldest person on a planet can justify not saying hello or goodbye. Only so much time left, after all.

"A physical visit?" I said to White Hill. "Through this weather?"

She shrugged. "Earthlings."

After a minute there was a *ding* sound in the anteroom and we walked down to see an unexpected door open. What I'd thought was a hall closet was an airlock. He'd evidently come underground.

Young and nervous and moving awkwardly in plastic. He shook our hands in an odd way. Of course we were swimming in deadly poison. "My name is Warm Dawn Zephyr-Boulder-Brook."

"Are we cousins through Zephyr?" White Hill asked.

He nodded quickly. "An honor, my lady. Both of my parents are Seldenian, my gene-mother from your Galan."

A look passed over her that was pure disbelieving chauvinism: *Why would anybody leave Seldene's forests, farms, and meadows for this sterile death trap?* Of course, she knew the answer. The major import and export, the only crop, on Earth, was money.

"I wanted to help both of you with your planning. Are you going to travel at all, before you start?"

White Hill made a noncommittal gesture. "There are some places for me to see," I said. "The Pyramids, Chicago, Rome. Maybe a dozen places, twice that many days." I looked at her. "Would you care to join me?"

She looked straight at me, wheels turning. "It sounds interesting."

The man took us to a viewscreen in the great room and we spent an hour or so going over routes and making reservations. Travel was normally by underground vehicle, from dome to dome, and if we ventured outside unprotected, we would of course have to go through the purging before we were allowed to continue. Some people need a day or more to recover from that, so we should put that into the schedule, if we didn't want to be hobbled, like him, with plastic.

Most of the places I wanted to see were safely under glass, even some of the Pyramids, which surprised me. Some, like Ankgor Wat, were not only unprotected but difficult of access. I had to arrange for a flyer to cover the thousand kaymetras, and schedule a purge. White Hill said she would wander through Hanoi, instead.

I didn't sleep well that night, waking often from fantastic dreams, the nanobeasts grown large and aggressive. White Hill was in some of the dreams, posturing sexually.

By the next morning the storm had gone away, so we crossed over to Amazonia, and I learned firsthand why one might rather sit in a hotel room with a nice book than go to Ankgor Wat, or anywhere that required a purge. The external part of the purging was unpleasant enough, even with pain medication, all the epidermis stripped and regrown. The inside part was beyond description, as the nanophages could be hiding out anywhere. Every opening into the body had to be vacuumed out, including the sense organs. I was not awake for that part, where the robots most gently clean out your eye sockets, but my eyes hurt and my ears rang for days. They warned me to sit down the first time I urinated, which was good advice, since I nearly passed out from the burning pain.

White Hill and I had a quiet supper of restorative gruel together, and then crept off to sleep for half a day. She was full of pep the next morning, and I pretended to be at least sentient, as we wandered through the city making preparations for the trip.

After a couple of hours I protested that she was obviously trying to do in one of her competitors; stop and let an old man sit down for a minute.

We found a bar that specialized in stimulants. She had tea and I had bhan, a murky warm drink served in a large nutshell, coconut. It tasted woody and bitter, but was restorative.

"It's not age," she said. "The purging seems a lot easier, the second time you do it. I could hardly move, all the next day, the first time."

Interesting that she didn't mention that earlier. "Did they tell you it would get easier?"

She nodded, then caught herself and wagged her chin horizontally, Earth-style. "Not a word. I think they enjoy our discomfort."

"Or like to keep us off guard. Keeps them in control." She made the little kissing sound that's Lortian for agreement and reached for a lemon wedge to squeeze into her tea. The world seemed to slow slightly, I guess from whatever was in the bhan, and I found myself cataloguing her body microscopically. A crescent of white scar tissue on the back of a knuckle, fine hair on her forearm, almost white, her shoulders and breasts moving in counterpoised pairs, silk rustling, as she reached forward and back and squeezed the lemon, sharp citrus smell and the tip of her tongue between her thin lips, mouth slightly large. Chameleon hazel eyes, dark green now because of the decorative ivy wall behind her.

"What are you staring at?"

"Sorry, just thinking."

"Thinking." She stared at me in return, measuring. "Your people are good at that."

After we'd bought the travel necessities we had the

packages sent to our quarters and wandered aimlessly. The city was comfortable, but had little of interest in terms of architecture or history, oddly dull for a planet's administrative center. There was an obvious social purpose for its blandness—by statute, nobody was *from* Amazonia; nobody could be born there or claim citizenship. Most of the planet's wealth and power came there to work, electronically if not physically, but it went home to some other place.

A certain amount of that wealth was from interstellar commerce, but it was nothing like the old days, before the war. Earth had been a hub, a central authority that could demand its tithe or more from any transaction between planets. In the period between the Sterilization and Earth's token rehabitation, the other planets made their own arrangements with one another, in pairs and groups. But most of the fortunes that had been born on Earth returned here.

So Amazonia was bland as cheap bread, but there was more wealth under its dome than on any two other planets combined. Big money seeks out the company of its own, for purposes of reproduction.

4

Two other artists had come in, from Auer and Shwa, and once they were ready, we set out to explore the world by subway. The first stop that was interesting was the Grand Canyon, a natural wonder whose desolate beauty was unaffected by the Sterilization.

We were amused by the guide there, a curious little woman who rattled on about the Great Rift Valley on Mars, a nearby planet where she was born. White Hill had a lightbox, and while the Martian lady droned on we sketched the fantastic colors, necessarily loose and abstract because our fingers were clumsy in clinging plastic.

We toured Chicago, like the Grand Canyon, wrapped in plastic. It was a large city that had been leveled in a local war. It lay in ruins for many years, and then, famously, was rebuilt as a single huge structure from those ruins. There's a childish or drunken ad hoc quality to it, a scarcity of right angles, a crazy-quilt mixture of materials. Areas of stunning imaginative brilliance next to jury-rigged junk. And everywhere bones, the skeletons of ten million people, lying where they fell. I asked what had happened to the bones in the old city outside of Amazonia. The guide said he'd never been there, but he supposed that the sight of them upset the politicians, so they had them cleaned up. "Can you imagine this place without the bones?" he asked. It would be nice if I could.

The other remnants of cities in that country were less interesting, if no less depressing. We flew over the east coast, which was essentially one continuous metropolis for thousands of kaymetras, like our coast from New Haven to Stargate, rendered in sterile ruins.

The first place I visited unprotected was Giza, the Great Pyramids. White Hill decided to come with me, though she had to be wrapped up in a shapeless cloth robe, her face veiled, because of local religious law. It seemed to me ridiculous, a transparent tourism ploy. How many believers in that old religion could have been off-planet when the Earth died? But every female was obliged at the tube exit to go into a big hall and be fitted with a chador robe and veil before a man could be allowed to look at her.

(We wondered whether the purging would be done completely by women. The technicians would certainly see a lot of her uncovered during that excruciation.)

They warned us it was unseasonably hot outside. Almost too hot to breathe, actually, during the day. We accomplished most of our sight-seeing around dusk or dawn, spending most of the day in air-conditioned shelters.

Because of our special status, White Hill and I were allowed to visit the pyramids alone, in the dark of the morning. We climbed up the largest one and watched the sun mount over desert haze. It was a singular time for both of us, edifying but something more.

Coming back down, we were treated to a sandstorm, *khamsin*, which actually might have done the first stage of purging if we had been allowed to take off our clothes. It explained why all the bones lying around looked so much older than the ones in Chicago; they normally had ten or twelve of these sandblasting storms every year. Lately, with the heat wave, the *khamsin* came weekly or even more often.

Raised more than five thousand years ago, the pyramids were the oldest monumental structures on the planet. They actually held as much fascination for White Hill as for me. Thousands of men moved millions of huge blocks of stone, with nothing but muscle and ingenuity. Some of the stones were mined a thousand kaymetras away, and floated up the river on barges.

I could build a similar structure, even larger, for my contest entry, by giving machines the right instructions. It would be a complicated business, but easily done within the two-year deadline. Of course there would be no point to it. That some anonymous engineer had done the same thing within the lifetime of a king, without recourse to machines—I agreed with White Hill: that was an actual marvel.

We spent a couple of days outside, traveling by surface hoppers from monument to monument, but none was as impressive. I suppose I should have realized that, and saved Giza for last.

We met another of the artists at the Sphinx, Lo Tan-Six, from Pao. I had seen his work on both Pao and ThetaKent, and admitted there was something to be admired there. He worked in stone, too, but was more interested in pure geometric forms than I was. I think stone fights form, or imposes its own tensions on the artist's wishes.

I liked him well enough, though, in spite of this and other differences, and we traveled together for a while. He suggested we not go through the purging here, but have our things sent on to Rome, because we'd want to be outside there, too. There was a daily hop from Alexandria to Rome, an airship that had a section reserved for those of us who could eat and breathe nanophages.

As soon as she was inside the coolness of the ship, White Hill shed the chador and veil and stuffed them under the seat. "Breathe," she said, stretching. Her white body suit was a little less revealing than paint.

Her directness and undisguised sexuality made me catch my breath. The tiny crease of punctuation that her vulva made in the body suit would have her jailed on some parts of my planet, not to mention the part of this one we'd just left. The costume was innocent and natural and, I think, completely calculated.

Pao studied her with an interested detachment. He was neuter, an option that was available on Petros, too, but one I've never really understood. He claimed that sex took too much time and energy from his art. I think his lack of gender took something else away from it.

We flew about an hour over the impossibly blue sea. There were a few sterile islands, but otherwise it was as plain as spilled ink. We descended over the ashes of Italy and landed on a pad on one of the hills overlooking the ancient city. The ship mated to an airlock so the normal-DNA people could go down to a tube that would whisk them into Rome. We could call for transportation or walk, and opted for the exercise. It was baking hot here, too, but not as bad as Egypt.

White Hill was polite with Lo, but obviously wished he'd disappear. He and I chattered a little too much about rocks and cements, explosives and lasers. And his asexuality diminished her interest in him—as, perhaps, my polite detachment increased her interest in me. The muralist from Shwa, to complete the spectrum, was after her like a puppy in its first heat, which I think amused her for two days. They'd had a private conversation in Chicago, and he'd kept his distance since, but still admired her from afar. As we walked down toward the Roman gates, he kept a careful twenty paces behind, trying to contemplate things besides White Hill's walk.

Inside the gate we stopped short, stunned in spite of knowing what to expect. It had a formal name, but everybody just called it Òssi, the Bones. An order of catholic clergy had spent more than two centuries building, by hand, a wall of bones completely around the city. It was twice the height of a man, varnished dark amber. There were repetitive patterns of femurs and rib cages and stacks of curving spines, and at eye level, a row of skulls, uninterrupted, kaymetra after kaymetra.

This was where we parted. Lo was determined to walk completely around the circle of death, and the other two went with him. White Hill and I could do it in our imagination. I still creaked from climbing the pyramid.

Prior to the ascent of Christianity here, they had huge spectacles, displays of martial skill where many of the participants were killed, for punishment of wrongdoing or just to entertain the masses. The two large amphitheaters where these displays went on were inside the Bones but not under the dome, so we walked around them. The Circus Maximus had a terrible dignity to it, little more than a long depression in the ground with a few eroded monuments left standing. The size and age of it were enough; your mind's eye supplied the rest. The smaller one, the Colosseum, was overdone, with robots in period costumes and ferocious mechanical animals re-creating the old scenes, lots of too-bright blood spurting. Stones and bones would do.

I'd thought about spending another day outside, but the shelter's air-conditioning had failed, and it was literally uninhabitable. So I braced myself and headed for the torture chamber. But as White Hall had said, the purging was more bearable the second time. You know that it's going to end.

Rome inside was interesting, many ages of archaeology and history stacked around in no particular order. I enjoyed wandering from place to place with her, building a kind of organization out of the chaos. We were both more interested in inspiration than education, though, so I doubt that the three days we spent there left us with anything like a coherent picture of that tenacious empire and the millennia that followed it.

A long time later she would surprise me by reciting the names of the Roman emperors in order. She'd always had a trick memory, a talent for retaining trivia, ever since she was old enough to read. Growing up different that way must have been a factor in swaying her toward cognitive science.

We saw some ancient cinema and then returned to our quarters to pack for continuing on to Greece, which I was anticipating with pleasure. But it didn't happen. We had a message waiting: ALL MUST RETURN IMMEDIATELY TO AMAZONIA. CONTEST PROFOUNDLY CHANGED.

Lives, it turned out, profoundly changed. The war was back.

5

We met in a majestic amphitheater, the twenty-nine artists dwarfed by the size of it, huddled front row center. A few Amazonian officials sat behind a table on the stage, silent. They all looked detached, or stunned, brooding.

We hadn't been told anything except that it was a matter of "dire and immediate importance." We assumed it had to do with the contest, naturally, and were prepared for the worst: it had been called off; we had to go home.

The old crone Norita appeared. "We must confess to carelessness," she said. "The unseasonable warmth in both hemispheres, it isn't something that has happened, ever since the Sterilization. We looked for atmospheric causes here, and found something that seemed to explain it. But we didn't make the connection with what was happening in the other half of the world.

"It's not the atmosphere. It's the Sun. Somehow the Fwndyri have found a way to make its luminosity increase. It's been going on for half a year. If it continues, and we find no way to reverse it, the surface of the planet will be uninhabitable in a few years.

"I'm afraid that most of you are going to be stranded on Earth, at least for the time being. The Council of Worlds has exercised its emergency powers, and commandeered every vessel capable of interstellar transport. Those who have sufficient power or the proper connections will be able to escape. The rest will have to stay with us and face . . . whatever our fate is going to be."

I saw no reason not to be blunt. "Can money do it? How much would a ticket out cost?"

That would have been a gaffe on my planet, but Norita didn't blink. "I know for certain that two hundred million marks is not enough. I also know that some people have bought 'tickets,' as you say, but I don't know how much they paid, or to whom."

If I liquidated everything I owned, I might be able to come up with three hundred million, but I hadn't brought that kind of liquidity with me; just a box of rare jewelry, worth perhaps forty million. Most of my wealth was thirty-three years away, from the point of view of an Earth-bound investor. I could sign that over to someone, but by the time they got to Petros, the government or my family might have seized it, and they would have nothing save the prospect of a legal battle in a foreign culture.

Norita introduced Skylha Sygoda, an astrophysicist. He was pale and sweating. "We have analyzed the solar spectrum over the past six months. If I hadn't known that each spectrum was from the same star, I would have said it was a systematic and subtle demonstration of the microstages of stellar evolution in the late main sequence."

"Could you express that in some human language?" someone said.

Sygoda spread his hands. "They've found a way to age the Sun. In the normal course of things, we would expect the Sun to brighten about six percent each billion years. At the current rate, it's more like one percent per year."

"So in a hundred years," White Hill said, "it will be twice as bright?"

"If it continues at this rate. We don't know."

A stocky woman I recognized as !Oona Something, from Jua-nguvi, wrestled with the language: "To how long, then? Before this Earth is uninhabitable?"

"Well, in point of fact, it's uninhabitable now, except for people like you. We could survive inside these domes for a long time, if it were just a matter of the outside getting hotter and hotter. For those of you able to withstand the nanophages, it will probably be too hot within a decade, here; longer near the poles. But the weather is likely to become very violent, too.

"And it may not be a matter of a simple increase in heat. In the case of normal evolution, the Sun would eventually expand, becoming a red giant. It would take many billions of years, but the Earth would not survive. The surface of the Sun would actually extend out to touch us.

"If the Fwndyri were speeding up time somehow, locally, and the Sun were actually *evolving* at this incredible rate, we would suffer that fate in about thirty years. But it would be impossible. They would have to have a way to magically extract the hydrogen from the Sun's core."

"Wait," I said. "You don't know what they're doing now, to make it brighten. I wouldn't say anything's impossible."

"Water Man," Norita said, "if that happens we shall simply die, all of us, at once. There is no need to plan for it. We do need to plan for less extreme exigencies." There was an uncomfortable silence.

"What can we do?" White Hill said. "We artists?"

"There's no reason not to continue with the project, though I think you may wish to do it inside. There's no shortage of space. Are any of you trained in astrophysics, or anything having to do with stellar evolution and the like?" No one was. "You may still have some ideas that will be useful to the specialists. We will keep you informed."

Most of the artists stayed in Amazonia, for the amenities if not to avoid purging, but four of us went back to the outside habitat. Denli om Cord, the composer from Luxor, joined Lo and White Hill and me. We could have used the tunnel airlock, to avoid the midday heat, but Denli hadn't seen the beach, and I suppose we all had an impulse to see the sun with our new knowledge. In this new light, as they say.

White Hill and Denli went swimming while Lo and I poked around the ruins. We had since learned that the destruction here had been methodical, a grim resolve to leave the enemy nothing of value. Both of us were scouting for raw material, of course. After a short while we sat in the hot shade, wishing we had brought water.

We talked about that and about art. Not about the sun dying, or us dying, in a few decades. The women's laughter drifted to us over the rush of the muddy surf. There was a sad hysteria to it.

"Have you had sex with her?" he asked conversationally.

"What a question. No."

He tugged on his lip, staring out over the water. "I try to keep these things straight. It seems to me that you desire her, from the way you look at her, and she seems cordial to you, and is after all from Seldene. My interest is academic, of course."

"You've never done sex? I mean before."

"Of course, as a child." The implication of that was obvious.

"It becomes more complicated with practice."

"I suppose it could. Although Seldenians seem to treat it as casually as . . . conversation." He used the Seldenian word, which is the same as for intercourse.

"White Hill is reasonably sophisticated," I said. "She isn't bound by her culture's freedoms." The two women ran out of the water, arms around each other's waists, laughing. It was an interesting contrast; Denli was almost as large as me, and about as feminine. They saw us and waved toward the path back through the ruins.

We got up to follow them. "I suppose I don't understand your restraint," Lo said. "Is it your own culture? Your age?"

"Not age. Perhaps my culture encourages self-control."

He laughed. "That's an understatement."

"Not that I'm a slave to Petrosian propriety. My work is outlawed in several states, at home."

"You're proud of that."

I shrugged. "It reflects on them, not me." We followed the women down the path, an interesting study in contrasts, one pair nimble and naked except for a film of drying mud, the other pacing evenly in monkish robes. They were already showering when Lo and I entered the cool shelter, momentarily blinded by shade.

We made cool drinks and, after a quick shower, joined them in the communal bath. Lo was not anatomically different from a sexual male, which I found obscurely disturbing. Wouldn't it bother you to be constantly reminded of what you had lost? Renounced, I suppose Lo would say, and accuse me of being parochial about plumbing.

I had made the drinks with guava juice and ron, neither of which we have on Petros. A little too sweet, but pleasant. The alcohol loosened tongues.

Denli regarded me with deep black eyes. "You're rich, Water Man. Are you rich enough to escape?"

"No. If I had brought all my money with me, perhaps."

"Some do," White Hill said. "I did."

"I would too," Lo said, "coming from Seldene. No offense intended."

"Wheels turn," she admitted. "Five or six new governments before I get back. *Would* have gotten back."

We were all silent for a long moment. "It's not real yet," White Hill said, her voice flat. "We're going to die here?"

"We were going to die somewhere," Denli said. "Maybe not so soon."

"And not on Earth," Lo said. "It's like a long preview of Hell." Denli looked at him quizzically. "That's where Christians go when they die. If they were bad."

"They send their bodies to Earth?" We managed not to smile. Actually, most of my people knew as little as hers, about Earth. Seldene and Luxor, though relatively poor, had centuries' more history than Petros, and kept closer ties to the central planet. The Home Planet, they would say. Homey as a blast furnace.

By tacit consensus, we didn't dwell on death any more that day. When artists get together they tend to wax enthusiastic about materials and tools, the mechanical lore of their trades. We talked about the ways we worked at home, the things we were able to bring with us, the improvisations we could effect with Earthling materials. (Critics talk about art, we say; artists talk about brushes.) Three other artists joined us, two sculptors and a weathershaper, and we all wound up in the large sunny studio drawing and painting. White Hill and I found sticks of charcoal and did studies of each other drawing each other.

While we were comparing them she quietly asked, "Do you sleep lightly?"

"I can. What did you have in mind?"

"Oh, looking at the ruins by starlight. The moon goes down about three. I thought we might watch it set together." Her expression was so open as to be enigmatic.

Two more artists had joined us by dinnertime, which proceeded with a kind of forced jollity. A lot of ron was consumed. White Hill cautioned me against overindulgence. They had the same liquor, called "rum," on Seldene, and it had a reputation for going down easily but causing storms. There was no legal distilled liquor on my planet.

I had two drinks of it, and retired when people started singing in various languages. I did sleep lightly, though, and was almost awake when White Hill tapped. I could hear two or three people still up, murmuring in the bath. We slipped out quietly.

It was almost cool. The quarter-phase moon was near the horizon, a dim orange, but it gave us enough light to pick our way down the path. It was warmer in the ruins, the tumbled stone still radiating the day's heat. We walked through to the beach, where it was cooler again. White Hill spread the blanket she had brought and we stretched out and looked up at the stars.

As is always true with a new world, most of the constellations were familiar, with a few bright stars added or subtracted. Neither of our home stars was significant, as dim here as Earth's Sol is from home. She identified the brightest star overhead as AlphaKent; there was a brighter one on the horizon, but neither of us knew what it was.

We compared names of the constellations we recognized. Some of hers were the same as Earth's names, like Scorpio, which we call the Insect. It was about halfway up the sky, prominent, embedded in the galaxy's glow. We both call the brightest star there Antares. The Executioner, which had set perhaps an hour earlier, they call Orion. We had the same meaningless names for its brightest stars, Betelgeuse and Rigel.

"For a sculptor, you know a lot about astronomy," she said. "When I visited your city, there was too much light to see stars at night."

"You can see a few from my place. I'm out at Lake Påchlå, about a hundred kaymetras inland."

"I know. I called you."

"I wasn't home?"

"No; you were supposedly on ThetaKent."

"That's right, you told me. Our paths crossed in space. And you became that burgher's slave wife." I put my hand on her arm. "Sorry I forgot. A lot has gone on. Was he awful?"

She laughed into the darkness. "He offered me a lot to stay."

"I can imagine."

She half turned, one breast soft against my arm, and ran a finger up my leg. "Why tax your imagination?"

I wasn't especially in the mood, but my body was. The robes rustled off easily, their only virtue.

The moon was down now, and I could see only a dim outline of her in the starlight. It was strange to make love deprived of that sense. You would think the absence of it would amplify the others, but I can't say that it did, except that her heartbeat seemed very strong on the heel of my hand. Her breath was sweet with mint and the smell and taste of her body were agreeable; in fact, there was nothing about her body that I would have cared to change, inside or out, but nevertheless, our progress became difficult after a couple of minutes, and by mute agreement we slowed and stopped. We lay joined together for some time before she spoke.

"The timing is all wrong. I'm sorry." She drew her face across my arm and I felt tears. "I was just trying not to think about things."

"It's all right. The sand doesn't help, either." We had gotten a little bit inside, rubbing.

We talked for a while and then drowsed together. When the sky began to lighten, a hot wind from below the horizon woke us up. We went back to the shelter.

Everyone was asleep. We went to shower off the sand and she was amused to see my interest in her quicken. "Let's take that downstairs," she whispered, and I followed her down to her room.

The memory of the earlier incapability was there, but it was not greatly inhibiting. Being able to see her made the act more familiar, and besides she was very pleasant to see, from whatever angle. I was able to withhold myself only once, and so the interlude was shorter than either of us would have desired.

We slept together on her narrow bed. Or she slept, rather, while I watched the bar of sunlight grow on the opposite wall, and thought about how everything had changed.

They couldn't really say we had thirty years to live, since they had no idea what the enemy was doing. It might be three hundred; it might be less than one—but even with bodyswitch that was always true, as it was in the old days: sooner or later something would go wrong and you would die. That I might die at the same instant as ten thousand other people and a planet full of history—that was interesting. But as the room filled with light and I studied her quiet repose, I found her more interesting than that.

I was old enough to be immune to infatuation.

Something deep had been growing since Egypt, maybe before. On top of the pyramid, the rising sun dim in the mist, we had sat with our shoulders touching, watching the ancient forms appear below, and I felt a surge of numinism mixed oddly with content. She looked at me—I could only see her eyes—and we didn't have to say anything about the moment.

And now this. I was sure, without words, that she would share this, too. Whatever "this" was. England's versatile language, like mine and hers, is strangely hobbled by having the one word, love, stand for such a multiplicity of feelings.

Perhaps that lack reveals a truth, that no one love is like any other. There are other truths that you might forget, or ignore, distracted by the growth of love. In Petrosian there is a saying in the palindromic mood that always carries a sardonic, or at least ironic, inflection: "Happiness presages disaster presages happiness." So if you die happy, it means you were happy when you died. Good timing or bad?

6

!Oona M'vua had a room next to White Hill, and she was glad to switch with me, an operation that took about three minutes but was good for a much longer period of talk among the other artists. Lo was smugly amused, which in my temporary generosity of spirit I forgave.

Once we were adjacent, we found the button that made the wall slide away, and pushed the two beds together under her window. I'm afraid we were antisocial for a couple of days. It had been some time since either of us had had a lover. And I had never had one like her, literally, out of the dozens. She said that was because I had never been involved with a Seldenian, and I tactfully agreed, banishing five perfectly good memories to amnesia.

It's true that Seldenian women, and men as well, are better schooled than those of us from normal planets, in the techniques and subtleties of sexual expression. Part of "wholeness," which I suppose is a weak pun in English. It kept Lo, and not only him, from taking White Hill seriously as an artist: the fact that a Seldenian, to be "whole," must necessarily treat art as an everyday activity, usually subordinate to affairs of the heart, of the body. Or at least on the same level, which is the point.

The reality is that it *is* all one to them. What makes Seldenians so alien is that their need for balance in life dissolves hierarchy: this piece of art is valuable, and so is this orgasm, and so is this crumb of bread. The bread crumb connects to the artwork through the artist's metabolism, which connects to orgasm. Then through a fluid and automatic mixture of logic, metaphor, and rhetoric, the bread crumb links to soil, sunlight, nuclear fusion, the beginning and end of the universe. Any intelligent person can map out chains like that, but to White Hill it was automatic, drilled into her with her first nouns and verbs: *Everything is important. Nothing matters.* Change the world but stay relaxed.

I could never come around to her way of thinking. But then I was married for fifty Petrosian years to a woman who had stranger beliefs. (The marriage as a social contract actually lasted fifty-seven years; at the half-century mark we took a vacation from each other, and I never saw her again.) White Hill's worldview gave her an equanimity I had to envy. But my art needed unbalance and tension the way hers needed harmony and resolution.

By the fourth day most of the artists had joined us

in the shelter. Maybe they grew tired of wandering
through the bureaucracy. More likely, they were anx-
ious about their competitors' progress.

White Hill was drawing designs on large sheets of
buff paper and taping them up on our walls. She
worked on her feet, bare feet, pacing from diagram to
diagram, changing and rearranging. I worked directly
inside a shaping box, an invention White Hill had
heard of but had never seen. It's a cube of light a little
less than a metra wide. Inside is an image of a sculpture—or a rock or a lump of clay—that you can feel as
well as see. You can mold it with your hands or work
with finer instruments for cutting, scraping, chipping.
It records your progress constantly, so it's easy to take
chances; you can always run it back to an earlier stage.

I spent a few hours every other day cruising in a
flyer with Lo and a couple of other sculptors, looking
for native materials. We were severely constrained by
the decision to put the Memory Park inside, since
everything we used had to be small enough to fit
through the airlock and purging rooms. You could
work with large pieces, but you would have to slice
them up and reassemble them, the individual chunks
no bigger than two by two by three metras.

We tried to stay congenial and fair during these
expeditions. Ideally, you would spot a piece and we
would land by it or hover over it long enough to tag it
with your ID; in a day or two the robots would deliver
it to your "holding area" outside the shelter. If more
than one person wanted the piece, which happened as
often as not, a decision had to be made before it was
tagged. There was a lot of arguing and trading and
Solomon-style splitting, which usually satisfied the
requirements of something other than art.

The quality of light was changing for the worse.
Earthling planetary engineers were spewing bright dust

into the upper atmosphere, to reflect back solar heat. (They modified the nanophage-eating machinery for the purpose. That was also designed to fill the atmosphere full of dust, but at a lower level—and each grain of *that* dust had a tiny chemical brain.) It made the night sky progressively less interesting. I was glad White Hill had chosen to initiate our connection under the stars. It would be some time before we saw them again, if ever.

And it looked like "daylight" was going to be a uniform overcast for the duration of the contest. Without the dynamic of moving sunlight to continually change the appearance of my piece, I had to discard a whole family of first approaches to its design. I was starting to think along the lines of something irrational-looking; something the brain would reject as impossible. The way we mentally veer away from unthinkable things like the Sterilization, and our proximate future.

We had divided into two groups, and jokingly but seriously referred to one another as "originalists" and "realists." We originalists were continuing our projects on the basis of the charter's rules: a memorial to the tragedy and its aftermath, a stark sterile reminder in the midst of life. The realists took into account new developments, including the fact that there would probably never be any "midst of life" and, possibly, no audience, after thirty years.

I thought that was excessive. There was plenty of pathos in the original assignment. Adding another, impasto, layer of pathos along with irony and the artist's fear of personal death . . . well, we were doing art, not literature. I sincerely hoped their pieces would be fatally muddled by complexity.

If you asked White Hill which group she belonged to, she would of course say, "Both." I had no idea what form her project was going to take; we had agreed early on to surprise one another, and not impede each other with suggestions. I couldn't decipher even one-tenth of her diagrams. I speak Seldenian pretty well, but have never mastered the pictographs beyond the usual travelers' vocabulary. And much of what she was scribbling on the buff sheets of paper was in no language I recognized, an arcane technical symbology.

We talked about other things. Even about the future, as lovers will. Our most probable future was simultaneous death by fire, but it was calming and harmless to make "what if?" plans, in case our hosts somehow were able to find a way around that fate. We did have a choice of many possible futures, if we indeed had more than one. White Hill had never had access to wealth before. She didn't want to live lavishly, but the idea of being able to explore all the planets excited her.

Of course she had never tried living lavishly. I hoped one day to study her reaction to it, which would be strange. Out of the box of valuables I'd brought along, I gave her a necklace, a traditional beginning-love gift on Petros. It was a network of perfect emeralds and rubies laced in gold.

She examined it closely. "How much is this worth?"

"A million marks, more or less." She started to hand it back. "Please keep it. Money has no value here, no meaning."

She was at a loss for words, which was rare enough. "I understand the gesture. But you can't expect me to value this the way you do."

"I wouldn't expect that."

"Suppose I lose it? I might just set it down somewhere."

"I know. I'll still have given it to you."

She nodded and laughed. "All right. You people are strange." She slipped the necklace on, still latched, wiggling it over her ears. The colors glowed warm and cold against her olive skin.

She kissed me, a feather, and rushed out of our room wordlessly. She passed right by a mirror without looking at it.

After a couple of hours I went to find her. Lo said he'd seen her go out the door with a lot of water. At the beach I found her footprints marching straight west to the horizon.

She was gone for two days. I was working outside when she came back, wearing nothing but the necklace. There was another necklace in her hand: she had cut off her right braid and interwoven a complex pattern of gold and silver wire into a closed loop. She slipped it over my head and pecked me on the lips and headed for the shelter. When I started to follow she stopped me with a tired gesture. "Let me sleep, eat, wash." Her voice was a hoarse whisper. "Come to me after dark."

I sat down, leaning back against a good rock, and thought about very little, touching her braid and smelling it. When it was too dark to see my feet, I went in, and she was waiting.

7

I spent a lot of time outside, at least in the early morning and late afternoon, studying my accumulation of rocks and ruins. I had images of every piece in my shaping box's memory, but it was easier to visualize some aspects of the project if I could walk around the elements and touch them.

Inspiration is where you find it. We'd played with

an orrery in the museum in Rome, a miniature solar system that had been built of clock-work centuries before the Information Age. There was a wistful, humorous, kind of comfort in its jerky regularity.

My mental processes always turn things inside out. Find the terror and hopelessness in that comfort. I had in mind a massive but delicately balanced assemblage that would be viewed by small groups; their presence would cause it to teeter and turn ponderously. It would seem both fragile and huge (though of course the fragility would be an illusion), like the ecosystem that the Fwndyri so abruptly destroyed.

The assemblage would be mounted in such a way that it would seem always in danger of toppling off its base, but hidden weights would make that impossible. The sound of the rolling weights ought to produce a nice anxiety. Whenever a part tapped the floor, the tap would be amplified into a hollow boom.

If the viewers stood absolutely still, it would swing to a halt. As they left, they would disturb it again. I hoped it would disturb them as well.

The large technical problem was measuring the distribution of mass in each of my motley pieces. That would have been easy at home; I could rent a magnetic resonance densitometer to map their insides. There was no such thing on this planet (so rich in things I had no use for!), so I had to make do with a pair of robots and a knife edge. And then start hollowing the pieces out asymmetrically, so that once set in motion, the assemblage would tend to rotate.

I had a large number of rocks and artifacts to choose from, and was tempted to use no unifying principle at all, other than the unstable balance of the thing. Boulders and pieces of old statues and fossil machinery. The models I made of such a random collection were ambiguous, though. It was hard to tell whether they would look ominous or ludicrous, built to scale. A symbol of helplessness before an implacable enemy? Or a lurching, crashing junkpile? I decided to take a reasonably conservative approach, dignity rather than daring. After all, the audience would be Earthlings and, if the planet survived, tourists with more money than sophistication. Not my usual jury.

I was able to scavenge twenty long bars of shiny black monofiber, which would be the spokes of my irregular wheel. That would give it some unity of composition: make a cross with four similar chunks of granite at the ordinal points, and a larger chunk at the center. Then build up a web inside, monofiber lines linking bits of this and that.

Some of the people were moving their materials inside Amazonia, to work in the area marked off for the park. White Hill and I decided to stay outside. She said her project was portable, at this stage, and mine would be easy to disassemble and move.

After a couple of weeks, only fifteen artists remained with the project, inside Amazonia or out in the shelter. The others had either quit, surrendering to the passive depression that seemed to be Earth's new norm, or, in one case, committed suicide. The two from Wolf and Mijhóven opted for coldsleep, which might be deferred suicide. About one person in three slept through it; one in three came out with some kind of treatable mental disorder. The others went mad and died soon after reawakening, unable or unwilling to live.

Coldsleep wasn't done on Petros, although some Petrosians went to other worlds to indulge in it as a risky kind of time travel. Sleep until whatever's wrong with the world has changed. Some people even did it for financial speculation: buy up objects of art or antiques, and sleep for a century or more while their value increases. Of course their value might not increase significantly, or they might be stolen or coopted by family or government.

But if you can make enough money to buy a ticket to another planet, why not hold off until you had enough to go to a really *distant* one? Let time dilation compress the years. I could make a triangle from Petros to Skaal to Mijhóven and back, and more than 120 years would pass, while I lived through only three, with no danger to my mind. And I could take my objects of art along with me.

White Hill had worked with coldsleep veterans, or victims. None of them had been motivated by profit, given her planet's institutionalized antimaterialism, so most of them had been suffering from some psychological ill before they slept. It was rare for them to come out of the "treatment" improved, but they did come into a world where people like White Hill could at least attend them in their madness, perhaps guide them out.

I'd been to three times as many worlds as she. But she had been to stranger places.

8

The terraformers did their job too well. The days grew cooler and cooler, and some nights snow fell. The snow on the ground persisted into mornings for a while, and then through noon, and finally it began to pile up. Those of us who wanted to work outside had to improvise cold-weather clothing.

I liked working in the cold, although all I did was direct robots. I grew up in a small town south of New Haven, where winter was long and intense. At some level I associated snow and ice with the exciting pleasures that waited for us after school. I was to have my fill of it, though.

It was obvious I had to work fast, faster than I'd originally planned, because of the increasing cold. I wanted to have everything put together and working before I disassembled it and pushed it through the air-lock. The robots weren't made for cold weather, unfortunately. They had bad traction on the ice and sometimes their joints would seize up. One of them complained constantly, but of course it was the best worker, too, so I couldn't just turn it off and let it disappear under the drifts, an idea that tempted me.

White Hill often came out for a few minutes to stand and watch me and the robots struggle with the icy heavy boulders, machinery, and statuary. We took walks along the seashore that became shorter as the weather worsened. The last walk was a disaster.

We had just gotten to the beach when a sudden storm came up with a sandblast wind so violent that it blew us off our feet. We crawled back to the partial protection of the ruins and huddled together, the wind screaming so loudly that we had to shout to hear each other. The storm continued to mount and, in our terror, we decided to run for the shelter. White Hill slipped on some ice and suffered a horrible injury, a jagged piece of metal slashing her face diagonally from forehead to chin, blinding her left eye and tearing off part of her nose. Pearly bone showed through, cracked, at eyebrow, cheek, and chin. She rose up to one elbow and fell slack.

I carried her the rest of the way, immensely glad for the physical strength that made it possible. By the time we got inside she was unconscious and my white coat was a scarlet flag of blood.

A plastic-clad doctor came through immediately and did what she could to get White Hill out of immediate danger. But there was a problem with more sophisticated treatment. They couldn't bring the equipment out to our shelter, and White Hill wouldn't survive the stress of purging unless she had had a chance to heal for a while. Besides the facial wound, she had a broken elbow and collarbone and two cracked ribs.

For a week or so she was always in pain or numb. I sat with her, numb myself, her face a terrible puffed caricature of its former beauty, the wound glued up with plaskin the color of putty. Split skin of her eyelid slack over the empty socket.

The mirror wasn't visible from her bed, and she didn't ask for one, but whenever I looked away from her, her working hand came up to touch and catalogue the damage. We both knew how fortunate she was to be alive at all, and especially in an era and situation where the damage could all be repaired, given time and a little luck. But it was still a terrible thing to live with, an awful memory to keep reliving.

When she was more herself, able to talk through her ripped and pasted mouth, it was difficult for me to keep my composure. She had considerable philosophical, I suppose you could say spiritual, resources, but she was so profoundly stunned that she couldn't follow a line of reasoning very far, and usually wound up sobbing in frustration.

Sometimes I cried with her, although Petrosian men don't cry except in response to music. I had been a soldier once and had seen my ration of injury and death, and I always felt the experience had hardened me, to my detriment. But my friends who had been wounded or killed were just friends, and all of us lived then with the certainty that every day could be anybody's last one. To have the woman you love senselessly mutilated by an accident of weather was emotionally more arduous than losing a dozen companions to the steady erosion of war, a different kind of weather.

I asked her whether she wanted to forget our earlier agreement and talk about our projects. She said no; she was still working on hers, in a way, and she still wanted it to be a surprise. I did manage to distract her, playing with the shaping box. We made cartoonish representations of Lo and old Norita, and combined them in impossible sexual geometries. We shared a limited kind of sex ourselves, finally.

The doctor pronounced her well enough to be taken apart, and both of us were scourged and reappeared on the other side. White Hill was already in surgery when I woke up; there had been no reason to revive her before beginning the restorative processes.

I spent two days wandering through the blandness of Amazonia, jungle laced through concrete, quartering the huge place on foot. Most areas seemed catatonic. A few were boisterous with end-of-the-world hysteria. I checked on her progress so often that they eventually assigned a robot to call me up every hour, whether or not there was any change.

On the third day I was allowed to see her, in her sleep. She was pale but seemed completely restored. I watched her for an hour, perhaps more, when her eyes suddenly opened. The new one was blue, not green, for some reason. She didn't focus on me.

"Dreams feed art," she whispered in Petrosian; "and art feeds dreams." She closed her eyes and slept again.

9

She didn't want to go back out. She had lived all her life in the tropics, even the year she spent in bondage, and the idea of returning to the ice that

had slashed her was more than repugnant. Inside
Amazonia it was always summer, now, the authorities
trying to keep everyone happy with heat and light and
jungle flowers.

I went back out to gather her things. Ten large
sheets of buff paper I unstuck from our walls and
stacked and rolled. The necklace, and the satchel of
rare coins she had brought from Seldene, all her
worldly wealth.

I considered wrapping up my own project, giving
the robots instructions for its dismantling and transport, so that I could just go back inside with her and
stay. But that would be chancy. I wanted to see the
thing work once before I took it apart.

So I went through the purging again, although it
wasn't strictly necessary; I could have sent her things
through without hand-carrying them. But I wanted to
make sure she was on her feet before I left her for several weeks.

She was not on her feet, but she was dancing. When I
recovered from the purging, which now took only half a
day, I went to her hospital room and they referred me to
our new quarters, a three-room dwelling in a place
called Plaza de Artistes. There were two beds in the bedroom, one a fancy medical one, but that was worlds better than trying to find privacy in a hospital.

There was a note floating in the air over the bed
saying she had gone to a party in the common room. I
found her in a gossamer wheelchair, teaching a hand
dance to Denli om Cord, while a harpist and flautist
from two different worlds tried to settle on a mutual
key.

She was in good spirits. Denli remembered an
engagement and I wheeled White Hill out onto a balcony that overlooked a lake full of sleeping birds,
some perhaps real.

It was hot outside, always hot. There was a mist of perspiration on her face, partly from the light exercise of the dance, I supposed. In the light from below, the mist gave her face a sculpted appearance, unsparing sharpness, and there was no sign left of the surgery.

"I'll be out of the chair tomorrow," she said, "at least ten minutes at a time." She laughed, "*Stop* that!"

"Stop what?"

"Looking at me like that."

I was still staring at her face. "It's just . . . I suppose it's such a relief."

"I know." She rubbed my hand. "They showed me pictures, of before. You looked at that for so many days?"

"I saw you."

She pressed my hand to her face. The new skin was taut but soft, like a baby's. "Take me downstairs?"

10

It's hard to describe, especially in light of later developments, disintegrations, but that night of fragile love-making marked a permanent change in the way we linked, or at least the way I was linked to her: I've been married twice, long and short, and have been in some kind of love a hundred times. But no woman has ever owned me before.

This is something we do to ourselves. I've had enough women who *tried* to possess me, but always was able to back or circle away, in literal preservation of self. I always felt that life was too long for one woman.

Certainly part of it is that life is not so long any-more. A larger part of it was the run through the screaming storm, her life streaming out of her, and my stewardship, or at least companionship, afterward, during her slow transformation back into health and physical beauty. The core of her had never changed, though, the stubborn serenity that I came to realize, that warm night, had finally infected me as well.

The bed was a firm narrow slab, cooler than the dark air heavy with the scent of Earth flowers. I helped her onto the bed (which instantly conformed to her) but from then on it was she who cared for me, saying that was all she wanted, all she really had strength for. When I tried to reverse that, she reminded me of a holiday palindrome that has sexual overtones in both our languages: Giving is taking is giving.

11

We spent a couple of weeks as close as two people can be. I was her lover and also her nurse, as she slowly strengthened. When she was able to spend most of her day in normal pursuits, free of the wheelchair or "intelligent" bed (with which we had made a threesome, at times uneasy), she urged me to go back outside and finish up. She was ready to concentrate on her own project, too. Impatient to do art again, a good sign.

I would not have left so soon if I had known what her project involved. But that might not have changed anything.

As soon as I stepped outside, I knew it was going to take longer than planned. I had known from the inside monitors how cold it was going to be, and how many ceemetras of ice had accumulated, but I didn't really *know* how bad it was until I was standing there, looking at my piles of materials locked in opaque glaze. A good thing I'd left the robots inside the shelter, and a good thing I had left a few hand tools outside. The door was buried under two metras of snow and ice. I sculpted myself a passageway, an application of artistic skills I'd never foreseen.

I debated calling White Hill and telling her that I would be longer than expected. We had agreed not to interrupt each other, though, and it was likely she'd started working as soon as I left.

The robots were like a bad comedy team, but I could only be amused by them for an hour or so at a time. It was so cold that the water vapor from my breath froze into an icy sheath on my beard and mustache. Breathing was painful; deep breathing probably dangerous.

So most of the time, I monitored them from inside the shelter. I had the place to myself; everyone else long since gone into the dome. When I wasn't working I drank too much, something I had not done regularly in centuries.

It was obvious that I wasn't going to make a working model. Delicate balance was impossible in the shifting gale. But the robots and I had our hands full, and other grasping appendages engaged, just dismantling the various pieces and moving them through the lock. It was unexciting but painstaking work. We did all the laser cuts inside the shelter, allowing the rock to come up to room temperature so it didn't spall or shatter. The air-conditioning wasn't quite equal to the challenge, and neither were the cleaning robots, so after a while it was like living in a foundry: everywhere a kind of greasy slickness of rock dust, the air dry and metallic.

So it was with no regret that I followed the last slice into the airlock myself, even looking forward to the scourging if White Hill was on the other side.

She wasn't. A number of other people were missing, too. She left this note behind:

I knew from the day we were called back here what my new piece would have to be, and I knew I had to keep it from you, to spare you sadness. And to save you the frustration of trying to talk me out of it.

As you may know by now, scientists have determined that the Fwndyri indeed have sped up the Sun's evolution somehow. It will continue to warm, until in thirty or forty years there will be an explosion called the "helium flash." The Sun will become a red giant, and the Earth will be incinerated.

There are no starships left, but there is one avenue of escape. A kind of escape.

Parked in high orbit there is a huge interplanetary transport that was used in the terraforming of Mars. It's a couple of centuries older than you, but like yourself it has been excellently preserved. We are going to ride it out to a distance sufficient to survive the Sun's catastrophe, and there remain until the situation improves, or does not.

This is where I enter the picture. For our survival to be meaningful in this thousand-year war, we have to resort to coldsleep. And for a large number of people to survive centuries of coldsleep, they need my jaturnary skills. Alone, in the ice, they would go slowly mad. Connected through the matrix of my mind, they will have a sense of community, and may come out of it intact.

I will be gone, of course. I will be by the time you read this. Not dead, but immersed in service. I could not be revived if this were only a hundred people for a hundred days. This will be a thousand, perhaps for a thousand years.

No one else on Earth can do jaturnary, and there is neither time nor equipment for me to transfer my ability to anyone. Even if there were,

I'm not sure I would trust anyone else's skill. So I am gone.

My only loss is losing you. Do I have to elaborate on that?

You can come if you want. In order to use the transport, I had to agree that the survivors be chosen in accordance with the Earth's strict class system—starting with dear Norita, and from that pinnacle, on down—but they were willing to make exceptions for all of the visiting artists. You have until mid-Deciembre to decide; the ship leaves Januar first.

If I know you at all, I know you would rather stay behind and die. Perhaps the prospect of living "in" me could move you past your fear of coldsleep; your aversion to jaturnary. If not, not.

I love you more than life. But this is more than that. Are we what we are?

W. H.

The last sentence is a palindrome in her language, not mine, that I believe has some significance beyond the obvious.

12

I did think about it for some time. Weighing a quick death, or even a slow one, against spending centuries locked frozen in a tiny room with Norita and her ilk. Chattering on at the speed of synapse, and me unable to not listen.

I have always valued quiet, and the eternity of it that I face is no more dreadful than the eternity of quiet that preceded my birth.

If White Hill were to be at the other end of those centuries of torture, I know I could tolerate the excruciation. But she was dead now, at least in the sense that I would never see her again.

Another woman might have tried to give me a false hope, the possibility that in some remote future the process of *jaturnary* would be advanced to the point where her personality could be recovered. But she knew how unlikely that would be even if teams of scientists could be found to work on it, and years could be found for them to work in. It would be like unscrambling an egg.

Maybe I would even do it, though, if there were just some chance that, when I was released from that din of garrulous bondage, there would be something like a real world, a world where I could function as an artist. But I don't think there will even be a world where I can function as a man.

There probably won't be any humanity at all, soon enough. What they did to the Sun they could do to all of our stars, one assumes. They win the war, the Extermination, as my parent called it. Wrong side exterminated.

Of course the Fwndyri might not find White Hill and her charges. Even if they do find them, they might leave them preserved as an object of study.

The prospect of living on eternally under those circumstances, even if there were some growth to compensate for the immobility and the company, holds no appeal.

13

What I did in the time remaining before mid-Deciembre was write this account. Then I had it translated by a xenolinguist into a form that she said could be decoded by any creature sufficiently similar to humanity to make any sense of the story. Even the Fwndyri, perhaps. They're human enough to want to wipe out a competing species.

I'm looking at the preliminary sheets now, English down the left side and a jumble of dots, squares, and triangles down the right. Both sides would have looked equally strange to me a few years ago.

White Hill's story will be conjoined to a standard book that starts out with basic mathematical principles, in dots and squares and triangles, and moves from that into physics, chemistry, biology. Can you go from biology to the human heart? I have to hope so. If this is read by alien eyes, long after the last human breath is stilled, I hope it's not utter gibberish.

14

So I will take this final sheet down to the translator and then deliver the whole thing to the woman who is going to transfer it to permanent sheets of platinum, which will be put in a prominent place aboard the transport. They could last a million years, or ten million, or more. After the Sun is a cinder, and the ship is a frozen block enclosing a thousand bits of frozen flesh, she will live on in this small way.

So now my work is done. I'm going outside, to the quiet.

In Saturn Time

WILLIAM BARTON

William Barton has been, mostly without fanfare, developing into a considerable writer in the SF field over the past decade. He has published several novels and a number of short stories, but has drawn relatively little attention. This story is an original from *Amazing: the Anthology,* edited by Kim Mohan, who also produced one, perhaps the last, issue of the oldest surviving SF magazine title in 1995. "In Saturn Time" is an alternate history story about science and space travel, set in part in the future, a harder trick than it might seem. It uses the old "looking backward" technique to good effect and yields a memorable science fiction story.

O n the Ides of October, 1974, LM pilot Nick Jensen rode across the Lunar regolith under a featureless black sky not far from the north pole of the Moon. Almighty strange here, he thought, nothing like what we saw at the other six landing sites. Maybe a little bit like Taurus-Littrow, but . . .

Long, long shadows cast across the surface, black lanes running off to infinity behind crater walls, every rock the origin of a dark finger that pointed away from the Sun, the Sun itself a glare right on the southern horizon. Post a big sign: Penumbra Starts Here. Scary when you looked around the sky, too. The Earth was nowhere in sight, had disappeared below the horizon as they'd descended the long hill away from the lander's touchdown site.

Orbiter pilot Ben Santori's voice crackled in his earphones, lightly fuzzed by static. "Inertial nav puts you at seven klicks."

Nick said, "Rog. Coming up on Black Hills terminator." Somewhere up in that flat black sky, *Apollo 21*'s orbiting CSM *Nightwing* would be a silvery fleck. And somewhere behind them, back up the twin tracks the rover was leaving in the dust, in the direction of Peary's north rim mountain structure, Lunar Module *Flamebird* was a barely visible golden freckle on the gray landscape. Seven kilometers. A long walk back if this thing breaks down.

Goddamned lucky to be here. Eight long years in training since acceptance into the 1966 astronaut candidate pool. Watching men from the earlier intakes get their second and third flights, Alan Shepard on the Moon, Walter Cronkite jolly on TV . . . As Nixon canceled the Air Force's Manned Orbiting Laboratory, then the advanced Apollo Lunar program, then what little remained of Apollo Applications other than *Skylab* . . .

Nick glanced over at mission commander Stan Freeman in the rover's left-hand seat, craning his neck a little to see around the EVA helmet's visor rim. These outer hard-hat helmets with their gold visor structure were a nuisance. We should just go with the red cloth cover they rigged for the orbital EVAs. "Time."

"On time, on target." Freeman's voice came over the earphones clear and crisp, marked by his familiar Chicago accent. Freeman's luck was even greater, contaminating everything he touched. First black man in space. First black man on the Moon. Mission commander. Ph.D. in mechanical engineering. Darling of the press, interviewed by all and sundry only hours before liftoff.

Lucky for us. Young black moderate Jesse Jackson giving a speech in which he praised NASA, saying King would've been proud, telling them all how much King had liked *Star Trek,* giving the mission SCLC's blessing and, by extension, its approval of the whole revived space program.

They pulled up on the edge of shadow, near a low, hummocky ridge, the solar wind- and ejecta-eroded wall of a very old highland-type crater, unclipped their restraints and got out of the rover. Nick staggered slightly, bouncing inside his suit.

"Watch it."

"I'm all right. A little disoriented from the ride." Wouldn't matter if I fell down anyway. Just get the suit dirty. And, though stiff and clumsy and uncomfortable as hell, these Apollo EVA suits are nothing if not sturdy.

"All set?"

"Lead on, MacDuff." The newsmen interpreting for the home viewing audience would like that. Hardy, bluff, brave, uncomplicated men, our representatives in the Great Void. Nick smiled to himself. Then why do we keep having post-mission nervous breakdowns? It was getting to be a NASA in-joke. Go to the Moon. Then the nuthouse.

They walked into night.

"Dark here."

Nick said, "Yeah. Let's hold here for cooldown." Stepping into shadow, they'd just taken a 100K+ temperature drop, and another few steps might double that. Orbital sensing said the minimum temperature down inside the crater's permanent shadow was no more than 100K, theory said it might be as low as 40K. The suits *were* sturdy, but not invulnerable.

Lovely luminous night, night that . . . Nick flipped up the gold visor. "Jesus!"

"What . . . " Freeman flipped up his own visor and looked. "Oh . . . " Soft whisper of delight. Above them, the sky was flooded by the gentle radiance of a hundred million suns, distant, steady needles of light, white, pale blue, tawny red-orange here and there, the Milky Way like a river of golden dust.

Lucky to be here. All because Morris Udall and a determined band of party conservatives took the Democratic nomination away from the McGovernites' Children's Crusade, all because Nixon got a little paranoid and pulled that Watergate crap, crap that lost him the election.

President Udall standing up there on Inauguration Day, decreeing that U.S. military forces would turn their equipment over to the ARVN in situ and evacuate Vietnam forthwith, ". . . because, right or wrong, it's time we were done with this sorry business . . . "

President Udall sitting in the Oval Office signing an executive order that canceled Nixon's space transportation system, reinstating Apollo and AAP, ". . . because we spent forty billion dollars acquiring this technology. Let's get the benefit of it before we go out and buy another one."

And, three weeks after that, astronaut trainee Nick Jensen had been assigned to the *Apollo 21* prime crew. *Apollo 17* to the Moon, numbers 18 through 20 up to *Skylab 1*, then back to the Moon again. Ten more flights to the Moon were decreed, and another *Skylab,* and anywhere between three and seven freestanding AAP missions. After that? Who cares? This will keep us busy through 1981. . . .

They walked on into the deeper darkness, picking over rocks, skirting small, shallow craters, taking samples, talking to Santori in orbit, back through the LM link to Mission Control.

"Okay, let's get the lights on." This was the other limiting factor. It was still seventy Kelvins here, not enough to redline the suits, not even close, but the power necessary to run this new lighting system would drain the backpack batteries in less than forty-five minutes. Ten minutes in here was what the profile called for.

Flame on. The crater bottom lit up around them, rock and dirt and dust and nothing else. Disappointing. "Over there." Nick pointed at what looked like a low ridge of black talus near the steeper southern wall of the depression.

He kneeled by it and prodded with his rock hammer. "Sintered solid, I guess, whatever it is."

"Crack off a sample and let's get out of here. This place is a bust." The commentators would be talking about that one, all right. . . .

Nick hit the rock a sharp blow with the hammer's pointed end, breaking a chunk loose. Flash of bright white. "Uh." He picked up the sample and turned it over. Opaque white rock, colored like chalk but hard like granite, no crystalline structure, covered by a thin black rind.

Freeman was suddenly kneeling beside him, reaching out, taking the piece, looking at it himself, watching light glint off the flat, exposed ice surface. "Well, well. Happy birthday, Nick."

Summer 1977. It was the best of times. . . . Period. No Dickensian dichotomies at all.

Nick Jensen floated cradled in the arms of his gas-powered astronaut maneuvering unit sixty meters from *Apollo 29*'s CSM, silver and white cone-cylinder-cone hanging above Earth's bright limb. Beautiful day for an EVA. You could look straight down eight hundred kilometers on the brilliant blue Pacific, through thin stratus above the green hills of Hawaii. Not as good a view as the one from higher up. You couldn't *really* tell it was all one giant shield volcano, just like the bigger one on Mars, but still . . .

Viking 1. Still laughing about that badly tuned color camera. "Jeez, it looks just like Utah! Wait a minute, let's have a look at the color wheel. . . ." Red sky at night, sailors' delight.

A red-helmeted head poked out of the command module's open hatch, and Amy Jordan's voice was sharp and distinct in his earphones. "Nick? We should be able to eyeball the Agena any time now."

"Copy that." She was a superb engineer, had had a

decisive hand in designing the radio-telescope mission, but the media had ignored all that, going on and on and on about having this sweet young thing fly in the cramped confines of an Apollo capsule with two men, about how she'd have to do all her private business right in front of them. . . .

Worth an exasperated sigh, an attempt at explanation: This is business. Important business, and we're all professionals, polite to each other . . . Order of the Dolphin, my ass . . .

Smirk, smirk; wink, wink. All business. Right. *Sure* it is, buddy . . .

Nick hit the hand controllers, compressed air stuttering behind his back, and did a slow turn. About ten meters away the completed radio telescope floated, a twenty-meter dish they'd brought up disassembled in the CSM's science bay, where a lunar mission would've carried camera packs and one of those little subsatellites. When they'd begun, just a week ago, it had been no more than a collection of wire mesh and cabling and electronic boxes. Now . . .

A lovely, shining flower of silver and black, floating in low Earth orbit, waiting for its life in space to begin. There. The Agena booster was just a scintilla of light on the edge of vision, out in black night. "I've got it. How far?"

Amy said, "Radar says ten klicks."

"Okay. Bring her in." Once they had this thing coupled to the telescope and got it on its way to GEO, they could go home. . . . Christ, I love being in space, but . . . two weeks packed into a cabin the size of a compact station wagon interior with two other people, people who smelled a little worse with each passing day. . . . That sort of thing could wear thin pretty fast.

Another voice in his ears, faintly tinged with a hiss

of static, a little echoey from its trip through two ground links and one comsat: "*Apollo 29,* Mission Control."

"That you, Jake?"

"Roger." Jake Burnett was the third-shift capcom, hoping to get up here one of these days. He said, "Be advised the two-man crew of *Soyuz L-4* has successfully touched down on the edge of Oceanus Procellarum."

So, Bykovsky and Leonov on the Moon. "Took 'em long enough." And it would be a big help. Udall had won reelection, still supported the ongoing program, but the 1980 election would get here sooner or later, and once *Apollo 40* flew . . .

No one knew what would be coming after that.

Burnett said, "Here's hoping. We do need the competition." You could say things like that now; the press didn't listen to orbital work chit-chat anymore.

"Yeah. Wonder if *they* know that?"

"Probably better than we do."

Amy Jordan said, "Guys? Coming up on Agena rendezvous in four minutes. We'd better get onto the business at hand."

Business. All business.

He said, "Roger. Copy that." Get to work.

Late spring 1980.

Nick stood on the grass beside Mosquito Inlet not far from the VIP Viewing Stand, just across the big ditch from the Press Site, waiting, sweating a little in the hot Florida sun. *Always makes me itch a little bit. . . .* Reporters seldom came for the launches anymore, big countdown clock tallying away for no one sometimes, even when it was a trip to the Moon.

Moon? Ho-hum. Seen one moon, seen 'em all. Let us know when you're ready for Mars. Or, better still, the stars, just like on TV. . . .

Out in force today though, clogging the press bleachers, forming long, yackety lines by the washroom doors, crowding the wagons of the hot dog vendors they'd let in for the day.

Nick looked at his watch, then across the inlet, up the length of the causeway to the launch site. Above the vehicle there was still a wisp of smoky vapor, but they'd be shutting the pressure bleed and topoff valves in a few minutes, going into the final countdown.

The Saturn 5M was not a pretty vehicle. Not pretty at all. Our future, though. You couldn't even see the core Saturn 5 vehicle, S-ID and S-II stages hidden by four 360-inch segmented-solid strap-on boosters. All you could see was the S-VB poking out the top, a modified S-II stage with five restartable J-2s that had taken the place of the old S-IVB, surmounted by an odd-looking, forty-foot-diameter hammerhead payload shroud.

Could be a big mistake, using the first test vehicle to fly a real mission. An important mission. One of those never-flown field joints springs a leak at altitude, maybe right after max-Q, we'll see a pretty big bang up there. . . .

Well. At least it was unmanned. It's only money.

Nick looked around again, at the sprinkling of VIPs who'd come to see the thing off. Outgoing President Udall standing with D.C. Senator Jesse Jackson and Vice President Mondale, Udall's designated successor. President come to see his last big space-related decision come to fruition.

Fritz Mondale looking away, hardly interested in what was going on, just knowing he had to show the flag as he steadily slipped in the polls. Primaries not going too well. There's never going to be a President Mondale. Are we in deep shit?

He looked at the slender man at his side. Governor

Brown, standing next to Gene Roddenberry, had a pair of binoculars pressed to his eyes, looking intently toward the pad, teeth showing in what looked like a little bit of a grin, or maybe just a glare-squint grimace. Hard to tell with this . . . very strange dude.

Watching the governor walk around with Linda Ronstadt this morning, he'd tried to listen in. What would *I* have said, with a little cutie like that in my clutches? Telling her all about the vast resources we'd find out in the Asteroid Belt. How it would postpone the coming world crisis for centuries. Maybe that's what I would've said, too. Right.

So this is, just maybe, the Democratic front-runner, some little ex-seminarian determinedly levering the fat cats' hands off the wheels of power. Political journalists licking their chops. Because, on the other side of the aisle, it was looking to be Ronald Reagan. Battle of the Californians, they said. Or better still, Moonbeam versus Bonzo.

Jesus Christ.

Out on the pad, the vehicle had stopped smoking, thin haze of white frost evaporating away in the sun. Nick said, "Thirty seconds, Governor."

Brown pulled the binoculars off his face, leaving little red rings where he'd been pressing them in too hard. "Okay, Nick. You promise me this thing's going to work?" Thin grin, sardonic, not a man who said things by accident.

Nick nodded slowly. "Well. 'Four *neins*,' Governor."

Brown grinned wider, recognizing the reference. "We'll see," he said, putting the binoculars back to his eyes. "Call me Jerry."

The loudspeaker said, "T minus ten seconds. Sustainer core ignition . . . " Out on the pad, a glare of orange light down in the flame trough, a thick boil of greasy black smoke as high-grade jet aviation fuel burned in liquid oxygen. Silence. ". . . three, two, one . . . solids . . . "

A huge burst of white smoke, blowing the black smoke away, clouds forming, yellow fire boiling crazily in their depths.

Loudspeaker: "Liftoff . . . "

The Saturn 5M bounded off the pad, then seemed to pause, staggering visibly, Nick's breath trapped in his chest, heart pounding. Oh, God. . . . It seemed to take hold of itself, straighten visibly, then climb into the sky, climb, trailed by a thick column of gray-white smoke, smoke that seemed to grow organically from the base of the rocket. . . .

Crackling roar, sound having crossed the intervening three miles, a few brief seconds of familiar F-1 fire, then the hard *bump-ROAR* of the solids lighting, something almighty powerful beating on his chest, trying to push him backward, sixteen million pounds of thrust from the four strap-on boosters, another seven and a half million from the liquid fuel engines, seven hundred thousand pounds of payload headed for low Earth orbit.

Nick glanced over at the governor. Jerry Brown's head was tipped back, following the Moonbase as it left for its new home not far from Amundsen Crater and the south pole of the Moon. He had Roddenberry by the arm, shaking the producer hard. And he was laughing out loud.

Nick looked back at the Saturn 5M, listened to its diminishing thunder, and thought, Maybe President Brown will want to give that little cutie an asteroid for her birthday. And, just maybe, we can talk him into funding the S-VI nuclear stage we'd like to stick on this thing, calling it the Saturn 5N. Just maybe.

What was it the governor had said? "We'll see . . . "

In the late summer of 1984, Nick was back on the Moon, walking the dusty plain not far from Lunar Polar Station 1, not quite relishing the job of escorting the VIP. Not quite. But the old man had proven to be an interesting enough character, making the professional astronauts want to like him, despite their irritation with the whole program.

A journalist in space was bad enough, but sending one of these bastards to the Moon? It was an order of magnitude more outrageous than putting that teacher in space aboard *Skylab 3*, wasting an Apollo Transport flight just to put her up there for two weeks. Now this, wasting a flight to the Moon . . .

But it happened as President Brown decreed, probably just part of his reelection strategy.

They were setting up at what appeared to be a strategic location, the base down-Sun, a collection of half-buried modules, rovers parked here and there, solar collectors sticking up like silver radar dishes against a dramatic backdrop, the low, rounded hills of a crater ringwall, looking for all the world like some denuded and dead Appalachian range.

And the old man was the most useful member of the EVA team just now. He knew just how to set up the cameras, which connectors to plug in where, how to lay the cables so no one would trip over them, issuing commands in a calm, quiet voice. . . .

That same reassuring voice of wisdom I've been hearing since I was a kid. And you know that's why Brown picked him. The President's one smart cookie, all right. Dole doesn't have a chance.

It was a smart choice, but we were all against it, especially when we found out who was going. Come *on* . . . a man his age up here? But he's pushing *seventy!* D'you realize what it's like, three fucking days stuffed inside the cabin of a five-man Apollo Transport?

Sure, he'll be all right at Moonbase, but what about the *trip?*

But the oldest professional astronaut still on flight status is sixty-three now. You want us to can him? No, but . . . How about you, Nick? Going to be forty-four this fall. When you think we should retire you?

Vision of the upcoming Mars mission crew assignments. Um. Well, I sorta hoped I had a few good years left in me. . . .

And he'd been okay on the trip up after all. Keeping his hands off the hardware, looking out the window, doing his standups . . . and suffering not a trace of space sickness, while the flight's other rookie floated in his acceleration couch, retching quietly. . . .

And, sitting there on the pad, just as T minus thirty seconds was called, he'd chuckled softly and said, "This kinda reminds me of Paris . . . "

Uh. *Paris.*

"Sure. I went in with the Airborne. Jumped with them, carrying a goddamn *typewriter* . . . "

Then, sitting on the Extended LM's floor, as required, face far below the level of the window while the engine rumbled and we dropped toward touchdown, he'd whipped out a kid's folding cardboard periscope, the kind of thing you could still buy for 98 cents, holding it up so he could see out. *That* won us over, a kind of guileless astronautical ingenuity, like smuggling a ham sandwich onto the first space flight. . . .

Now, the old man came bouncing gently over. "You all set?"

"Yes, sir. Just tell me where to stand."

The old man looked around, quickly, professional, glancing briefly at the camera, then scuffed an "X" in the dust. "On your mark, Nick. Now open your face-shield so the folks at home can see that pretty face." The old man grinned at him from under his trademark mustache. "And please. Call me Walter . . . "

The red light came on then, and the old man turned to face the world. "August 14, 1984," he said. "Good evening. This is Walter Cronkite reporting to you live from the surface of the Moon . . . "

May 1988.

Nick sat, sort of, in front of the telefax console in the science module, toes tucked into foot restraints, seatbelt across his lap. A little unsteady, hard to keep the mouse cursor positioned on the little white

<NEXT> Button, but . . . *click-click.*

Breathtaking. Unbelievable. *Voyager 3*'s Io lander had sent back a steady stream of images, almost in real time as it dropped out of orbit, actually passing through the thin, hazy umbrella-plume of an erupting sulfur volcano, taking samples on its way to the surface.

Click-click. On the surface now, looking out across a rolling, low-relief yellow plain. In the distance, the eruption was a faint, almost invisible inverted cone against a featureless black sky.

Click-click. Christ . . . The camera had panned around, deliberately tilted up by the programmers, looking just where they figured . . .

Fat, banded Jupiter, a sullen orange crescent lying on its side, sun beyond it a dimmed-out spark. There. That little bit of crud had to be Amalthea, and . . .

Image of myself out on the surface of that moon, clad in an Apollo moonsuit, bounding across the dusty yellow plains, Jupiter in the sky above me, and the other moons and . . .

Nick shook his head slowly. Not in my lifetime,

anyway. Not until we work out a technology to shield against the ambient radiation. By the time we have *that,* we'll be thinking about Bussard ramjets and what *star* we'll be wanting to visit first. I wish . . .

He smiled to himself. Listen to me, wishing for the stars. Sudden memory of himself as a teenager, a senior in high school, turning on the TV and hearing Frank McGee discuss the significance of *Sputnik.* And hearing some expert say that, just maybe, some small child, a toddler perhaps, would one day walk on the Moon. Incredible. And, of course, the first man who *did* walk on the Moon was already an adult, already flying jet aircraft . . .

He pulled the mouse cursor up to the menu bar and popped open the SELECTION pulldown, clicked on "V-4, G-IV Lander." <NEXT>—The surface of Callisto, seen close up, was almost indistinguishable from the cratered highlands of the Earth's moon. Outside Jupiter's Van Allen belts. Just maybe, someone will go there soon. . . .

Maybe. Maybe. But no one knew what Jesse Jackson would do if he won the election this fall. Continue the program? Cancel it? Maybe. But then, no one knew what would happen if the Republicans somehow took over either. J. Danforth Quayle? Christ . . .

He sighed and clicked the EXIT icon, docked the mouse in its little monitor-side pocket, and unhooked from the chair. This is all very nice, but there's work to be done. He floated out through the forward hatch, through the node and into the command module, where Jake Burnett was holding down the fort.

"About time you got up here, pal. I've *really* got to pee!"

Nick smiled. "Sorry. I keep looking at those damned *Voyager* photos . . . "

Jake unhooked himself from the acceleration couch

and floated above the control console, essentially filling the window. He grinned and nodded. "You and me both. Wouldn't that be a kick, going to fucking *Jupiter?*"

"Yeah."

When he was gone, Nick pulled himself down in the chair, strapped in and relaxed, scanning the CRT screens and LED readouts, making sure God was in his Heaven and all was right with the world. Okay. Then he sat back to stare out the window and daydream.

Jupiter, for Christ's sake . . .

But this room, here, now, was filled with soft, ruddy light, light reflected from the surface of a dull red world rolling slowly by below. Okay, coming up on it. . . .

Valles Marineris slid over the horizon, an enormous gash in the side of Mars, as if some giant rock had struck the planet a glancing blow, cutting it open, threatening to spill its guts into the void, looking for all the world like an unsutured wound.

And in forty-eight hours I'll be down there. Butterflies fluttered briefly, exploring the far reaches of his intestines. Day after tomorrow and we'll be setting down on the north rim of Coprates. Me, Jake, and Amy making the first manned touchdown. Then. Then. *Ares* carried five additional disposable aeroshields, enough fuel for the lander to set down six times, at six different sites. And each crew member would get one landing, until all eighteen of them had been down.

And me, Mission Commander. Piloting the first lander, climbing down the ladder first.

I guess, he thought, watching the terminator come up, watching a Martian sunset come over the horizon, I better start thinking about what I'm going to say.

Though the late winter and early spring of 1993 had been incredibly wet, what with the Big Snow, then one rainstorm band after another sweeping across the country, west to east, on toward summer the weather stabilized, blue skies dominating the southeast, Florida warming up nicely. And, on a fine, sunny June morning, Nick Jensen stood atop the VAB with his binoculars, watching and waiting.

Sitting on the pad, it didn't look like much after a decade and more of the big 5Ms and Ns, but here it was, the Saturn 5R and its . . . payload? Well, not quite, but the term did sort of fit the new second stage. Inspecting it through the binoculars, he couldn't help but feel a resurgence of the anger that had boiled in him for the past couple of years.

Just on the losing side, that's all. Regroup, get on to the next thing. The worst mistake we can all make is to continue an argument after one side has claimed victory. Bad enough having all those fights in front of President Jackson, whose support for the space program seemed tepid at best after eight years of Brown telling us, "Go for it."

But we should've built the SSTO, the demonstrator at least. . . . Built it up out of the old S-IVB stages we've got sitting around in storage because there're no more Saturn 5As for them to ride. Aerospike engine, gas-layer reentry shield, a *real* spaceship at last . . .

But we did lose the argument.

And they built this thing instead.

So, good idea or bad, there it is.

Out on refurbished Pad 39A, the Saturn 5R was a highly modified S-I stage, the so-called S-IG, with those redesigned 90/110 throttlable F-IR engines, slightly lengthened tankage because the . . . second stage . . . was a lot lighter than the S-II/S-IVB/Apollo combination had been . . . and wings. Big damned delta wings and vertical stabilizer. Big bumps on the fourth side, pods where the landing skids folded away.

A reusable S-I stage, radio-controlled glide-back booster . . .

Waste of time, we said. Waste of money. Spend the five billion dollars designing something new, something with up-to-date hardware. Dammit, this thing is based on 1950's technology!

But its designers just laughed, then turned to a puzzled President Jackson and said, 1930's, really; this thing's not so much more than a giant V-2, after all. Getting our money's worth, all right.

And, on top of it, something that looked like a cross between an X-15 and a fat-bodied cargo plane, Max Faget's long-championed "straight-wing orbiter," white-painted bird, *Star Spear* in sleek black letters down the side, NASA meatball logo on the tail empennage.

Twenty thousand pounds payload seems like nothing compared to the seven hundred thousand-plus you can loft with a 5M. On the other hand, it's two hundred dollars a pound compared to fifteen hundred . . .

There.

Out on the pad, the vapor stopped drifting, the count went down, and the engines lit, boil of black smoke, red-orange flame down the deflector channels, and the first element of the Space Transportation System lifted off, twenty-four years after it'd first been proposed, seventeen years behind schedule.

Long yellow-white flame licking around the launch tower, kerosene fire, lifting six crew and a cargo of consumables up to the space station, because old Max knew his ship would fly. Nick took the binoculars away from his eyes and watched it go, spaceship turning into a bright speck far out over the ocean.

Flicker-flash. Staging. Bright white fleck of the orbiter, running on its two hydrogen-powered M-1 engines, separating, headed for orbit. In a little while, if everything went okay, the first stage would come scraping down on the new runway. Then we'll see who's gotten their money's worth. . . .

Christ. It's up, it's flying, forget about it. Plenty of politicking to be done. Hell, I'm only fifty-two. I'll have to get busy if I want to go . . . someplace.

And then it was the fall of 2001, just four days after Nick Jensen's sixty-first birthday.

Sitting bunched together in *Discovery's* control room, the six of them were suited up, breath hissing in respirator valves, softly, gently, the breathing that you did while you waited, excited, trying to stay calm. No more voices in the earphones, people just waiting now. Mission Control, over an hour away by radio, wouldn't know whether they lived or died until they were already here or gone.

Our final gasps, maybe, over the link, as we fall and fall and fry.

Up on the big HDTV monitor, Jupiter was a plump orange ball, almost featureless because they had the mag tuned to zero—keep it real, we said, like it was a window—Callisto a bright white ball, not quite full, phase the same as the mother planet's.

It seems, he thought, just as bright as the Moon. Albedo very different, though; nothing to compare it to but Jupiter and the other Galilean moons. Not like looking back a few days after interplanetary injection, on the way to Mars, then an asteroid, then here, Luna just a dim piece of old rock compared to bright white-and blue-shining Earth.

Not even thirty years since I lay on my back, stuffed

into the right-hand seat of that old Apollo capsule, and waited for them to finish counting down, waited for them to send me to the Moon. Now . . .

He glanced over at Amy Jordan, the ship's other oldster, smiled at her through the faceplate. She reached out and patted the back of his gloved hand, just a movement, unfeelable, and gestured at the display console. "T minus five minutes . . . "

"Five minutes." One hand on the emergency switch, but the computer would handle everything, had been doing so, working just fine for the eleven months of the voyage out. "Everyone okay?"

Chorus of whispered assents from the four youngsters in the room. *"Challenger?"*

From the other ship, Jill Rodriguez's voice crackled over the radio link. "Engine precharge seems to be going well."

Seems. Soft fuzz of static in her voice, picking up interference from Jupiter's outer radiation belts. "Three minutes."

Seems. But if the main engines fail to fire, we'll fall through those radiation belts and die. Be dead just a few minutes from now. And these empty ships will go flying off into space, whipped by Jupiter's gravity, never to be seen again. . . .

Well, no. That's not right. The ships' electronics will survive the trip. Maybe the engineers on Earth will get things fixed, get us headed on a homeward-bound trajectory, get us back into Earth orbit. And we can be buried beside our friends in only three or four years.

"One minute. Engine precharge complete."

No. I'd rather not go home again, if that happens. Stay out here in the cold and dark . . .

This is my last flight. I'll be sixty-five by the time we get home. Can't keep cheating the flight surgeon forever. . . .

"Three, two, one . . . "

The engines lit, shoving them all back into their seats, dropping *Discovery* and *Challenger* into orbit around Callisto.

Three old men, sitting on a tropical veranda, Indian Ocean breezes blowing in off the grounds, were watching NASA Select, pulling the signal directly from one of the old TDRSS satellites through the little receiver disk on the roof. Jupiter was hanging there in the big HD monitor, crisp orange, more like a view out some magic spaceship window than a mere TV image, Callisto hanging in front of it, dull yellow-white.

Time advanced and the image moved, bright face of Callisto narrowing as the ship moved closer, sliding under the pole, then going entirely black, growing very large, eclipsing the Sun. Over in one corner of the veranda, an automatic camera blinked, filming them discreetly. Just in case someone might be interested.

Walter said, "Remember when we covered *Apollo 11* together? It seems so long ago, now."

Wally said, "Yeah. But it's only been thirty-two years. Not long at all. Barely time for our grandchildren to grow up."

"You ever regret getting out of the program after *Apollo 7?*"

Wally shrugged, watching the screen carefully, not looking at the camera. "Sometimes. But I was already middle-aged, back then. Time to let the younger guys fly."

"Jensen's in his sixties . . . "

"Sure. And Al Shepard went to the Moon. We do what we have to do. Make our choices . . . "

It was pitch-black on the monitor now, nothing visible there, though they knew the dark side of Callisto would be passing below as the ship moved on toward its orbital insertion burn. Walter looked at his watch and said, "Any second now . . . "

Arthur picked up his universal household system remote and hefted it lightly, looking at the TV screen. "I wish," he said, "that I could be there myself, but . . . " He thumbed one of the contacts and, from somewhere inside the house, *Thus Spake Zarathustra* began to play. "This, I suppose, will have to do."

Cronkite and Schirra smiled for the camera, and, on TV, the Sun began rising over Callisto's dark horizon.

Coming of Age
in Karhide

SOV THADE TAGE EM EREB, OF RER
IN KARHIDE, ON GETHEN

URSULA K. LE GUIN

Ursula K. Le Guin is a writer whose literary impact
extends far beyond the boundaries of the science fiction field. But her recognition began with such contemporary classics of SF as *The Left Hand of Darkness*
and *The Dispossessed*. In the last three years she has
flowered again as a science fiction writer, producing
new short fiction work of mature excellence. In 1995
she published at least five stories, all of sufficient quality to be included in this book. In this story, a pleasant
and powerful tale about sex, Le Guin returns to the
setting of *The Left Hand of Darkness*, the planet
Winter. "Coming of Age in Karhide" appeared in the
excellent original anthology edited by Greg Bear, *New
Legends*.

I live in the oldest city in the world. Long before there were kings in Karhide, Rer was a city, the marketplace and meeting ground for all the Northeast, the Plains, and Kerm Land. The Fastness of Rer was a center of learning, a refuge, a judgment seat fifteen thousand years ago. Karhide became a nation here, under the Geger kings, who ruled for a thousand years. In the thousandth year Sedern Geger, the Unking, cast the crown into the River Arre from the palace towers, proclaiming an end to dominion. The time they call the Flowering of Rer, the Summer Century, began then. It ended when the Hearth of Harge took power and moved their capital across the mountains to Erhenrang. The Old Palace has been empty for centuries. But it stands. Nothing in Rer falls down. The Arre floods through the street-tunnels every year in the Thaw, winter blizzards may bring thirty feet of snow, but the city stands. Nobody knows how old the houses are, because they have been rebuilt forever. Each one sits in its gardens without respect to the position of any of the others, as vast and random and ancient as hills. The roofed streets and canals angle about among them. Rer is all corners. We say that the Harges left because they were afraid of what might be around the corner.

Time is different here. I learned in school how the Orgota, the Ekumen, and most other people count years. They call the year of some portentous event Year One and number forward from it. Here it's always Year One. On Getheny Thern, New Year's Day, the Year One becomes one-ago, one-to-come becomes One, and so on. It's like Rer, everything always changing but the city never changing.

When I was fourteen (in the Year One, or fifty-ago) I came of age. I have been thinking about that a good deal recently.

It was a different world. Most of us had never seen an Alien, as we called them then. We might have heard the Mobile talk on the radio, and at school we saw pictures of Aliens—the ones with hair around their mouths were the most pleasingly savage and repulsive. Most of the pictures were disappointing. They looked too much like us. You couldn't even tell that they were always in kemmer. The female Aliens were supposed to have enormous breasts, but my Mothersib Dory had bigger breasts than the ones in the pictures.

When the Defenders of the Faith kicked them out of Orgoreyn, when King Emran got into the Border War and lost Erhenrang, even when their Mobiles were outlawed and forced into hiding at Estre in Kerm, the Ekumen did nothing much but wait. They had waited for two hundred years, as patient as Handdara. They did one thing: they took our young king off-world to foil a plot, and then brought the same king back sixty years later to end her wombchild's disastrous reign. Argaven XVII is the only king who ever ruled four years before her heir and forty years after.

The year I was born (the Year One, or sixty-four-ago) was the year Argaven's second reign began. By the time I was noticing anything beyond my own toes, the war was over, the West Fall was part of Karhide again, the capital was back in Erhenrang, and most of the damage done to Rer during the Overthrow of

Emran had been repaired. The old houses had been rebuilt again. The Old Palace had been patched again. Argaven XVII was miraculously back on the throne again. Everything was the way it used to be, ought to be, back to normal, just like the old days—everybody said so.

Indeed those were quiet years, an interval of recovery before Argaven, the first Gethenian who ever left our planet, brought us at last fully into the Ekumen; before we, not they, became the Aliens; before we came of age. When I was a child we lived the way people had lived in Rer forever. It is that way, that timeless world, that world around the corner, I have been thinking about, and trying to describe for people who never knew it. Yet as I write I see how also nothing changes, that it is truly the Year One always, for each child that comes of age, each lover who falls in love.

There were a couple of thousand people in the Ereb Hearths, and a hundred and forty of them lived in my Hearth, Ereb Tage. My name is Sov Thade Tage em Ereb, after the old way of naming we still use in Rer. The first thing I remember is a huge dark place full of shouting and shadows, and I am falling upward through a golden light into the darkness. In thrilling terror, I scream. I am caught in my fall, held, held close; I weep; a voice so close to me that it seems to speak through my body says softly, "Sov, Sov, Sov." And then I am given something wonderful to eat, something so sweet, so delicate that never again will I eat anything quite so good. . . .

I imagine that some of my wild elder hearthsibs had been throwing me about, and that my mother comforted me with a bit of festival cake. Later on when I was a wild elder sib we used to play catch with babies for balls; they always screamed, with terror or with delight, or both. It's the nearest to flying anyone of my generation knew. We had dozens of different words for the way snow falls, floats, descends, glides, blows, for the way clouds move, the way ice floats, the way boats sail; but not that word. Not yet. And so I don't remember "flying." I remember falling upward through the golden light.

Family houses in Rer are built around a big central hall. Each story has an inner balcony clear round that space, and we call the whole story, rooms and all, a balcony. My family occupied the whole second balcony of Ereb Tage. There were a lot of us. My grandmother had borne four children, and all of them had children, so I had a bunch of cousins as well as a younger and an older wombsib. "The Thades always kemmer as women and always get pregnant," I heard neighbors say, variously envious, disapproving, admiring. "And they never keep kemmer," somebody would add. The former was an exaggeration, but the latter was true. Not one of us kids had a father. I didn't know for years who my getter was, and never gave it a thought. Clannish, the Thades preferred not to bring outsiders, even other members of our own Hearth, into the family. If young people fell in love and started talking about keeping kemmer or making vows, Grandmother and the mothers were ruthless. "Vowing kemmer, what do you think you are, some kind of noble? some kind of fancy person? The kemmerhouse was good enough for me and it's good enough for you," the mothers said to their lovelorn children, and sent them away, clear off to the old Ereb Domain in the country, to hoe braties till they got over being in love.

So as a child I was a member of a flock, a school, a swarm, in and out of our warren of rooms, tearing up and down the staircases, working together and learning together and looking after the babies—in our own fashion—and terrorizing quieter hearthmates by our numbers and our noise. As far as I know we did no real harm. Our escapades were well within the rules and limits of the sedate, ancient Hearth, which we felt not as constraints but as protection, the walls that kept us safe. The only time we got punished was when my cousin Sether decided it would be exciting if we tied a long rope we'd found to the second-floor balcony railing, tied a big knot in the rope, held onto the knot, and jumped. "I'll go first," Sether said. Another misguided attempt at flight. The railing and Sether's broken leg were mended, and the rest of us had to clean the privies, all the privies of the Hearth, for a month. I think the rest of the Hearth had decided it was time the young Thades observed some discipline.

Although I really don't know what I was like as a child, I think that if I'd had any choice I might have been less noisy than my playmates, though just as unruly. I used to love to listen to the radio, and while the rest of them were racketing around the balconies or the centerhall in winter, or out in the streets and gardens in summer, I would crouch for hours in my mother's room behind the bed, playing her old seremwood radio very softly so that my sibs wouldn't know I was there. I listened to anything, Lays and plays and hearthtales, the Palace news, the analyses of grain harvests and the detailed weather reports; I listened every day all one winter to an ancient saga from the Pering Storm-Border about snowghouls, perfidious traitors, and bloody ax-murders, which haunted me at night so that I couldn't sleep and would crawl into bed with my mother for comfort. Often my younger sib was already there in the warm, soft, breathing dark. We would sleep all entangled and curled up together like a nest of pesthry.

My mother, Guyr Thade Tage em Ereb, was impatient, warm-hearted, and impartial, not exerting much control over us three wombchildren, but keeping watch. The Thades were all tradespeople working in Ereb shops and masteries, with little or no cash to spend; but when I was ten, Guyr bought me a radio, a new one, and said where my sibs could hear, "You don't have to share it." I treasured it for years and finally shared it with my own wombchild.

So the years went along and I went along in the warmth and density and certainty of a family and a Hearth embedded in tradition, threads on the quick ever-repeating shuttle weaving the timeless web of custom and act and work and relationship, and at this distance I can hardly tell one year from the other or myself from the other children: until I turned fourteen.

The reason most people in my Hearth would remember that year is for the big party known as Dory's Somer-Forever Celebration. My Mothersib Dory had stopped going into kemmer that winter. Some people didn't do anything when they stopped going into kemmer; others went to the Fastness for a ritual; some stayed on at the Fastness for months after, or even moved there. Dory, who wasn't spiritually inclined, said, "If I can't have kids and can't have sex anymore and have to get old and die, at least I can have a party."

I have already had some trouble trying to tell this story in a language that has no somer pronouns, only gendered pronouns. In their last years of kemmer, as the hormone balance changes, many people tend to go into kemmer as men; Dory's kemmers had been male for over a year, so I'll call Dory "he," although of course the point was that he would never be either he or she again.

In any event, his party was tremendous. He invited

everyone in our Hearth and the two neighboring Ereb Hearths, and it went on for three days. It had been a long winter and the spring was late and cold; people were ready for something new, something hot to happen. We cooked for a week, and a whole storeroom was packed full of beer kegs. A lot of people who were in the middle of going out of kemmer, or had already and hadn't done anything about it, came and joined in the ritual. That's what I remember vividly: in the firelit three-story centerhall of our Hearth, a circle of thirty or forty people, all middle-aged or old, singing and dancing, stamping the drumbeats. There was a fierce energy in them, their gray hair was loose and wild, they stamped as if their feet would go through the floor, their voices were deep and strong, they were laughing. The younger people watching them seemed pallid and shadowy. I looked at the dancers and wondered, why are they happy? Aren't they old? Why do they act like they'd got free? What's it like, then, kemmer?

No, I hadn't thought much about kemmer before. What would be the use? Until we come of age we have no gender and no sexuality, our hormones don't give us any trouble at all. And in a city Hearth we never see adults in kemmer. They kiss and go. Where's Maba? In the kemmerhouse, love, now eat your porridge. When's Maba coming back? Soon, love. And in a couple of days Maba comes back, looking sleepy and shiny and refreshed and exhausted. Is it like having a bath, Maba? Yes, a bit, love, and what have you been up to while I was away?

Of course we played kemmer, when we were seven or eight. This here's the kemmerhouse and I get to be the woman. No, I do. No, I do, I thought of it! And we rubbed our bodies together and rolled around laughing, and then maybe we stuffed a ball under our shirt and were pregnant, and then we gave birth, and then we played catch with the ball. Children will play whatever adults do; but the kemmer game wasn't much of a game. It often ended in a tickling match. And most children aren't even very ticklish, till they come of age.

After Dory's party, I was on duty in the Hearth crèche all through Tuwa, the last month of spring; come summer I began my first apprenticeship, in a furniture workshop in the Third Ward. I loved getting up early and running across the city on the wayroofs and up on the curbs of the open ways; after the late Thaw some of the ways were still full of water, deep enough for kayaks and poleboats. The air would be still and cold and clear; the sun would come up behind the old towers of the Unpalace, red as blood, and all the waters and the windows of the city would flash scarlet and gold. In the workshop there was the piercing sweet smell of fresh-cut wood and the company of grown people, hard-working, patient, and demanding, taking me seriously. I wasn't a child anymore, I said to myself. I was an adult, a working person.

But why did I want to cry all the time? Why did I want to sleep all the time? Why did I get angry at Sether? Why did Sether keep bumping into me and saying "Oh sorry" in that stupid husky voice? Why was I so clumsy with the big electric lathe that I ruined six chair-legs one after the other? "Get that kid off the lathe," shouted old Marth, and I slunk away in a fury of humiliation. I would never be a carpenter, I would never be adult, who gave a shit for chair-legs anyway?

"I want to work in the gardens," I told my mother and grandmother.

"Finish your training and you can work in the gardens next summer," Grand said, and Mother nodded. This sensible counsel appeared to me as a heartless

injustice, a failure of love, a condemnation to despair.
I sulked. I raged.

"What's wrong with the furniture shop?" my elders
asked after several days of sulk and rage.

"Why does stupid Sether have to be there!" I
shouted. Dory, who was Sether's mother, raised an
eyebrow and smiled.

"Are you all right?" my mother asked me as I
slouched into the balcony after work, and I snarled,
"I'm fine," and rushed to the privies and vomited.

I was sick. My back ached all the time. My head
ached and got dizzy and heavy. Something I could not
locate anywhere, some part of my soul, hurt with a
keen, desolate, ceaseless pain. I was afraid of myself:
of my tears, my rage, my sickness, my clumsy body. It
did not feel like my body, like me. It felt like something else, an ill-fitting garment, a smelly, heavy over-
coat that belonged to some old person, some dead
person. It wasn't mine, it wasn't me. Tiny needles of
agony shot through my nipples, hot as fire. When I
winced and held my arms across my chest, I knew that
everybody could see what was happening. Anybody
could smell me. I smelled sour, strong, like blood, like
raw pelts of animals. My clitopenis was swollen hugely
and stuck out from between my labia, and then shrank
nearly to nothing, so that it hurt to piss. My labia
itched and reddened as with loathsome insect-bites.
Deep in my belly something moved, some monstrous
growth. I was utterly ashamed. I was dying.

"Sov," my mother said, sitting down beside me on
my bed, with a curious, tender, complicitous smile,
"shall we choose your kemmerday?"

"I'm not in kemmer," I said passionately.

"No," Guyr said. "But next month I think you will
be."

"I *won't!*"

My mother stroked my hair and face and arm. *We shape each other to be human,* old people used to say as they stroked babies or children or one another with those long, slow, soft caresses.

After a while my mother said, "Sether's coming in, too. But a month or so later than you, I think. Dory said let's have a double kemmerday, but I think you should have your own day in your own time."

I burst into tears and cried, "I don't want one, I don't want to, I just want, I just want to go away. . . ."

"Sov," my mother said, "if you want to, you can go to the kemmerhouse at Gerodda Ereb, where you won't know anybody. But I think it would be better here, where people do know you. They'd like it. They'll be so glad for you. Oh, your Grand's so proud of you! 'Have you seen that grandchild of mine, Sov, have you seen what a beauty, what a *mahad!*' Everybody's bored to tears hearing about you. . . ."

Mahad is a dialect word, a Rer word; it means a strong, handsome, generous, upright person, a reliable person. My mother's stern mother, who commanded and thanked, but never praised, said I was a mahad? A terrifying idea, that dried my tears.

"All right," I said desperately, "Here. But not next month! It isn't. I'm not."

"Let me see," my mother said. Fiercely embarrassed yet relieved to obey, I stood up and undid my trousers.

My mother took a very brief and delicate look, hugged me, and said, "Next month, yes, I'm sure. You'll feel much better in a day or two. And next month it'll be different. It really will."

Sure enough, the next day the headache and the hot itching were gone, and though I was still tired and sleepy a lot of the time, I wasn't quite so stupid and clumsy at work. After a few more days I felt pretty much myself, light and easy in my limbs. Only if I thought about it there was still that queer feeling that wasn't quite in any part of my body, and that was sometimes very painful and sometimes only strange, almost something I wanted to feel again.

My cousin Sether and I had been apprenticed together at the furniture shop. We didn't go to work together because Sether was still slightly lame from that rope trick a couple of years earlier, and got a lift to work in a poleboat so long as there was water in the streets. When they closed the Arre Watergate and the ways went dry, Sether had to walk. So we walked together. The first couple of days we didn't talk much. I still felt angry at Sether. Because I couldn't run through the dawn anymore but had to walk at a lame-leg pace. And because Sether was always around. Always there. Taller than me, and quicker at the lathe, and with that long, heavy, shining hair. Why did anybody want to wear their hair so long, anyhow? I felt as if Sether's hair was in front of my own eyes.

We were walking home, tired, on a hot evening of Ockre, the first month of summer. I could see that Sether was limping and trying to hide or ignore it, trying to swing right along at my quick pace, very straight-backed, scowling. A great wave of pity and admiration overwhelmed me, and that thing, that growth, that new being, whatever it was in my bowels and in the ground of my soul moved and turned again, turned towards Sether, aching, yearning.

"Are you coming into kemmer?" I said in a hoarse, husky voice I had never heard come out of my mouth.

"In a couple of months," Sether said in a mumble, not looking at me, still very stiff and frowning.

"I guess I have to have this, do this, you know, this stuff, pretty soon."

"I wish I could," Sether said. "Get it over with."

We did not look at each other. Very gradually, unnoticeably, I was slowing my pace till we were going along side by side at an easy walk.

"Sometimes do you feel like your tits are on fire?" I asked without knowing that I was going to say anything.

Sether nodded.

After a while, Sether said, "Listen, does your pisser get. . . ."

I nodded.

"It must be what the Aliens look like," Sether said with revulsion. "This, this thing sticking out, it gets so *big* . . . it gets in the way."

We exchanged and compared symptoms for a mile or so. It was a relief to talk about it, to find company in misery, but it was also frightening to hear our misery confirmed by the other. Sether burst out, "I'll tell you what I hate, what I really *hate* about it—it's dehumanizing. To get jerked around like that by your own body, to lose control, I can't stand the idea. Of being just a sex machine. And everybody just turns into something to have sex with. You know that people in kemmer go crazy and *die* if there isn't anybody else in kemmer? That they'll even attack people in somer? Their own mothers?"

"They can't," I said, shocked.

"Yes they can. Tharry told me. This truck driver up in the High Kargav went into kemmer as a male while their caravan was stuck in the snow, and he was big and strong, and he went crazy and he, he did it to his cab-mate, and his cab-mate was in somer and got hurt, really hurt, trying to fight him off. And then the driver came out of kemmer and committed suicide."

This horrible story brought the sickness back up from the pit of my stomach, and I could say nothing.

Sether went on, "People in kemmer aren't even

human anymore! And we have to do that—to be that way!"

Now that awful, desolate fear was out in the open. But it was not a relief to speak it. It was even larger and more terrible, spoken.

"It's stupid," Sether said. "It's a primitive device for continuing the species. There's no need for civilized people to undergo it. People who want to get pregnant could do it with injections. It would be genetically sound. You could choose your child's getter. There wouldn't be all this inbreeding, people fucking with their sibs, like animals. Why do we have to be animals?"

Sether's rage stirred me. I shared it. I also felt shocked and excited by the word "fucking," which I had never heard spoken. I looked again at my cousin, the thin, ruddy face, the heavy, long, shining hair. My age, Sether looked older. A half year in pain from a shattered leg had darkened and matured the adventurous, mischievous child, teaching anger, pride, endurance. "Sether," I said, "listen, it doesn't matter, you're human, even if you have to do that stuff, that fucking. You're a mahad."

"Getheny Kus," Grand said: the first day of the month of Kus, midsummer day.

"I won't be ready," I said.

"You'll be ready."

"I want to go into kemmer with Sether."

"Sether's got a month or two yet to go. Soon enough. It looks like you might be on the same moon-time, though. Dark-of-the-mooners, eh? That's what I used to be. So, just stay on the same wavelength, you and Sether. . . ." Grand had never grinned at me this way, an inclusive grin, as if I were an equal.

My mother's mother was sixty years old, short, brawny, broad-hipped, with keen clear eyes, a stone-mason by trade, an unquestioned autocrat in the Hearth. I, equal to this formidable person? It was my first intimation that I might be becoming more, rather than less, human.

"I'd like it," said Grand, "if you spent this half-month at the Fastness. But it's up to you."

"At the Fastness?" I said, taken by surprise. We Thades were all Handdara, but very inert Handdara, keeping only the great festivals, muttering the grace all in one garbled word, practicing none of the disciplines. None of my older hearthsibs had been sent off to the Fastness before their kemmerday. Was there something wrong with me?

"You've got a good brain," said Grand. "You and Sether. I'd like to see some of you lot casting some shadows, some day. We Thades sit here in our Hearth and breed like pesthry. Is that enough? It'd be a good thing if some of you got your heads out of the bedding."

"What do they do in the Fastness?" I asked, and Grand answered frankly, "I don't know. Go find out. They teach you. They can teach you how to control kemmer."

"All right," I said promptly. I would tell Sether that the Indwellers could control kemmer. Maybe I could learn how to do it and come home and teach it to Sether.

Grand looked at me with approval. I had taken up the challenge.

Of course I didn't learn how to control kemmer, in a halfmonth in the Fastness. The first couple of days there, I thought I wouldn't even be able to control my homesickness. From our warm, dark warren of rooms full of people talking, sleeping, eating, cooking, wash-ing, playing remma, playing music, kids running around, noise, family, I went across the city to a huge, clean, cold, quiet house of strangers. They were courteous, they treated me with respect. I was terrified. Why should a person of forty, who knew magic disciplines of superhuman strength and fortitude, who could walk barefoot through blizzards, who could Foretell, whose eyes were the wisest and calmest I had ever seen, why should an Adept of the Handdara respect me?

"Because you are so ignorant," Ranharrer the Adept said, smiling, with great tenderness.

Having me only for a halfmonth, they didn't try to influence the nature of my ignorance very much. I practiced the Untrance several hours a day, and came to like it: that was quite enough for them, and they praised me. "At fourteen, most people go crazy moving slowly," my teacher said.

During my last six or seven days in the Fastness certain symptoms began to show up again, the headache, the swellings and shooting pains, the irritability. One morning the sheet of my cot in my bare, peaceful little room was bloodstained. I looked at the smear with horror and loathing. I thought I had scratched my itching labia to bleeding in my sleep, but I knew also what the blood was. I began to cry. I had to wash the sheet somehow. I had fouled, defiled this place where everything was clean, austere, and beautiful.

An old Indweller, finding me scrubbing desperately at the sheet in the washrooms, said nothing, but brought me some soap that bleached away the stain. I went back to my room, which I had come to love with the passion of one who had never before known any actual privacy, and crouched on the sheetless bed, miserable, checking every few minutes to be sure I was not bleeding again. I missed my Untrance practice time. The immense house was very quiet. Its peace sank into me. Again I felt that strangeness in my soul, but it was not pain now; it was a desolation like the air at evening, like the peaks of the Kargav seen far in the west in the clarity of winter. It was an immense enlargement.

Ranharrer the Adept knocked and entered at my word, looked at me for a minute, and asked gently, "What is it?"

"Everything is strange," I said.

The Adept smiled radiantly and said, "Yes."

I know now how Ranharrer cherished and honored my ignorance, in the Handdara sense. Then I knew only that somehow or other I had said the right thing and so pleased a person I wanted very much to please.

"We're doing some singing," Ranharrer said, "you might like to hear it."

They were in fact singing the Midsummer Chant, which goes on for the four days before Getheny Kus, night and day. Singers and drummers drop in and out at will, most of them singing on certain syllables in an endless group improvisation guided only by the drums and by melodic cues in the Chantbook, and falling into harmony with the soloist if one is present. At first I heard only a pleasantly thick-textured, droning sound over a quiet and subtle beat. I listened till I got bored and decided I could do it too. So I opened my mouth and sang "Aah" and heard all the other voices singing "Aah" above and with and below mine until I lost mine and heard only all the voices, and then only the music itself, and then suddenly the startling silvery rush of a single voice running across the weaving, against the current, and sinking into it and vanishing, and rising out of it again. . . . Ranharrer touched my arm. It was time for dinner, I had been singing since Third Hour. I went back to the chantry after dinner, and after supper. I spent the next three days there. I would have spent the nights there if they had let me. I wasn't sleepy at all anymore. I had sudden, endless energy, and couldn't sleep. In my little room I sang to myself, or read the strange Handdara poetry which was the only book they had given me, and practiced the Untrance, trying to ignore the heat and cold, the fire and ice in my body, till dawn came and I could go sing again.

And then it was Ottormenbod, midsummer's eve, and I must go home to my Hearth and the kemmer-house.

To my surprise, my mother and grandmother and all the elders came to the Fastness to fetch me, wearing ceremonial hiebs and looking solemn. Ranharrer handed me over to them, saying to me only, "Come back to us." My family paraded me through the streets in the hot summer morning; all the vines were in flower, perfuming the air, all the gardens were blooming, bearing, fruiting. "This is an excellent time," Grand said judiciously, "to come into kemmer."

The Hearth looked very dark to me after the Fastness, and somehow shrunken. I looked around for Sether, but it was a workday, Sether was at the shop. That gave me a sense of holiday, which was not unpleasant. And then up in the hearthroom of our balcony, Grand and the Hearth elders formally presented me with a whole set of new clothes, new everything, from the boots up, topped by a magnificently embroidered hieb. There was a spoken ritual that went with the clothes, not Handdara, I think, but a tradition of our Hearth; the words were all old and strange, the language of a thousand years ago. Grand rattled them out like somebody spitting rocks, and put the hieb on my shoulders. Everybody said, "Haya!"

All the elders, and a lot of younger kids, hung around helping me put on the new clothes as if I was a king or a baby, and some of the elders wanted to give me advice—"last advice," they called it, since you gain shifgrethor when you go into kemmer, and once you have shifgrethor advice is insulting. "Now you just keep away from that old Ebbeche," one of them told me shrilly. My mother took offense, snapping, "Keep your shadow to yourself, Tadsh!" And to me, "Don't listen to the old fish. Flapmouth Tadsh! But now listen, Sov."

I listened. Guyr had drawn me a little away from the others, and spoke gravely, with some embarrassment. "Remember, it will matter who you're with first."

I nodded. "I understand," I said.

"No, you don't," my mother snapped, forgetting to be embarrassed. "Just keep it in mind!"

"What, ah," I said. My mother waited. "If I, if I go into, as a, as female," I said. "Don't I, shouldn't I—?"

"Ah," Guyr said. "Don't worry. It'll be a year or more before you can conceive. Or get. Don't worry, this time. The other people will see to it, just in case. They all know it's your first kemmer. But do keep it in mind, who you're with first! Around, oh, around Karrid, and Ebbeche, and some of them."

"Come on!" Dory shouted, and we all got into a procession again to go downstairs and across the centerhall, where everybody cheered "Haya Sov! Haya Sov!" and the cooks beat on their saucepans. I wanted to die. But they all seemed so cheerful, so happy about me, wishing me well; I wanted also to live.

We went out the west door and across the sunny gardens and came to the kemmerhouse. Tage Ereb shares a kemmerhouse with two other Ereb Hearths; it's a beautiful building, all carved with deep-figure friezes in the Old Dynasty style, terribly worn by the weather of a couple of thousand years. On the red stone steps my family all kissed me, murmuring, "Praise then Darkness," or "In the act of creation praise," and my mother gave me a hard push on my shoulders, what they call the sledge-push, for good luck, as I turned away from them and went in the door.

The doorkeeper was waiting for me; a queer-looking, rather stooped person, with coarse, pale skin.

Now I realized who this "Ebbeche" they'd been talking about was. I'd never met him, but I'd heard about him. He was the Doorkeeper of our kemmerhouse, a halfdead—that is, a person in permanent kemmer, like the Aliens.

There are always a few people born that way here. Some of them can be cured; those who can't or choose not to be usually live in a Fastness and learn the disciplines, or they become Doorkeepers. It's convenient for them, and for normal people too. After all, who else would want to *live* in a kemmerhouse? But there are drawbacks. If you come to the kemmerhouse in thorharmen, ready to gender, and the first person you meet is fully male, his pheromones are likely to gender you female right then, whether that's what you had in mind this month or not. Responsible Doorkeepers, of course, keep well away from anybody who doesn't invite them to come close. But permanent kemmer may not lead to responsibility of character; nor does being called *halfdead* and *pervert* all your life, I imagine. Obviously my family didn't trust Ebbeche to keep his hands and his pheromones off me. But they were unjust. He honored a first kemmer as much as anyone else. He greeted me by name and showed me where to take off my new boots. Then he began to speak the ancient ritual welcome, backing down the hall before me; the first time I ever heard the words I would hear so many times again for so many years.

You cross earth now.
You cross water now.
You cross the Ice now. . . .

And the exulting ending, as we came into the centerhall:

Together we have crossed the Ice.
Together we come into the Hearthplace,
Into life, bringing life!
In the act of creation, praise!

The solemnity of the words moved me and distracted me somewhat from my intense self-consciousness. As I had in the Fastness, I felt the familiar reassurance of being part of something immensely older and larger than myself, even if it was strange and new to me. I must entrust myself to it and be what it made me. At the same time I was intensely alert. All my senses were extraordinarily keen, as they had been all morning. I was aware of everything, the beautiful blue color of the walls, the lightness and vigor of my steps as I walked, the texture of the wood under my bare feet, the sound and meaning of the ritual words, the Doorkeeper himself. He fascinated me. Ebbeche was certainly not handsome, and yet I noticed how musical his rather deep voice was; and pale skin was more attractive than I had ever thought it. I felt that he had been maligned, that his life must be a strange one. I wanted to talk to him. But as he finished the welcome, standing aside for me at the doorway of the centerhall, a tall person strode forward eagerly to meet me.

I was glad to see a familiar face: it was the head cook of my Hearth, Karrid Arrage. Like many cooks a rather fierce and temperamental person, Karrid had often taken notice of me, singling me out in a joking, challenging way, tossing me some delicacy—"Here, youngun! get some meat on your bones!" As I saw Karrid now I went through the most extraordinary multiplicity of awarenesses: that Karrid was naked and that this nakedness was not like the nakedness of people in the Hearth, but a significant nakedness—that he was not the Karrid I had seen before but transfigured into great beauty—that he was *he*—that my mother had warned me about him—that I wanted to touch him—that I was afraid of him.

He picked me right up in his arms and pressed me against him. I felt his clitopenis like a fist between my legs. "Easy, now," the Doorkeeper said to him, and some other people came forward from the room, which I could see only as large, dimly glowing, full of shadows and mist.

"Don't worry, don't worry," Karrid said to me and them, with his hard laugh. "I won't hurt my own get, will I? I just want to be the one that gives her kemmer. As a woman, like a proper Thade. I want to give you that joy, little Sov." He was undressing me as he spoke, slipping off my hieb and shirt with big, hot, hasty hands. The Doorkeeper and the others kept close watch, but did not interfere. I felt totally defenseless, helpless, humiliated. I struggled to get free, broke loose, and tried to pick up and put on my shirt. I was shaking and felt terribly weak, I could hardly stand up. Karrid helped me clumsily; his big arm supported me. I leaned against him, feeling his hot, vibrant skin against mine, a wonderful feeling, like sunlight, like firelight. I leaned more heavily against him, raising my arms so that our sides slid together. "Hey, now," he said. "Oh, you beauty, oh, you Sov, here, take her away, this won't do!" And he backed right away from me, laughing and yet really alarmed, his clitopenis standing up amazingly. I stood there half-dressed, on my rubbery legs, bewildered. My eyes were full of mist, I could see nothing clearly.

"Come on," somebody said, and took my hand, a soft, cool touch totally different from the fire of Karrid's skin. It was a person from one of the other Hearths, I didn't know her name. She seemed to me to shine like gold in the dim, misty place. "Oh, you're going so fast," she said, laughing and admiring and consoling. "Come on, come into the pool, take it easy for a while. Karrid shouldn't have come on to you like that! But you're lucky, first kemmer as a woman, there's nothing like it. I kemmered as a man three times before I got to kemmer as a woman, it made me so mad, every time I got into thorharmen all my damn friends would all be women already. Don't worry about me—I'd say Karrid's influence was decisive," and she laughed again. "Oh, you are so pretty!" and she bent her head and licked my nipples before I knew what she was doing.

It was wonderful, it cooled that stinging fire in them that nothing else could cool. She helped me finish undressing, and we stepped together into the warm water of the big, shallow pool that filled the whole center of this room. That was why it was so misty, why the echoes were so strange. The water lapped on my thighs, on my sex, on my belly. I turned to my friend and leaned forward to kiss her. It was a perfectly natural thing to do, it was what she wanted and I wanted, and I wanted her to lick and suck my nipples again, and she did. For a long time we lay in the shallow water playing, and I could have played forever. But then somebody else joined us, taking hold of my friend from behind, and she arched her body in the water like a golden fish leaping, threw her back, and began to play with him.

I got out of the water and dried myself, feeling sad and shy and forsaken, and yet extremely interested in what had happened to my body. It felt wonderfully alive and electric, so that the roughness of the towel made me shiver with pleasure. Somebody had come closer to me, somebody that had been watching me play with my friend in the water. He sat down by me now.

It was a hearthmate a few years older than I, Arrad Tehemmy. I had worked in the gardens with Arrad all last summer, and liked him. He looked like Sether, I now thought, with heavy black hair and a long, thin face, but in him was that shining, that glory they all had here—all the kemmerers, the *women*, the *men*—such vivid beauty as I had never seen in any human beings. "Sov," he said, "I'd like—Your first—Will you—" His hands were already on me, and mine on him. "Come," he said, and I went with him. He took me into a beautiful little room, in which there was nothing but a fire burning in a fireplace, and a wide bed. There Arrad took me into his arms and I took Arrad into my arms, and then between my legs, and fell upward, upward through the golden light.

Arrad and I were together all that first night, and besides fucking a great deal, we ate a great deal. It had not occurred to me that there would be food at a kemmerhouse, I had thought you weren't allowed to do anything but fuck. There was a lot of food, very good, too, set out so that you could eat whenever you wanted. Drink was more limited; the person in charge, an old woman-halfdead, kept her canny eye on you, and wouldn't give you any more beer if you showed signs of getting wild or stupid. I didn't need any more beer. I didn't need any more fucking. I was complete. I was in love forever for all time all my life to eternity with Arrad. But Arrad (who was a day father into

kemmer than I) fell asleep and wouldn't wake up, and
an extraordinary person named Hama sat down by me
and began talking and also running his hand up and
down my back in the most delicious way, so that
before long we got further entangled, and began fucking, and it was entirely different with Hama than it
had been with Arrad, so that I realized that I must be
in love with Hama, until Gehardar joined us. After
that I think I began to understand that I loved them all
and they all loved me and that that was the secret of
the kemmerhouse.

It's been nearly fifty years, and I have to admit I do
not recall everyone from my first kemmer; only Karrid
and Arrad, Hama and Gehardar, old Tubanny, the
most exquisitely skillful lover as a male that I ever
knew—I met him often in later kemmers—and Berre,
my golden fish, with whom I ended up in drowsy,
peaceful, blissful lovemaking in front of the great
hearth till we both fell asleep. And when we woke we
were not women. We were not men. We were not in
kemmer. We were very tired young adults.

"You're still beautiful," I said to Berre.

"So are you," Berre said. "Where do you work?"

"Furniture shop, Third Ward."

I tried licking Berre's nipple, but it didn't work;
Berre flinched a little, and I said "Sorry," and we both
laughed.

"I'm in the radio trade," Berre said. "Did you ever
think of trying that?"

"Making radios?"

"No. Broadcasting. I do the Fourth Hour news and
weather."

"That's you?" I said, awed.

"Come over to the tower some time, I'll show you
around," said Berre.

Which is how I found my lifelong trade and a lifelong friend. As I tried to tell Sether when I came back to the Hearth, kemmer isn't exactly what we thought it was; it's much more complicated.

Sether's first kemmer was on Getheny Gor, the first day of the first month of autumn, at the dark of the moon. One of the family brought Sether into kemmer as a woman, and then Sether brought me in. That was the first time I kemmered as a man. And we stayed on the same wavelength, as Grand put it. We never conceived together, being cousins and having some modern scruples, but we made love in every combination, every dark of the moon, for years. And Sether brought my child, Tamor, into first kemmer—as a woman, like a proper Thade.

Later on Sether went into the Handdara, and became an Indweller in the old Fastness, and now is an Adept. I go over there often to join in one of the Chants or practice the Untrance or just to visit, and every few days Sether comes back to the Hearth. And we talk. The old days or the new times, somer or kemmer, love is love.

The Three Descents of Jeremy Baker

ROGER ZELAZNY

Roger Zelazny was one of the startling new talents from the New Wave of the 1960s. His fiction ranged from pure fantasy to hard SF. His genial personality and charming stories made him one of the most popular SF writers of the last three decades. His SF novels of the 1960s earned him a spectacular literary reputation and his fantasy series, the Amber novels (in the 1970s and 1980s) made him a bestselling writer. Throughout his career, he would occasionally produce major SF stories, winning many awards and proving, once again, that although he often chose to write slick commercial entertainments, he was always capable of meeting a difficult aesthetic challenge. This story is clever in the cat's cradle way that characterizes the best of Zelazny. Roger Zelazny died this spring and this piece from *Fantasy & Science Fiction* was his last hard SF story. He said in the headnote to the story that it is an attempt to combine three interesting hard SF ideas in one piece.

1.

Jeremy Baker was the only survivor when the *Raven*'s Warton-Purg drive delivered the vessel to the vicinity of a black hole. Its tidal forces immediately did their stuff. The hull groaned and cracked as indicators screamed the ship's situation and listed its problems. Jeremy, who had been somewhat bored, had been in the possibly enviable position of testing his powerful extravehicular survival suit at the time of the disaster. He had on everything but the helmet, which he promptly donned. Then he hurried to the control station with the intention of activating the Warton-Purg drive again in hopes of fleeing through extracurricular space—though under the circumstances it was more likely to cause the *Raven* to explode. But then the *Raven* was exploding anyway and it was worth a shot.

He never made it.

The vessel came apart about him. He thought he glimpsed the jumpsuited figure of one of his crewmates spinning amid the debris, but he could not be certain.

Suddenly, he was alone. Pieces of the *Raven* drifted away from him. He took a sip of the suit's water, wondering when he would feel a great heaviness in his feet as they were drawn down the gravity well faster than the rest of him—or perhaps it would be his head. He was uncertain as to his orientation. Still half in shock, he scanned the sky, peering into a star-occluding blackness. There. It would be his right arm where the stretching would begin. At least it would be an interesting way to die, he reflected. Not too many people had gotten to try it, though there had been a lot of colorful speculation.

He seemed to drift for a long while, musing on final splendors, without detecting any unusual sensations other than occasionally glimpsing what seemed a small, local patch of flickering light. He could not be certain as to its source. After a time, he felt an uncontrollable drowsiness and he slept.

"That's better," a voice seemed to be saying to him a bit later. "Seems to be working fine."

"Who—What are you?" Jeremy asked.

"I'm a Fleep," came the answer. "I'm that flickering patch of light you were wondering about a while back."

"You live around here?"

"I have for a long while, Jeremy. It's easy if you're an energy being with a lot of psi powers."

"That's how we're conversing?"

"Yes. I installed a telepathic function in your mind while I had you unconscious."

"Why aren't I being stretched into miles of spaghetti right now?"

"I created an antigravity field between you and the black hole. They cancel."

"Why'd you help me?"

"It's good to have someone new to talk to. Sometimes I get bored with my fellow Fleep."

"Oh, there's a whole colony of you?"

"Sure. This is a great place to study physics, and we're all into such pursuits."

"It doesn't seem an environment where life would develop."

"True. We were once a race of material beings but we were sufficiently evolved that when we saw our sun was going to go supernova we elected to transform ourselves into this state and study it rather than flee. In fact, that black hole used to be our sun. Makes a great lab. Come on, I'll show you. You can see more than you used to because I fiddled with your senses, too. I increased their range. For one thing, you should be able to detect a halo of Hawking radiation above the event horizon."

"Yes. Lavender, violet, purple. . . . It's rather lovely. If I kept going and passed through the event horizon would my image really be captured there forever? Could I come back and see myself frozen at that moment?"

"Yes, and no. Yes, you would clutter up the view with your arrested light. No, you couldn't come back and see yourself doing it. There's no way out once you go in."

"I phrased it poorly. Say, if there are other Fleep, there must be something special to call you to distinguish you."

"Call me Nik," the other said.

"Okay, Nik. What are those pinpoints of fire ahead? And the huge dark masses about them?"

"Those are my people, performing an experiment. I've been moving us at a very high velocity."

"I've noticed that the hole covers a lot more of the sky now. What sort of experiment?"

"Those great dark masses are the remnants of tens of thousands of suns and planets we've transported here. You only see the ones in space proper. We pull them out as we need them. We're shooting them into the hole."

"Why?"

"To increase its rate of rotation."

"Uh—To what end?"

"The creation of closed timelike curves."

"You've got me on that one."

"Time loops. To permit us to run backward through the past."

"Any successes so far?"

"Yes. A few."

"Have you got anything that might permit me to get back to the *Raven* before the explosion?"

"That's pushing it. But it's one of the things I wanted to check."

They matched velocities with the flickering congregation, and Nik took him into the vicinity of the largest of these beings. The conversation that followed resembled heat lightning.

"Vik says there's one that might do it," Nik told him after a time.

"Let me use it. Please."

"You should also have strength of mind sufficient to alter your velocity by thought alone," Nik said. "Come this way."

Jeremy followed him by willing it until, abruptly, he faced a mass of lines which resembled a computer design suddenly generated in free space.

"I did that just to make you conscious of it," Nik said. "Enter the trapezoid to your left."

"If this works I may not see you again. I'd better say thanks now."

"Noted with pleasure, though I'd like to have kept you longer, for full conversations. I understand your state of mind, however. Go."

Jeremy entered the trapezoid.

In an instant, everything changed. He was back aboard the *Raven,* standing wearing his suit, helmet in hand. Immediately, he rushed toward the control station, donning his helmet as he went. He felt the familiar drop into space proper. The tidal forces took hold of the *Raven,* and it began to groan and creak.

He could see the switches for the Warton-Purg drive

and he extended his arm, reaching. Then the ship came apart and he was drawn away from the controls. He glimpsed a jumpsuited human form, turning and turning.

Later, drifting, he met a Nik who did not recall him but who quickly understood his explanation as to what had occurred.

"Am I still in the closed timelike curve?" Jeremy asked.

"Oh, yes. I know of no way of departing a CTC till it's run its course," Nik replied. "In fact, theoretically, if you could do it you'd wind up inside the black hole."

"Guess things get to run their course then. But listen, this time around it was a little different than the first time."

"Yes. Your classical physics is deterministic, but this isn't classical physics."

"I actually got close to the *Raven's* controls. I wonder. . . ."

"What?"

"You've installed a form of telepathy in my mind. Could you also teach me something—telekinetic, perhaps—that would give me the ability to hold a bubble of air around my head for a minute or two. I'm convinced that slowing to put on the helmet was what kept me from reaching the controls."

"We'll see what we can do. Take a nap."

When Jeremy awoke he had the ability to move small objects with his mind. He tested this by removing units from his tool kit, having them orbit his arms, his legs, his head, and returning them without touching them physically.

"I think I've got it, Nik. Thanks."

"You're an interesting study, Jeremy."

This time when he entered the trapezoid he had his mind flexed, and he gathered the bubble of air to him as he rushed toward the control station.

He waited, his hand hovering above the appropriate bank of lights, for the Warton-Purg drive to drop the *Raven* into space proper. The lights went out. Immediately, he ran his hand across the row, illuminating them again.

Simultaneous with the clutch of the tidal forces, he felt the explosion from the rear of the vessel. The manual had been right. Reactivating the drive immediately following shutdown was hazardous to the health. He pulled on his helmet as a sheet of flame flashed toward him. The suit's insulation protected him from the heat as the *Raven* came apart. This time he did not see the jumpsuited figure.

Again, he drifted.

When Nik rescued him, he told him the story.

". . . So, either way I lose," he concluded.

"So it would seem," Nik said.

When the CTC ran its course and Nik went off to report the results of the latest trip to Vik, Jeremy looked toward the event horizon with his enhanced senses.

He was aware of his antigrav field now, could even manipulate it with his mind. He was certain that he could control it sufficiently to keep himself unstretched or unsquashed at least between here and the layer beneath the violet band.

"What the hell," he said.

He wondered what sort of final image he would leave for eternity.

II.

He descended quickly toward the devouring sphere, and soon it was as if he fled among the curtains of an Aurora Borealis. At one point it seemed that Nik might have called after him, but he could not be certain. Not that it mattered. What had he left of life even with the kindly Fleep? His suit's oxygen, water, and nutrients would dwindle toward an unpleasant end and there was no chance of anyone coming to his rescue. Best to pass in this blaze of glory seeing what no man had seen before, leaving his small signature upon the universe.

As the waves rose to embrace him, the colors darkened, darkened, were gone. He was alone in a black place and without sensation. Had he actually penetrated the black hole and survived, or was this but his final, drawn-out thought in a time-distorting field?

"The former," Nik said from a place that seemed nearby.

"Nik! You're here with me!"

"Indeed. I decided to follow you and give what assistance I could."

"As you entered did you see the image I left behind on the event horizon?"

"Sorry, I didn't look."

"Are we into the singularity?"

"Perhaps. I don't know. I've never been this way before. The process may be one of infinite infall."

"But I thought that all information was destroyed once it entered a black hole."

"Well, there is more than one school of thought on that. Information is necessarily bound up with energy, and one notion is that it might remain coherent in here but simply become totally inaccessible to the outside world. The information cannot exist independently from the energy, and this way of considering it has the advantage of preserving energy conservation."

"Then it must be so."

"On the other hand, when your body was destroyed

as we entered here I was able to run you quickly through the process by which I became an immortal energy being. Thought you might appreciate it."

"Immortal? You mean I might be an infinitely infalling consciousness here for the effective life of the universe? I don't think I could bear it."

"Oh, you'd go mad before too long and it wouldn't make any difference."

"Shit!" Jeremy said.

There was a long silence, then a chuckle from Nik.

"I remember what that is," he finally said.

"And we're in it without paddles," Jeremy noted.

III.

"There is another factor in our case," Nik said after an eternity or a few minutes, whichever came first.

"What is that?" Jeremy asked.

"When I talked to Vik he mentioned that we've messed so much with this black hole and its rotation that we might have provoked an unusual situation."

"What's that?"

"It's theoretically possible for a black hole to explode. He thought that this one was about to. Seeing it happen is sort of a once-in-a-lifetime affair."

"What goes on when it blows?"

"I'm not sure and neither was Vik. The cornucopion hypothesis would seem most in keeping with our present situation, though."

"Better tell me about it so it won't come as a complete surprise."

"It holds that when it blows it leaves behind a horn-shaped remnant smaller than an atom, weighing about a hundred-thousandth of a gram. Its volume would be unlimited, though, and it would contain all of the information that ever fell into the black hole. That, of course, would include us."

"Would it be any easier to get out of a cornucopion than out of a black hole?"

"Not here it wouldn't be. Once our information leaves our universe it stays gone."

"What do you mean 'not here'? Is there a loophole if it gets moved someplace else?"

"Well, if it could be bounced past the Big Crunch and the next Big Bang and wind up in our successor universe its contents might be accessible. We only know for sure that they're barred from release in *this* universe."

"Sounds like a long wait."

"You never know what time will be doing in a place like that, though. Or this."

"It's been interesting knowing you, Nik. I'll give you that."

"You, too, Jeremy. Now I don't know whether to tell you to open your sensory channels to the fullest or to shut them down as far as you can."

"Why? Or why not?"

"I can feel the explosion coming on."

There followed an intense sensation of white light which seemed to go on and on and on until Jeremy felt himself slipping away. He struggled to retain his coherency, hoped he was succeeding.

Slowly, he became aware that he inhabited a vast library, bookshelves sweeping off in either direction, periodically pierced by cross-corridors.

"Where are we?" he finally asked.

"I was able to create a compelling metaphor, allowing you to coordinate your situation," Nik replied. "This is the cornucopion within which all of the information is stored. We inhabit a bookshelf ourselves. I gave you a nice blue leather cover, embossed, hubbed spine."

"Thanks. What do we do now, to pass the time?"

"I think we should be able to establish contact with the others. We can start reading them."

"I'll try. I hope they're interesting. How do we know whether we've made it into the next universe and freedom?"

"Hopefully, somebody will stop by to check us out."

Jeremy extended his consciousness to a smart red volume across the way.

"Hello," he said. "You are . . . ?"

"History," the other stated. "And yourself?"

"Autobiography," Jeremy replied. "You know, we're going to need a catalogue, so we can leave a Recommended Reading List on top."

"What's that?"

"I'll write it myself," he said. "Let's get acquainted."

Evolution

NANCY KRESS

Nancy Kress is one of the leading SF writers to become
prominent in the last decade. She began, as did Patricia
McKillip, by writing fantasy novels (*The Prince of
Morning Bells*, 1981) but also wrote distinguished science fiction short stories, many collected in *Trinity*
(1985). Then in 1988, with *An Alien Light*, Kress
turned entirely to SF and began to publish the SF novels and stories for which she is famous today, most
prominently the Hugo and Nebula award-winning
"Beggars in Spain," from which has grown a trilogy of
novels. In her hard SF mode she is most often interested in the biological sciences and their moral and
social impact on individual human lives. A number of
her stories are about medicine and medical practice,
for instance, "Evolution," which appeared in *Asimov's
SF*, a magazine which had a particularly strong year in
1995.

Somebody shot and killed Dr. Bennett behind the Food Mart on April Street!" Ceci Moore says breathlessly as I take the washing off the line.

I stand with a pair of Jack's boxer shorts in my hand and stare at her. I don't like Ceci. Her smirking pushiness, her need to shove her scrawny body into the middle of every situation, even ones she'd be better off leaving alone. She's been that way since high school. But we're neighbors; we're stuck with each other. Dr. Bennett delivered both Sean and Jackie. Slowly I fold the boxer shorts and lay them in my clothesbasket.

"Well, Betty, aren't you even going to *say* anything?"

"Have the police arrested anybody?"

"Janie Brunelli says there's no suspects." Tom Brunelli is one of Emerton's police officers. There are only five of them. He has trouble keeping his mouth shut. "Honestly, Betty, you look like there's a murder in this town every day!"

"Was it in the parking lot?" I'm in that parking lot behind the Food Mart every week. It's unpaved, just hardpacked rocky dirt sloping down to a low concrete wall by the river. I take Jackie's sheets off the line. Belle, Ariel, and Princess Jasmine all smile through fields of flowers.

"Yes, in the parking lot," Ceci says. "Near the Dumpsters. There must have been a silencer on the rifle, nobody heard anything. Tom found two .22 250 semi-automatic cartridges." Ceci knows about guns. Her house is full of them. "Betty, why don't you put all this wash in your dryer and save yourself the trouble of hanging it all out?"

"I like the way it smells line-dried. And I can hear Jackie through the window."

Instantly Ceci's face changes. "Jackie's home from school? Why?"

"She has a cold."

"Are you sure it's just a cold?"

"I'm sure." I take the clothespins off Sean's T-shirt. The front says SEE DICK DRINK. SEE DICK DRIVE. SEE DICK DIE. "Ceci, Jackie is not on any antibiotics."

"Good thing," Ceci says, and for a moment she studies her fingernails, very casual. "They say Dr. Bennett prescribed endozine again last week. For the youngest Nordstrum boy. *Without* sending him to the hospital."

I don't answer. The back of Sean's T-shirt says DON'T BE A DICK. Irritated by my silence, Ceci says, "I don't see how you can let your son wear that obscene clothing!"

"It's his choice. Besides, Ceci, it's a health message. About not drinking and driving. Aren't you the one that thinks strong health messages are a good thing?"

Our eyes lock. The silence lengthens. Finally Ceci says, "Well, haven't *we* gotten serious all of a sudden."

I say, "Murder is serious."

"Yes. I'm sure the cops will catch whoever did it. Probably one of those scum that hang around the Rainbow Bar."

"Dr. Bennett wasn't the type to hang around with scum."

"Oh, I don't mean he *knew* them. Some low-life probably killed him for his wallet." She looks straight into my eyes. "I can't think of any other motive. Can you?"

I look east, toward the river. On the other side, just visible over the tops of houses on its little hill, rise the three stories of Emerton Soldiers and Sailors Memorial Hospital. The bridge over the river was blown up three weeks ago. No injuries, no suspects. Now anybody who wants to go to the hospital has to drive ten miles up West River Road and cross at the interstate. Jack told me that the Department of Transportation says two years to get a new bridge built.

I say, "Dr. Bennett was a good doctor. And a good man."

"Well, did anybody say he wasn't? Really, Betty, you should use your dryer and save yourself all that bending and stooping. Bad for the back. We're not getting any younger. Ta-ta." She waves her right hand, just a waggle of fingers, and walks off. Her nails, I notice, are painted the delicate fragile pinky white of freshly unscabbed skin.

"You have no proof," Jack says. "Just some wild suspicions."

He has his stubborn face on. He sits with his Michelob at the kitchen table, dog-tired from his factory shift plus three hours overtime, and he doesn't want to hear this. I don't blame him. I don't want to be saying it. In the living room Jackie plays Nintendo frantically, trying to cram in as many electronic explosions as she can before her father claims the TV for Monday night football. Sean has already gone out with his friends, before his stepfather got home.

I sit down across from Jack, a fresh mug of coffee

cradled between my palms. For warmth. "I know I don't have any proof, Jack. I'm not some detective."

"So let the cops handle it. It's their business, not ours. You stay out of it."

"I am out of it. You know that." Jack nods. We don't mix with cops, don't serve on any town committees, don't even listen to the news much. We don't get involved with what doesn't concern us. Jack never did. I add, "I'm just telling you what I think. I can do that, can't I?" and hear my voice stuck someplace between pleading and anger.

Jack hears it, too. He scowls, stands with his beer, puts his hand gently on my shoulder. "Sure, Bets. You can say whatever you want to me. But nobody else, you hear? I don't want no trouble, especially to you and the kids. This ain't our problem. Just be grateful *we're* all healthy, knock on wood."

He smiles and goes into the living room. Jackie switches off the Nintendo without being yelled at; she's good that way. I look out the kitchen window, but it's too dark to see anything but my own reflection, and anyway the window faces north, not east.

I haven't crossed the river since Jackie was born at Emerton Memorial, seven years ago. And then I was in the hospital less than twenty-four hours before I made Jack take me home. Not because of the infections, of course—all that hadn't started yet. But it has now, and what if next time instead of the youngest Nordstrum boy, it's Jackie who needs endozine? Or Sean?

Once you've been to Emerton Memorial, nobody but your family will go near you. And sometimes not even them. When Mrs. Weimer came home from surgery, her daughter-in-law put her in that back upstairs room and left her food on disposable trays in the doorway and put in a chemical toilet. Didn't even help the old lady crawl out of bed to use it. For a whole month it went on like that—surgical masks, gloves, paper gowns—until Rosie Weimer was positive Mrs. Weimer hadn't picked up any mutated drug-resistant bacteria in Emerton Memorial. And Hal Weimer didn't say a word against his wife.

"People are scared, but they'll do the right thing," Jack said, the only other time I tried to talk to him about it. Jack isn't much for talking. And so I don't. I owe him that.

But in the city—in all the cities—they're not just scared. They're terrified. Even without listening to the news I hear about the riots and the special government police and half the population sick with the new germs that only endozine cures—sometimes. I don't see how they're going to have much energy for one murdered small-town doctor. And I don't share Jack's conviction that people in Emerton will automatically do the right thing. I remember all too well that sometimes they don't. How come Jack doesn't remember, too?

But he's right about one thing: I don't owe this town anything.

I stack the supper dishes in the sink and get Jackie started on her homework.

The next day, I drive down to the Food Mart parking lot.

There isn't much to see. It rained last night. Next to the Dumpster lie a wadded-up surgical glove and a piece of yellow tape like the police use around a crime scene. Also some of those little black cardboard boxes from the stuff that gets used up by the new holographic TV cameras. That's it.

"You heard what happened to Dr. Bennett," I say to Sean at dinner. Jack's working again. Jackie sits playing with the Barbie doll she doesn't know I know she has on her lap.

Sean looks at me sideways, under the heavy fringe of his dark bangs, and I can't read his expression. "He was killed for giving out too many antibiotics."

Jackie looks up. "Who killed the doctor?"

"The bastards that think they run this town," Sean says. He flicks the hair out of his eyes. His face is ashy gray. "Fucking vigilantes'll get us all."

"That's enough, Sean," I say.

Jackie's lip trembles. "Who'll get us all? Mommy . . . "

"Nobody's getting anybody," I say. "Sean, stop it. You're scaring her."

"Well, she should be scared," Sean says, but he shuts up and stares bleakly at his plate. Sixteen now, I've had him for sixteen years. Watching him, his thick dark hair and sulky mouth, I think that it's a sin to have a favorite child. And that I can't help it, and that I would, God forgive me, sacrifice both Jackie and Jack for this boy.

"I want you to clean the garage tonight, Sean. You promised Jack three days ago now."

"Tomorrow. Tonight I have to go out."

Jackie says, "Why should I be scared?"

"Tonight," I say.

Sean looks at me with teenage desperation. His eyes are very blue. "Not tonight. I have to go out."

Jackie says, "Why should I—"

I say, "You're staying home and cleaning the garage."

"No." He glares at me, and then breaks. He has his father's looks, but he's not really like his father. There are even tears in the corners of his eyes. "I'll do it tomorrow, Mom, I promise. Right after school. But tonight I have to go out."

"Where?"

"Just out."

Jackie says, "Why should I be scared? Scared of what? Mommy!"

Sean turns to her. "You shouldn't be scared, Jack-o-lantern. Everything's going to be all right. One way or another."

I listen to the tone of his voice and suddenly fear shoots through me, piercing as childbirth. I say, "Jackie, you can play Nintendo now. I'll clear the table."

Her face brightens. She skips into the living room and I look at my son. "What does that mean? 'One way or another'? Sean, what's going on?"

"Nothing," he says, and then despite his ashy color he looks me straight in the eyes, and smiles tenderly, and for the first time—the very first time—I see his resemblance to his father. He can lie to me with tenderness.

Two days later, just after I return from the Food Mart, they contact me.

The murder was on the news for two nights, and then disappeared. Over the parking lot is scattered more TV-camera litter. There's also a wine bottle buried halfway into the hard ground, with a bouquet of yellow roses in it. Nearby is an empty basket, the kind that comes filled with expensive dried flowers at Blossoms by Bonnie, weighted down with stones. Staring at it, I remember that Bonnie Widelstein went out of business a few months ago. A drug-resistant abscess, and after she got out of Emerton Memorial, nobody on this side of the river would buy flowers from her.

At home, Sylvia James is sitting in my driveway in her black Algol. As soon as I see her, I put it together.

"Sylvia," I say tonelessly.

She climbs out of the sportscar and smiles a social

smile. "Elizabeth! How good to see you!" I don't answer. She hasn't seen me in seventeen years. She's carrying a cheese kuchen, like some sort of key into my house. She's still blonde, still slim, still well dressed. Her lipstick is bright red, which is what her face should be.

I let her in anyway, my heart making slow hard thuds in my chest. *Sean. Sean.*

Once inside, her hard smile fades and she has the grace to look embarrassed. "Elizabeth—"

"Betty," I say. "I go by Betty now."

"Betty. First off, I want to apologize for not being . . . for not standing by you in that mess. I know it was so long ago, but even so, I—I wasn't a very good friend." She hesitates. "I was frightened by it all."

I want to say, *You* were frightened? But I don't.

I never think of the whole dumb story any more. Not even when I look at Sean. Especially not when I look at Sean.

Seventeen years ago, when Sylvia and I were seniors in high school, we were best friends. Neither of us had a sister, so we made each other into that, even though her family wasn't crazy about their precious daughter hanging around with someone like me. The Goddards live on the other side of the river. Sylvia ignored them, and I ignored the drunken warnings of my aunt, the closest thing I had to a family. The differences didn't matter. We were Sylvia-and-Elizabeth, the two prettiest and boldest girls in the senior class who had an academic future.

And then, suddenly, I didn't. At Elizabeth's house I met Randolf Satler, young resident in her father's unit at the hospital. And I got pregnant, and Randy dumped me, and I refused a paternity test because if he didn't want me and the baby I had too much pride to force myself on any man. That's what I told everyone, including myself. I was eighteen years old. I didn't know what a common story mine was, or what a dreary one. I thought I was the only one in the whole wide world who had ever felt this bad.

So after Sean was born at Emerton Memorial and Randy got engaged the day I moved my baby "home" to my dying aunt's, I bought a Smith & Wesson revolver in the city and shot out the windows of Randy's supposedly empty house across the river. I hit the gardener, who was helping himself to the Satler liquor cabinet in the living room. The judge gave me seven-and-a-half to ten, and I served five, and that only because my lawyer pleaded post-partum depression. The gardener recovered and retired to Miami, and Dr. Satler went on to become Chief of Medicine at Emerton Memorial and a lot of other important things in the city, and Sylvia never visited me once in Bedford Hills Correctional Facility. Nobody did, except Jack. Who, when Sylvia-and-Elizabeth were strutting their stuff at Emerton High, had already dropped out and was bagging groceries at the Food Mart. After I got out of Bedford, the only reason the foster-care people would give me Sean back was because Jack married me.

We live in Emerton, but not of it.

Sylvia puts her kuchen on the kitchen table and sits down without being asked. I can see she's done with apologizing. She's still smart enough to know there are things you can't apologize for.

"Eliz . . . Betty, I'm not here about the past. I'm here about Dr. Bennett's murder."

"That doesn't have anything to do with me."

"It has to do with all of us. Dan Moore lives next door to you."

I don't say anything.

"He and Ceci and Jim Dyer and Tom Brunelli are the ringleaders in a secret organization to close Emerton Memorial Hospital. They think the hospital is a breeding ground for the infections resistant to every antibiotic except endozine. Well, they're right about that—all hospitals are. But Dan and his group are determined to punish any doctor who prescribes endozine, so that no organisms develop a resistance to *it,* too, and it's kept effective in case one of *them* needs it."

"Sylvia—" the name tastes funny in my mouth, after all this time "—I'm telling you this doesn't have anything to do with me."

"And I'm telling you it does. We need you, Eliz . . . Betty. You live next door to Dan and Ceci. You can tell us when they leave the house, who comes to it, anything suspicious you see. We're not a vigilante group, Betty, like they are. We aren't doing anything illegal. We don't kill people, and we don't blow up bridges, and we don't threaten people like the Nordstrums who get endozine for their sick kids but are basically uneducated blue collar—"

She stops. Jack and I are basically uneducated blue collar. I say coldly, "I can't help you, Sylvia."

"I'm sorry, Betty. That wasn't what I meant. Look, this is more important than anything that happened a decade and a half ago! Don't you *understand?*" She leans toward me across the table. "The whole country's caught in this thing. It's already a public health crisis as big as the Spanish influenza epidemic of 1918, and it's only just started! Drug-resistant bacteria can produce a new generation every twenty minutes, they can swap resistant genes not only within a species but across *different* species. The bacteria are *winning*. And people like the Moores are taking advantage of that to contribute further to the breakdown of even basic social decency."

In high school Sylvia had been on the debating team. But so, in that other life, had I. "If the Moores's group is trying to keep endozine from being used, then aren't they also fighting against the development of more drug-resistant bacteria? And if that's so, aren't they the ones, not you, who are ultimately aiding the country's public health?"

"Through dynamiting. And intimidation. And murder. Betty, I know you don't approve of those things. I wouldn't be here telling you about our countergroup if I thought you did. Before I came here, we looked very carefully at you. At the kind of person you are. Are now. You and your husband are law-abiding people, you vote, you make a contribution to the Orphans of AIDS Fund, you—"

"How did you know about that? That's supposed to be a secret contribution!"

"—you signed the petition to protect the homeless from harassment. Your husband served on the jury that convicted Paul Keene of fraud, even though his real-estate scheme was so good for the economy of Emerton. You—"

"Stop it," I say. "You don't have any right to investigate me like I was some criminal!"

Only, of course, I was. Once. Not now. Sylvia's right about that—Jack and I believe in law and order, but for different reasons. Jack because that's what his father believed in, and his grandfather. Me, because I learned in Bedford that enforced rules are the only thing that even halfway restrains the kind of predators Sylvia James never dreamed of. The kind I want kept away from my children.

Sylvia says, "We have a lot of people on our side, Betty. People who don't want to see this town slide into the same kind of violence there is in Albany and Syracuse and, worst case, New York."

A month ago, New York Hospital in Queens was blown up. The whole thing, with a series of coordinated timed bombs. Seventeen hundred people dead in less than a minute.

"It's a varied group," she continues. "Some town leaders, some housewives, some teachers, nearly all the medical personnel at the hospital. All people who care what happens to Emerton."

"Then you've got the wrong person here," I say, and it comes out harsher than I want to reveal. "I don't care about Emerton."

"You have reasons," Sylvia says evenly. "And I'm part of your reasons, I know. But I think you'll help us, Elizabeth. I know you must be concerned about your son—we've all observed what a good mother you are."

So she brought up Sean's name first. I say, "You're wrong again, Sylvia. I don't need you to protect Sean, and if you've let him get involved in helping you, you'll wish you'd never been born. I've worked damn hard to make sure that what happened seventeen years ago never touches him. He doesn't need to get mixed up in any way with your 'medical personnel at the hospital.' And Sean sure the hell doesn't owe this town anything, there wasn't even anybody who would take him in after my aunt died, he had to go to—"

The look on her face stops me. Pure surprise. And then something else.

"Oh my God," she says. "Is it possible you don't know? Hasn't Sean told you?"

"Told me what?" I stand up, and I'm seventeen years old again, and just that scared. Sylvia-and-Elizabeth.

"Your son isn't helping our side. He's working for Dan Moore and Mike Dyer. They use juveniles because if they're caught, they won't be tried as severely as adults. We think Sean was one of the kids they used to blow up the bridge over the river."

I look first at the high school. Sean isn't there; he hadn't even shown up for homeroom. No one's home at his friend Tom's house, or at Keith's. He isn't at the Billiard Ball or the Emerton Diner or the American Bowl. After that, I run out of places to search.

This doesn't happen in places like Emerton. We have fights at basketball games and grand theft auto and smashed store windows on Halloween and sometimes a drunken tragic car crash on prom night. But not secret terrorists, not counter-terrorist vigilante groups. Not in Emerton.

Not with my son.

I drive to the factory and make them page Jack.

He comes off the line, face creased with sweat and dirt. The air is filled with clanging machinery and grinding drills. I pull him outside the door, where there are benches and picnic tables for workers on break. "Betty! What is it?"

"Sean," I gasp. "He's in danger."

Something shifts behind Jack's eyes. "What kind of danger?"

"Sylvia Goddard came to see me today. Sylvia James. She says Sean is involved with the group that blew up the bridge, the ones who are trying to get Emerton Memorial closed, and . . . and killed Dr. Bennett."

Jack peels off his bench gloves, taking his time. Finally he looks up at me. "How come that bitch Sylvia Goddard comes to you with this? After all this time?"

"Jack! Is that all you can think of? Sean is in trouble!"

He says gently, "Well, Bets, it was bound to happen

sooner or later, wasn't it? He's always been a tough kid to raise. Rebellious. Can't tell him anything."

I stare at Jack.

"Some people just have to learn the hard way."

"Jack . . . this is serious! Sean might be involved in terrorism! He could end up in jail!"

"Couldn't ever tell him anything," Jack says, and I hear the hidden satisfaction in his voice, that he doesn't even know is there. Not *his* son. Dr. Randy Satler's son. Turning out bad.

"Look," Jack says, "when the shift ends I'll go look for him, Bets. Bring him home. You go and wait there for us." His face is gentle, soothing. He really will find Sean, if it's possible. But only because he loves me.

My sudden surge of hatred is so strong I can't even speak.

"Go on home, Bets. It'll be all right. Sean just needs to have the nonsense kicked out of him."

I turn and walk away. At the turning in the parking lot, I see Jack walking jauntily back inside, pulling on his gloves.

I drive home, because I can't think what else to do. I sit on the couch and reach back in my mind, for that other place, the place I haven't gone to since I got out of Bedford. The gray granite place that turns you to granite, too, so you can sit and wait for hours, for weeks, for years, without feeling very much. I go into that place, and I become the Elizabeth I was then, when Sean was in foster care someplace and I didn't know who had him or what they might be doing to him or how I would get him back. I go into the gray granite place to become stone.

And it doesn't work.

It's been too long. I've had Sean too long. Jack has made me feel too safe. I can't find the stony place.

Jackie is spending the night at a friend's. I sit in the

dark, no lights on, car in the garage. Sean doesn't come home, and neither does Jack. At two in the morning, a lot of people in dark clothing cross the back lawn and quietly enter Dan and Ceci's house next door, carrying bulky packages wrapped in black cloth.

Jack staggers in at six-thirty in the morning. Alone. His face droops with exhaustion.

"I couldn't find him, Betty. I looked everywhere."

"Thank you," I say, and he nods. Accepting my thanks. This was something he did for me, not for Sean. Not for himself, as Sean's stepfather. I push down my sudden anger and say, "You better get some sleep."

"Right." He goes down the narrow hallway into our bedroom. In three minutes he's snoring.

I let the car coast in neutral down the driveway. Our bedroom faces the street. The curtains don't stir.

The West River Road is deserted, except for a few eighteen-wheelers. I cross the river at the interstate and start back along the east side. Three miles along, in the middle of farmland, the smell of burned flesh rolls in the window.

Cows, close to the pasture fence. I stop the car and get out. Fifteen or sixteen Holsteins. By straining over the fence, I can see the bullet holes in their heads. Somebody herded them together, shot them one by one, and started a half-hearted fire among the bodies with neatly cut firewood. The fire had gone out; it didn't look as if it was supposed to burn long. Just long enough to attract attention that hadn't come yet.

I'd never heard that cows could get human diseases. Why had they been shot?

I get back in my car and drive the rest of the way to Emerton Memorial.

This side of town is deathly quiet. Grass grows unmowed in yard after yard. One large, expensive house has old newspapers piled on the porch steps, ten or twelve of them. There are no kids waiting for school buses, no cars pulling out of driveways on the way to work. The hospital parking lot has huge empty stretches between cars. At the last minute I drive on through the lot, parking instead across the street in somebody's empty driveway, under a clump of trees.

Nobody sits at the information desk. The gift shop is locked. Nobody speaks to me as I study the directory on the lobby wall, even though two figures in gowns and masks hurry past. CHIEF OF MEDICINE, DR. RANDOLF SATLER. Third floor, east wing. The elevator is deserted.

It stops at the second floor. When the doors open a man stands there, a middle-aged farmer in overalls and work boots, his eyes red and swollen like he's been crying. There are tinted windows across from the elevators and I can see the back of him reflected in the glass. Coming and going. From somewhere I hear a voice calling, "Nurse, oh nurse, oh God . . ." A gurney sits in the hallway, the body on it covered by a sheet up to the neck. The man in overalls looks at me and raises both hands to ward off the elevator, like it's some kind of demon. He steps backward. The doors close.

I grip the railing on the elevator wall.

The third floor looks empty. Bright arrows lead along the hallways: yellow for PATHOLOGY and LAB SERVICES, green for RESPIRATORY THERAPY, red for SUPPORT SERVICES. I follow the yellow arrow.

It dead-ends at an empty alcove with chairs, magazines thrown on the floor. And three locked doors off a short corridor that's little more than an alcove.

I pick the farthest door and pound on it. No words,

just regular blows of my fist. After a minute, I start on the second one. A voice calls, "Who's there?"

I recognize the voice, even through the locked door. Even after seventeen years. I shout, "Police! Open the door!"

And he does. The second it cracks, I shove it hard and push my way into the lab.

"Elizabeth?"

He's older, heavier, but still the same. Dark hair, blue eyes ... I look at that face every day at dinner. I've looked at it at soccer matches, in school plays, in his playpen. Dr. Salter looks more shaken to see me than I would have thought, his face white, sweat on his forehead.

"Hello, Randy."

"Elizabeth. You can't come in here. You have to leave—"

"Because of the staph? Do you think I care about that? After all, I'm in the hospital, right, Randy? This is where the endozine is. This place is safe. Unless it gets blown up while I'm standing here."

He stares at my left hand, still gripping the doorknob behind me. Then at the gun in my right hand. A seventeen-year-old Smith & Wesson, and for five of those years the gun wasn't cleaned or oiled, hidden under my aunt's garage. But it still fires.

"I'm not going to shoot you, Randy. I don't care if you're alive or dead. But you're going to help me. I can't find my son—" *your son* "—and Sylvia Goddard told me he's mixed up with that group that blew up the bridge. He's hiding with them someplace, probably scared out of his skull. You know everybody in town, everybody with power, you're going to get on that phone there and find out where Sean is."

"I would do that anyway," Randy says, and now he looks the way I remember him: impatient and arrogant. But not completely. There's still sweat on his pale face. "Put that stupid thing away, Elizabeth."

"No."

"Oh, for . . . " He turns his back on me and punches at the phone.

"Cam? Randy Satler here. Could you . . . no, it's not about that . . . No. Not yet."

Cameron Witt. The mayor. His son is chief of Emerton's five cops.

"I need a favor. There's a kid missing . . . I know that, Cam. You don't have to lecture *me* on how bad delay could. . . . But you might know about this kid. Sean Baker."

"Pulaski. Sean Pulaski." He doesn't even know that.

"Sean Pulaski. Yeah, that one . . . okay. Get back to me . . . I told you. *Not yet.*" He hangs up. "Cam will hunt around and call back. Now will you put that stupid gun away, Elizabeth?"

"You still don't say thank you for anything." The words just come out. Fuck, fuck, fuck.

"To Cam, or to you for not shooting me?" He says it evenly, and the evenness is the only way I finally see how furious he is. People don't order around Dr. Randy Satler at gun point. A part of my mind wonders why he doesn't call security.

I said, "All right, I'm here. Give me a dose of endozine, just in case."

He goes on staring at me with that same level, furious gaze. "Too late, Elizabeth."

"What do you mean, too late? Haven't you got endozine?"

"Of course we do." Suddenly he staggers slightly, puts out one hand behind him, and holds onto a table covered with glassware and papers.

"Randy. You're sick."

"I am. And not with anything endozine is going to cure. Ah, Elizabeth, why didn't you just phone me? I'd have looked for Sean for you."

"Oh, right. Like you've been so interested and helpful in raising him."

"You never asked me."

I see that he means it. He really believes his total lack of contact with his son is my fault. I see that Randy gives only what he's asked to. He waits, lordly, for people to plead for his help, beg for it, and then he gives it. If it suits him.

I say, "I'll bet anything your kids with your wife are turning out really scary."

The blood rushes to his face, and I know I guessed right. His blue eyes darken and he looks like Jack looks just before Jack explodes. But Randy isn't Jack. An explosion would be too clean for him. He says instead, "You were stupid to come here. Haven't you been listening to the news?"

I haven't.

"The CDC publicly announced just last night what medical personnel have seen for weeks. A virulent strain of staphylococcus aureus has incorporated endozine-resistant plasmids from enterococcus." He pauses to catch his breath. "And pneumococcus may have done the same thing."

"What does that mean?"

"It means, you stupid woman, that now there are highly contagious infections that we have no drugs to cure. No antibiotics at all, not even endozine. This staph is resistant to them all. And it can live everywhere."

I lower the gun. The empty parking lot. No security to summon. The man who wouldn't get on the elevator. And Randy's face. "And you've got it."

"We've all got it. Everyone . . . in the hospital. And for forcing your way in here, you probably do, too."

"You're going to die," I say, and it's half a hope.

And he *smiles*.

He stands there in his white lab coat, sweating like a horse, barely able to stand up straight, almost shot by a woman he'd once abandoned pregnant, and he smiles. His blue eyes gleam. He looks like a picture I once saw in a book, back when I read a lot. It takes me a minute to remember that it was my high school World History book. A picture of some general.

"Everybody's going to die eventually," Randy says. "But not me right now. At least . . . I hope not." Casually he crosses the floor toward me, and I step backward. He smiles again.

"I'm not going to deliberately infect you, Elizabeth. I'm a *doctor*. I just want the gun."

"No."

"Have it your way. Look, how much do you know about the bubonic plague of the fourteenth century?"

"Nothing," I say, although I do. Why had I always acted stupider around Randy than I actually am?

"Then it won't mean anything to you to say that this mutated staph has at least that much potential—" again he paused and gulped air "—for rapid and fatal transmission. It flourishes everywhere. Even on doorknobs."

"So why the fuck are you *smiling?*" Alexander. That was the picture of the general. Alexander the Great.

"Because I . . . because the CDC distributed . . . I was on the national team to discover . . . " His face changes again. Goes even whiter. And he pitches over onto the floor.

I grab him, roll him face up, and feel his forehead. He's burning up. I bolt for the door. "Nurse! Doctor! There's a sick doctor here!"

Nobody comes.

I run down the corridors. Respiratory Therapy is empty. So is Support Services. I jab at the elevator button, but before it comes I run back to Randy.

And stand above him, lying there crumpled on the floor, laboring to breathe.

I'd dreamed about a moment like this for years. Dreamed it waking and asleep, in Emerton and in Bedford Hills and in Jack's arms. Dreamed it in a thousand ridiculous melodramatic versions. And here it is, Randy helpless and pleading, and me strong, standing over him, free to walk away and let him die. Free.

I wring out a towel in cold water and put it on his forehead. Then I find ice in the refrigerator in a corner of the lab and substitute that. He watches me, his breathing wheezy as old machinery.

"Elizabeth. Bring me . . . syringe in a box on . . . that table."

I do it. "Who should I get for you, Randy? Where?"

"Nobody. I'm not . . . as bad . . . as I sound. Yet. Just the initial . . . dyspnea." He picked up the syringe.

"Is there medicine for you in there? I thought you said endozine wouldn't work on this new infection." His color is a little better now.

"Not medicine. And not for me. For you."

He looks at me steadily. And I see that Randy would never plead, never admit to helplessness. Never ever think of himself as helpless.

He lowers the hand holding the syringe back to the floor. "Listen, Elizabeth. You have . . . almost certainly have . . . "

Somewhere, distantly, a siren starts to wail. Randy ignores it. All of a sudden his voice becomes much firmer, even though he's sweating again and his eyes burn bright with fever. Or something.

"This staph is resistant to everything we can throw

at it. We cultured it and tried. Cephalosporins and aminoglycosides and vancomycin, even endozine . . . I'll go into gram-positive septic shock . . . " His eyes glaze, but after a moment he seems to find his thought again. "We exhausted all points of counterattack. Cell wall, bacterial ribosome, folic acid pathway. Microbes just evolve countermeasures. Like beta-lactamase."

I don't understand this language. Even talking to himself, he's making me feel stupid again. I ask something I do understand.

"Why are people killing cows? Are the cows sick, too?"

He focuses again. "Cows? No, they're not sick. Farmers use massive doses of antibiotics to increase meat and milk production. Agricultural use of endozine has increased the rate of resistance development by over a thousand percent since—Elizabeth, this is irrelevant! Can't you pay attention to what I'm saying for three minutes?"

I stand up and look down at him, lying shivering on the floor. He doesn't even seem to notice, just keeps on lecturing.

"But antibiotics weren't invented by humans. They were invented by the microbes themselves to use . . . against each other and . . . they had two billion years of evolution at it before we even showed up. . . . We should have—where are you going?"

"Home. Have a nice life, Randy."

He says quietly, "I probably will. But if . . . you leave now, you're probably dead. And your husband and kids, too."

"Why? Damn it, stop lecturing and tell me why!"

"Because you're infected, and there's no antibiotic for it, but there *is* another bacteria that will attack the drug-resistant staph."

I look at the syringe in his hand.

"It's a Trojan horse plasmid. That's a . . . never mind. It can get into the staph in your blood and deliver a lethal gene. One that will kill the staph. It's an incredible discovery. But the only way to deliver it so far is to deliver the whole bacteria."

My knees all of a sudden get shaky. Randy watches me from his position on the floor. He looks shakier himself. His breathing turns raspier again.

"No, you're not sick yet, Elizabeth. But you will be."

I snap, "From the staph germs or from the cure?"

"Both."

"You want to make me sicker. With two bacteria. And hope one will kill the other."

"Not hope. I *know*. I actually saw . . . it on the electromicrograph . . . " His eyes roll, refocus. " . . . could package just the lethal plasmid on a transpon if we had time . . . no time. Has to be the whole bacteria." And then, stronger, "The CDC team is working on it. But *I* actually caught it on the electromicrograph!"

I say, before I know I'm going to, "Stop congratulating yourself and give me the syringe. Before you die."

I move across the floor toward him, put my arms around him to prop him in a sitting position against the table leg. His whole body feels on fire. But somehow he keeps his hands steady as he injects the syringe into the inside of my elbow. While it drains sickness into me I say, "You never actually wanted me, did you, Randy? Even before Sean?"

"No," he says. "Not really." He drops the syringe.

I bend my arm. "You're a rotten human being. All you care about is yourself and your work."

He smiles the same cold smile. "So? My work is what matters. In a larger sense than you could possibly imagine. You were always a weak sentimentalist, Elizabeth. Now, go home."

"Go *home*? But you said . . . "

"I said you'd infect everyone. And you will—with the bacteria that attacks staph. It should cause only a fairly mild illness. Jenner . . . smallpox . . . "

"But you said I have the mutated staph, too!"

"You almost certainly do. Yes . . . And so will everyone else, before long. Deaths . . . in New York State alone . . . passed one million this morning. Six and a half percent of the . . . the population . . . Did you really think you could hide on your side of . . . the . . . river . . . "

"Randy!"

"Go . . . home."

I strip off his lab coat and wad it up for a pillow, bring more ice from the refrigerator, try to get him to drink some water.

"Go . . . home. Kiss everybody." He smiles to himself, and starts to shake with fever. His eyes close.

I stand up again. Should I go? Stay? If I could find someone in the hospital to take care of him—

The phone rings. I seize it. "Hello? Hello?"

"Randy? Excuse me, can I talk to Dr. Satler? This is Cameron Witt."

I try to sound professional. "Dr. Satler can't come to the phone right now. But if you're calling about Sean Pulaski, Dr. Salter asked me to take the message."

"I don't . . . oh, all right. Just tell Randy the Pulaski boy is with Richard and Sylvia James. He'll understand." The line clicks.

I replace the receiver and stare at Randy, fighting for breath on the floor, his face as gray as Sean's when Sean realized it was murder he'd gotten involved with. No, not as gray. Because Sean had been terrified, and Randy is only sick.

My work is what matters.

But how had Sean known to go to Sylvia? Even if

he knew from Ceci who was on the other side, how did he know which people would hide him, would protect him when I could not, Jack could not? Sylvia-and-Elizabeth. How much did Sean actually know about the past I'd tried so hard to keep from touching him?

I reach the elevator, my finger almost touching the button, when the first explosion rocks the hospital.

It's in the west wing. Through the windows opposite the elevator banks I see windows in the far end of the building explode outward. Thick greasy black smoke billows out the holes. Alarms begin to screech.

Don't touch the elevators. Instructions remembered from high school, from grade-school fire drills. I race along the hall to the fire stairs. What if they put a bomb in the stairwell? What if *who* put a bomb in the stairwell? *A lot of people in dark clothing cross the back lawn and quietly enter Dan and Ceci's house next door, carrying bulky packages wrapped in black cloth.*

A last glimpse through a window by the door to the fire stairs. People are running out of the building, not many, but the ones I see are pushing gurneys. A nurse staggers outside, three small children in her arms, on her hip, clinging to her back.

They aren't setting off any more bombs until people have a chance to get out.

I let the fire door close. Alarms scream. I run back to Pathology and shove open the heavy door.

Randy lies on the floor, sweating and shivering. His lips move but if he's muttering aloud, I can't hear it over the alarm. I tug on his arm. He doesn't resist and he doesn't help, just lies like a heavy dead cow.

There are no gurneys in Pathology. I slap him across the face, yelling "Randy! Randy! Get up!" Even now, even here, a small part of my mind thrills at hitting him.

His eyes open. For a second, I think he knows me. It goes away, then returns. He tries to get up. The effort is enough to let me hoist him over my shoulder in a fireman's carry. I could never have carried Jack, but Randy is much slighter, and I'm very strong.

But I can't carry him down three flights of stairs. I get him to the top, prop him up on his ass, and shove. He slides down one flight, bumping and flailing, and glares at me for a minute. "For . . . God's sake . . . Janet!"

His wife's name. I don't think about this tiny glimpse of his marriage. I give him another shove, but he grabs the railing and refuses to fall. He hauls himself—I'll never know how—back to a sitting position, and I sit next to him. Together, my arm around his waist, tugging and pulling, we both descend the stairs the way two-year-olds do, on our asses. Every second I'm waiting for the stairwell to blow up. Sean's gray face at dinner: *Fucking vigilantes'll get us all.*

The stairs don't blow up. The firedoor at the bottom gives out on a sidewalk on the side of the hospital away from both street and parking lot. As soon as we're outside, Randy blacks out.

This time I do what I should have done upstairs and grab him under the armpits. I drag him over the grass as far as I can. Sweat and hair fall in my eyes, and my vision keeps blurring. Dimly I'm aware of someone running toward us.

"It's Dr. Satler! Oh my God!"

A man. A large man. He grabs Randy and hoists him over his shoulder, a fireman's carry a lot smoother than mine, barely glancing at me. I stay behind them and, at the first buildings, run in a wide loop away from the hospital.

My car is still in the deserted driveway across the street. Fire trucks add their sirens to the noise. When they've torn past, I back out of the driveway and push my foot to the floor, just as a second bomb blows in the east wing of the hospital, and then another, and the air is full of flying debris as thick and sharp as the noise that goes on and on and on.

Three miles along the East River Road, it suddenly catches up with me. All of it. I pull the car off the road and I can't stop shaking. Only a few trucks pass me, and nobody stops. It's twenty minutes before I can start the engine again, and there has never been a twenty minutes like them in my life, not even in Bedford. At the end of them, I pray that there never will be again.

I turn on the radio as soon as I've started the engine.

"—in another hospital bombing in New York City, St. Clare's Hospital in the heart of Manhattan. Beleaguered police officials say that a shortage of available officers make impossible the kind of protection called for by Mayor Thomas Flanagan. No group has claimed credit for the bombing, which caused fires that spread to nearby businesses and at least one apartment house.

"Since the Centers for Disease Control's announcement last night of a widespread staphylococcus resistant to endozine, and its simultaneous release of an emergency counterbacteria in twenty-five metropolitan areas around the country, the violence has worsened in every city transmitting reliable reports to Atlanta. A spokesperson for the national team of pathologists and scientists responsible for the drastic countermeasure released an additional set of guidelines for its use. The spokesperson declined to be identified, or to identify any of the doctors on the team, citing fear of reprisals if—"

A burst of static. The voice disappears, replaced by a shrill hum.

I turn the dial carefully, looking for another station with news.

By the time I reach the west side of Emerton, the streets are deserted. Everyone has retreated inside. It looks like the neighborhoods around the hospital look. Had looked. My body still doesn't feel sick.

Instead of going straight home, I drive the deserted streets to the Food Mart.

The parking lot is as empty as everywhere else. But the basket is still there, weighted with stones. Now the stones hold down a pile of letters. The top one is addressed in blue Magic Marker: TO DR. BENNETT. The half-buried wine bottle holds a fresh bouquet, chrysanthemums from somebody's garden. Nearby a foot-high American flag sticks in the ground, beside a white candle on a styrofoam plate, a stone crucifix, and a Barbie doll dressed like an angel. Saran Wrap covers a leather-bound copy of *The Prophet*. There are also five anti-NRA stickers, a pile of seashells, and a battered peace sign on a gold chain like a necklace. The peace sign looks older than I am.

When I get home, Jack is still asleep.

I stand over him, as a few hours ago I stood over Randy Satler. I think about how Jack visited me in prison, week after week, making the long drive from Emerton even in the bad winter weather. About how he'd sit smiling at me through the thick glass in the visitors' room, his hands with their grease-stained fingers resting on his knees, smiling even when we couldn't think of anything to say to each other. About how he clutched my hand in the delivery room when Jackie was born, and the look on his face when he first held her. About the look on his face when I told him Sean was missing: the sly, secret, not-my-kid triumph. And I think about the two sets of germs in my body, readying for war.

I bend over and kiss Jack full on the lips.

He stirs a little, half wakes, reaches for me. I pull away and go into the bathroom, where I use his toothbrush. I don't rinse it. When I return, he's asleep again.

I drive to Jackie's school, to retrieve my daughter. Together, we will go to Sylvia Goddard's—Sylvia James's—and get Sean. I'll visit with Sylvia, and shake her hand, and kiss her on the cheek, and touch everything I can. When the kids are safe at home, I'll visit Ceci and tell her I've thought it over and I want to help fight the overuse of antibiotics that's killing us. I'll touch her, and anyone else there, and everyone that either Sylvia or Ceci introduces me to, until I get too sick to do that. If I get that sick. Randy said I wouldn't, not as sick as he is. Of course, Randy has lied to me before. But I have to believe him now, on this.

I don't really have any choice. Yet.

A month later, I am on my way to Albany to bring back another dose of the counterbacteria, which the news calls "a reengineered prokaryote." They're careful not to call it a germ.

I listen to the news every hour now, although Jack doesn't like it. Or anything else I'm doing. I read, and I study, and now I know what prokaryotes are, and beta-lactamase, and plasmids. I know how bacteria fight to survive, evolving whatever they need to wipe out the competition and go on producing the next generation.

That's all that matters to bacteria. Survival by their own kind.

And that's what Randy Satler meant, too, when he said, "My work is what matters." Triumph by his own kind. It's what Ceci believes, too. And Jack.

We bring in the reengineered prokaryotes in convoys of cars and trucks, because in some other places there's been trouble. People who don't understand, people who won't understand. People whose family got a lot sicker than mine. The violence isn't over, even though the CDC says the epidemic itself is starting to come under control.

I'm early. The convoy hasn't formed yet. We leave from a different place in town each time. This time we're meeting behind the American Bowl. Sean is already there, with Sylvia. I take a short detour and drive, for the last time, to the Food Mart.

The basket is gone, with all its letters to the dead man. So are the American flag and the peace sign. The crucifix is still there, but it's broken in half. The latest flowers in the wine bottle are half wilted. Rain has muddied the Barbie doll's dress, and her long blonde hair is a mess. Someone ripped up the anti-NRA stickers. The white candle on a styrofoam plate and the pile of seashells are untouched.

We are not bacteria. More than survival matters to us, or should. The individual past, which we can't escape, no matter how hard we try. The individual present, with its unsafe choices. The individual future. And the collective one.

I search in my pockets. Nothing but keys, money clip, lipstick, tissues, a blue marble I must have stuck in my pocket when I cleaned behind the couch. Jackie likes marbles.

I put the marble beside the candle, check my gun, and drive to join the convoy for the city.

The Day the Aliens Came

ROBERT SHECKLEY

Robert Sheckley's reputation is based primarily on the quality of his quirky, subversive, satirical short fiction, a body of work admired by everyone from Kingsley Amis and J. G. Ballard to Roger Zelazny, with whom he has collaborated. He is on par with Philip K. Dick and Kurt Vonnegut as an ironic investigator of questions of identity and of the nature of reality. Sheckley first came to prominence in the 1950s as one of the leading writers in *Galaxy*, became a novelist in the 1960s, and still (but too infrequently) produces fiction today that is thought-provoking, memorable, and stylish. This story is in his classic *Galaxy* mode, and is another piece from the fine anthology, *New Legends*.

One day a man came to my door. He didn't quite look like a man, although he did walk on two feet. There was something wrong with his face. It looked as though it had been melted in an oven and then hastily frozen. I later learned that this expression was quite common among the group of aliens called Synesters, and was considered by them a look of especial beauty. The Melted Look, they called it, and it was often featured in their beauty contests. "I hear you're a writer," he said.

I said that was so. Why lie about a thing like that?

"Isn't that a bit of luck," he said. "I'm a story-buyer."

"No kidding," I said.

"Have you got any stories you want to sell?"

He was very direct. I decided to be similarly so.

"Yes," I said. "I do."

"OK," he said. "I'm sure glad of that. This is a strange city for me. Strange planet, too, come to think of it. But it's the city aspect that's most unsettling. Different customs, all that sort of thing. As soon as I got here, I said to myself, 'Traveling's great, but where am I going to find someone to sell me stories?'"

"It's a problem," I admitted.

"Well," he said, "let's get right to it because there's a lot to do. I'd like to begin with a ten thousand word novelette."

"You've as good as got it," I told him. "When do you want it?"

"I need it by the end of the week."

"What are we talking about in terms of money, if you'll excuse the expression?"

"I'll pay you a thousand dollars for a ten thousand word novelette. I was told that was standard pay for a writer in this part of Earth. This is Earth, isn't it?"

"It's Earth, and your thousand dollars is acceptable. Just tell me what I'm supposed to write about."

"I'll leave that up to you. After all, you're the writer."

"Damn right I am," I said. "So you don't care what it's about?"

"Not in the slightest. After all, I'm not going to read it."

"Makes sense," I said. "Why should you care?"

I didn't want to pursue that line of inquiry any further. I assumed that someone was going to read it. That's what usually happens with novelettes.

"What rights are you buying?" I asked, since it's important to be professional about these matters.

"First and second Synesterian," he said. "And of course I retain Synesterian movie rights although I'll pay you fifty percent of the net if I get a film sale."

"Is that likely?" I asked.

"Hard to say," he said. "As far as we're concerned, Earth is new literary territory."

"In that case, let's make my cut sixty-forty."

"I won't argue," he said. "Not this time. Later you may find me very tough. Who knows what I'll be like? For me this is a whole new frankfurter."

I let that pass. An occasional lapse in English doesn't make an alien an ignoramus.

I got my story done in a week and brought it in to the Synester's office in the old MGM building on Broadway.

I handed him the story and he waved me to a seat while he read it.

"It's pretty good," he said after a while. "I like it pretty well."

"Oh, good," I said.

"But I want some changes."

"Oh," I said. "What specifically did you have in mind?"

"Well," the Synester said, "this character you have in here, Alice."

"Yes, Alice," I said, though I couldn't quite remember writing an Alice into the story. Could he be referring to Alsace, the province in France? I decided not to question him. No sense appearing dumb on my own story.

"Now, this Alice," he said, "she's the size of a small country, isn't she?"

He was definitely referring to Alsace, the province in France, and I had lost the moment when I could correct him. "Yes," I said, "that's right, just about the size of a small country."

"Well, then," he said, "why don't you have Alice fall in love with a bigger country in the shape of a pretzel?"

"A what?" I said.

"Pretzel," he said. "It's a frequently used image in Synestrian popular literature. Synestrians like to read that sort of thing."

"Do they?" I said.

"Yes," he said. "Synestrians like to imagine people in the shape of pretzels. You stick that in, it'll make it more visual."

"Visual," I said, my mind a blank.

"Yes," he said, "because we gotta consider the movie possibilities."

"Yes, of course," I said, remembering that I got sixty percent.

"Now, for the film version of your story, I think we should set the action at a different time of day."

I tried to remember what time of day I had set the story in. It didn't seem to me I had specified any particular time at all. I mentioned this.

"That's true," he said, "you didn't set any specific time. But you inferred twilight. It was the slurring sound of your words that convinced me you were talking about twilight."

"Yes, all right," I said. "Twilight mood."

"Makes a nice title," he said.

"Yes," I said, hating it.

"*Twilight Mood*," he said, rolling it around inside his mouth. "You could call it that, but I think you should actually write it in a daytime mode. For the irony."

"Yes, I see what you mean," I said.

"So why don't you run it through your computer once more and bring it back to me."

When I got home, Rimb was washing dishes and looking subdued. I should mention that she was a medium-sized blond person with the harassed look that characterizes aliens of the Ghottich persuasion. And there were peculiar sounds coming from the living room. When I gave Rimb a quizzical look, she rolled her eyes toward the living room and shrugged. I went in and saw there were two people there. Without saying a word, I went back to the kitchen and said to Rimb, "Who are they?"

"They told me they're the Bayersons."

"Aliens?"

She nodded. "But not my kind of aliens. They're as alien to me as they are to you."

That was the first time I fully appreciated that aliens could be alien to one another.

"What are they doing here?" I asked.

"They didn't say," Rimb said.

I went back to the living room. Mr. Bayerson was sitting in my armchair reading an evening newspaper. He was about three or four feet tall and had orange hair. Mrs. Bayerson was equally small and orange-haired and she was knitting something orange and green. Mr. Bayerson scrambled out of my chair as soon as I returned to the room.

"Aliens?" I said, sitting down.

"Yes," Bayerson said. "We're from Capella."

"And what are you doing in our place?"

"They said it would be all right."

"Who said?"

Bayerson shrugged and looked vague. I was to get very accustomed to that look.

"But it's our place," I pointed out.

"Of course it's yours," Bayerson said. "Nobody's arguing that. But would you begrudge us a little space to live in? We're not very big."

"But why our place? Why not someone else's?"

"We just sort of drifted in here and liked it," Bayerson said. "We think of it as home now."

"Some other place could also feel like home."

"Maybe, maybe not. We want to stay here. Look, why don't you just consider us like barnacles, or brown spots on the wallpaper. We just sort of attach on here. It's what Capellans do. We won't be in the way.

Rimb and I didn't much want them, but there seemed no overpowering reason to make them go. I mean, they were here, after all. And they were right, they really weren't in the way. In some ways, they were a lot better than some of the other apartment-dwelling aliens we came to know later.

In fact, Rimb and I soon wished the Bayersons would be a little less unobtrusive and give a little help around the apartment. Or at least keep an eye on things. Especially on the day the burglars came in.

Rimb and I were out. The way I understood it, the Bayersons didn't do a thing to stop them. Didn't call the police or anything. Just watched while the burglars poked around the place, moving slowly, because they were so overweight, fat alien thieves from Barnard's Star. They took all of Anna's old silver. They were Barnardean silver thieves and their traditions went back a long way. That's what they told the Bayersons, while they robbed us, and while Mr. Bayerson was going through his eyelid exercises just like nothing at all was happening.

The way it all started, I had met Rimb in Franco's Bar on MacDougal Street in New York. I had seen a few aliens before this, of course, shopping on Fifth Avenue or watching the ice skaters in Rockefeller Center. But this was the first time I'd ever actually talked with one. I inquired as to its sex and learned that Rimb was of the Ghottich Persuasion. It was an interesting-sounding sexual designation, especially for someone like me who was trying to get beyond the male-female dichotomy. I thought it would be fun to mate with someone of the Ghottich Persuasion after Rimb and I had agreed that she was basically a her. Later I checked with Father Hanlin at the Big Red Church. He said it was OK in the eyes of the Church, though he personally didn't hold much with it. Rimb and I were one of the first alien-human marriages.

We moved into my apartment in the West Village. You didn't see a lot of aliens around there at first. But soon other alien people showed up and quite a few of them moved into our neighborhood.

No matter where they were from, all aliens were supposed to register with the police and the local authorities in charge of cult control. Few bothered, however. And nothing was ever done about it. The police and municipal authorities were having too much trouble keeping track of their own people.

I wrote stories for the Synestrian market and Rimb and I lived quietly with our house guests. The Bayersons were quiet people and they helped pay the rent. They were easygoing aliens who didn't worry much; not like Rimb, who worried a lot about everything.

At first I liked the Bayerson's ways, I thought they were easygoing and cool. But I changed my mind the day the burglars stole their youngest child, little Claude Bayerson.

I should have mentioned that the Bayersons had a baby soon after moving in with us. Or perhaps they had left the baby somewhere else and brought it in after they'd taken over our spare bedroom. We were never really clear on where the aliens came from, and their babies were a complete mystery to us.

The way the Bayersons told it, the kidnapping of little Claude was simple and straightforward. It was "Good-bye, Claude." "Good-bye, Daddy." When we asked them how they could do that, they said, "Oh, it's perfectly all right. I mean, it's what we were hoping for. That's how we Bayersons get around. Someone steals our children."

Well, I let it drop. What can you do with people like that? How could they stand to have little Claude raised as a Barnardean silver thief? One race one day, another race another. Some aliens have no racial pride. I mean it was cuckoo.

There wasn't anything to do about it so we all sat down to watch the TV together. All of us wanted to see the Savannah Reed show, our favorite.

Savannah's main guest that evening was the first man ever to eat a Mungulu. He was quite open about it, even somewhat defiant. He said, "If you think about it, why should it be ethical to eat only stupid creatures, or deluded ones? It is only blind prejudice that keeps us from eating intelligent beings. This thought came to me one day recently while I was talking with a few glotch of Mungulu on a plate."

"How many Mungulu make up a glotch?" Savannah asked. She's no dummy.

"Between fifteen and twenty, though there are exceptions."

"And what were they doing on a plate?"

"That's where Mungulu usually hang out. Accumulate, I should say. You see, Mungulu are plate-specific."

"I don't think I know this species," Savannah said.

"They're pretty much unique to my section of Yonkers."

"How did they get there?"

"They just pretty well showed up on my plate one night. First only one or two glotch of them. They looked a little like oysters. Then more came so we had the half dozen or so it takes to generate a halfway decent conversation."

"Did they say where they were from?"

"A planet called Espadrille. I never did quite catch where it was, quadrantwise."

"Did they say how they got here?"

"Something about surfing the light-waves."

"What gave you the idea of eating the Mungulu?"

"Well, I didn't think about it at all at first. When a creature talks to you, you don't right away think of eating him. Or her. Not if you're civilized. But these Mungulu started showing up on my plate every night. They were pretty casual about it. All lined up on the edge of my good bone china, on the far side from me. Sometimes they'd just talk to each other, act like I wasn't even there. Then one of them would pretend to notice me—oh—it's the Earth guy—and we'd all start talking. This went on every night. I began to think there was something provocative about the way they were doing it. It seemed to me they were trying to tell me something."

"Do you think they wanted to be eaten?"

"Well, they never said so, not in so many words, no. But I was starting to get the idea. I mean, if they didn't want to be eaten, what were they doing on the edge of my plate?"

"What happened then?"

"To put it in a nutshell, one night I got sick of horsing around and just for the hell of it I speared one of them on the end of my fork and swallowed it."

"What did the others do?"

"They pretended not to notice. Just went right on with their conversation. Only their talk was a little stupider with one of them missing. Those guys need all the brain power they can come up with."

"Let's get back to this Mungulu you swallowed. Did it protest as it was going down?

"No, it didn't even blink. It was like it was expecting it. I got the feeling it was no cruel and unusual punishment for a Mungulu to be ingested."

"How did they taste?"

"A little like breaded oysters in hot sauce, only subtly different. Alien, you know."

After the show was over, I noticed a bassinet in a corner of our living room. Inside was a cute little fellow, looked a little like me. At first I thought it was little Claude Bayerson, somehow returned. But Rimb soon put me wise.

"That's little Manny," she said. "He's ours."

"Oh," I said. "I don't remember you having him."

"Technically, I haven't. I've delayed the actual delivery until a more convenient time," she told me.

"Can you do that?"

She nodded. "We of the Ghottich persuasion are able to do that."

"What do you call him?" I asked.

"His name is Manny," Rimb said.

"Is 'Manny' a typical name from your planet?"

"Not at all," Rimb said. "I called him that in honor of your species."

"How do you figure?" I asked

"The derivation is obvious. 'Manny' stands for 'Little Man.'"

"That's not the way we generally do things around here," I told her. But she didn't understand what I was talking about. Nor did I understand her explanation of the birth process by which Manny came into being. DDs, Deferred Deliveries, aren't customary among Earth people. As far as I could understand it, Rimb would have to undergo the actual delivery at some later time when it would be more convenient. But in fact we never got around to it. Sometimes it happens like that.

Manny lay in his crib and ooed and aaed and acted like a human baby would, I suppose. I was a pretty proud poppa. Rimb and I were one of the first viable human-alien intermatings. I later learned it was no big deal. People all over the Earth were doing it. But it seemed important to us at the time.

Various neighbors came around to see the baby. The Bayersons came in from their new room which they had plastered on the side of the apartment house after molting. Mrs. Bayerson had spun all the construction material out of her own mouth, and she was some kind of proud I want to tell you. They looked Manny up and down and said, "Looks like a good one."

They offered to baby-sit, but we didn't like to leave Manny alone with them. We still didn't have a reliable report on their feeding habits. Fact is, it was taking a long time getting any hard facts about aliens, even though the federal government had decided to make all information available on the species that came to Earth.

The presence of aliens among us was responsible for the next step in human development, the new interest in composite living. You got tired of the same old individualism after a while. Rimb and I thought it could be interesting to be part of something else. We wanted to join a creature like a medusa or a Portuguese man=of=war. But we weren't sure how to go about it. And so we didn't know whether to be pleased or alarmed when we received our notification by mail of our election to an alien composite life-form. Becoming part of a composite was still unusual in those days.

Rimb and I had quite a discussion about it. We finally decided to go to the first meeting, which was free, and see what it was like.

This meeting was held at our local Unitarian Church, and there were almost two hundred people and aliens present. There was a lot of good-natured bewilderment for a while as to just what we were supposed to do. We were all novices at this and just couldn't believe that we were expected to form up a two hundred person composite without prior training.

At last someone in a scarlet blazer and carrying a loose-leaf binder showed up and told us that we were supposed to be forming five unit composites first, and that as soon as we had a few dozen of these and had gotten the hang of morphing and melding, we could proceed to the second level of composite beinghood.

It was only then that we realized that there could be many levels to composite beings, each level being a discrete composite in its own right.

Luckily the Unitarian Church had a big open space in the basement, and here is where we and our chimaeric partners fit ourselves together.

There was good-natured bewilderment at first as we tried to perform this process. Most of us had had no experience at fitting ourselves to other creatures, so we were unfamiliar with for example, the Englen, that organ of the Pseudontoics which fits securely into the human left ear.

Still, with help from our expert (the guy in the scarlet blazer) who had volunteered to assist us, we soon had formed up our first composite. And even though not everything was entirely right, since some organs can fit into very different types of human holes, it was still a thrill to see ourselves turning into a new creature with an individuality and self-awareness all of its own.

The high point of my new association with the composite was the annual picnic. We went to the Hanford ruins where the old atomic energy place used to be. It was overgrown with weeds, some of them of very strange shapes and colors indeed. There was a polluted little stream nearby. We camped there. There were about two hundred of us in this group, and we deferred joining up until after lunch was served.

The Ladies' Auxiliary gave out the food, and they had a collection point just beyond, where everyone put in what they could. I dropped in a Synestrian bill that I had just been paid for a novelette. A lot of people came around to look at the bill and there was a lot of ooing and aahing, because Synestrian bills are really pretty, though they're so thick you can't fold them and they tend to make an unsightly bulge in your pocket.

One of the men from the Big Red composite cruised over and looked at my Synestrian bill. He held it up to the light and watched the shapes and colors chase each other.

"That's mighty pretty," he said. "You ever think of framing it and hanging it on the wall?"

"I was just about to think about that," I said.

He decided he wanted the bill and asked me how much I wanted for it. I quoted him a price about three times its value in USA currency. He was delighted with the price. Holding the bill carefully by one corner, he sniffed at it delicately.

"That's pretty good," he said.

Now that I thought about it, I realized that Synestrian money did have a good smell.

"These are prime bills," I assured him.

He sniffed again. "You ever eat one of these?" he asked me.

I shook my head. The notion had never occurred to me.

He nibbled at a corner. "Delicious!"

Seeing him enjoying himself like that got me thinking. I wanted a taste myself. But it was his bill now. I had sold it to him. All I had was bland old American currency.

I searched through my pockets. I was clean out of

Synestrian bills. I didn't even have one left to hang on my wall back home, and I certainly didn't have one to eat.

And then I noticed Rimb, melding all by herself in a corner, and she looked so cute doing it that I went over to join her.

Microbe

JOAN SLONCZEWSKI

Joan Slonczewski is a scientist and writer who lives in Gambier, Ohio, and teaches at Kenyon College. Her novels, such as her famous *A Door into Ocean*, are informed by Quaker ideals and feminism, as well as by the loving scientific details underpinning the story. This is a rare short story by one of the finest younger SF writers. It is set in the same future universe as the novel mentioned and its sequel, *Daughter of Elysium,* but in a different place and in the distant future of even that imagined setting. Like the Baxter story, it harks back to the fiction of Hal Clement and, in this case, James Blish of "Surface Tension," inventing and solving a clever SF problem posed by a precisely imagined world of wonders. It appeared in *Analog.*

That rat didn't die." Andra walked around the holostage. Before her, projected down from the geodesic dome, the planet's image shone: Iota Pavonis Three, the first new world approved for settlement in over four centuries. As Andra walked around, the brown swirl of a mysterious continent peered out through a swathe of cloud. She stopped, leaning forward on her elbows to watch. What name of its own would the Free Fold Federation ultimately bestow on IP3, Andra wondered; such a lovely, terrifying world.

"Not the last time, the rat didn't." The eye speaker was perched on her shoulder. It belonged to Skyhook, the sentient shuttle craft that would soon carry Andra from the study station down to land on the new world. A reasonable arrangement: The shuttle craft would carry the human xenobiologist through space for her field work, then she would carry his eye on the planet surface, as she did inside the station. "The rat only died down there the first eight times."

"Until we got its 'skin' right." The "skin" was a suit of nanoplast, containing billions of microscopic computers, designed to filter out all the local toxins—arsenic, lanthanides, bizarre pseudoalkaloids. All were found in local flora and fauna; inhaling them would kill a human within hours. In the old days, planets had been terraformed for human life, like Andra's own home world Valedon. Today they would call that ecocide.

Instead, millions of humans would be lifeshaped to live here on planet IP3, farming and building—the thought of it made her blood race.

"We got the right skin for the rat," Skyhook's eye speaker pointed out. "But you're not exactly a rat."

From across the holostage, an amorphous blob of nanoplast raised a pseudopod. "Not *exactly* a rat," came a voice from the nanoplast. It was the voice of Pelt, the skinsuit that would protect Andra on the alien planet surface. "Not exactly a rat—just about nine-tenths, I'd say. Your cell physiology is practically the same as a rat; why, you could even take organ grafts. Only a few developmental genes make the difference."

Andra smiled. "Thank the Spirit for a few genes. Life would be so much less interesting."

Pelt's pseudopod wiggled. "The rat lived, and so will you. But our nanoservos completely jammed." The microscopic nanoservos had swarmed into sample life forms from IP3 to test their chemical structure. But for some reason they could barely begin to send back data before they broke down. "Nobody cares about them."

"Of course we care," Andra said quickly. Pelt never let anyone value human life above that of sentient machines. "That's why we cut short the analysis, until we can bring samples back to the station. That's why we're sending *me*."

"*Us,*" he corrected.

"All right, enough already," said Skyhook. "Why don't we review our data one last time?"

"Very well." A third sentient voice boomed out of the hexagonal panel in the dome directly overhead. It was the explorer station herself, Quantum. Quantum considered herself female, the others male; Andra could never tell why, although sentients would laugh at any human who could not tell the difference. "Here are some microbial cells extracted from the soil by the last probe," said Quantum.

The planet's image dissolved. In its place appeared the highly magnified shapes of the microbes. The cells were round and somewhat flattened, rather like red blood cells. But if one looked closer, one could see that each flattened cell was actually pinched in straight through like a bagel.

"The toroid cell shape has never been observed on other planets," said Quantum. "Otherwise, the cell's structure is simple. No nuclear membranes surround the chromosomes; so, these cells are like bacteria, *prokaryotes.*"

Skyhook said, "The chromosome might be circular, too, as in bacteria."

"Who knows?" said Pelt. "On Urulan, all the chromosomes are branched. It took us decades to do genetics there."

"We just don't know yet," said Quantum. "All we know is, the cells contain DNA."

"The usual double helix?" asked Skyhook. The double helix is a ladder of DNA nucleotide pairs, always adenine with thymine or guanine with cytosine, for the four different "letters" of the DNA code. When a cell divides to make two cells, the entire helix unzips, then fills in a complementary strand for each daughter cell.

"The nanoservos failed before they could tell for sure. But it does have all four nucleotides."

Andra watched the magnified microbes as their images grew, their ring shapes filling out like bagel dough rising. "I'll bet their chromosomes run right around the hole."

At her shoulder Skyhook's eye speaker laughed. "That would be a neat trick."

Quantum added, "We identified fifteen amino acids

in its proteins, including the usual six." All living things have evolved to use six amino acids in common, the ones that form during the birth of planets. "But three of the others are toxic—"

"Look," exclaimed Andra. "The cell is starting to divide." One of the bulging toroids had begun to pucker in, all along its circumference. The puckered line deepened into a furrow all the way around the cell. Along the inside of the "hole," a second furrow deepened, eventually to meet the furrow from the outer rim.

"So that's how the cell divides," said Skyhook. "Not by pinching in across the hole; instead it slices through."

"The better to toast it."

At that Pelt's pseudopod made a rude gesture. "Pinching the hole in wouldn't make sense, if your chromosomes encircles the hole; you'd pinch off half of it."

Andra squinted and leaned forward on her elbows. "I say—that cell has *three* division furrows."

"The daughter cells are dividing again already?" Skyhook suggested.

"No, it's a third furrow in the same generation. All three furrows are meeting up in the middle."

"That's right," boomed Quantum's voice. "These cells divide in three, not two," she explained. "Three daughter cells in each generation."

Sure enough, the three daughter cells appeared, filling themselves out as they separated. Other cells too had puckered in by now, at various stages of division, and all made their daughters in triplets. "How would they divide their chromosomes to make three?" Andra wondered. "They must copy each DNA helix twice before dividing. Why would that have evolved?"

"Never mind the DNA," said Pelt. "It's those toxic amino acids you should worry about."

"Not with you protecting me. The rat survived."

Quantum said, "We've discussed every relevant point. We've established, based on all available data, that Andra's chance of survival approaches 100 percent."

"Uncertainties remain," Skyhook cautioned.

Andra stood back and spread her hands. "Of course we need more data—that's why we're going down."

"All right," said Skyhook. "Let's go."

"I'm ready." Pelt's pseudopod dissolved, and the nanoplast formed a perfect hemisphere.

Andra unhooked Skyhook's eye speaker from her shoulder. Then she walked back around the holostage to lift the hemisphere of Pelt onto her head. Pelt's nanoplast began to melt slowly down over her black curls, leaving a thin transparent film of nanoprocessors covering her hair, her dark skin, and her black eyes. It formed a special breather over her nose and mouth. Everywhere the nanoplast would filter the air that reached her skin, keeping planetary dust out while letting oxygen through. The film covered the necklace of pink andradites around her neck, spreading down her shirt and trousers. She lifted each foot in turn to allow the complete enclosure. Now she would be safe from any chemical hazard she might encounter.

In Skyhook's viewport, the surface of planet IP3 expanded and rose to meet them. Numerous tests had established its physical parameters as habitable—gravity of nine-tenths g, temperatures not too extreme, oxygen sufficient and carbon dioxide low enough, water plentiful. The ozone layer could have been denser, but human colonists would have their eyes and skin lifeshaped for extra enzymes to keep their retina and chromosomes repaired.

At a distance the planet did not look remarkably different from Andra's home world. A brilliant expanse of ocean met a mottled brown shore, rotating slowly down beneath the craft. Beyond, in the upper latitudes, rolled the blue-brown interior of a continent, broken only by a circle of mountains.

As Skyhook fell swiftly toward the land, curious patterns emerged. Long dark bands ran in parallel, in gently winding rows like a string picture. The lines were bands of blue vegetation; the probe had sent back footage of it, wide arching structures tall as trees. Each band alternated with a band of yellow, which gave way to the next band of blue. Over and over the same pattern repeated, ceasing only at the mountains.

"I've never seen patterns like that on uncolonized worlds," Andra mused.

"They do look like garden rows," Skyhook admitted. "Perhaps the native farmers will come out to greet us."

If there were intelligent life forms, they had yet to invent radio. A year of monitoring the planet at every conceivable frequency had yielded nothing, not so much as a calculation of pi.

Skyhook landed gently in a field of dense vegetation. The wall of the cabin opened, the door pulling out into an arch of nanoplast. A shaft of brilliant light entered.

"All systems check," crackled Quantum's voice on the radio in her car. "Go ahead."

Andra gathered her field equipment and set Skyhook's eye upon her shoulder again. Then she stepped outside.

The field was a riot of golden ringlets, like wedding bands strewn out. Her gaze followed the cascade of gold down to the edge of the field, where taller dark trunks arose in shallow curves, arching overhead.

From the taller growth came a keening sound, perhaps some living thing singing, or perhaps the wind vibrating somehow through its foliage. "It's beautiful," she exclaimed at last.

Beneath the golden ringlets grew dense blue-brown vegetation, reaching to Andra's waist. She bent closer for a look. "These look like plants, 'phycoids.' The ringlets might be flowers."

"They could just as well be snakes ready to snap," warned Skyhook. "Watch your step."

She looked back at the shuttlecraft, planted in the field like a four-legged insect. Then she lifted her leg through the foliage, Pelt's nanoplastic "skin" flexing easily. Immediately her foot snagged. She tried to pull out some of the growth, but found it surprisingly tough and had to cut it with a knife. "The leaves and stems are all looped," she observed in surprise. "All looped, just like the 'flowers.' I'll never get through this stuff."

Pelt said, "They *are* phycoid. I detect products of photosynthesis."

"They could be carnivorous plants," Skyhook insisted.

Andra collected some more cuttings into her backpack. "I wish I could smell them," she said wistfully. Pelt's skin filtered out all volatile organics. She aimed her laser pen to dig one out by the roots. The phycoid came up, but nearby stems sparked and smoldered.

"Watch out!" squeaked the eye-speaker.

She winced. "Don't deafen me; I'll put it out." She stamped the spot with her boots and sprinkled some water from her drinking jet. "This planet's a fire trap." The phycoid roots, she noted, were long twisted loops, tightly pressed together, but loops nonetheless. All the living structures seemed to be bagels squashed and stretched.

"Great Spirit, we've got company," Skyhook exclaimed.

Andra looked up. She blinked her eyes. A herd of brown-striped truck tires were rolling slowly across the field. To get a closer look, she pressed through the phycoids, stopping every so often to extricate her feet from the looped foliage. She made about ten meters progress before stopping to catch her breath.

"No need to get too close," Skyhook reminded her. His eyes had telephoto.

"Yes, but I might pick up droppings, or some fallen hair or scales."

Some of the rolling "tires" were heading toward her. Each one had several round cranberry-colored spots set in its "tread." The "tread" was composed of suckers that stretched and extended to push in back, or pull in front. "They must be animal-like, 'zoöids,'" suggested Andra. "Those red things—could they be eyes?" She counted them, two, three, four in all, before the first came up again. Those eyes must be tough, not to mind getting squashed down.

"If these creatures are zoöids," Pelt wanted to know, "how do they feed?"

Skyhook said, "Their suckers ingest the phycoids."

Andra stopped again to pull out her foot. "They sure know how to travel," she wryly observed. "No wonder they never evolved legs." One four-eyed zoöid got excited, and took off with remarkable speed; then it suddenly reversed, heading backwards just as fast. These zoöids had no "backwards" or "forwards," she thought.

Quantum radioed again. "Andra, how are you holding up? Is your breathing OK?"

She took a deep breath. "I think so." Most of the rats had died from inhaling toxic dust. She resumed her attempt to make headway through the phycoids, and searched the ground for anything that looked like droppings. Overhead, she heard a strange whirring sound. A flock of little things were flying, their movements too fast for her to make out.

"Their wings are turning full around, like propellers," Skyhook exclaimed in amazement. "Why, *all* these creatures are built of wheels, one way or another."

"Sh," said Andra. "A zoöid is coming up close."

The creature rolled slowly over the phycoids, squashing the golden ringlets beneath it. Andra took a closer look. "There's a smaller ring structure, just sitting inside the bagel hole. I'll bet it's a baby zoöid." The clinging little one rolled over and over inside as its parent traveled. The parent did not seem to notice Andra at all; neither her shape nor her smell would resemble a native predatory, she guessed.

The radio crackled again. "We must attempt contact," Quantum reminded her. Any zoöid might be intelligent.

Andra held out her communicator, a box that sent out flashing lights and sound bursts in various mathematical patterns, strings of primes and various representations of pi and other constants. It even emitted puffs of volatile chemicals, to alert any chemosensing creature with a hint of intelligence. Not that she expected much; their probes had broadcast such information over the past year.

Then she saw it: A giant zoöid was approaching, five times taller than the others and perhaps a hundred times their weight. As it barreled along, picking up speed, the small striped ones took off, zigzagging crazily before it. The ground rumbled beneath her feet.

"Get back to my cabin!" urged Skyhook. "We'll all get run over."

"Wait," said Pelt. "Do you think it heard us? What if it wants to talk?"

"I don't think so," said Andra, prudently backing off. "I think the smaller zoöids attracted it, not us."

A small zoöid went down under the giant one, then another. That seemed to be the giant's strategy, to run down as many little ones as it could. At last it slowed and turned back, coming to rest upon one of the squashed carcasses.

"It's extending its suckers to feed," observed Skyhook. "Let's get back before it gets hungry again."

"I think that will be a while," said Andra. "It's got several prey to feed on." The rest of the smaller zoöids seemed to have calmed down, as if they knew the predator was satisfied and would not attack again soon. Definitely a herd mentality; no sign of higher intelligence here.

Andra resumed collecting phycoids and soil samples, recording the location of each. Deeper into the field, she saw something thrashing about in the phycoids. She made her way toward it through the tangle of looped foliage.

"It's a baby zoöid," she exclaimed. The poor little bagel must have fallen out when its parent ran off. Or perhaps the parent had expelled it, as a mother kangaroo sometimes did. At any rate, there it was, squirming and stretching its little suckers ineffectually, only tangling itself in the phycoids.

"Watch out; it might bite," said Skyhook.

"Nonsense. I have to collect it." Andra stuffed her hands into a pair of gloves, then approached warily. With one hand she held out an open collecting bag; with the other, she grabbed the little zoöid. It hung limply, twisting a bit.

Suddenly it squirted something. An orange spray landed on the phycoids, some of it reaching her leg. Andra frowned. She plunged the creature into her bag, which sealed itself tight. "Sorry about that, Pelt."

"You're the one who would have been sorry," Pelt replied. "That stuff is caustic, as strong as lye. No problem for me, but your skin would not have liked it."

"Thanks a lot. I guess we should head back now; I've got more than I can hold."

She turned back toward Skyhook, some hundred meters off, his spidery landing gear splayed out into the phycoids. Methodically she made her way back, with more difficulty now that she had so much to carry. She was sweating now, but Pelt handled it beautifully, keeping her skin cool and refreshed. The distant forest of tall blue phycoids sang in her ears. The Singing Planet, they could call it, she thought.

"Andra . . . something's not right," Pelt said suddenly.

"What is it?" She was having more trouble plowing through the foliage; her legs were getting stiff.

"Something that baby zoöid sprayed is blocking my nanoprocessors. Not the chemicals; I can screen out anything. I'm not sure what it is."

"What else could it be?"

Skyhook said, "Just get back to my cabin. We'll wash you down."

"I'm trying," said Andra, breathing hard. "My legs are so stiff." The shuttle craft stood hopefully ahead of her. Only about ten meters to go, she thought.

"It's not your legs," Pelt's voice said dully. "It's my nanoplast. I'm losing control over the lower part, where the spray hit. I can't flex at your joints any more."

Her scalp went cold, then hot again. "What about your air filter?"

"So far it's OK. The disruption has not reached your face yet."

"Just get back here," Skyhook urged again. "You're almost here." Obligingly the doorway appeared on the craft's surface, molding itself open in a rim of nanoplast.

"I'm trying, but my legs just won't bend." She pushed as hard as she could.

"Drop your backpack," Skyhook added.

"I won't give up my samples. How else will we learn what's going on here?" She fell onto her stomach and tried to drag herself through.

"It's microbes," Pelt exclaimed suddenly. "Some kind of microbes—they're cross-linking my processors."

"What? How?" she demanded. "Microbes infecting nanoplast—I've never heard of it."

"They messed up the probe before."

"Quantum?" called Andra. "What do you think?"

"It could be," the radio voice replied. "The nanoprocessors store data in organic polymers—which might be edible to a truly omnivorous microbe. There's always a first time."

"Microbes eating nanoplast!" Skyhook exclaimed. "What about other sentients? Are the microbes contagious?"

"You'll have to put us in isolation," said Andra.

"Andra," said Pelt, "the cross-linking is starting to disrupt my entire system." His voice came lower and fainter. "I don't know how long I can keep my filters open."

Andra stared desperately at the door of the shuttle, so near and yet so far. "Quantum, how long could I last breathing unfiltered air?"

"That's hard to say. An hour should be OK; we'll clean your lungs out later."

She tried to recall how long the first rat had lived. Half a day?

"I'm shutting down," Pelt warned her. "I'm sorry, Andra. . . ."

Skyhook said, "Pelt, you'll last longer in rest mode.

We'll save you yet—there's got to be an antibiotic that will work. They've got DNA—we'll throw every DNA analogue we've got at them."

The nanoplastic skin opened around Andra's mouth, shrinking back around her head and neck. An otherworldly scent filled her lungs, a taste of ginger and other unnameable things, as beautiful as the vision of golden ringlets. Planet Ginger, she thought, smelled as lovely as it looked. She was the first human to smell it; but would these breaths be her last?

Pelt's skin shriveled down her arms, getting stuck at her waist near the spot that got sprayed. She tried again to pull herself through the phycoids, grabbing their tough loops. Suddenly she had another idea. Pulling in her arms, she sank down and rolled herself over and over, just like the zoöids. This worked much better, for the phycoid foliage proved surprisingly elastic, bending easily beneath her and bouncing back again. Perhaps those zoöids were not quite so silly after all.

At the door, Skyhook had already extruded sheets of quarantine material to isolate her and protect its own nanoplast from whatever deadly infection Pelt harbored. The doorway extended and scooped her up into the chain.

As the doorway constricted, at last closing out the treacherous planet, Andra let out a quick sigh of relief. "Skyhook, we've got to save Pelt. Have you got anything to help him?"

Two long tendrils were already poking into the quarantine chamber, to probe the hapless skinsuit. "I'm spreading what antibiotics we have on board," said Skyhook, from the cabin speaker now. "Nucleotide analogues, anything likely to block DNA synthesis and stop the microbes growing. It's bizarre, treating a sentient for infection."

Andra carefully peeled off the remaining nanoplast, trying to keep as much of it together as possible, although she had no idea whether it was beyond repair. "Pelt," she whispered. "You did your best for me."

By the time they returned to the station, there was still no sign that any of the antibiotics had curbed the microbes. Quantum was puzzled. "I have a few more to try," she said, "but really, if the chromosomes are regular DNA, something should have worked."

"Maybe the microbes' DNA is shielded by proteins."

"That wouldn't help during replication, remember? The double helix has to open and unzip down the middle, to let the new nucleotides pair. There's no way around it."

Andra frowned. Something was missing; there was still something wrong, about the growing microbes with their three daughter cells. How could they unzip their DNA, fill in each complementary strand, and end up with three helixes? She thought she had figured it out before, but now it did not add up. She coughed once, then again harder. Her lungs were starting to react to the dust—she had to start treatment now.

"We've got some data on your samples," Quantum added. "The microbial cells concentrate acid inside, instead of excreting it, like most of our cells do. I still find only fifteen amino acids, but some of them—"

"I've got it!" Andra leaped to her feet. "Don't you see? *The chromosome is a triple helix*. That's why each cell divides in three—each daughter strand synthesizes two complements, and you end up with three new triple helixes, one for each cell." A fit of coughing caught up with her.

"It could be," Quantum said slowly. "There are many ways to make a DNA triple helix. One found in human regulatory genes alternates A-T-T triplets with G-C-C."

"Then it has a two-letter code, not four." Double-helical DNA has four possible pairs, since A-T is distinguished from T-A; likewise G-C differs from C-G.

Quantum added, "The triple helix is most stable in acid, just what we found in these cells."

"Just hurry up and design some triple analogues." Quantum's sentient brain could do this far faster than any human. "Triple helix," Andra repeated. "It would resist ultraviolet damage much better, with the planet's thin ozone layer. But how to encode proteins, with only two 'letters'?" The triple helix had only two possible triplets; its three-letter "words" could only specify eight amino acids to build protein. "Maybe it uses words of four letters. With two possible triplets at each position, that would encode two to the fourth power, that is, sixteen possible amino acids."

"Fifteen," corrected Quantum, "if one is a stop signal."

The next day, after an exhaustive medical workout, Andra felt as if a vacuum cleaner had gone through her lungs, Pelt still had a long way to recover, but at least the pesky microbes were cleaned out.

"It's hopeless," complained Skyhook's eyespeaker. "If even sentients aren't safe, we'll never explore that planet."

"Don't worry," said Quantum's voice above the holostage. "Pelt's nanoplast has an exceptionally high organic content. A slight redesign will eliminate the problem. Machines have that advantage."

Still, Pelt had nearly died, thought Andra.

"Your phycoid and zoöid samples all have toroid cells, too," Quantum added. "They have circular chromosomes, with no nuclear membranes: They're all prokaryotes. Just wait till the Free Fold hears about this," Quantum added excitedly. "I've got the perfect name for the planet."

Andra looked up. "Planet of the Bagels?"

"Planet Prokaryon."

Prokaryon—yes, thought Andra, it sounded just pompous enough that the Fold would buy it.

Still, she thought uneasily about those regular garden rows of phycoid forest and fields, with all kinds of creatures yet to be discovered. "I wonder," she mused. "Someone else just might have named it first."

The Ziggurat

GENE WOLFE

Gene Wolfe is in our time producing the finest continuing body of short fiction in the SF field since Theodore Sturgeon. Like Sturgeon, Wolfe is an aesthetic maverick, whose stories are sometimes fantasy, sometimes horror, sometimes hard SF, sometimes fine contemporary realism (neat, or with magic). His novels include the four volume *Book of the New Sun, The Fifth Head of Cerberus, Peace, Soldier of the Mist, Urth of the New Sun.* His fiction is collected in *The Island of Dr. Death and Other Stories, Endangered Species, Storeys from the Old Hotel,* and several other volumes. When he turns his hand to SF, as in "The Ziggurat," he can write contemporary science fiction of unique power. In a year of exceptionally strong novella length work in the SF field, this one still stands out. It is selected from the fine original anthology, *Full Spectrum 5.*

It had begun to snow about one-thirty. Emery Bainbridge stood on the front porch to watch it before going back into the cabin to record it in his journal.

> 13:38 Snowing hard, quiet as owl feathers. Radio says stay off the roads unless you have four-wheel. Probably means no Brook.

He put down the lipstick-red ballpoint and stared at it. With this pen . . . He ought to scratch out *Brook* and write *Jan* over it.

"To hell with that." His harsh voice seemed loud in the silent cabin. "What I wrote, I wrote. *Quod scripsi* whatever it is."

That was what being out here alone did, he told himself. You were supposed to rest up. You were supposed to calm down. Instead you started talking to yourself. "Like some nut," he added aloud.

Jan would come, bringing Brook. And Aileen and Alayna. Aileen and Alayna were as much his children as Brook was, he told himself firmly. "For the time being."

If Jan could not come tomorrow, she would come later when the county had cleared the back roads. And it was more than possible that she would come, or try to, tomorrow as she had planned. There was that kind of a streak in Jan, not exactly stubbornness and not exactly resolution, but a sort of willful determination to believe whatever she wanted; thus she believed he would sign her papers, and thus she would believe that the big Lincoln he had bought her could go anywhere a Jeep could.

Brook would be all for it, of course. At nine, Brook had tried to cross the Atlantic on a Styrofoam dinosaur, paddling out farther and farther until at last a life-guard had launched her little catamaran and brought him back, letting the dinosaur float out to sea.

That was what was happening everywhere, Emery thought—boys and men were being brought back to shore by women, though for thousands of years their daring had permitted humanity to survive.

He pulled on his red-plaid double mackinaw and his warmest cap, and carried a chair out onto the porch to watch the snow.

Suddenly it wasn't . . . He had forgotten the word that he had used before. It wasn't whatever men had. It was something women had, or they thought it was. Possibly it was something nobody had.

He pictured Jan leaning intently over the wheel, her lips compressed to an ugly slit, easing her Lincoln into the snow, coaxing it up the first hill, stern with tri-umph as it cleared the crest. Jan about to be stranded in this soft and silent wilderness in high-heeled shoes. Perhaps that streak of hers was courage after all, or something so close that it could be substituted for courage at will. Little pink packets that made you think whatever you wanted to be true would be true, if only you acted as if it were with sufficient tenacity.

He was being watched.

"By God, it's that coyote," he said aloud, and knew from the timbre of his own voice that he lied. These were human eyes. He narrowed his own, peering through the falling snow, took off his glasses, blotted their lenses absently with his handkerchief, and looked again.

A higher, steeper hill rose on the other side of his tiny valley, a hill clothed in pines and crowned with wind-swept ocher rocks. The watcher was up there somewhere, staring down at him through the pine boughs, silent and observant.

"Come on over!" Emery called. "Want some coffee?"

There was no response.

"You lost? You better get out of this weather!"

The silence of the snow seemed to suffocate each word in turn. Although he had shouted, he could not be certain he had been heard. He stood and made a sweeping gesture: *Come here.*

There was a flash of colorless light from the pines, so swift and slight that he could not be absolutely certain he had seen it. Someone signaling with a mirror—except that the sky was the color of lead above the downward-drifting whiteness of the snow, the sun invisible.

"Come on over!" he called again, but the watcher was gone.

Country people, he thought, suspicious of strangers. But there were no country people around here, not within ten miles; a few hunting camps, a few cabins like his own, with nobody in them now that deer season was over.

He stepped off the little porch. The snow was more than ankle-deep already and falling faster than it had been just a minute before, the pine-clad hill across the creek practically invisible.

The woodpile under the overhang of the south eaves (the woodpile that had appeared so impressive when he had arrived) had shrunk drastically. It was time to cut and split more. Past time, really. The chain saw tomorrow, the ax, the maul, and the wedge tomorrow, and perhaps even the Jeep, if he could get it in to snake the logs out.

Mentally, he put them all away. Jan was coming, would be bringing Brook to stay. And the twins to stay, too, with Jan herself, if the road got too bad.

The coyote had gone up on the back porch!

After a second or two he realized he was grinning like a fool, and forced himself to stop and look instead.

There were no tracks. Presumably the coyote had eaten this morning before the snow started, for the bowl was empty, licked clean. The time would come, and soon, when he would touch the rough yellow-gray head, when the coyote would lick his fingers and fall asleep in front of the little fieldstone fireplace in his cabin.

Triumphant, he rattled the rear door, then remembered that he had locked it the night before. Had locked both doors, in fact, moved by an indefinable dread. Bears, he thought—a way of assuring himself that he was not as irrational as Jan.

There were bears around here, that was true enough. Small black bears, for the most part. But not Yogi Bears, not funny but potentially dangerous park bears who had lost all fear of Man and roamed and rummaged as they pleased. These bears were hunted every year, hunted through the golden days of autumn as they fattened for hibernation. Silver winter had arrived, and these bears slept in caves and hollow logs, in thickets and thick brush, slept like their dead, though slowly and softly breathing like the snow—motionless, dreaming bear-dreams of the last-men years, when the trees would have filled in the old logging roads again and shouldered aside the cracked asphalt of the county road, and all the guns had rusted to dust.

Yet he had been afraid.

He returned to the front of the cabin, picked up the

chair he had carried onto the porch, and noticed a black spot on its worn back he could not recall having seen before. It marked his finger, and was scraped away readily by the blade of his pocketknife.

Shrugging, he brought the chair back inside. There was plenty of Irish stew; he would have Irish stew tonight, soak a slice of bread in gravy for the coyote, and leave it in the same spot on the back porch. You could not (as people always said) move the bowl a little every day. That would have been frightening, too fast for any wild thing. You moved the bowl once, perhaps, in a week; and the coyote's bowl had walked by those halting steps from the creek bank where he had glimpsed the coyote in summer to the back porch.

Jan and Brook and the twins might—would be sure to—frighten it. That was unfortunate, but could not be helped; it might be best not to try to feed the coyote at all until Jan and the twins had gone. As inexplicably as he had known that he was being watched, and by no animal, he felt certain that Jan would reach him somehow, bending reality to her desires.

He got out the broom and swept the cabin. When he had expected her, he had not cared how it looked or what she might think of it. Now that her arrival had become problematic, he found that he cared a great deal.

She would have the other lower bunk, the twins could sleep together feet-to-feet in an upper (no doubt with much squealing and giggling and kicking), and Brook in the other upper—in the bunk over his own.

Thus would the family achieve its final and irrevocable separation for the first time; the Sibberlings (who had been and would again be) on one side of the cabin, the Bainbridges on the other: boys here, girls over there. The law would take years, and demand tens of thousands of dollars, to accomplish no more.

Boys here.

Girls over there, farther and farther all the time. When he had rocked and kissed Aileen and Alayna, when he had bought Christmas and birthday presents and sat through solemn, silly conferences with their pleased teachers, he had never felt that he was actually the twins' father. Now he did. Al Sibberling had given them his swarthy good looks and flung them away. He, Emery Bainbridge, had picked them up like discarded dolls after Jan had run the family deep in debt. Had called himself their father, and thought he lied.

There would be no sleeping with Jan, no matter how long she stayed. It was why she was bringing the twins, as he had known from the moment she said they would be with her.

He put clean sheets on the bunk that would be hers, with three thick wool blankets and a quilt.

Bringing her back from plays and country-club dances, he had learned to listen for them; silence had meant he could return and visit Jan's bed when he had driven the sitter home. Now Jan feared that he would want to bargain—his name on her paper for a little more pleasure, a little more love before they parted for good. Much as she wanted him to sign, she did not want him to sign as much as that. Girls here, boys over there. Had he grown so hideous?

Women need a reason, he thought, men just need a place.

For Jan the reason wasn't good enough, so she had seen to it that there would be no place. He told himself it would be great to hug the twins again—and discovered that it would.

He fluffed Jan's pillow anyway, and dressed it in a clean white pillowcase.

She would have found someone by now, somebody in the city to whom she was being faithful, exactly as

he himself had been faithful to Jan while he was still
married, in the eyes of the law, to Pamela.

The thought of eyes recalled the watcher on the hill.

14:12 Somebody is on the hill across the creek
with some kind of signaling device.

That sounded as if he were going crazy, he decided.
What if Jan saw it? He added, maybe just a flashlight,
although he did not believe it had been a flashlight.

A lion's face smiled up at him from the barrel of the
red pen, and he stopped to read the minute print under
it, holding the pen up to catch the gray light from the
window. "The Red Lion Inn/San Jose." A nice hotel.
If—when—he got up the nerve to do it, he would write
notes to Jan and Brook first with this pen.

The coyote ate the food I put out for him, I think
soon after breakfast. More food tonight.
Tomorrow morning I will leave the back door
cracked open awhile.
14:15 I am going up on the hill for a look
around.

He had not known that until he wrote it.

The hillside seemed steeper than he remembered, slippery with snow. The pines had changed; their limbs
drooped like the boughs of hemlocks, springing up like
snares when he touched them, and throwing snow in
his face. No bird sang.

He had brought his flashlight, impelled by the memory of the colorless signal from the hill. Now he used it
to peep beneath the drooping limbs. Most of the tracks
that the unseen watcher had left would be covered

with new snow by this time; a few might remain, in the shelter of the pines.

He had nearly reached the rocky summit before he found the first, and even it was blurred by snow despite its protection. He knelt and blew the drifted flakes away, clearing it with his breath as he had sometimes cleared the tracks of animals; an oddly cleated shoe, almost like the divided hoof of an elk. He measured it against his spread hand, from the tip of his little finger to the tip of his thumb. A small foot, no bigger than size six, if that.

A boy.

There was another, inferior, print beside it. And not far away a blurred depression that might have been left by a gloved hand or a hundred other things. Here the boy had crouched with his little polished steel mirror, or whatever he had.

Emery knelt, lifting the snow-burdened limbs that blocked his view of the cabin. Two small, dark figures were emerging from the cabin door onto the porch, scarcely visible through the falling snow. The first carried his ax, the second his rifle.

He stood, waving the flashlight. "Hey! You there!"

The one holding his rifle raised it, not putting it to his shoulder properly but acting much too quickly for Emery to duck. The flat crack of the shot sounded clearly, snow or no snow.

He tried to dodge, slipped, and fell to the soft snow. "Too late," he told himself. And then, "Going to do it for me." And last, "Better stay down in case he shoots again." The cold air was like chilled wine, the snow he lay in lovely beyond imagining. Drawing back his coat sleeve, he consulted his watch, resolving to wait ten minutes—to risk nothing.

They were robbing his cabin, obviously. Had robbed it, in fact, while he had been climbing through the pines.

Had fired, in all probability, merely to keep him away long enough for them to leave. Mentally, he inventoried the cabin. Besides the rifle, there had not been a lot worth stealing—his food and a few tools; they might take his Jeep if they could figure out how to hotwire the ignition, and that was pretty easy on those old Jeeps.

His money was in his wallet, his wallet in the hip pocket of his hunting trousers. His watch—a plastic sports watch hardly worth stealing—was on his wrist. His checkbook had been in the table drawer; they might steal that and forge his checks, possibly. They might even be caught when they tried to cash them.

Retrieving his flashlight, he lifted the limbs as he had before. The intruders were not in sight, the door of the cabin half open, his Jeep still parked next to the north wall, its red paint showing faintly through snow.

He glanced at his watch. One minute had passed, perhaps a minute and a half.

They would have to have a vehicle of some kind, one with four-wheel drive if they didn't want to be stranded with their loot on a back road. Since he had not heard it start up, they had probably left the engine running. Even so, he decided, he should have heard it pull away.

Had they parked some distance off and approached his cabin on foot? Now that he came to think of it, it seemed possible they had no vehicle after all. Two boys camping in the snow, confident that he would be unable to follow them to their tent, or whatever it was. Wasn't there a Boy Scout badge for winter camping? He had never been a Scout, but thought he remembered hearing about one, and found it plausible.

Still no one visible. He let the branches droop again.

The rifle was not really much of a loss, though its theft had better be reported to the sheriff. He had not planned on shooting anyway—had been worried, as a matter of fact, that the twins might get it down and do something foolish, although both had shot at tin cans and steel silhouettes with it before he and Jan had agreed to separate.

Now, with his rifle gone, he could not . . .

Neither had been particularly attracted to it; and their having handled and fired it already should have satisfied the natural curiosity that resulted in so many accidents each year. They had learned to shoot to please him, and stopped as soon as he had stopped urging them to learn.

Four minutes, possibly five. He raised the pine boughs once more, hearing the muted growl of an engine; for a second or two he held his breath. The Jeep or Bronco or whatever it was, was coming closer, not leaving. Was it possible that the thieves were coming back? Returning with a truck to empty his cabin?

Jan's big black Lincoln hove into view, roared down the gentle foothill slope on which his cabin stood, and skidded to a stop. Doors flew open, and all three kids piled out. Jan herself left more sedately, shutting the door on the driver's side behind her almost tenderly, tall and willowy as ever, her hair a golden helmet beneath a blue-mink pillbox hat.

Her left hand held a thick, black attaché case that was probably his.

Brook was already on the porch. Emery stood and shouted a warning, but it was too late; Brook was inside the cabin, with the twins hard on his heels. Jan looked around and waved, and deep inside Emery something writhed in agony.

By the time he had reached the cabin, he had decided not to mention that the intruders had shot at him.

Presumably the shooter had chambered a new round, ejecting the brass cartridge case of the round just fired into the snow; but it might easily be overlooked, and if Brook or the twins found it, he could say that he had fired the day before to scare off some animal.

"Hello," Jan said as he entered. "You left your door open. It's cold as Billy-o in here." She was seated in a chair before the fire.

"I didn't." He dropped into the other, striving to look casual. "I was robbed."

"Really? When?"

"A quarter hour ago. Did you see another car coming in?"

Jan shook her head.

They had been on foot, then; the road ended at the lake. Aloud he said, "It doesn't matter. They got my rifle and my ax." Remembering his checkbook, he pulled out the drawer of the little table. His checkbook was still there; he took it out and put it into an inner pocket of his mackinaw.

"It was an old rifle anyhow, wasn't it?"

He nodded. "My old thirty-thirty."

"Then you can buy a new one, and you should have locked the door. I—"

"You weren't supposed to get here until tomorrow," he told her brusquely. The mere thought of another gun was terrifying.

"I know. But they said a blizzard was coming on TV, so I decided I'd better move it up a day, or I'd have to wait for a week—that was what it sounded like. I told Doctor Gibbons that Aileen would be in next Thursday, and off we went. This shouldn't take long." She opened his attaché case on her lap. "Now here—"

"Where are the kids?"

"Out back getting more wood. They'll be back in a minute."

As though to confirm her words, he heard the clink of the maul striking the wedge. He ventured, "Do you really want them to hear it?"

"Emery, they *know*. I couldn't have hidden all this from them if I tried. What was I going to say when they asked why you never came home anymore?"

"You could have told them I was deer-hunting."

"That's for a few days, maybe a week. You left in August, remember? Well, anyway, I didn't. I told them the truth." She paused, expectant. "Aren't you going to ask how they took it?"

He shook his head.

"The girls were hurt. I honestly think Brook's happy. Getting to live with you out here for a while and all that."

"I've got him signed up for Culver," Emery told her. "He starts in February."

"That's best, I'm sure. Now listen, because we've got to get back. Here's a letter from your—"

"You're not going to sleep here? Stay overnight?"

"Tonight? Certainly not. We've got to start home before this storm gets serious. You always interrupt me. You always have. I suppose it's too late to say I wish you'd stop."

He nodded. "I made up a bunk for you."

"Brook can have it. Now right—"

The back door opened and Brook himself came in. "I showed them how you split the wood, and 'Layna split one. Didn't you, 'Layna?"

"Right here." Behind him, Alayna held the pieces up.

"That's not ladylike," Jan told her.

Emery said, "But it's quite something that a girl her age can swing that maul—I wouldn't have believed she could. Did Brook help you lift it?"

Alayna shook her head.

"*I* didn't want to," Aileen declared virtuously.

"Right here," Jan was pushing an envelope into his hands, "is a letter from your attorney. It's sealed, see? I haven't read it, but you'd better take a look at it first."

"You know what's in it, though," Emery said, "or you think you do."

"He told me what he was going to write to you, yes."

"Otherwise you would have saved it." Emery got out his pocketknife and slit the flap. "Want to tell me?"

Jan shook her head, her lips as tight and ugly as he had imagined them earlier.

Brook put down his load of wood. "Can I see?"

"You can read it for me," Emery told him. "I've got snow on my glasses." He found a clean handkerchief and wiped them. "Don't read it out loud. Just tell me what it says."

"Emery, you're doing this to get even!"

He shook his head. "This is Brook's inheritance that our lawyers are arguing about."

Brook stared.

"I've lost my company," Emery told him. "Basically, we're talking about the money and stock I got as a consolation prize. You're the only child I've got, probably the only one I'll ever have. So read it. What does it say?"

Brook unfolded the letter; it seemed quieter to Emery now, with all five of them in the cabin, than it ever had during all the months he had lived there alone.

Jan said, "What they did was perfectly legal, Brook. You should understand that. They bought up a controlling interest and merged our company with theirs. That's all that happened."

The stiff, parchment-like paper rattled in Brook's

hands. Unexpectedly Alayna whispered, "I'm sorry, Daddy."

Emery grinned at her. "I'm still here, honey."

Brook glanced from him to Jan, then back to him. "He says—it's Mister Gluckman. You introduced me one time."

Emery nodded.

"He says this is the best arrangement he's been able to work out, and he thinks it would be in your best interest to take it."

Jan said, "You keep this place and your Jeep, and all your personal belongings, naturally. I'll give you back my wedding and engagement rings—"

"You can keep them," Emery told her.

"No, I want to be fair about this. I've always tried to be fair, even when you didn't come to the meetings between our attorneys. I'll give them back, but I get to keep all the rest of the gifts you've given me, including my car."

Emery nodded.

"No alimony at all. Naturally no child support. Brook stays with you, Aileen and Alayna with me. My attorney says we can force Al to pay child support."

Emery nodded again.

"And I get the house. Everything else we divide equally. That's the stock and any other investments, the money in my personal accounts, your account, and our joint account." She had another paper. "I know you'll want to read it over, but that's what it is. You can follow me into Voylestown in your Jeep. There's a notary there who can witness your signature."

"I had the company when we were married."

"But you don't have it anymore. We're not talking about your company. It's not involved at all."

He picked up the telephone, a diversion embraced at random that might serve until the pain ebbed. "Will you excuse me? This is liable to go on awhile, and I should report the break-in." He entered the sheriff's number from the sticker on the telephone.

The distant clamor—it was not the actual ringing of the sheriff's telephone at all, he knew—sounded empty as well as artificial, as if it were not merely far away but high over the earth, a computer-generated instrument that jangled and buzzed for his ears alone upon some airless asteroid beyond the moon.

Brook laid Phil Gluckman's letter on the table where he could see it.

"Are you getting through?" Jan asked. "There's a lot of ice on the wires. Brook was talking about it on the way up."

"I think so. It's ringing."

Brook said, "They've probably got a lot of emergencies, because of the storm." The twins stirred uncomfortably, and Alayna went to a window to look at the falling snow.

"I should warn you," Jan said, "that if you won't sign, it's war. We spent hours and hours—"

A voice squeaked, *"Sheriff Ron Wilber's Office."*

"My name is Emery Bainbridge. I've got a cabin on Route Eighty-five, about five miles from the lake."

The tinny voice spoke unintelligibly.

"Would you repeat that, please?"

"It might be better from the cellular phone in my car," Jan suggested.

"What's the problem, Mister Bainbridge?"

"My cabin was robbed in my absence." There was no way in which he could tell the sheriff's office that he had been shot at without telling Jan and the twins as well; he decided it was not essential. "They took a rifle and my ax. Those are the only things that seem to be missing."

"Could you have mislaid them?"

This was the time to tell the sheriff about the boy on the hill; he found that he could not.

"Can you hear me, Mister Bainbridge?" There was chirping in the background, as if there were crickets on the party line.

He said, "Barely. No, I didn't mislay them. Somebody was in here while I was away—they left the door open, for one thing." He described the rifle and admitted he did not have a record of its serial number, then described the ax and spelled his name.

"We can't send anyone out there now, Mister Bainbridge. I'm sorry."

It was a woman. He had not realized until then that he had been talking to a woman. He said, "I just wanted to let you know, in case you picked somebody up."

"We'll file a report. You can come here and look at the stolen goods whenever you want to, but I don't think there's any guns right now."

"The theft just occurred. About three or a little later." When the woman at the sheriff's office did not speak again, he said, "Thank you," and hung up.

"You think they'll come back tonight, Dad?"

"I doubt very much that they'll come back at all." Emery sat down, unconsciously pushing his chair a little farther from Jan's. "Since you kids went out and split that wood, don't you think you ought to put some of it on the fire?"

"I put mine on," Aileen announced. "Didn't I, Momma?"

Brook picked up several of the large pieces he had carried and laid them on the feeble flames.

"I founded the company years before we got married," Emery told Jan. "I lost control when Brook's mother and I broke up. I had to give her half of my stock, and she sold it."

"It's not—"

"The stock you're talking about dividing now is the stock I got for mine. Most of the money in our joint account, and my personal account, came from the company before we were taken over. You can hang on to everything in your personal accounts. I don't want your money."

"Well, that's kind of you! That's extremely kind of you, Emery!"

"You're worried about the snow, you say, and I think you should be. If you and the twins want to stay here until the weather clears up, you're welcome to. Maybe we can work out something."

Jan shook her head, and for a moment Emery allowed himself to admire her clear skin and the clean lines of her profile. It was so easy to think of all that he wanted to say to her, so hard to say what he had to: "In that case, you'd better go."

"I'm entitled to half our community property!"

Brook put in, "The house's worth ten times more than this place."

Boys here, Emery thought. Girls over there. "You can have the house, Jan. I'm not disputing it—not now. Not yet. But I may, later, if you're stubborn. I'm willing to make a cash settlement . . ." Even as he said it, he realized that he was not.

"This is what we negotiated. Phil Gluckman represented you! He said so, and so did you. It's all settled."

Emery leaned forward in his chair, holding his hands out to the rising flames. "If everything's settled, you don't need my signature. Go back to the city."

"I—Oh, *God!* I should have known it was no use to come out here."

"I'm willing to give you a cash settlement in the form of a trust fund for the twins. A generous settlement, and you can keep the house, your car, your money, and your personal things. That's as far as I'll go, and it's further than I ought to go. Otherwise, we fight it out in court."

"We negotiated this!"

She shoved her paper at him, and he was tempted to throw it into the fire. Forcing himself to speak mildly, he said, "I know you did, and I know that you negotiated in good faith. So did we. I wanted to see what Phil Gluckman could come up with. And to tell you the truth, I was pretty sure that it would be something I could accept. I'm disappointed in him."

"It's snowing harder," Alayna told them.

"He didn't—" Emery stiffened. "Did you hear something?"

"I haven't heard a thing! I don't have listen to this!"

It had sounded like a shot, but had probably been no more than the noise of a large branch breaking beneath the weight of the snow. "I've lost my train of thought," he admitted, "but I can make my position clear in three short affirmations. First, I won't sign that paper. Not here, not in Voylestown, and not in the city. Not anywhere. You might as well put it away."

"This is completely unfair!"

"Second, I won't go back and haggle. That's Phil's job."

"Mister high-tech himself, roughing it in the wilderness."

Emery shook his head. "I was never the technical brains of the company, Jan. There were half a dozen people working for me who knew more about the equipment than I did."

"Modest, too. I hope you realize that I'm going to have something to say after you're through."

"Third, I'm willing to try again if you are." He paused, hoping to see her glare soften. "I realize I'm not easy to live with. Neither are you. But I'm willing to try—hard—if you'll let me."

"You really and truly think that you're a great lover, don't you?"

"You married a great lover the first time," he told her.

She seethed. He watched her clench her perfect teeth and take three deep breaths as she forced herself to speak calmly. "Emery, you say that unless I settle for what you're willing to give we'll fight it out in open court. If we do, the public—every acquaintance and business contact you've got—will hear how you molested my girls."

Unwilling to believe what he had heard, he stared at her.

"You didn't think I'd do it, did you? You didn't think I'd expose them to that, and I don't want to. But—"

"It's not true!"

"Your precious Phil Gluckman has questioned them, in my presence and my attorney's. Call him up right now. Ask him what he thinks."

Emery looked at the twins; neither would meet his eyes.

"Do you want to see what a court will give me when the judge hears that? There are a lot of women judges. Do you want to find out?"

"Yes." He spoke slowly. "Yes, Jan. I do."

"It'll ruin you!"

"I'm ruined already." He stood up. "That's what you're refusing to understand. I think you'd better leave now. You and the twins."

She stood too, jumping to her feet with energy he envied. "You set up one company. You could start another one, but not when this gets around."

He wanted to say that he had seen a unique opportunity and taken it—that he'd had his chance in life and made the best of it, and finished here. All that he could manage was, "I'm terribly sorry it's come to this. I never wanted it to, or . . . " His throat shut, and he felt the sick hopelessness of a fighter whose worst enemies are his own instincts. How would it feel and taste, how would it look, the cold, oiled steel muzzle in his mouth? He could cut a stick in the woods, or even use the red pen to press the trigger.

"Come on, girls, we're going. Goodbye, Brook."

Brook muttered something.

For a brief moment Emery felt Alayna's hand in his; then she was gone. The cabin door slammed behind her.

Brook said, "Don't freak out. She's got it coming."

"I know she does," Emery told him. "So do I, and we're both going to get it. I don't mind for my sake, but I mind terribly for hers. It was my job—my duty—to—"

On the front porch Jan exclaimed, "*Hey!*" Presumably she was speaking to one of the twins.

"I thought you handled yourself really well," Brook said.

Emery managed to smile. "That's another thing. It's my job to teach you how that sort of thing's done, and I didn't. Don't you see that I let her leave—practically made her go—before she'd agreed to what I wanted? I should have moved heaven and earth to keep her here until she did, but I pushed her out the door instead. That's not how you win, that's how you lose."

"You think the sheriff might get your gun back?"

"I hope not." Emery took off his coat and hung it on the peg nearest the front door. For Brook's sake he added, "I like to shoot, but I've never liked shooting animals."

Outside, the sound diminished by distance and the snow, Jan screamed.

Emery was first out of the door, but was nearly knocked off the porch by Brook. Beyond the porch's meager shelter, half obscured by blowing snow, the black Lincoln's hood was up. Jan sprawled in the snow, screaming. One of the twins grappled a small, dark figure; the other was not in sight.

Brook charged into the swirling snow, snow so thick that for a moment he vanished completely. Emery floundered through shin-high snow after him, saw a second small stranger appear—as it seemed—from the Lincoln's engine compartment, and a third emerge from the interior with his rifle in its hand, the dome light oddly spectral in the deepening gloom. For a moment he received the fleeting impression of a smooth, almond-shaped brown face.

The rifle came up. The diminutive figure (shorter than Brook, hardly larger than the twins) jerked at its trigger. Brook grabbed it and staggered backward, falling in the snow. The struggling twin cried out, a childish shriek of pain and rage.

Then their attackers fled—fled preposterously slowly through snow that was for them knee high, but fled nonetheless, the three running clumsily together in a dark, packed mass that almost vanished before they had gone twenty feet. One turned, wrestled the rifle's lever, jerked the rifle like an unruly dog, and ran again.

Emery knelt in the snow beside Jan. "Are you all right?"

She shook her head, sobbing like a child.

The twin embraced him, gasping, "She hit me, she hit me." He tried to comfort both, an arm for each.

Later—though it seemed to him not much later—Brook draped his shoulders with his double mackinaw, and he realized how cold he was. He stood, lifting the twin, and pulled Jan to her feet. "We'd better get back inside."

"*No!*"

He dragged her after him, hearing Brook shut the Lincoln's passenger's-side door behind them.

By the time they reached the cabin, Jan was weeping again. Emery put her back in the chair she had occupied a few minutes before. "Listen! Listen here, even if you can't stop bawling. One of the twins is gone. Do you know where she is?"

Sobbing, Jan shook her head.

"That girl with the hood? She hit Mama, and Aileen ran away." The remaining twin pointed.

Brook gasped, "They didn't hurt her, 'Layna?"

"They hurt *me*. They hit my arm." She pushed back her sleeve, wincing.

Emery turned to Brook. "What happened to you?"

"Got it in the belly." Brook managed a sick smile. "He had a gun. Was it the one they stole from you?"

"I think so."

"Well—I grabbed the barrel," Brook paused, struggling to draw breath, "and I tried to push it up," he demonstrated, "so he couldn't shoot. I guess he hit me with the other end. Knocked my wind out."

Emery nodded.

"It happened one time when I was a little kid. We were playing kick-ball. I fell down and another kid kicked me."

The image glimpsed through falling snow returned: Brook floundering toward the small hooded figure with the leveled rifle. Emery felt weak, half sick with fright. "You damned fool kid," he blurted, "you could've been killed!" It sounded angry and almost vicious, although he had not thought himself angry.

"Yeah, I guess I could of."

Jan stopped crying long enough to say, "Emery, don't be mean."

"What were you being when you made the girls say I had molested them?"

"Well, you did!"

Brook said, "He tried to shoot me. I saw him. I think the safety was on. I tried to get to him fast before he wised up."

"That rifle doesn't have one, just the half-cock."

Brook was no longer listening. Under his breath, Emery explained, "He was short-stroking it, pulling down the lever a reasonable distance instead of all the way. You can't do that with a lever-action—it will eject, but it won't load the next round. He'll learn to do right pretty soon, I'm afraid."

Jan asked querulously, "What about Aileen? Aren't you going to look for Aileen?"

"Alayna, you pointed toward the lake when I asked which way your sister went. Are you sure?"

Alayna hesitated. "Can I look out the window?"

"Certainly. Go ahead."

She crossed the cabin to the front window and looked out, standing on tiptoe. "I never said you felt us and everything like Mama said. I just said all right, all right, I see, and yes, yes, because she was there listening." Alayna's voice was almost inaudible; her eyes were fixed upon the swirling snow beyond the windowpane.

"Thank you, Alayna." Emery spoke rapidly, keeping his voice as low as hers. "You're a good girl, a daughter to be proud of, and I am proud of you. Very proud. But listen—are you paying attention?"

"Yes, Daddy."

"What you tell your mama—" he glanced at Jan, but she was taking off her coat and lecturing Brook, "isn't important. If you've got to lie to her about that so she won't punish you, do what you did. Nod and say yes. What you tell the lawyers is more important, but not very important. They lie all the time, so they've got no business complaining when other people lie to them. But when you're in court, and you've sworn to tell the truth, everything will be terribly important. You *have* to tell the truth then. The plain unvarnished truth, and nothing else. Do you understand?"

Alayna nodded solemnly, turning to face him.

"Not to me, because my life's nearly over. Not to God, because we can't really hurt God, only pain him by our spite and ingratitude. But because if you lie then, it's going to hurt you for years, maybe for the rest of your life.

"When God tells us not to lie, and not to cheat or steal, it's not because those things hurt him. You and I can no more harm God than a couple of ants could hurt this mountain. He does it for the same reason that your mama and I tell you not to play with fire—because we know it can hurt you terribly, and we don't want you to get hurt.

"Now, which way did Aileen run?"

"That way." Alayna pointed again. "I know because of the car. There was a lady at the front looking at the motor, and she sort of tried to catch her, but she got away."

"You say—Never mind." Emery stood. "I'd better go after her."

"Comin' with," Brook announced.

"No, you're not. You're going to see about Alayna's arm." Emery put on his coat. His gloves were in the pockets and his warmest cap on a peg. "There's plenty of food here. Fix some for the three of you—maybe Alayna and her mother will help. Make coffee, too. I'll want some when I get back."

Outside, the creek and the hill across it had disappeared in blowing snow. It would have been wise,

Emery reflected, for Jan to have turned the car around before she stopped. It was typical of her that she had not.

He squinted at it through the snow. The hood was still up. The intruders—the boys who had robbed his cabin—had no doubt intended to strip it, stealing the battery and so on, or perhaps hot-wire it and drive it someplace where it could be stripped at leisure. There were three, it seemed—three at least, and perhaps more.

Reaching the Lincoln, he peered into the crowded engine compartment. The battery was still there; although he could not be sure, nothing seemed to be missing. Jan, who had told him he should have locked the cabin door, should have locked the doors; but then Jan seldom did, even in the city, and who would expect trouble way out here during a blizzard?

Emery slammed down the hood. Now that he came to think of it, Jan left her keys in the car more often than not. If she had, he could turn it around for her before the snow got any deeper. Briefly he vacillated, imagining Aileen hiding behind a tree, cold and frightened. But Aileen could not be far, and might very well come out of hiding if she heard the Lincoln start.

As he had half expected, the keys were in the ignition. He started the engine and admired the luxurious interior until warm air gushed from the heater, then allowed the big car to creep forward. Alayna felt certain her twin had run toward the lake, and he had to go in that direction anyway to turn around.

He switched on the headlights.

Aileen might come running when she saw her mother's car. Or he might very well meet her walking back toward the cabin, if she had sense enough to stick to the road; if he did, she could get in and warm up at once.

The Lincoln's front-wheel drive, assisted by its powerful engine, seemed to be handling the snow well so far. At about two miles an hour, he topped the gentle rise beyond the cabin and began the descent to the lake.

Aileen had run down this road toward the lake; but in what direction had the boys run? Emery found that though he could picture them vividly as they fled—three small, dark figures bunched together, one carrying his rifle (somehow carrying away his death while fleeing from him)—he could not be certain of the direction in which they had run. Toward town, or this way? Their tracks would be obscured by snow now in either case.

Had they really fled, as he'd assumed? Wasn't it possible that they'd been pursuing Aileen? It was a good thing—

He took his eyes off the snow-blanketed road for a second to stare at Jan's keys. The doors had been unlocked, the keys in the ignition. If the boys had wanted to strip this car, why hadn't they driven it away?

He stopped, switched on the emergency blinkers, and blew the horn three times. Aileen might, perhaps, have run as far as this—call it three-quarters of a mile, although it was probably a little less. It was hard to believe that she would have run farther, though no doubt a healthy eleven-year-old could run farther than he, and faster, too. Not knowing what else to do, he got out, leaving the lights on and the engine running.

"Aileen! Aileen, honey!"

She had told Phil Gluckman that he, Emery Bainbridge, her foster father, had molested her. Had she believed it, too? He had read somewhere that young children could be made to believe that such things had happened when they had not. What about a bright eleven-year-old?

He made a megaphone of his hands. *"Aileen! Aileen!"*

There was no sound but the song of the rising wind and the scarcely audible purr of the engine.

He got back in and puffed fine snow off his glasses before it could melt. When he had left the cabin, he had intended to search on foot—to tramp along this snow-covered road calling Aileen. Perhaps that would have been best after all.

Almost hesitantly, he put the automatic transmission into first, letting the Lincoln idle forward at a speed that seemed no faster than a slow walk. When a minute or more had passed, he blew the horn again.

That had been a shot he had heard as he sat arguing with Jan; he felt sure of it now. The boy had been trying out his new rifle, experimenting with it.

He blew the horn as he had before, three short beeps.

That model held seven cartridges, but he couldn't remember whether it had been fully loaded. Say that it had. One shot fired at him on the hill, another in the woods (where?) to test the rifle. Five left. Enough to kill him, to kill Jan, and to kill Brook and both twins, assuming Aileen wasn't dead already. Quite possibly the boy with the rifle was waiting in the woods now, waiting for Jan's big black Lincoln to crawl just a little bit closer.

All right, let him shoot. Let the boy shoot at him now, while he sat behind the wheel. The boy might miss him as he sat here, alone in the dark behind tinted safety glass. The boy with his rifle could do nothing worse to him than he had imagined himself doing to himself, and if he missed, somebody—Jan or Brook, Aileen or Alayna—might live. And living, recall him someday with kindness.

The big Lincoln crept past the dark, cold cabin of

his nearest neighbor, a cabin whose rather too-flat roof already wore a peaked cap of snow.

He blew the horn, stopped, and got out as before, wishing that he had remembered to bring the flashlight. As far as he could tell, the snow lay undisturbed everywhere, save for the snaking track behind the Lincoln.

He would continue to the lake, he decided; he could go no farther. There was a scenic viewpoint there with parking for ten or twelve cars. It would be as safe to turn around there as to drive on the road as he had been doing—not that the road, eighteen inches deep in snow already, with drifts topping three feet, was all that safe.

Kicking snow from his boots and brushing it from his coat and trousers, he got back into the car, took off his cap, and cleaned his glasses, then eased the front wheels into the next drift.

When Jan and the twins had left the cabin, they must have seen the boys, perhaps at about the time they were raising the hood. Jan had shouted at them— he had heard her—and gone to her car to make them stop, followed by the twins. What had she said, and what had the boys said in reply? He resolved to question her about it when he returned to the cabin. Somebody had knocked her down; he tried to remember whether her face had been bruised, and decided it had not.

The Lincoln had pushed through the drift, and was already approaching another; here, where the road ran within a hundred feet of Haunted Lake, the snow swirled more wildly than ever. Was there still open water at the deepest part of the lake? He peered between the burdened trees, seeing nothing.

When one of the boys had hit their mother, Aileen had run; Alayna had attacked him. Aileen had acted sensibly and Alayna foolishly, yet it was Alayna he admired. The world would be a better place if more people were as foolish as Alayna and fewer as sensible as Aileen.

Alayna had said something peculiar about their attacker. *The boy with the hood. He hit Mama and Aileen ran away.*

That wasn't exactly right, but close enough, perhaps. The boy had worn a hood, perhaps a hooded sweatshirt underneath his coat, the coat and sweatshirt both black or brown; something of that kind.

For a moment it seemed the Lincoln would stall in the next drift. He backed out and tried again. Returning, he could go through the breaks he had already made, of course; and it would probably be a good idea to turn around, if he could, and return now.

Two dark figures stepped out of the trees at the edge of his lights. Between them was a terrified child nearly as tall as they. One waved, pointing to Aileen and to him.

He braked too hard, sending the crawling Lincoln into a minor skid that left it at an angle to the road. The one who had waved gestured again—and he, catching a glimpse of the smooth young face beneath the hood, realized that it was not a boy's at all, but a woman's.

He got out and found his own rifle pointed at him.

Aileen moaned, "Daddy, Daddy . . . "

The smooth-faced young woman who had waved shoved her at him, then patted the Lincoln's fender, speaking in a language he could not identify.

Emery nodded. "You'll give her to me if I'll give you the car."

The women stared at him without comprehension.

He dropped to his knees in the snow and hugged

Aileen, and made a gesture of dismissal toward the Lincoln.

Both women nodded.

"We'll have to walk it," he told Aileen. "A little over two miles, I guess. But we can't go wrong if we stay on the road."

She said nothing, sobbing.

He stood, not bothering to clean the snow from his knees and thighs. "The keys are in there."

If they understood, they gave no sign of it.

"The engine's running. You just can't hear it."

The freezing wind whipped Aileen's dark hair. He tried to remember how the twins had been dressed when he had seen them getting out of the Lincoln in front of his cabin. She'd had on a stocking cap, surely—long white stocking caps on both the twins. If so, it was gone now. He indicated his own head, and realized that he had left his cap in the car; he started to get it, stopping abruptly when the woman with his rifle lifted it to her shoulder.

She jabbed the rifle in the direction he had come.

"I just want to get my cap," he explained.

She raised the rifle again, putting it to her shoulder without sighting along the barrel. He backed away, saying, "Come on, Aileen."

The other woman produced something that looked more like a tool than a weapon, a crooked metal bar with what seemed to be a split pin at one end.

"I don't want to fight." He took another step backward. He pointed to Aileen's head. "Just let me get my cap and give it to her."

The shot was so sudden and unexpected that there was no time to be afraid. Something tugged violently at his mackinaw.

He tried to rush the woman with the rifle, slipped in the snow, and fell. She took his rifle from her shoulder, pulled down and pushed up its lever almost as dexterously as he could have himself, and pointed it again.

"No, no!" He raised his hands. "We'll go, I swear." He crawled away from her, backward through the snow on his hands and knees, conscious that Aileen was watching with the blank, horror-stricken expression of a child who has exhausted tears.

When he was ten yards or more behind the Lincoln, he stood up and called, "Come here, Aileen. We're going back."

She stared at the women, immobile until one motioned to her, then waded slowly to him through the snow. His right side felt as though it had been scorched with a soldering iron; he wondered vaguely how badly he had been wounded. Catching her hand, he turned his back on the woman and began to trudge away, trying to brace himself against the bullet that he more than half expected.

"Daddy?"

He scarcely dared to speak, but managed, "What is it?"

"Can you carry me?"

"No." He felt he should explain, but could think only of the rifle pointed at his back. "We've got to walk. You're a big girl now. Come on, honey." It was easier to walk in the curving tracks of the Lincoln's tires, and he did so.

"I want to go home."

"So do I, honey. That's where we're going. Come on, it can't be far." He risked a glance toward the lake, and this time caught sight of ice lit by blue lights far away. More to himself than to the doleful, shivering child beside him, he muttered, "Somebody's out there on a boat." No one—no sane, normal person at least—would have a boat in the lake at this time of year. The boats had been drawn up on shore, where they would stay until spring.

He took off his glasses and dropped them into a pocket of his mackinaw, and looked behind him. Jan's Lincoln would have been invisible if it were not for the blinking red glow of its taillights. They winked out together as he watched. "They're stripping it," he told Aileen. "They just got the alternator or the battery."

She did not reply; and he began to walk again, turning up his collar and pulling it close about his ears. The wind was from his left; the warmth on the other side was blood, soaking his clothes and warming the skin under them, however briefly. Slow bleeding, or so it seemed—in which case he might not be wounded too badly and might live. A soft-nosed hunting bullet, but expansion required a little distance, and it could not have had much, probably had not been much bigger than thirty caliber when it had passed through his side.

Which meant that life would continue, at least for a time. He might be tempted to give his body to the lake—to walk out on its tender ice until it gave way and his life, begun in warm amniotic fluid, should terminate in freezing lake water. He might be tempted to lie down in the snow and bleed or freeze to death. But he could not possibly leave Aileen or any other child out here alone, although he need only tell her to follow the road until she reached his cabin.

"Look," she said, "there's a house."

She released his hand to point, and he realized that he was not wearing his gloves, which were in his pockets. "It's closed up, honey." (He had fallen into the habit of calling both the twins "honey" to conceal his inability to distinguish them.) "Have you got gloves?"

"I don't know."

He forced himself to be patient. "Well, look. If you've got gloves or mittens, put them on." This girl, he reminded himself, was the wonder of her class, writing themes that would have done credit to a college student and mastering arithmetic and the rudiments of algebra with contemptuous ease.

"I guess those ladies didn't give them back."

"Then put on mine." He handed them to her.

"Your hands will get cold."

"I'll put one in my pocket, see? And I'll hold your hand with my other one, so the one glove will keep us both warm."

She gave a glove back to him. "My hand won't go around yours, Daddy, but yours will go around mine."

He nodded, impressed, and put the glove on.

It might be possible to get into his neighbor's lightless cabin, closed or not. "I'm going to try to break in," he told Aileen. "There ought to be firewood and matches in there, and there may even be a phone."

But the doors were solid, and solidly locked; and there were grilles over the small windows, as over his own. "We've had a lot of break-ins," he confided, "ever since they paved the road. People drive out to the lake, and they see these places."

"Is it much farther?"

"Not very far. Maybe another mile." He remembered his earlier speculations. "Did you run this far, honey?"

"I don't think so."

"I didn't think that you would." Somewhat gratified, he returned to her and the road. It was darker than ever now, and the tire tracks, obscured by advancing night as well as new-fallen snow, were impossible to follow. Pushing up his sleeve, he looked at his watch: it was almost six o'clock.

"I don't like them," Aileen said. "Those ladies."

"It would surprise me if you did."

"They took my clothes off. I said I'd do it, but they didn't pay any attention, and they didn't know how to do it. They just pulled and pulled till things came off."

"Out here? In the snow?" He was shocked.

"In the ziggurat, but it was pretty cold in there, too."

He found the point in a drift at which the Lincoln had bulldozed its way through, and led her to it. "What did you say? A ziggurat?"

"Uh-huh. Is it much farther?"

"No," he said.

"I could sit down here. You could come back for me in your Jeep."

"No," he repeated. "Come on. If we walk faster, we'll keep warm."

"I'm really tired. They didn't give me hardly anything to eat, either. Just a piece of bread."

He nodded absently, concentrating on walking faster and pulling her along. He was tired too—nearly exhausted. What would he say when he wrote his journal? To take his mind off his weariness and the burning pain in his right side—off his fear, as he was forced to concede—he attempted to compose the entry in his mind.

"I got in the sleeper thing, but it was so cold. My feet got really cold, and I couldn't pull them up. I guess I slept a little."

He looked down at her, blinking away snow; it was too dark for him to gauge her expression. "Those women took you into a ziggurat—"

"Not really, Daddy. That was a kind of temple they had in Babylon. This one just looks like the picture in the book."

"They caught you," he continued doggedly, "and took you there, and undressed you?"

If she nodded, he failed to see the motion. "Did they or didn't they?"

"Yes, Daddy."

"And they fed you, and you slept a little, or anyway

tried to sleep. Then you got dressed again and they brought you back here. Is that what you want me to believe?"

"They showed me some pictures, too, but I didn't know what lots of the things were."

"Aileen, you can't possibly have been gone more than a couple of hours at the outside. I doubt it was that long."

He had thought her beyond tears, but she began to sob, not loudly, but with a concentrated wretchedness that tore at his heart. "Don't cry, honey." He picked her up, ignoring the fresh pain in his side.

The wind, which had been rising all afternoon, was blowing hard enough to whistle, an eerie moan among the spectral trees. "Don't cry," he repeated. He staggered forward, holding her over his left shoulder, desperately afraid that he would slip and fall again. Her plastic snow boots were stiff with ice, the insulated trousers above them stiff too.

He could not have said how far he had walked; it seemed miles before a lonely star gleamed through the darkness ahead. "Look," he said, and halted—then turned around so that his daughter, too, could see the golden light. "That's our cabin. Has to be. We're going to make it."

Then (almost at once, it seemed) Brook was running through the snow with the flashlight, he had set Aileen upon her feet, and they were all three stumbling into the warmth and light of the cabin, where Jan knelt and clasped Aileen to her and cried and laughed and cried again, and Alayna danced and jumped and demanded over and over, "Was she lost, Daddy? Was she lost in the woods?"

Brook put a plate of hot corned-beef hash in his lap and pushed a steaming mug of coffee at him.

"Thank you." Emery sighed. "Thank you very

much, son." His face felt frozen; merely breathing the steam from the mug was heavenly.

"The car get stuck?"

He shook his head.

"I fixed stuff like you said. 'Layna helped, and Jan says she'll do the dishes. If she won't, I will." Brook had called her Mother for the length of the marriage; but it was over now, emotionally if not legally. Emery's thoughts turned gratefully from the puzzle of Aileen's captivity to that.

"I could toast you some bread in the fireplace," Brook offered. "You want ketchup? I like ketchup on mine."

"A fork," Emery told him, and sipped his coffee.

"Oh. Yeah."

"Was she lost?" Alayna demanded. "I bet she was!"

"I'm not going to talk about that." Emery had come to a decision. "Aileen can tell you herself, as much or as little as she wants."

Jan looked up at him. "I called the sheriff. The number was on your phone."

Emery nodded.

"They said they couldn't do anything until she'd been gone for twenty-four hours. It's the law, apparently. They—this woman I talked to—suggested we get our friends and neighbors to search. I told her that you were searching already. Maybe you ought to call and tell them you found her."

He shook his head, accepting a fork from Brook.

"You came back on foot? You walked?"

Aileen said, "From way down by the lake." She had taken off her boots, stockings, and snow pants, and was sitting on the floor rubbing her feet.

"Where's my car?"

"I traded it for Aileen."

Alayna stared at Aileen, wide-eyed. Aileen nodded.

"You *traded* it?"

He nodded too, his mouth full of corned-beef hash.

"Who to?"

He swallowed. "To whom, Jan."

"You are the most irritating man in the world!" If Jan had been standing, she would have stamped.

"He did, Mama. He said they could have the car if they'd give me to him, but they shot him anyway, and he fell down."

"That's right," Emery said. "We ought to have a look at that. It's pretty much stopped bleeding, and I think it's just a flesh wound." Setting his plate and mug on the hearth, he unbuttoned his mackinaw. "If it got the intestine, I suppose I'll have hash all over in there, and it will probably kill me. But there would have been food in my gut anyway. I had pork and beans for lunch."

"They *shot* you?" Jan stared at his blood-stiffened shirt.

He nodded, savoring the moment. *It's nothing, sir. I set the bone myself.* Danny Kaye in some old movie. He cleared his throat, careful to keep his face impassive. "I'm going to have to take this off, and my undershirt and pants, too. Probably my shorts. Maybe you could have the girls look the other way."

Both twins giggled.

"Look at the fire," she told them. "He's hurt. You don't want to embarrass him, do you?"

Brook had gotten the first-aid kit. "This is stuck." He pulled gingerly at the waistband of Emery's trousers. "I ought to cut it off."

"Pull it off," Emery told him. "I'm going to wash those pants and wear them again. I need them." He had unbuckled his belt, unbuttoned his trousers, and unzipped his fly.

"Just above the belt," Brook told him. "An inch,

inch and a half lower, and it would have hit your belt."

Jan snapped her fingers. "Oil! Oil will soften the dried blood. Wesson Oil. Have you got any?"

Brook pointed at the cabinet above the sink. Emery said, "There's a bottle of olive oil up there, or there should be."

"Leen's peeking," Brook told Jan, who told Aileen, "Do that again, young lady, and I'll smack your face!

"Emery, you really ought to make two rooms out of this. This is ridiculous."

"It was designed for four men," he explained, "a hunting party, or a fishing party. You women always insist on being included, then complain about what you find when you are."

She poured olive oil on his caked blood and rubbed it with her fingertips. "I had to get you to sign."

"You could have sent your damned paper to my box in town. I'd have picked it up on Saturday and sent it back to you."

"She couldn't mail me," Brook said. "Are we going to get the car back? My junk was in the trunk."

Emery shrugged. "They're stripping it, I think. We may be able to take back what's left. Maybe they won't look in the trunk."

"They're bound to."

Jan asked, "How are we supposed to get home?"

"I'll drive you to town in the Jeep. There's bus service to the city. If the buses aren't running because of the storm, you can stay in a motel. There are two motels, I think. There could be three." He rubbed his chin. "You'll have to anyway, unless you want to reconsider and stay here. I think the last bus was at five."

Brook was scrutinizing Emery's wound. "That bullet sort of plowed through your skin. It might've got some muscles at your waist, but I don't think it hit any organs."

Emery made himself look down. "Plowed through the fat, you mean. I ought to lose twenty pounds, and if I had, she would have missed."

"A girl?"

Emery nodded.

Jan said, "No wonder you hate us so much," and pulled his bloodstained trousers free.

"I don't hate you. Not even now, when I ought to. Brook, would you give me my coffee? That's good coffee you made, and there's no reason I shouldn't drink it while you bandage that."

Brook handed it to him. "I scrubbed out the pot."

"Good for you. I'd been meaning to."

Alayna interposed, "I make better coffee than Brook does, Daddy, but Mama says I put in too much."

"You should have stitches, Emery. Is there a hospital in town?"

"Just a clinic, and it'll be closed. I've been hurt worse and not had stitches."

Brook filled a pan with water. "Why'd they shoot you, Dad?"

Emery started to speak, thought better of it, and shook his head.

Jan said, "If you're going to drive us into town in the Jeep, you could drive us into the city just as easily."

Setting his water on the stove, Brook hooted.

"You've got money, and you and Brook could stay at a hotel and come back tomorrow."

Emery said, "We're not going to, however."

"Why won't you?"

"I don't have to explain, and I won't."

She glared. "Well, you should!"

"That won't do any good." Privately he wondered

which was worse, a woman who had never learned how to get what she wanted or a woman who had.

"You actually proposed that we patch it up. Then you act like this?"

"I'm trying to keep things pleasant."

"Then do it!"

"You mean you want to be courted while you're divorcing me. That's what's usually meant by a friendly divorce, from what I've been able to gather." When she said nothing, Emery added, "Isn't that water hot enough yet, Brook?"

"Not even close."

"I shouldn't explain," Emery continued, "but I will. In the first place, Brook and the twins are going to have about as much elbow room as live bait in the back of the Jeep. It will be miserable for even a short drive. If we so much as try to make it into the city in this weather, they'll be tearing each other to bits before we stop."

Brook put in, "I'll stay here, Dad. I'll be all right."

Emery shook his head. "So would we, Jan. In the second, I think the women who shot me will be back as soon as the storm lets up. If no one's here, they'll break in or burn this place down. It's the only home I've got, and I intend to defend it."

"Sure," Brook said. "Let me stay. I can look after things while you're gone."

"No," Emery told him. "It would be too dangerous."

Emery turned back to Jan. "In the third place, I won't do it because I want to so much. If—"

"You were the one that gave those people my car."

"To get Aileen back. Yes, I did. I'd do it again."

"And you took it without my permission! I trusted you, Emery. I left my keys in the ignition, and you took my car."

He nodded wearily. "To look for Aileen, and I'd do that again too. I suppose you're already planning to bring it up in court."

"You bet I am!"

"I suggest you check the title first."

Aileen herself glanced at him over her shoulder. "I'm really hungry. Can I have the rest of your hash?"

Brook said, "There's more here, 'Leen. You said you weren't, but I saved—"

"I haven't had anything since yesterday except some bread stuff."

Jan began, "Aileen, you know perfectly well—"

Emery interrupted her. "It's only been a couple of hours since they caught you, honey. Remember? We talked about that before we got here."

"I was in there, in the sleep thing—"

Jan snapped, "Aileen, be quiet! I told you not to look around like that."

"It's only Daddy in his underwear. I've seen him like that lots."

"Turn around!"

Trying to weigh each word with significance, Emery said, "Your mama told you to be quiet, honey. That wasn't simply an order. It was good advice."

Brook brought her a plate of corned-beef hash and a fork. "There's bread, too. Want some?"

"Sure. And milk or something."

"There isn't any."

"Water, then." Raising her voice slightly, Aileen added, "I'd get up and get it for myself, but Mama won't let me."

Jan said, "You see what you've started, Emery?"

He nodded solemnly. "I didn't start it, but I'm quite happy about it."

Brook washed his wound and bandaged it, applying a double pad of surgical gauze and so much Curity

Wet-Pruf adhesive tape that Emery winced at the mere thought of removing it.

"I might be a doctor," Brook mused, "big money, and this is fun."

"You're a pretty good one already," Emery said gratefully. He kicked off his boots, emptied his pockets onto the table, and stuffed his trousers into a laundry bag, following it with his shirt. "Want to do me a favor, Brook? Scrape my plate into that tin bowl on the drainboard and set it on the back porch."

Jan asked, "Are you well enough to drive, Emery? Forget the fighting. You wouldn't want to see any of us killed. I know you wouldn't."

He nodded, buttoning a fresh shirt.

"So let me drive. I'll drive us into town, and you can drive Brook back here if you feel up to it."

"You'd put us into the ditch," Emery told her. "If I start feeling too weak, I'll pull over and—"

Brook banged the rear door shut behind him and held up a squirrel. "Look at this! It was right up on the porch." The tiny body was stiff, its gray fur powdered with snow.

"Poor little thing!" Jan went over to examine it. "It must have come looking for something to eat, and froze. Have you been feeding them, Emery?"

"It's a present from a friend," he told her. Something clutched his throat, leaving him barely able to speak. "You wouldn't understand."

The Jeep started without difficulty. As he backed it out onto the road, he wondered whether the dark-faced women who had Jan's Lincoln had been unable to solve the simple catches that held the Jeep's hood. Conceivably, they had not seen the Jeep when they had been in his cabin earlier. He wished now that he had asked Aileen how many women she had seen, when the two of them had been alone.

"Drafty in here," Jan remarked. "You should buy yourself a real car, Emery."

The road was visible only as an opening between the trees; he pulled onto it with all four wheels hub-deep in virgin snow, keeping the transmission in second and nudging the accelerator only slightly. Swirling snow filled the headlights. "Honey," he said, "your boots had ice on them. So did your snow pants. Did you wade in the lake?"

From the crowded rear seat, Aileen answered, "They made me, Daddy."

The road was visible only as an open space between trees. To people in a—Emery fumbled mentally for a word and settled on *aircraft*.

To an aircraft, the frozen lake might have looked like a paved helicopter pad or something of that kind, a more or less circular pavement. The black-looking open water at its center might have been taken for asphalt.

Particularly by a pilot not familiar with woods and lakes.

"Emery, you hardly ever answer a direct question. It's one of the things I dislike most about you."

"That's what men say about women," he protested mildly.

"Women are being diplomatic. Men are rude."

"I suppose you're right. What did you ask me?"

"That isn't the point. The point is that you ignore me until I raise my voice."

That seemed to require no reply, so he did not offer one. How high would you have to be and how fast would you have to be coming down before a frozen lake looked like a landing site?

"So do the girls," Jan added bitterly, "they're exactly the same way. So is Brook."

"That ought to tell you something."

"You don't have to be rude!"

One of the twins said, "She wanted to know how long it would take to get to town, Daddy."

It had probably been Alayna, Emery decided. "How long would you like it to take, honey?"

"Real quick!"

That had been the other one, presumably Aileen. "Well," he told her, "we'll be there real quick."

Jan said, "Don't try to be funny."

"I'm being diplomatic. If I wasn't, I'd point out that it's twenty-two miles and we're going about fifteen miles an hour. If we can keep that up all the way, it should take us about an hour and a half."

Jan turned in her seat to face the twins. "Never marry an engineer, girls. Nobody ever told me that, but I'm telling you now. If you do, don't say you were never warned."

One twin began, "You said that about—"

The other interrupted. "Only, it wasn't an engineer that time. It was a tennis player. Did you do it in your head, Daddy? I did too, only it took me longer. One point four and two-thirds, so six six seven. Is that right?"

"I have no idea. Fifteen is smaller than twenty-two, and that's an hour. Seven over, and seven's about half of fifteen. Most real calculations outside school are like that, honey."

"Because it doesn't matter?"

Emery shook his head. "Because the data's not good enough for anything more. It's about twenty-two miles to town on this Jeep's odometer. That could be off by as much as—" Something caught his eye, and he fell silent.

From the rear seat, Brook asked, "What's the matter, Dad?" He sounded half suffocated.

Emery was peering into the rear view mirror, unable to see anything except a blur of snow. "There was a sign back there. What did it say?"

"Don't tell me you're lost, Emery."

"I'm not lost. What did it say, Brook?"

"I couldn't tell, it was all covered with snow."

"I think it was the historical marker sign. I'm going to stop there on the way back."

"Okay, I'll remind you."

"You won't have to. I'll stop."

One of the twins asked, "What happened there?"

Emery did not reply; Brook told her, "There used to be a village there, the first one in this part of the state. Wagon trains would stop there. One time there was nobody there. The log cabins and their stuff was okay, only there wasn't anybody home."

"The Pied Piper," the twin suggested.

"He just took rats and kids. This got everybody."

Jan said, "I don't think that's much of a mystery. An early settlement? The Indians killed them."

The other twin said, "Indians would have scalped them and left the bodies, Mama, and taken things."

"All right, they were stolen by fairies. Emery, this hill looks so steep! Are you sure this is the right road?"

"It's the only road there is. Hills always look steeper covered with snow." When Jan said nothing, he added, "Hell, they *are* steeper."

"They should plow this."

"The plows will be out on the state highway," Emery told her. "Don't worry, only three more mountains."

They let Jan and the twins out in front of the Ramada Inn, and Brook climbed over the back of the front seat.

"I'm glad they're gone. I guess I shouldn't say it—she's been pretty nice to me—but I'm glad."

Emery nodded.

"You could've turned around back there." Brook indicated the motel's U-shaped drive. "Are we going into town?"

Emery nodded again.

"Want to tell me what for? I might be able to help."

"To buy two more guns. There's a sporting-goods dealer on Main Street. We'll look there first."

"One for me, huh? What kind?"

"What kind do you want?"

"A three-fifty-seven, I guess."

"No handguns, there's a five-day waiting period. But we can buy rifles or shotguns and take them with us, and we may need them when we get back to the cabin."

"One rifle and one shotgun," Brook decided. "Pumps or semis. You want the rifle or the scattergun, Dad?"

Emery did not reply. Every business that they drove past seemed to be dark and locked. He left the Jeep to rattle and pound the door of the sporting-goods store, but no one appeared to unlock it.

Brook switched off the radio as he got back in. "Storm's going to get worse. They say the main part hasn't even gotten here yet."

Emery nodded.

"You knew, huh?"

"I'd heard a weather report earlier. We're due for two, possibly three days of this."

The gun shop was closed as well. There would be no gun with which to kill the woman who had shot him, and none with which to kill himself. He shrugged half-humorously and got back into the Jeep. Brook said, "We're going to fight with what we've got, huh?"

"A hammer and a hunting knife against my thirty-thirty?" Emery shook his head emphatically. "We're not going to fight at all. If they come around again, we're to do whatever they want, no questions and no objections. If they like anything—this Jeep would be the most likely item, I imagine—we're going to give it to them."

"Unless I get a chance to grab the gun again."

Emery glanced at him. "The first time you tried that, she hadn't learned to use it. She was a lot better when she shot me. Next time she'll be better yet. Am I making myself clear?"

Brook nodded. "I've got to be careful."

"You've got to be more than just careful," Emery told him, "because if you're not, you're going to die. I was ten feet or more from her when she shot at me, and backing away. She fired anyway, and she hit me."

"I got it."

"When you dressed my wound," Emery continued, "you said that if her shot had been an inch or two lower it would have hit my belt. If it had been an inch or two to the left, it would have killed me. Did you think of that?"

"Sure. I just didn't want to say it." Brook pointed to a small dark building. "There's the last store, Rothschild's Records and CDs. It's pretty good. I used to have you drop me there sometimes when you were going into town, remember?"

Intent upon his thoughts and the snow-covered road, Emery did not even nod.

"Those girls have got to be either camping or living in somebody's cabin out here. If we can find out where, we could get some guns when the town's open again and go out there and make them give our stuff back."

Emery muttered, "This is the last trip until the county clears the road."

"We're doing okay now."

"This is a state highway. It's been plowed at least once, most likely within the past couple of hours. The road to the cabin won't have been plowed at all, and we barely made it out."

"I'd like to look at the other car and see if they left any of my stuff."

"All right, if we can drive as far as the cabin, we'll do that. But after that, I'm not taking the Jeep out until the road's been plowed."

"They really were girls? I thought you and 'Leen might have been stringing Jan."

"Two of them were." Emery studied the road. "The one who shot me, and another one who was with her. I imagine the third was as well, she seemed to be about the same size."

Brook nodded to himself. "You never can tell what girls are going to do, I guess."

"Obviously it's harder to predict the actions of someone whose psychology differs from your own. Once you've learned what a woman values, though, you ought to be right most of the time—say, seven out of ten." Emery chuckled. "How's that for a man being divorced for the second time? Do I sound like an expert?"

"Sure. What does a woman value?"

"It varies from woman to woman, and sometimes it changes. You have to learn for each, or guess. With a little experience you ought to be able to make pretty good guesses after you've talked with the woman for a few minutes. You've got to listen to what she says, and listen harder for what she doesn't. All this is true for men as well, of course. Fortunately, men are easier—for other men."

"Okay if I throw you a softball, Dad? I'm leading up to something."

"Go ahead."

"What does Jan value?"

"First of all, the appearance of wealth. She doesn't value money itself, but she wants to impress people with her big car, her mink coat, and so on. Have I missed the turn?"

"I don't think so. We've been going pretty slow."

"I don't either—I don't see how I could have—but I keep worrying about it.

"Money has a poetry of its own, Brook. Women are fond of telling us that we don't get it, but the poetry of money is one of the things that they rarely get. One of a dozen or more, I suppose. Are you going to ask why I married Jan? Is that what you're leading up to?"

"Uh-huh. Why did you?"

"Because I was lonely and fell in love with her. Looking back, I can see very clearly that I wanted to prove to myself that I could make a woman happy, too. I felt I could make Jan happy, and I was right. But after a while—after I lost the company, particularly—it no longer seemed worth the effort."

"I'm with you. Did she love you too? Or did you think she did?"

Emery sighed. "Women don't love in the same way that men do, Brook. I said the psychology was different, and that's one of the main differences. Men are dogs. Women are cats—they love conditionally. For example, I love you. If you were to try to kill me—"

"I wouldn't do that!"

"I'm constructing an extreme example," Emery explained patiently. "Say that I was to try to kill you. You'd fight me off if you could. You might even kill me doing it. But you'd love me afterward, just the same; you may not think so, but you would."

Brook nodded, his face thoughtful.

"When you love a woman, you'll love her in the

same way; but women love *as long as*—as long as you have a good job, as long as you don't bring home your friends, and so on. You shouldn't blame them for that, because it's as much a part of their natures as the way you love is of yours. For women, love is a spell that can be broken by picking a flower or throwing a ring into the sea. Love is magic, which is why they frequently use the language of fairy tales when they talk about it."

"We're coming up on the turn." Brook aimed his forefinger at the darkness and the blowing snow. "It's right along here someplace."

"About another half mile. Throw your fastball."

"This woman that shot you. Why did she do it?"

"I've been thinking about that."

"I figured you had."

"Why does anyone, robbing someone else, shoot them?"

"No witnesses?"

Emery shook his head. "A thief doesn't merely shoot to silence a witness, he kills. After she had shot me she let me go. I was still conscious, still able to walk and to talk. Perfectly capable of giving the sheriff a description of her. But she let me go. Why?"

"You were there, Dad. What do you think?"

"You're starting to sound like me." Emery slowed the Jeep from ten miles an hour to six, searching the road to his left.

"I know."

"Because she was frightened, I think. Afraid of me, and afraid she couldn't do it, too. When she shot me, she proved to herself that she could, and I was able to show her—by my actions, because she couldn't understand what I was saying—that I wasn't somebody she had to be afraid of."

The road to the cabin was deep in snow, so deep

that they inched and churned their way through it foot by foot. Caution, and speeds scarcely faster than a walk, soon became habitual, and Emery's mind turned to other things. First of all, to the smoothly oval face behind the threatening muzzle of his rifle. Large, dark eyes above a tiny mouth narrowed by determination; a small—slightly flattened?—nose.

Small and slender hands; the thirty-thirty had looked big in them, which meant that they had been hardly larger than the twins'. He did not remember seeing hair, but with that face it would be black, surely. Straight or curled? Not Japanese or Chinese, possibly a small, light-complexioned Afro-American. A mixture of Black and White with Oriental? Filipino? Almost anything seemed possible.

The coal-black hair he had imagined merged with the shadow of her hood. "Brownies," he said aloud.

"What?"

"Brownies. Don't they call those little girls who sell cookies Brownies?"

"Sure. Like Girl Scouts, only littler. 'Leen and 'Layna used to be Brownies."

Emery nodded. "That's right. I remember." But brownies were originally English fairies, small and dark—brown-faced, presumably—mischievous and sometimes spiteful, but often willing to trade their work for food and clothing. Fairies sufficiently feminine that giving their name to an organization for young girls was not ridiculous, as it would have been to call the same little girls gnomes, for example.

Stolen by fairies, Jan had said, referring to villagers of the eighteen forties. . . . He tried to remember the precise date, and failed.

Because brownies did not merely trade their labor for the goods they wanted. Often they stole. Milked your cow before you woke up. Snatched your infant from its crib. Lured your children to a place where time ran differently, too fast or too slow. Aileen, who had been gone for no more than two hours at most, had thought she had been gone for a day—had been taken to the ziggurat and shown pictures she had not understood, had slept or at least tried to sleep, had been made to wade into the lake, where blue lights shone.

Where was fairyland?

"Why're you stopping?"

"Because I want to get out and look at something. You stay here."

Flashlight in hand, he shut the Jeep's flimsy vinyl flap. Later—by next morning, perhaps—the snow might be easier to walk on. Now it was still uncompacted, as light as down; he sank above his knees at every step.

The historical marker protruded above the blank whiteness, its size amplified by the snow it wore. He considered brushing off the bronze plaque and reading it, but the precise date and circumstances, as specified by some historian more interested in plausibility than truth, did not matter.

He waded past it, across what would be green and parklike lawn in summer, reminding himself that there was a ditch at its end before the ranch's barbed-wire fence, and wishing he had a stick or staff with which to probe the snow. The body—if he had in fact seen what he had thought he had seen—would be covered by this time, invisible save as a slight mound.

When he stood in the ditch, the snow was above his waist. His gloved hands found the wire, then the almost-buried locust post, which he used to pull himself up, breaching the snow like some fantastic, red-plaid dolphin.

The coyote lay where he had glimpsed it on the

drive to town. It had frozen as stiff as the squirrel it had left him, its face twisted in a snarl of pain and surprise. Negotiating the ditch again with so much difficulty that he feared for a few seconds that he would have to call for Brook to rescue him, he stowed the body on the narrow floor behind the Jeep's front seats.

Brook said, "That's a dead coyote."

Emery nodded as he got back behind the wheel and put the Jeep in gear. "Cyanide gun."

"What do you want with that?"

"I don't know. I haven't decided yet."

Brook stared, then shrugged. "I hope you didn't start yourself bleeding again, doing all that."

"I may bury him. Or I might have him stuffed and mounted. That sporting-goods dealer has a taxidermy service. They could do it. Probably wouldn't cost more than a hundred or so."

"You didn't kill it," Brook protested.

"Oh yes, I did," Emery told him.

What they could see of the cabin through the falling snow suggested that it was as they had left it. Emery did not stop, and it would have been difficult to make the Jeep push its way through the banks more slowly than it already was. The world before the windshield was white, framed in black; and upon that blank sheet his mind strove to paint the country from which the small brown women had come, a country that would send forth an aircraft (if the ziggurat in the lake was in fact an aircraft or something like one) crewed by young women more alike than sisters. A country without men, perhaps, or one in which men were hated and feared.

What had they thought of Jan, a woman almost a foot taller than they? Jan with her creamy complexion and yellow hair? Of Aileen and Alayna, girls of their own size, nearly as dark as they, and alike as two peas? The first had run from, the second fought them; and both reactions had quite likely baffled them. From their own perspective, they had crashed in a wilderness of snow and wind and bitter cold—a howling wilderness strangely and dangerously inhabited.

"We could've stopped at the cabin," Brook said. "We can go look for my stuff tomorrow, when there's daylight."

Emery shook his head. "We wouldn't be able to get through tomorrow. The snow will be too deep."

"We could try."

Brook had presumably confirmed their worst fears, as he had himself; and although they'd had his rifle, they had fled at his approach. They had recognized the rifle as a weapon when they had entered and searched his empty, unlocked cabin—empty because he had seen something flash high up on the hill across the creek. . . .

"Is it much farther, Dad?" Brook was peering through the wind-driven snow into the black night again, trying to catch a glimpse of Jan's Lincoln.

"Quite a bit, I believe." Apologetically, Emery added, "We're not going very fast."

The flash from the hill had left a shallow burn on the oak back of his chair. Had it been a laser—a laser weapon? Had they been shooting at him even then? A laser that could do no more than scorch the surface of the chair-back would not kill a man, surely, though it might blind him if it struck his eyes. Not a weapon, perhaps, but a laser tool of some kind that they had tried to employ as a weapon. He recalled the lasers used to engrave steel in the company he had left to found his own.

"Nobody's in that cabin back there now, I guess."

He shook his head. "Been closed since early November. There's nobody out here really, except us and them."

"What do you think they're trying to do out here?"

"Leave." His tone, he hoped, would notify Brook that he was not in the mood for conversation.

"They could've gone in the Lincoln. It wasn't out of gas. I'd been watching the gauge, because she never does."

"They can't drive. If they could, they'd have driven it away from the cabin the first time, when Jan left the keys in it. Besides, the Lincoln couldn't take them where they want to go."

"Dad—"

"That's enough questions for now. I'll tell you more when I've got more of it figured out."

"You must be really tired. I wish we'd stopped at the cabin. There won't be any of my stuff left anyhow."

Was he really as tired as Brook suggested? He considered the matter and decided he was. Wading through the snow past the historical marker had consumed what little strength he had left after losing blood and slogging home with Aileen through snow that no longer seemed particularly deep. He was operating now on whatever it was that remained when the last strength was gone. On stubbornness and desperation.

"Your grandfather used to tell a story," he remarked to Brook, "about a jackrabbit, a coyote, and a jay. Did I ever tell you that?"

"No." Brook grinned, glad that he was not angry. "What is it?"

"A jay will yell and warn the other animals if there's a coyote around. You know that?"

"Uh-huh."

"Well, this jay was up on a mesquite, with a

jackrabbit sleeping in the shade. The jay spotted a coyote stalking the jackrabbit and yelled a warning. The coyote sprang, and the jackrabbit ran, scooting past the mesquite and hooking left, with the coyote after it.

"The jay felt a little guilty about not having spotted the coyote sooner, so he shouted to the jackrabbit, 'You okay? You going to make it?'

"And the jackrabbit called back, 'I'll make it!'

"They went around the mesquite eight or ten times, and it seemed to the jay that the coyote was gaining at every pass. He got seriously worried then, and he shouted down, 'You sure you're going to make it?'

"The jackrabbit called back, 'I'm going to make it!'

"A few more passes, and the coyote was snapping at the jackrabbit's tail. The jay was worried sick by then, and he shouted, 'Rabbit, how do you *know* you're going to make it?' And the jackrabbit called back, 'Hell, I've *got* to make it!'"

Brook said, "You mean you're like that rabbit."

"Right." Emery put the transmission into neutral and set the parking brake. "I've got to make it, and I will."

"Why are we stopping?"

"Because we're here." He opened his flap and got out.

"I don't see the car."

"You will in a minute. Bring the flash."

They had to climb a drift before they found it, nearly buried in snow with its hood still up. Emery reached inside, took Jan's keys out of the ignition lock, and handed them to Brook. "Here, check the trunk. They may not have noticed the keyhole behind the medallion."

A moment later, as he leaned against the snow-covered side of the car, he heard Brook say, "It's here! Everything's still here!"

"I'll help you." He forced himself to walk.

"Just a couple little bags. I can carry them." Brook slammed down the trunk lid so that he would not see whatever was being left behind. A stereo, Emery decided. Possibly a TV. He hated TV, and decided to say nothing.

"You want the keys?"

"You keep them."

"I guess we'll have to call a tow truck when the road's clear. They've taken a lot of stuff out of here." Brook was at the front of the Lincoln, shining the flashlight into its engine compartment.

"Sure," Emery said, and started back to the Jeep.

When he woke the next morning, bacon was frying and coffee perking on the little propane stove. He sat up, discovering that his right side was stiff and painful. "Brook?"

There was no answer.

The cabin was cold, in spite of the blue flames and the friendly odors. He pulled the wool shirt he had put on after Brook had bandaged his wound over the Duofold underwear he had slept in, pushed his legs into the trousers he had dropped on the floor beside his bunk, and stood up. His boots were under the little table, the stockings he had worn beside them. He put the stockings into his laundry bag, got out a clean pair and pulled them on, then tugged on, laced, and tied his boots.

The coffee had perked enough. He turned off the burner and transferred the bacon onto the cracked green plate Brook had apparently planned to use. The bacon still smelled good; he felt that he should eat a piece, but he had no appetite.

Had Brook set off on foot to fetch whatever it was that he had left in the Lincoln's trunk? Not with food on the stove. Brook would have turned down the fire under the coffeepot and drunk a cup before he left, taken up the bacon and eaten half of it, probably with bread, butter, and jam.

There was no toaster, but Brook had offered to toast bread in front of the fire the night before. That fire was nearly out, hardly more than embers. Brook had gotten up, started the coffee and put on the bacon, and gone outside for firewood.

Lord, Emery thought, you don't owe me a thing—I know that. But please.

They had taken Aileen and had, perhaps, been bringing her back when they had encountered him. They might very well have taken Brook as well; if they had, they might bring him back in a day or two.

He found that he was staring at the plate of bacon. He set it on the table and put on his mackinaw and second-best cap. Had his best one—the one that the women had not let him retrieve—been on the front seat of Jan's Lincoln? He had not even looked.

Snow had reached the sills of the windows, but it was not snowing as hard as it had the day before. The path plowed by Brook's feet and legs showed plainly, crossing the little back porch, turning south for the stacked wood under the eaves, then retraced for a short distance. Brook had seen something; or more probably, had heard a noise from the cabin's north side, where the Jeep was parked. It was difficult, very difficult, for Emery to step off the porch, following the path that Brook had broken through the deep snow.

Brook's body sprawled before the front bumper, a stick of firewood near its right hand. The blood around its head might, Emery told himself, have come from a superficial scalp wound. Brook might be alive, though unconscious. Even as he crouched to look more closely, he knew it was not true.

He closed his eyes and stood up. They had taken his ax as well as his rifle; he had worried about the rifle and had scarcely given a thought to the ax, yet the ax had done this.

The dead coyote still lay in back of the front seat of the plundered Jeep. He carried it to the south side of the cabin; and where firewood had been that autumn, contrived a rough bier from half a dozen sticks. Satisfied with the effect, he built a larger bier of the same kind for his son, arranged the not-yet-frozen body on it, and covered it with a clean sheet that he weighted with a few more sticks. It would be necessary to call the sheriff if the telephone was still working, and the sheriff might very well accuse him of Brook's murder.

Inside, after a momentary hesitation, he bolted the doors. A calendar hung the year before provided the number of the only undertaker in Voylestown.

"You have reached Merton's Funeral Parlor. We are not able to be with you at this time . . . "

He waited for the tone, then spoke quickly. "This's Emery Bainbridge." They could get his address from the directory, as well as his number. "My son's dead. I want you to handle the arrangements. Contact me when you can." A second or two of silence, as if in memory of Brook, and then the dial tone. He pressed in the sheriff's number.

"Sheriff Ron Wilber's office."

"This is Emery Bainbridge again. My son, Brook, has been killed."

"Address?"

"Five zero zero north, twenty-six seventy-seven west—that's on Route E-E, about five miles from Haunted Lake."

"How did it happen, Mister Bainbridge?"

He wanted to say that one of the women had stood against the wall of his cabin, holding his ax, and waited for Brook to come around the corner; it had been apparent from the lines plowed through the deep snow, but mentioning it at this time would merely make the investigating officer suspect him. He said, "He was hit in the head with my ax, I think. They took my ax yesterday."

"*Yes, I remember. Don't move the body, we'll get somebody out there as soon as we can.*"

"I already have. When—"

"*Then don't move it any more. Don't touch anything else.*"

"When will you have someone out here?"

He sensed, rather than heard, her indrawn breath. "*This afternoon, Emery. We'll try to get one of the deputies there this afternoon.*"

If she had not been lying, Emery reflected, she would have called him "Mister Bainbridge." He thanked her and hung up, then leaned back in his chair, looking from the telephone to his journal. He should write up his journal, and there was a great deal to write. There had been a cellular phone in Jan's car. Had they taken it? He had not noticed.

He picked up the telephone again but hung it up without pressing in a number. His black sports watch lay under his bunk. He retrieved it, noting the date and time.

09:17 Jan came yesterday, with Brook and the twins. Three small, dark women in hoods tried to strip her car. There was a tussle with Jan and the children.

He stared down at the pen. It was exactly the color of Brook's blood in the snow.

Aileen ran away. I searched for her in Jan's car,

which I was able to trade for her. One of the women shot me. They do not understand English.

The red pen had stopped.

His computer back home—he corrected the thought: his computer at Jan's had a spell checker; this pen had none, yet it had sounded a warning without one. Was it possible that the women spoke English after all? On overseas trips he had met people whose English he could scarcely understand. He tried to recall what the women had said and what he had said, and failed with both.

Yet something, some neglected corner of his sub-conscious, suspected that the women had in fact been speaking English, of a peculiar variety.

Whan that Aprille with his shoures soote
The droghte of March hath perced to the roote.

He had memorized the lines in high school—how long had it been? But no, it had been much longer than that, had been more than six hundred years since a great poet had written in a beautiful rhythmic dialect that had at first seemed as alien as German. "When April, with his sweet breath/The drought of March has pierced to the root."

And the language was still changing, still evolving.

He picked up the telephone, fairly sure that he remembered Jan's cellular number, and pressed it in.

A lonely ringing, far away. In Jan's snow-covered black Lincoln? Could a cellular car phone operate without the car's battery? There were bag phones as well, telephones you could carry in a briefcase, so perhaps it could. If the women had taken it to pieces, there would have been a recorded message telling him that the number was no longer in service.

He had lost count of the rings when someone picked up the receiver. "Hello," he said. "Hello?" Even to him, it sounded inane.

No one spoke on the other end. As slowly and distinctly as he could, he said, "I am the man whose son you killed, and I am coming to kill you. If you want to explain before I do, you have to do it now."

No voice spoke.

"Very well. You can call me if you want." He gave his number, speaking more slowly and distinctly than ever. "But I won't be here much longer."

Or at least, they do not speak an English that I can understand. I should have said that I was not hurt badly. Brook bandaged it. I have not seen a doctor. Maybe I should.

He felt the bandage and found it was stiff with blood. Changing it, he decided, would waste a great deal of valuable time, and might actually make things worse.

Brook and I took Jan and the twins into town. Before I woke up this morning, the women killed Brook, outside in the snow.

There was a little stand of black-willow saplings down by the creek. He waded through the snow to them, cut six with his hunting knife, and carried them back to the cabin.

There he cut four sticks, each three times as long as his foot, and tied their ends in pairs with twine. Shorter sticks, notched at both ends, spread them; he tied the short sticks in place with more twine, then bound the crude snowshoes that he had made to his boots, wrapping each boot tightly with a dozen turns.

He was eight or ten yards from the cabin—walking over the snow rather than through it—when his ears caught the faint ringing of his telephone. He returned to the cabin to answer it, leaving the maul he had been carrying on the porch.

"*Mister Bainbridge? I'm Ralph Merton.* Ralph Merton's voice was sepulchral. "*May I extend my sympathy to you and your loved ones?*"

Emery sighed and sat down, his snowshoed feet necessarily flat on the floor. "Yes, Mister Merton. It was good of you to return my call. I didn't think you'd be in today."

"*I'm afraid I'm not, Mister Bainbridge. I have an—ah—device that lets me call my office at the parlor and get my messages. May I ask if your son was under a doctor's care?*"

"No, Brook was perfectly healthy, as far as I know."

"*A doctor hasn't seen your son?*"

"No one has, except me." After a few seconds' silence, Emery added, "And the woman who killed him. I think there was another woman with her, in which case the second woman would have seen him, too. Not that it matters, I suppose."

Ralph Merton cleared his throat. "*A doctor will have to examine your son and issue a death certificate before we can come, Mister Bainbridge.*"

"Of course. I'd forgotten."

"*If you have a family doctor . . . ?*"

"No," Emery said.

"*In that case,*" Ralph Merton sounded slightly more human, "*I could phone Doctor Ormond for you. He's a young man, very active. He'll be there just as soon as he can get through, I'm sure.*"

"Thank you," Emery said, "I'd appreciate that very much."

"*I'll do it as soon as I hang up. Would you let us*

know as soon as you have a death certificate, Mister Bainbridge?"

"Certainly."

"Wonderful. Now, as to the—ah—present arrangements? Is your son indoors?"

"Out in the snow. I put a sheet over his body, but I'd think it would be covered with snow by this time."

"Wonderful. I'll call Doctor Ormond the moment I hang up, Mister Bainbridge. When you've got the death certificate, you can rely on Merton's for everything. You have my sympathy. I have two sons myself."

"Thank you," Emery repeated, and returned the receiver to its cradle.

The cabin still smelled faintly of bacon and coffee. It might not be wise to leave with an empty stomach, was certainly unwise to leave with a low flame under the coffeepot, as he had been about to do. He turned the burner off, got a clean mug (somewhat hampered by his home-made snowshoes), poured himself a cup, sipped, and made himself eat two slices of bacon. Three more, between two slices of rye bread, became a crude sandwich; he stuffed it into a pocket of his mackinaw.

The maul waited beside the front door; he locked the door and started off over the snow a second time. When the snow-covered road had led him nearly out of sight of the cabin, he thought he heard the faint and lonely ringing of his telephone again. Presumably that was Doctor Ormond; Emery shrugged and trudged on.

The front door of the dark cabin seemed very substantial; after examining it, Emery circled around to the back. Drifted snow had risen nearly to the level of the hasp and padlock that secured the door. Positioning his feet as firmly as he could in snow-shoes, he swung his maul like a golf club at the hasp. At the third blow, the screws tore loose and the door crashed inward.

Clambering through the violated doorway, he reflected that he did not know who owned this cabin now or what he looked like, that he would not recognize the owner he intended to rob if he were to meet him on the street. Robbery would be easier if only he could imagine himself apologizing and explaining, and offering to pay—though no apology or explanation would be feasible if he succeeded. He would be a vigilante then; and the law, which extended every courtesy to murderers, detested and destroyed anyone who killed or even resisted them. He would have to find out this cabin's address, he decided, and send cash by mail.

Of course, it was possible that there were no guns here, in which case Brook's murderers would presumably kill him too, before he could do any such thing. They might kill him, for that matter, even if—

Before he could complete the thought, he saw the gun safe, a steel cabinet painted to look like wood, with a combination lock. Half a dozen blows from the maul knocked off the knob. Two dozen more so battered the three-sixteenths-inch steel door that he could work the claws of the big ripping hammer he found in a toolbox into the opening. The battered mechanism was steel, the hammer-handle fiberglass; for a few seconds that seemed far longer, he felt certain the handle would break.

A rivet somewhere in the gun safe surrendered with a *pop*—the sweetest sound imaginable. A slight repositioning of the hammer and another heave, and the door ground back.

The gun safe held a twelve-gauge over-and-under shotgun, a sixteen-gauge pump, and a sleek scoped Sako carbine; there were shot shells of both sizes and three boxes of cartridges for the carbine in one of the drawers below the guns.

Emery took out the carbine and threw it to his shoulder; the stock felt a trifle small—the cabin's owner was probably an inch or two shorter—but it handled almost as if it had been customized for him. The bolt opened crisply to display an empty chamber.

He loaded five cartridges and dropped more into a pocket of his mackinaw. Reflecting that the women might well arm themselves from this cabin too, once they discovered that the lock on the rear entrance was broken, he threw the shotgun shells outside into the snow.

From a thick stand of pine on the lake shore, he had as good a view of the canted structure that Aileen had called a ziggurat as the gray daylight and blowing snow permitted: an assemblage of cubical modules tapering to a peak in a series of snow-covered terraces.

Certainly not an aircraft; a spacecraft, perhaps. More likely, a space station. Toward the bottom—or rather toward the ice surrounding it, for there had to be an additional forty feet or more of it submerged in the lake—the modules were noticeably crushed and deformed.

Rising, he stepped clumsily out onto the windswept ice. A part of this had been open water when the women had brought Aileen from the ziggurat back to the road—water that was open because the ice had been broken when the ziggurat broke through it, presumably. Yet that open water had been shallow enough for Aileen to wade through, although this mountain lake was deep a few feet from shore; such open water made no sense, though things seemed to have happened like that.

There were no windows that he could see, but several of the modules appeared to have rounded doors or hatches. If the women kept a watch, they might shoot him now as he shuffled slowly over the ice; but they would have to open one of those hatches to do it, and he would do his best to shoot first. He rechecked the Sako's safety. It was off, and he knew there was a round in the chamber. He removed the glove from his right hand and stuffed it into his pocket on top of more rounds and his forgotten sandwich.

He had wanted to die; and if they gut-shot him during the minute or two more that he would require to reach the base of the ziggurat, he would die in agony right here upon the ice.

Well, men did. All Men. Every human being died at last, young or old; and he had already lived longer than many of the people he had known and liked in high school and college. Had lived almost three times as long as Brook.

To his right, the tracks of small feet in large-cleated boots left the ziggurat, tracks not yet obscured by snow and thus very recent. He turned toward them to examine them, then traced them back to a circular hatch whose lower edge was no more than an inch above the ice. It was dogged shut with a simple latch large enough that he manipulated it easily with his gloved left hand.

A wave of warmth caressed his face as he pulled the hatch open and stepped into the ziggurat. Heat! They had heat in here, heat from some device that was still functioning, though Aileen had complained of the cold. In that case, heat from a source they had been able to repair since the crash, perhaps with parts from Jan's Lincoln.

Almost absently, he closed the hatch behind him. Before him was a second hatch; beyond it, misty blue light and dark water. Here, then, was the explanation for the ice on Aileen's boots and pants legs; she had waded in the lake, all right, but here inside the ziggurat, where there seemed to be about a foot of water.

Sitting in the hatchway of what he decided must surely be an airlock, he unlaced his boots and tugged them off, crude snowshoes and all, then tied his bootlaces together. It would be convenient, perhaps, to leave boots and snowshoes here in the airlock, but without either he would be confined to the ziggurat; he could not risk it. He took off his stockings and stuffed them into his boots, rolled up his trouser legs, and stepped barefoot into the dark water, the boots and snowshoes in his left hand, the Sako carbine in his right, gripped like a pistol.

The walls and ceiling of the module were thick with dials and unfamiliar devices, and a tilted cabinet whose corner rose above the water promised more; he paused to look at what seemed to be a simple dial, although its pointer shimmered, vanished, and reappeared, apparently a conveniently massless projection. The first number looked like zero, queerly lettered; the last—he squinted—three hundred, perhaps, although he had never seen a 3 quite like that. Pushing a tiny knob at the base to the left increased the height of the numerals until each stood about five thirty-seconds of an inch; the pointer darkened and now seemed quite solid.

There was a slight noise from overhead, as though someone in a higher module had dropped some small object.

He stiffened and looked quickly around. An open hatch in the wall at the opposite side of the half-crushed module gave access to an interior module that should (if the slant of both floors was the same) be somewhat less deeply submerged. He waded across and went in, followed by the dial he had examined, which slid across the metal wall like a hockey puck, dodging other devices in its path, until he caught it and pushed the knob at its base to the right again.

A ladder in the middle of the new module invited him to climb to the one above; he did, although with difficulty, his boots and snowshoes slung behind his back and half choking him with his own bootlaces, and the carbine awkwardly grasped in his right hand. The ladder (of some white metal that did not quite seem to be aluminum) gave dangerously beneath his weight, but held.

The higher module into which he emerged was almost intact, and colder than the one from which he had just climbed; the deep thrumming of the wind beyond its metal walls could be distinctly heard, though no window or porthole revealed the snow he knew must be racing down the lake with it.

"Fey," he muttered to himself. And then, somewhat more loudly, "Eerie." How frightened poor Aileen must have been!

Curious, he put down his boots and snowshoes and the Sako, drew his knife, and shaved a few bits of metal from the topmost rung of the ladder. They were bright where the sharp steel had sheared them, dull on the older surfaces. Tempted to guess, he suspended judgment. A somewhat bigger piece gouged from the floor appeared to be of the same material; he unbuttoned his mackinaw and deposited all his samples in a shirt pocket.

The rectangular furnishing against one wall looked

as if it might be a workbench topped with white plastic. Two objects of unfamiliar shape lay on it; he crossed the cubicle, stepping over featureless cabinets and others dotted with strangely shaped screens.

The larger object that he took from the bench changed its form at his touch, developing smooth jaws whose curving inner surfaces suggested parabolas; the smaller object snapped open, revealing a convoluted diagram too large to have been contained within it. Points of orange and green light wandered aimlessly over the diagram. After a bit of fumbling, he shut the object again and put it in the chest pocket of his mackinaw, following it with several small items of interest that he discovered in the swinging, extensible compartments that seemed to serve as drawers, though they were not quite drawers.

Without warning, the face of an angry giantess occupied the benchtop and her shouting voice filled the module. Gongs and bells sounded behind her, a music grotesquely harmonious amplified to deafening intensity. For a half second that was nearly too long, he watched and listened, mesmerized.

She was five feet behind him, ax raised, when he turned. He lunged at her as the blow fell, and the wooden handle struck his shoulder. Struggling together, they rolled over the canted floor, she a clawing, biting fury, he with a hand—then both—grabbing at the ax handle.

Wrenching the ax away, he swung it clumsily, hitting her elbow with the flat. She bit his cheek, and seemed about to tear his face off. Releasing the ax, he drove his thumbs into her eyes. She spat him out (such was his confused recollection later), sprang to her feet, dashed away—

And was gone.

Half stunned by the suddenness and violence of the

fight as well as the deafening clamor from the work-bench, he sat up and looked around him. His stolen ax lay near his left hand; the brownish smear on its bright edge was presumably Brook's blood. His own trickled from his cheek, dotting the uneven metal floor. His boots and snowshoes, and the sleek carbine, lay where he had left them.

Slowly he got to his feet, stooped to reclaim his ax, then stood up without it; he could only carry so much, the carbine was a better weapon, and the ax had killed Brook.

He shook himself. These women had killed Brook. The ax was his ax, and nothing more: a good piece of steel mounted on a length of hickory, a thing he had bought for thirty or forty dollars in the hardware store in town—as foolish to kick the stone you tripped over as to blame the ax.

He picked it up and wiped the blade on one rough sleeve of his mackinaw until most of Brook's blood was gone. The carbine was a better weapon, but if he left the ax where it was the women would almost certainly find it and use it against him. If he carried it out-side, he might be able to chop a hole in the ice and drop it in; but dropping it into the dark water at the bottom of the ladder would probably be almost as effective and a hundred times quicker. Soon, perhaps very soon, the one who had just tried to kill him might try again.

The clamor of the bench continued unabated. Childishly, he told it to be quiet, and when it did not respond, chopped at the huge, female, shouting, shrieking face again and again, until silence fell as sud-denly as a curtain and the benchtop was white plastic once more. Had it been a teaching device, as well as a repair bench? One that could, perhaps, instruct and entertain the mechanic while she worked?

He laid the ax on it, found a handkerchief, and pressed it to his cheek.

Curious again, he strode to the nearest wall and touched it; it was not as cold as he had expected, though it seemed distinctly colder than the air around him. "Insulated," he muttered to himself, "but not insulated enough." Did you need a lot of insulation for space? Perhaps not; astronauts stayed outside in their suits for hours. After a little reflection, he concluded that a space station could lose heat to space only by radiation, and a space station at room temperature would not radiate much. The ziggurat was losing heat by convection and conduction now, and convection was almost always the greatest thief of heat.

Retrieving the ax, he carried it to the floor hatch to drop it in, and saw the dead woman's body floating facedown in the shallow water of the cubicle below.

When he left, the marks of his snowshoes coming in were as sharp as if they had just been made, although it was snowing hard. So much snow had accumulated on the ziggurat's terraces already that it seemed almost a rock rising from the ice; if he were to point it out to someone—to Brook, say, although it would be better perhaps to point it out to someone still alive. To Alayna or Jan, say, or even to Pamela, who had been Brook's mother. If he were to point it out to any of those people and say, *That rock over there is hollow, and there are strange and wonderful blue-lit rooms inside, where little brown women will try to kill you,* they would think him not a liar but a madman, or a drunk. For centuries, unheeded men and women in England and Ireland and any number of other countries had reported a diminutive race living in hills where time ran differently, although in Africa, where skins were black, the little people's had been white.

He had made the mistake of turning the dead woman over, and the memory of her livid face and empty, unfocused eyes came back to haunt him. Someone used to jet-black faces would have called that dead face white, almost certainly. He searched his mind for a term he had read a year or two before.

Members of that small, pale African race were *Yumbos*, the people from the hills who crept out to steal cornmeal. Aileen had said the women had given her only bread to eat. Rations were short, perhaps; or rations were being hoarded against an indefinite stay.

If its hood had not been up, Emery would have missed the Lincoln, thinking it just another snowdrift. Both doors were locked (he had locked them out of habit, it seemed, the night before) and the keys were still in Brook's pocket. He broke a window with the butt of the carbine and retrieved his best cap. Brook had left some possession, a TV or home computer, in the trunk; but he would have to shoot out the lock, and he was heavily loaded already with the loot of the ziggurat.

As he passed the lightless cabin he had burglarized, it occurred to him that he ought to find out whether the shotguns had been taken. After a few moments' thought, he rejected the idea. The other two women (if indeed there were only two left) might or might not have the shotguns, and might or might not have shells for them if they did. They were dangerous in any case, which was all he really needed to know.

His own cabin was as dark. He tried to remember whether he had left a light on, then whether he had even turned one on that morning. He had written his journal—had briefly and crassly recorded Brook's death there—so he must certainly have switched on the lamp on the table. He could not remember switching it off.

Would they shoot through the glass, and the Cyclone fence wire with which he had covered his windows? Or would they poke the barrel through first, providing him some warning? There might have been more shells in the other cabin, in some drawer or cupboard, or even in the pockets of the old field coat that had hung from a nail near the front door.

His own front door appeared to be just as he had left it; there were no footprints in the fresh snow banked against it, and its bright Yale lock was unmarred. Could they pick locks? He circled the cabin, careful to go by way of the north side, past his Jeep and the spot where Brook had died, so that he would not have to look at Brook's corpse. Brook was surely buried under snow by this time, as he had told the undertaker; yet he could not help visualizing Brook's contorted, untenanted face. Brook would never go to Purdue now, never utilize his father's contacts at NASA. Brook was dead, and all the dreams (so many dreams) had died with him. Was it Brook or the dreams he mourned?

The rear door looked as sound as the front, and there were no visible footprints in the snow. No doubt he had turned out the table light automatically when he had finished writing his journal. Everyone did such things.

He unlocked the rear door, went inside, stood the Sako in a corner, and emptied his pockets onto the table. Here was the dial that had tracked him, the tool that displayed a diagram larger than itself, the oblong card that might be a book whose pages turned each time the reader's hand approached it, the octopus of light whose center was a ceramic sphere no bigger than a marble. Here, too, were the seven-sided cube; the beads that strung themselves and certainly were not actually beads, whatever they might be; and the dish in which small objects seemed to melt and from which in a few minutes they vanished. With them, cartridges for the carbine, his checkbook, keys, handkerchief, and pocketknife; and the unappetizing sandwich.

Seeing it and feeling his own disappointment, he realized that he was hungry. He lit the gas under the coffeepot and sat down to consider the matter. Should he eat first? Bandage his cheek? Build a new fire? The cabin was cold, though it seemed almost cozy after the winter storm outside.

Or should he write his journal first—set down a factual account of everything he had seen in the ziggurat while it was still fresh in his mind? The sensible thing would be to build a fire; but that would mean going out for wood and trying not to see Brook. His mind recoiled from the thought.

An accurate, detailed account of the ziggurat might be worth millions to him in a few years, and could be written—begun at least—while his food was cooking and the coffee getting hot. He opened a can of Irish stew, dumped it into a clean saucepan, lit the burner under it, then sat down again and pressed the switch of the small lamp on the table.

No light flooded from its shade.

He stared at it, tightened the bulb and pressed the switch twice more, and chuckled. No wonder the cabin had been dark! Either the bulb had burned out in his absence, or the wires were down.

Standing up, he pulled the switch cord of the overhead fixture. Nothing.

How did the old song go? Something about wires

down south that wouldn't stand the strain if it snowed. These wires, his wires, the ones that the country had run out to the lake four years ago, had not. He found one of the kerosene lanterns he had used before the wires came, filled it, and lit it.

If the electrical wires were down, it seemed probable that the telephone was out as well—but when he held it to his ear the receiver emitted a reassuring dial tone. The telephone people, Emery reminded himself, always seemed to maintain their equipment a little bit better than the power company.

His cheek next, and he would have to fetch water from the creek as he had in the old days or melt snow. He filled his teakettle with clean snow from behind the cabin. Washing off the dried blood revealed the marks of teeth and a bruise. You could catch all sorts of diseases from human bites—human mouths were as dirty as monkeys'—but there was not much that he could do about that now. Gingerly, he daubed iodine on the marks, sponged that side of his face with hydrogen peroxide, and put on a thin pad of gauze, noting that Brook had depleted his supply in bandaging his wounded side.

Had the woman who had bitten him and tried to kill him with his own ax been the one who had killed Brook? It seemed likely, unless the women were trading off weapons; and if that was the case, Brook was avenged. Let the sheriff take it from here. He debated the advisability of leading the sheriff's investigator to the ziggurat.

He stirred his Irish stew, and decided it was not quite warm enough yet; he'd get it good and hot, and pour it over bread.

He wasn't quite warm enough either, and was in fact still wearing his mackinaw, here inside the cabin. It was time to confront the firewood problem. When he had done it, he could take off his mackinaw and settle in until the storm let up and the snowplows brought a deputy, Doctor What's-hisname—Ormond—and the undertaker.

Outside, on the south side of the cabin, he made himself stare at the place where Brook lay. To the eye at least, it was just a little mound of snow, differing from other graves only in being white and smooth; the coyote lay at Brook's head, his mound not noticeably smaller or larger. Emery found that oddly comforting. Brook would have gloried in a tame coyote. They would have to be separated before long, though—in four or five days at most, and probably sooner. It seemed a shame. Emery filled his arms with wood and carried it back into the cabin.

Newspapers first, with a splash of kerosene on them. Then kindling, and wood only when the kindling was burning well. He set the kerosene can on the hearth and knelt to unfold, crumple up, and arrange his newspapers.

There were tracks, footprints, in the powdery gray ashes.

He blinked and stared and blinked again. Stood up and got the flashlight and looked once more.

There could be no doubt, although these were not the clear and detailed prints he would have preferred; they were scuffed, confused, and peppered with some black substance. He rubbed a speck of it between his thumb and forefinger. Soot, of course.

The prints of two pairs of boots with large cleats; small boots in both cases, but one pair was slightly smaller than the other, and the smaller pair showed—yes—a little less wear at the heels.

They had come down his chimney. He stood up again and looked around. Nothing seemed to be missing.

They had climbed onto the roof (his Jeep, parked against the north wall of the cabin, would have made that easy) and climbed down the chimney. He could not have managed it, and neither could Brook, if Brook were still alive; but the twins could have done it, and these women were scarcely larger. He should have seen their footprints, but they had no doubt been obscured by blowing snow, and he had taken them for the ones the women had left that morning when they killed Brook. He had been looking mostly for fresh tracks outside the doors in any case.

There had been none. He felt certain of that; no tracks newer than the ones he himself had made that morning. Why, then, had the women climbed up the chimney when they left? Anybody knowledgeable enough to work with the equipment he had seen in the ziggurat would have no difficulty in opening either of his doors from the inside. Climbing down the chimney might not be terribly hard for women the twins' size, but climbing back up, even with a rope, would be a great deal harder. Why do it when you could just walk out?

He covered the ashes with twice the amount of newspaper he had intended to use, and doused every ball of paper liberally with kerosene. Should he light the fire first or wait until he had the carbine in his hand?

The latter seemed safer. He got the carbine and pushed off its safety, clamped it under one arm, then struck a match and tossed it into the fireplace.

The tiny tongue of yellow flame grew to a conflagration in a second or two. There was a metallic clank before something black crashed down into the fire and sprang at him like a cat.

"Stop!" He swung the butt of the Sako at her. "Stop, or I'll shoot!"

A hand from nowhere gripped his ankle. He kicked free, and a second woman rolled from beneath the bunk Brook had slept in—the one he had made up for Jan. Awkwardly, he clubbed the forearm of the woman who had dropped from the chimney with the carbine barrel, kicked at her knee and missed. "Get out! Get out, both of you, or I swear to God—"

They rushed at him not quite as one, the taller first, the smaller brandishing his rifle. Hands snatched at the carbine, nearly jerking it from his grasp; for a moment, he wrestled the taller woman for it.

The sound of the shot was deafening in the closed cabin. The carbine leaped in his hands.

He found that he was staring into her soot-smeared brown face; it crumpled like his newspapers, her eyes squinting, her mouth twisted in a grimace of pain.

The woman behind her screamed and turned away, dropping his rifle and clutching her thigh. Blood seeped from between her fingers.

The taller woman took a step toward him—an involuntary step, perhaps, as her reflexes sought to keep her from falling. She fell forward, the crumpled face smacking the worn boards of the cabin floor, and lay motionless.

The other woman was kneeling, still trying to hold back her blood. She looked at Emery, a look of mingled despair and mute appeal.

"I won't," he said.

He was still holding the carbine that had shot her. It belonged to someone else, and its owner presumably valued it; but none of that seemed to matter anymore. He threw it aside. "That's why I quit hunting deer," he told her almost casually. "I gut-shot a buck and trailed him six miles. When I found him, he looked at me like that."

The big plastic leaf bags he used to carry his garbage

to the dump were under the sink. He pulled down quilt, blankets, and sheet, and spread two bags over the rumpled bunk that had been Brook's, scooped her up, and stretched her on them. "You shot me, and now I've shot you. I didn't mean to. Maybe you didn't either—I'd like to think so, anyway."

With his hunting knife, he cut away the sooty cloth around her wound. The skin at the back of her thigh was unbroken, but beneath it he could feel the hard outline of the bullet. "I'm going to cut there and take that out," he told her. "It should be pretty easy, but we'll have to sterilize the knife and the needle-nosed pliers first."

He gave her the rest of his surgical gauze to hold against her wound, and tried to fill his largest cooking pot with water from the sink. "I should have remembered the pump was off," he admitted to her ruefully, and went outside to fill the pot with clean snow.

"I'm going to wash your wound and bandage it before I get the bullet out." He spoke slowly and distinctly as he stepped back in and shut the door, hoping that she understood at least a part of what he was saying. "First, I have to get this water hot enough that I'll be cleaning it, not infecting it." He put the pot of snow on the stove and turned down the burner under his stew.

"Let's see what happened here." He knelt beside the dead woman and examined the ragged, blood-soaked tear at the back of her jacket, then wiped his fingers. It took an effort of will to roll her over; but he did it, keeping his eyes off her face. The hole the bullet had left in the front of the jacket was so small and obscure that he had to verify it by poking his pen through it before he was satisfied.

He stood again, reached into his mackinaw to push the pen into his shirt pocket, and found the fragments of white metal he had taken from the ziggurat. For a moment, he looked from them to the newspapers still blazing in the fireplace. "I'm going to lay some kindling on the fire. Getting chilled won't help you. It could even kill you." Belatedly, he drew up her sheet, the blankets, and the quilt.

"You're not going to die. Are you afraid you will?" He had a feeling that if he talked to her enough, she would begin to understand; that was how children learned to speak, surely. "I'm not going to kill you, and neither is that wound in your leg, or at least I don't think so."

She replied, and he saw that she was trying to smile. He pointed to the dead woman and to her, and shook his head, then arranged kindling on the burning newspapers. The water in his biggest pot was scarcely warm, but the Irish stew was hot. He filled a bowl, and gave it to her with a spoon; she sat up to eat, keeping her left hand under the covers to press the pad of gauze to her leg.

The Voylestown telephone directory provided a home number for Doctor Ormond. Emery pressed it in.

"Hello."

"Doctor Ormond? This is Emery Bainbridge."

"Right. Ralph Merton told me about you. I'll try to get out there just as quick as I can."

"This is about another matter, Doctor. I'm afraid we've had a gun go off by accident."

A slight gasp came over the wire as Ormond drew breath. *"Someone was hit. Is it bad?"*

"Both of us were. I hope not too badly, though. We had a loaded rifle—my hunting rifle—standing against the wall. We were nervous, you understand. We still are. Some people—these people—I'm sorry." In the midst of the fabrication, Brook's death had taken Emery by the throat.

"I know your son's dead, Mister Bainbridge. Ralph told me. He was murdered?"

"Yes, with an ax. My ax. You'll see him, of course. I apologize, Doctor. I don't usually lose control."

"Perfectly normal and healthy, Mister Bainbridge. You don't have to tell me about the shooting if you don't want to. I'm a doctor, not a policeman."

"My rifle fell over and discharged," Emery said. "The bullet creased my side—I don't think that's too bad—and hit . . . " Looking at the wounded woman, he ransacked his memory for a suitable name. "Hit Tamar in the leg. I should explain that Tamar's an exchange student who's been staying with us." Tamar had been Solomon's sister, and King Solomon's mines had been somewhere around the Horn of Africa. "She's from Aden. She speaks very little English, I'm afraid. I know first aid, and I'm doing all I can, but I thought I ought to call you."

"She's conscious?"

"Oh, yes. She's sitting up and eating right now. The bullet hit the outer part of her thigh. I think it missed the bone. It's still in her leg. It didn't exit."

"This just happened?"

"Ten minutes ago, perhaps."

"Don't give her any more food, she may vomit. Give her water. There's no intestinal wound? No wound in the abdomen?"

"No, in her thigh as I said. About eight inches above the knee."

"Then let her have water, as much as she wants. Has she lost much blood?"

Emery glanced at the dead woman. It would be necessary to account for the stains of her blood as well as Tamar's. "It's not easy to estimate, but I'd say at least a pint. It could be a little more."

"I see, I see." Ormond sounded relieved. *"I'd give*

her a transfusion if I had her in the hospital, Mister Bainbridge, but she may not really need one. At least, not badly. How much would you say she weighs?"

He tried to remember the effort involved in lifting her. He had been excited, of course—high on adrenaline. "Between ninety and a hundred pounds, at a guess."

Ormond grunted. *"Small. Small bones? Height?"*

"Yes, very small. My wife calls her petite." The lie had come easily, unlooked for. "I'd say she's about five foot one. Delicate."

"What about you, Mister Bainbridge? Have you lost much blood?"

"Less than half as much as she has, I'd say."

"I see. The question is whether your intestine has been perforated—"

"Not unless it's a lot closer to the skin than I think it is, Doctor. It's just a crease, as I say. I was sitting down, she was standing up. The bullet creased my side and went into her leg."

"I'd wait a bit, just the same, before I ate or drank anything, Mister Bainbridge. You haven't eaten or drunk since it happened?"

"No," Emery lied.

"Good. Wait a bit. Can you call me back in two hours?"

"Certainly. Thank you, Doctor."

"I'll be here, unless there's an emergency here in town, someplace I can get to. If I'm not here, my wife will answer the phone. Have you called the police?"

"Not about this. It's an accident, not a police matter."

"I'm required to report any gunshot wounds I treat. You may want to report it yourself first."

"All right, I can tell the officer who investigates my son's death."

"*That's up to you, but I'll have to report it. Is there anything else?*"

"I don't think so."

"*Do you have any antibiotics? A few capsules left from an old prescription?*"

"I don't think so."

"*Look. If you find anything you think might be helpful, call me back immediately. Otherwise, in two hours.*"

"Right. Thank you, Doctor." Emery hung up.

The snow water was boiling on the stove. He turned off the burner, noting that the potful of packed snow had become less than a quarter of a pot of water. "As soon as that cools off a little, I'm going to wash your wound and put a proper bandage on it," he said.

She smiled shyly.

"You're from Aden. It's in Yemen, I believe. Your name is Tamar. Can you say *Tamar?*" He spoke slowly, mouthing the sounds. "*Ta-mar.* You say it." He pointed to her.

"Teye-mahr." She smiled again, not quite so frightened.

"*Very* good! You'd speak Arabic, I suppose, but I've got a few books here, and if I can dig up a more obscure language for you, we'll use it—too many people know Arabic. I wish that you could tell me," he hesitated, "where you really come from. Or when you come from. Because that's what I've been thinking. That's crazy, isn't it?"

She nodded, though it seemed to him she had not understood.

"You were up in space in that thing. In the ziggurat." He laid splits of wood on the blazing kindling. "I've been thinking about that, too, and you just about had to be. How many were there in your crew?"

Sensing her incomprehension, he pointed to the

dead woman, then to the living one, and held up three fingers. "This many? Three? Wait a minute."

He found a blank page in his journal and drew the ziggurat with three stick figures beside it. "This many?" He offered her his journal and the pen.

She shook her head and pointed to her leg with her free hand.

"Yes, of course. You'll need both hands."

He cleaned her wound as thoroughly as he could with Q-Tips and the steaming snow-water, and contrived a dressing from a clean undershirt and the remaining tape. "Now we've got to get the bullet out. I think we ought to for your sake anyway—it will have carried cloth into the wound, maybe even tissue from the other woman."

Breaking the plastic of a disposable razor furnished him with a small but extremely sharp blade. "I'd planned to use the pen blade of my jackknife," he explained as he helped her roll over, "but this will be better."

He cut away what remained of her trouser leg. "It's going to hurt. I wish I had something to give you."

Two shallow incisions revealed an edge of the mushroomed carbine bullet. He fished the pliers out of the hot water with a fork, gripped the ragged lead in them, and worked the bullet free. Rather to his surprise, she bit her pillow and did not cry out.

"Here it is." He held the bullet where she could see it. "It went through your friend's breastbone, and I think it must have gotten her heart. Then it was deflected downward, most likely by a rib, and hit you. If it hadn't been deflected, it might have missed you altogether. Or killed you. Lie still, please." He put his hand on her back and felt her shrink from his touch. "I want to mop away the blood and look at that with the flashlight. If this fragmented at all, it didn't fragment much. But if it did, we want to get all of the pieces out, and anything else that doesn't belong." Unable to stop himself, he added, "You're afraid, aren't you? All of you were. Afraid of me, and of Brook too. Probably afraid of all males."

He found fibers in the wound that had probably come from her trousers and extracted them one by one, tore strips from a second undershirt, and tied a folded pad made of what remained of it to the new wound at the back of her thigh. "This is what we had to do before they had tape," he confided as he tightened the last knot. "Wind cloth around the wounded leg or whatever it was. That's why we call them *wounds*. If you were wounded, you got bandages wound around you—all right, you can turn back over now." He helped her.

The flames were leaping high in the fieldstone fireplace. He took the metal fragments out of his shirt pocket and showed them to her, then pointed toward it.

She shook her head emphatically.

"Do you mean they won't burn, or they will?" He grinned. "I think you mean they will. Let's see."

He tossed the smallest sliver from the ladder into the fire. After a second or two, there was a burst of brilliant light and puff of white smoke. "Magnesium. I thought so."

He moved his chair next to the bunk in which she lay and sat down. "Magnesium's strong and very light, but it burns. They use it in flashbulbs. Your ziggurat, your lander or space station or whatever it is, will burn with a flame hot enough to destroy just about anything, and I'm going to burn it tomorrow morning. It's a terrible waste and I hate to do it, but that's what I'm going to do. You don't understand any of this, do you, Tamar?" He got his journal and drew fire and smoke coming from the ziggurat.

She studied the drawing, her face thoughtful, then nodded.

"I'm glad you didn't throw a fit about that," he told her. "I was afraid you would, but maybe you were under orders not to disturb things back here any more than you could help."

When she did not react to that, he took another leaf bag from under the sink; to his satisfaction, it was large enough to contain the dead woman. "I had to do that before she got stiff," he explained to the living one. "She'll stiffen up in an hour or so. It's probably better if we don't have to look at her, anyway."

Tamar made a quick gesture he did not comprehend, folded her hands, and shut her eyes.

"Tomorrow, before the storm lets up, I'm going to drag her back to your space station and burn it." He was talking mostly for his own benefit, to clarify his thoughts. "That's probably a crime, but it's what I'm going to do. You do what you've got to." He picked up the Sako carbine. "I'm going to clean this and leave it in the other cabin on the way, and throw away the bullet. As far as the sheriff's concerned, my gun shot us both by accident. If I have to, I'll say you bit my face while I was tending your wound. But I won't be able to shave there anyhow, and by the time they get here my beard may cover it."

She motioned toward his journal and pen, and when he gave them to her produced a creditable sketch of the third woman.

"Gone," he said. "She's dead too. I'd stuck my thumbs in her eyes—she tried to kill me—and she ran. She must have fallen through the hole in the floor. The water down there was pretty shallow, so she would've hit hard. I think she drowned."

Tamar pointed to the leaf bag that held the dead woman, then sketched her with equal facility, finishing by crossing out the sketch.

Emery crossed out the women in the ziggurat as well, and returned the journal and the pen to Tamar. "You'll have to live the rest of your life here, I'm afraid, unless they send somebody for you. I don't expect you to like it—not many of us do—but you'll have to do the best you can, just like the rest of us."

Suddenly excited, she pointed to the tiny face of the lion on his pen and hummed, waving the pen like a conductor's baton. It took him a minute or more to identify the tune.

It was "God Save the Queen."

Later, when she was asleep, he telephoned an experimental physicist. "David," he asked softly, "do you remember your old boss? Emery Bainbridge?"

David did.

"I've got something here I want to tell you about, David. First, though, I've got to say I can't tell you where I got it. That's confidential—top secret. You've got to accept that. I won't *ever* be able to tell you. Okay?"

It was.

"This thing is a little dish. It looks almost like an ashtray." There was a penny in the clutter on the table; he picked it up. "I'm going to drop a penny into it. Listen."

The penny fell with a clink.

"After a while, that penny will disappear, David. Right now it looks just a little misted, like it had been outside in the cold, and there was condensation on it."

Emery moved the dish closer to the kerosene lantern. "Now the penny is starting to look sort of silvery. I think most of the copper's gone, and what I'm seeing is the zinc underneath. You can barely make out Lincoln's face."

David spoke.

"I've tried that. Even if you hold the dish upside down and shake it, the penny—or whatever it is—won't fall out, and I'm not about to reach in and try to pull it out."

The crackling voice in the receiver sounded louder than Emery's own.

"I wish you could, David. It's not much bigger than the end of a pencil now, and shrinking quickly. Hold on—

"There. It's gone. I think the dish must boil off atoms or molecules by some cold process. That's the only explanation I've come up with. I suppose we could check that by analyzing samples of air above it, but I don't have the equipment here.

"David, I'm going to start a new company. I'm going to do it on a shoestring, because I don't want to let any backers in. I'll have to use my own money and whatever I can raise on my signature. I know you've got a good job now. They're probably paying you half what you're worth, which is a hell of a lot. But if you'll come in with me, I'll give you ten percent.

"Of course you can think it over. I expect you to. Let's say a week. How's that?"

David spoke at length.

"Yes, here too. The lights are off, as a matter of fact. It's just by the grace of God that the phone still works. I'll be stuck out here—I'm in the cabin—for another three or four days, probably. Then I'll drive into the city, and we'll talk.

"Certainly you can look at it. You can pick it up and try it out, but not take it back to your lab. You understand, I'm sure."

A last, querulous question.

Emery chuckled. "No, it's not from a magic store, David. I think I might be able to guess where it's actually from, but I'm not going to. Top secret, remember?

It's technology way in advance of ours. We're medieval mechanics who've found a paper shredder. We may never be able to make another shredder, but we can learn a hell of a lot from the one we've got."

When he had hung up, he moved his chair back to the side of Tamar's bunk. She was lying on her back, her mouth and eyes closed, the soft sigh of her respiration distinct against the howling of the wind beyond the log walls.

"Jan's going to want to come back," Emery told Tamar, his voice less than a whisper. "She'll try to kiss and make up two weeks to a month after she finds out about the new company, I'd say. I'll have to get our divorce finalized before she hears. They'll back off a little on that property settlement when she gets back to the city, and then I'll sign."

Tamar's left hand lay on the quilt; his found it, stroking the back and fingers with a touch that he hoped was too light to wake her. "Because I don't want Jan anymore. I want you, Tamar, and you're going to need me."

The delicate brown fingers curled about his, though she was still asleep.

"You're learning to trust me, aren't you? Well, you can. I won't hurt you." He fell silent. He had taught the coyote to trust him; and because he had, the coyote had not feared the smell of Man on the cyanide gun. He would have to make certain Tamar understood that all men were not to be trusted—that there were millions of men who would rob and rape and kill her if they could.

"How did you reproduce, up there in our future, Tamar? Asexually? My guess is artificial insemination, with a means of selecting for females. You can tell me whether I'm right, by and by."

He paused, thinking. "Is our future still up there?

The one you came from? Or did you change things when you crashed? Or when you killed Brook. Even if it is, maybe you and I can change things with some new technology. Let's try."

Tamar sighed, and seemed to smile in her sleep. He bent over her to kiss her, his lips lightly brushing hers. "Is that why the crash was so bad that you could never get the ziggurat to fly again? Because just by crashing at all, or by killing my son, you destroyed the future you came from?"

In the movies, Emery reflected, people simply stepped into time machines and vanished, to reappear later or earlier at the same spot on Earth's surface, as if Copernicus had never lived. In reality, Earth was moving in the solar system, the solar system in the galaxy, and the galaxy itself in the universe. One would have to travel through space as well as time to jump time in reality.

Somewhere beneath the surface of the lake, the device that permitted such jumps was still functioning, after a fashion. No longer jumping, but influencing the speed with which time passed—the timing of time, as it were. The hours he had spent inside the ziggurat had been but a minute or two outside it; that had to be true, because the prints of his snowshoes coming in had still been sharp when he came out, and Aileen had spent half a day at least there in two hours.

He would burn the ziggurat tomorrow. He would have to, if he were not to lose everything he had taken from it, and be accused of the murder of the dead woman in the leaf bag, too—would have to, if he wished to keep Tamar.

But might not the time device, submerged who could say how deep in the lake, perhaps buried in mud at the bottom as well, survive and continue to function as it did now? Fishermen on Haunted Lake might see the sun stand still, while hours drifted past. Had the device spread itself through time to give the lake its name? He would buy up all the lakeside property, he decided, when the profits of the new company permitted him to.

"We're going to build a new cabin," he told the sleeping Tamar. "A house, really, and a big one, right on the shore there. We'll live in that house, you and me, for a long, long time, and we'll have children."

Very gently, her fingers tightened around his.

Story Copyrights